CIANAN PUCKETT

Never Without Hope

The Void-Sleeper War: I

I owe my spark of creativity to Suzanne Hamilton, who helped me break out of the mundane and into a world of inspiration.

To my mother, Joy Puckett, who always showed me support for my dreams, even if she wasn't aware of it.

Contents

Preface

So, just to get this out of the way, this book's happenings occur within the medieval time period for the world of Seran. As such, some words, actions, and phrases we may find terribly offensive nowadays may be used throughout it. This serves as my statement of intent to not offend, injure, or traumatize (or re-traumatize, as the case may be) people. As well, there are depictions of gruesome injuries and illnesses, as well as the burning of bodies.

You know, normal things.

What you are about to read is a labor of love and tears at least nine years in the making. I have spent countless hours sweating the small details and trying to realize a world bigger than I could conceive alone. Countless other folk have given me inspiration to craft this novel and indeed the world it is set in, and if I were to thank them all (or even just the ones I remember) by name, we would have about sixty more pages.

So, to all who believed in me through this ridiculous project, I say a heartfelt thank you. Thank you for your ideas, for listening to my incessant questions and inane babbling as I fought to realize one of the biggest dreams in my life. Thank you for providing the ideas that later morphed to become names, events, and other happenings in the world of Seran.

And thank you, dear reader, for taking the chance on an unknown author from the middle of basically nowhere. I do hope this novel excites you and gives you as much joy to read it as I had writing it. In many ways, I hope that you find the message of this novel as near and dear to your heart as I did, because I know we all need it. In times like these, and especially the time I am finishing the final touches on this book, I feel we are faced every day with new challenges and new insanity. Through it all, though, we know the truth. That life? Life is Never Without Hope.

Acknowledgments

Scott Bryden, who gave me the inspiration for Thäoldr and the Order of Gelvrentael, though they may deviate from his original image.

Alana Mayhem, whose tireless work editing and perfecting my work, has no doubt caused her much stress and annoyance. From her comes the inspiration for many things, the least of which is not Khula, though she deviates from Alana's idea of her.

I

The Gathering Storm

1

1: The Mootgrounds, Eversnow Forest, Northrealm

"**R**anger bold, where walk thee now?**"** A single voice rang out, pained enough that the owner's words became tremulous. Many others soon joined it to form a chorus of sorrow. A lamenting dirge issued forth, heard by all in the area and heard by the High Ancestors above. The line was repeated, this time stronger, as if numbers had bolstered the singer's courage against some terrible loss.

"Ranger bold, where walk thee now?
Does the dust lie heavy upon your brow?
Did you die with sword or bow in hand?
Were you cut down in your last stand?
Tell me where does the spirit go,
When dealt with death's final blow?
Where does the spirit rest when we die?
Does it rest upon the pyre, or fly up high?
Ranger ranger, how did you go?
Protecting the innocent or fighting lost souls?
Ranger bold, where sleep thee now?

'neath starry skies, 'neath ground stone-cold?"

From somewhere nearby, a torch was lit, fire springing to life, crackling at the air. An orange glow suffused the area in a harsh, warm light, combating the darkness of the moonless night. Fifty-three cloaked and hooded figures stood there, and all eyes were on a pyre in the center of the throng. Silently came six more, bearing a hastily made cot and followed by a weeping peasant woman, watching the body on what was little more than a cloak wrapped around two poles. Upon it lay the unmoving body of a teenage boy wrapped lovingly in a cloak of green, with a deeply cracked axe-head and broken handle laid upon his breast and a crude shield placed above his head.

"Was your blade the last,
was your bow steadfast?
Ranger bold, be you free?
Free voices now carry your legacy
Ranger bold, can you see?
Ranger bold, was this your place?
The years no longer touch your face.
Sadness no longer will you know,
To peaceful rest now you go."

Reverently, the circle opened, silently moving to allow the pallbearers access to the pyre. The song became six voices stronger, and the woman cried. The tears of many caught the light of the torch, reflecting the pain felt by all at the loss of this life. A tragic loss, for he was cut down young. Carefully, those carrying him lowered his body down onto the pyre, placed with the utmost of gentle hands onto the gathered wood. A pitcher formed of clay was brought from nearby. Upon it, in a tongue more ancient than the Clans of

Northrealm, were engraved. Within it was a viscous liquid, clear and smelling slightly of sage. The pitcher and the contents within were a sendoff for the Rangers own.

The Rangers reverently and lovingly finessed the pitcher. They passed it from person to person, and each added a pinch of sand, before giving it to the next. Around the circle it went until everyone had added their pinch. Then, the final Ranger handed it to the woman, whose grief rendered her barely able to stand.

"Ranger bold, were you alone?
For some sin, did you atone?
Veljra's rest you go to now,
Oh, Ranger bold, no longer alone.
Were sword and bow held in your name
Do free voices now sing your fame?
Oh ranger, ranger, no stone shall we cast
Holding the line, you breathed your last
Ranger, ranger, hold your ground
For we know your soul is around."

Supported on each side by a Ranger, the woman slowly raised the pitcher. Tilting it, she poured the mixture onto the body of the young man. As it left the pitcher, the liquid caught the light, glowing brilliantly orange with iridescent sparkles flashing within. Down it fell, until it struck the body of the teen and flowed, taking the path of least resistance around and soaking into fabric and flesh, until the pitcher was empty. The person holding the torch began walking toward the pyre, holding aloft the flame.

"Ranger, ranger, your tasks are done
For your memory is the song we have sung
Ranger, Ranger, the coals burn cold,

Join the hunt now in Veljra's fold
Shrouded in her cloak of gold,
Ranger bold, be now free."

On 'free', he plunged the burning torch into the wood of the pyre. Since they were soaked in oil long before, the branches and sticks immediately caught fire, springing into orange flames. As they climbed, the flames caught the liquid-soaked fabric, adding to the inferno. As the sand within caught fire and flared up, the colors of the flames changed, burning in a dazzling rainbow as a send-off worthy of one of their own. Revealed then were the forms standing around the fire. Fifty-nine Rangers of Seran, clad in the traditional garb of their station and one peasant woman, barely able to contain her grief. As the pyre's flames reached into the sky, a scream wrenched its way from her heaving breast, chilling all who heard it.

"My son! My son is dead!"

Gently, the Ranger nearest her caught her arm and drew her into a warm, compassionate embrace. Into their shoulder she sobbed, heaving and choking with emotion and tears. The ranger spoke after a moment, with a firm, kind voice that held the gentleness of a stream running over rocks and the authority of a tidal wave. It was a powerful voice, in the baritone range, though hushed out of deference for her grief. The voice of a man who had known pain throughout his life. The voice of a hero.

"Your son was strong in life and stood his ground against many." Slowly, the man brought the woman out to face him. What she could see of his face was known around Seran, a kind face, one that had seen its way through many trials and triumphs. Young though the face was, the scars were unmistakable. Here and there were the dots of freckles and difficult to see was the tan. But the eyes... Those chilled the woman the most. The eyes were of a warrior, older than her bloodline.

"He was just a boy... Just a farm-boy, a peasant like his father." Her voice still choked with emotion as she spoke, watching the fire dance in his eyes. Tears streamed down her face and onto her gown, the wet spots growing as her limitless grief flowed. She was unsure why the Rangers, of all people, would choose to honor him in this way. Sure, he had fell fighting raiders, but surely that courage was beneath the notice of people so great?

As if he had heard her thoughts, the man spoke. "No, milady... In life, he may have been but a poor farm-boy. But in his finest moments, he was a Ranger. In death, he stood fast against many foes and he shall hunt with Veljra in the Afterworld. And honored will be his ancestors to receive him at their table, alongside his father." He then gave her arms a gentle squeeze, before looking up to the multitude of Rangers assembled there. His voice raised, above the crackling of the flames, to address all gathered.

"Let it be known henceforth that when anyone speaks of Njall, Son of Sigmunt and Heli, they speak of a Ranger of Seran! That this lad will forevermore be in the company of Veljra of the Wilds and be received with honors by his ancestors in the halls of the Ancestors! Let him be witnessed among the heroes of our times!" Out came his sword, shining in the light. Like many weapons, including the young Njall's axe, they drank deeply that day. Others raised their weapons, and a cheer roared up through the mass of men and women.

"HEARD AND WITNESSED!" From sixty throats the shout

came, a send-off as the prismatic flames consumed the body. They shook weapons in the air, spears, swords, and axes alike. A few of them even clashed against shields, creating a cacophonous tribute. After a time, the tumult died down and the Rangers broke away. A few led the woman to the pyre, where she said her goodbye towards the flames and threw in colored sand. The inferno climbed for a moment, shimmering into a deep blue color, her son's favorite. Silently, she pressed her hands to her lips, then her breast, before raising them up to the sky in a silent farewell. Then, she turned away, to be attended to by other Rangers.

Around the Tent of Station a few hours later, many young men and women (and even a few older ones) sat, listening to every word spoken by a small group of Rangers. Glancing up, the speaker at the funeral smiled slightly to himself, before turning to slip towards the edge of the permanent camp. He had gotten no further than the watch-post before someone called out to him.

"Warden Ranger!" The voice of a woman, with the characteristic daintiness that identified the speaker as being an elf. The man, evidently one of high station, turned to face the one calling to him. She was beautiful beyond words, but long ago the man had learned to see past that beauty. Her silver hair fell in waves along her body and her face was akin to the representations of the Ancestors by the best painters of the time.

"Aye, Kiri? How might I help you?" The man looked almost worried as he studied the stern expression on the tanned, tattooed face of the wild-elf. Something was annoying her, and he guessed it was something recent.

"Do you *really* think that you are going to just slip away

unnoticed? You may be the best of us, *Warden*, but remember, I trained you." The man rolled his eyes. She was showing the pretense of anger, evidently out of want of some favor. Looking her in the eyes, the man smirked. She held his gaze, smirking, before they both laughed.

"Tell me what you want then, *mother hen*, and I shall make it so." She threw a rucksack at him and closed the distance, playfully smacking him upside the head. Quickly dropping back, Kiri extended her hand, palm toward the sky, and beckoned, challenging him to attack her. He retorted by sweeping her leg out from under her, in the hopes of off-balancing her. It worked, but far too well. As she fell, she threw her hands behind her and raised both legs, planting them squarely in his chest and knocking him back.

"The Moot is convening, and you are *required, ka teljt*. As our leader, it is up to you to decide how our might will be used, Karos." The woman reached up for her mask, swiftly pulling it up to hide her features. Karos did likewise, and the two walked back towards the Tent of Station. Silently, the eyes of the men and women sitting near the tent moved towards him, as did the eyes of the Rangers speaking to those people. Karos nodded and one of the Rangers, an older man supporting himself with a quarterstaff, stepped towards him.

"Karos, that was a wonderful eulogy you gave. We heard it from here. Well done lad." The old man reached out and grasped Karos' forearm, which prompted the younger to do likewise. He then spoke, addressing the elder. As he did, his eyes ranged across the gathered, watching as they nursed aching and abused feet. Some were doing better than others, but all were exhausted, having come from as far away as The Farlands and Khataar, walking with a Ranger over 2500 leagues to the Moot-lands for this night.

"Thank you, Wastan. 'tis terribly sad that it had to be said, for the loss of one so young is always lamentable. I pray he finds peace. Because of him, his mother survived... That is a victory enough." He struck his bracer against Wastan's and stepped inside the tent. Even through the privacy wards, he could still hear the Loremaster reciting tales of old glories. Tales many of these Tenderfeet would grow to hold closer than their own, even as they surpassed them.

This night was special for them and for all Rangers. Tonight was a celebration to Veljra and her husband Ybril, the patron deities of the Rangers. Goodbyes have been said and sorrows were still fresh for many. But they would move on, carrying the lost in their hearts and minds forevermore. And they would become stronger for it. Tonight was not a night for sorrow, or for self-doubt. It was the first of the Wild Nights, a week of celebration, during which they would celebrate and they would practice their skills. Hunts would bring meat to the table, and of course they would give the first meat as tribute to Veljra herself. She-who-walks and she-who-listens, the Ranger of Highest Station. It was she who seeded the wildlands with plant and beast and she who watched over the Rangers and protected them.

And it was she who would receive them when they passed into the Afterworld.

"Warden Ranger, good, you have arrived. What news from the world?"

Karos' first move was to bow when the voice addressed him, breaking his line of thought. The other Rangers within the tent bowed in similar fashion, before focusing on the cloth map on the table. It was a normal enough map of Seran, though the letters upon its surface were cryptic and all but impossible for one untrained in the language to decipher. They were the runes of the Sk'av'A, as seen on the pitcher of oil. The eldest of the gathered Rangers, the Moot, turned to Karos.

"Sahyrn, there is unrest brewing in the border towns of Nevian and Dragonmoor. Ranger Blazefur reports that dal'Korin troops pledged to the Scala'dun have harassed the town of Farwing. The local knights are keeping things civil... For now." Karos sounded annoyed, as if the actions undertaken by these creatures was an expected menace. He turned to another member of the Moot. "What news from Ranger Koz'Ta'Riin? We tasked him with monitoring the Scala'dun six months past.

The lizard-woman's tongue darted out for a moment, allowing her to 'smell' the air. She hissed slightly. "Warden Ranger, you reek of blood. Have you had no rest?" Karos shook his head, as much in answer as in displeasure at the derailing question. The Ranger, a dal'Korin named Tas'sa'Raath, blinked; her pupils contracting into slits. Her kind were natural hunters, able to read the heartbeat of their prey; and she could tell that Karos' was elevated. "Karos, you seem troubled. Speak, Warden Ranger."

"Tas, I have heard nothing from Koz'Ta'Riin in three sevendays. We must task a party of your egg-kin to see what has become of him." The lizard's pupils widened. Three weeks without contact was usually a bad sign, especially for a Ranger posted in Nevian, home of the dal'Korin. Even one of their own species was not safe there, especially if they allied with the Rangers and by extension the Empire. She shook her head, her neck-frill rustling.

"Of course, Karos. Who should we send? Perhaps Elz'Kal'Raan? He has always been good with search and rescue." She reached out to steady the Warden Ranger and once more, her tongue darted out of her mouth to taste the air. Abruptly, she let out a loud hiss of alarm, her frill flowering out. "Karos, you are injured! Why did you not tell us?" Two other Rangers joined her as she forced Karos into a seat. Another began unfastening his over tunic, to reveal a bloody chainmail shirt with a hole in the stomach. Then, they removed both his chainmail shirt and tunic to reveal the grisly wound left from an arrow. Some part of the arrow was still within the man, likely with the head still intact, such was the ferocity of the battle they'd recently went through.

"'tis naught but a scratch. You all worry too mu– AAUGH! Scorch it all, Argin! Give a man some warning before pulling an arrow from his stomach!" He was pale and sweating but had somehow managed not to bleed out before now, not to mention pass out from either the pain or the injury. It looked bad, but would not be mortal, at least. Tas'sa'Raath slapped him.

"*Valtagt!* you know better than to let an injury slip by untended." Immediately, a potion was passed from someone's pouch. Someone yanked the cork out and down Karos' throat the liquid went. He sputtered as they forced the liquid upon him and shook his head.

"You made your point. Now let me be. The wound will heal!" Despite his protests, however, he winced as they assaulted him with a poultice and bandages, grimacing as the application of the antiseptic mixture of plants stung the flesh. Only when they had bandaged him and checked for other injuries were the other Rangers satisfied. He reached for his shirt, only to have it whisked away from his grasp by a rather tall dokk. Gripping the shirt, the creature eyed Karos.

"I think not, Warden Ranger. This shirt needs washed and mended, as do your chainmail and tunic. Fear not, I shall ensure they get to Mairi. On with your briefing, comrades. I shan't miss much. Tas, be a dear and take notes of what I miss." With that, the lupine being was out the door, padding on his feet toward the tent of the Weaver. A Ranger she was and skilled as much with a needle, thread, or hammer as she was with her chosen spear. Covered in as many forge-burns as she was with scars, she and her fellows held the important task of ensuring a Ranger's gear was in working order.

"Now then, are we done torturing the Warden Ranger?" *Celedorn. Of course.* Karos chuckled inwardly as he heard the voice of the wood elf. He stepped into view, looking at the Warden Ranger and eyeing him curiously. "After all, I would like to know of the situation in Khataar, as I think you would, Cael."

"Of course, Celedorn. My homeland borders Nevian as well and in the past, they have sought to turn us against the Empire." A catlike creature stood there, having been silent until they spoke to him. Flexing his hands, he unsheathed his claws for a moment, inspecting them. "Of course, I know that Kuzi sends back a weekly raven to you wherever you might find yourself, Karos."

"Aye, Cael, that is true. Kuzi has been watchful, the two Rangers with her." He nodded slightly. Those were three incredibly capable Rangers. Not that there were any incapable Rangers. From the time someone recruits them, they train, ending a decade later for a week while older Rangers gave them the Life-Blessing to extend their longevity infinitely.

From there, they spend 9 decades under the watchful eye of a senior Ranger, training in their arts to become more capable than the greatest of warriors. A hard life, one of extreme toil and danger, but a rewarding one for sure.

Going silent for a moment, Karos listened as tables were being set up and fuel was being chopped for the fires. "By all accounts, the dal'Korin have been silent along that border. What concerns me most is the southern border of Westerspring. Rangers Kozlo ces'Dalri and Otho Narjas and the others we have along the border have all sent ravens indicating that larger than usual amounts of metals have been going into Nevian under guard. Not to mention the prevalence of slave-raids has gone higher than ever in that region."

Tas'sa'Raath spoke next, scratching her frill idly. "Of course. Few scale-kin alive still remember they attempted the last war against Westerspring. It did not go well for the scale-kin. The halflings are quite dangerous when roused." This brought a round of nods from everyone in the tent. A bunch of them had earned quite a few scars that day, alongside many diminutive berserkers. While hilarious to watch, their effectiveness was unquestionably intimidating. Even so, too many had fallen.

To interrupt where that train of thought had been leading, Karos pointed to the province of Dragonmoor on the map. "Sources show that The Temple of Enkar in Cúledan has started training a new class of Paladins. In fact, Master-At-Arms Kyal the White has informed me they have more than a few former slaves in this class, a fact which has pleased me greatly." Again, more nodding. To see freed slaves taking charge of their own future was a good thing. It meant that they had rehabilitated those people and wished to ensure no others faced the same fate. That they were becoming paladins and not Rangers was a slight blow to everyone's pride, but they were happy regardless to know that these people were becoming warriors and at least serving the Ancestors.

As the night wore on, it became more upbeat, more chaotic, and more playful, and The Moot took a break to involve themselves. Rangers and Tenderfeet competed against each other in contests of skill. Some battled in *ljas'atuk*, the ancient method of fighting with or without weapons, either as a method of training or settling grudges that naturally came up. After the bout, the Rangers would embrace each other, showing that no hard feelings remained or had cropped up from the fight. It was an ancient art, predating even the Rangers, to where there were only a few elves who could claim to have trained with the Tribal Northmen before the first Empire began.

Ljas'atuk is an abrupt, brutal art, focused on avoiding attack while simultaneously using any method available to remove the threat your opponent poses. Armed or unarmed, they fought with dangerous precision. Karos watched the fighting as he sipped a cup of hot cider, chuckling as he remembered his time learning *ljas'atuk*. He'd earned more than his fair share of lumps during that time, even ending up with a broken nose.

"Remind you of your time as a *valtagt*, Karos?"

The voice belonged to the Loremaster, Wastan. Karos turned to face the man, looking him over slowly. He was a head shorter than Karos, with salt-and-pepper hair decorating an otherwise unremarkable head. He knew the man's face, though it was hidden by the mask, and it was like the rest of him; plain, but not unattractive. Just unremarkable, as if whoever sculpted his face was growing tired when they got to him. It benefited him, though, as he seemed to blend in and out of crowds when needed. Nodding, Karos cleared his throat.

"It is refreshing to see the Tenderfeet make the same mistakes I made."

"You? Make mistakes? Come now, surely you can do better these days?"

"Perhaps, but my energy must be spent on other tasks, old friend."

He took another sip of his cider. They had made it well, causing him to smirk at the thoughts that came with the hot cup. It'd been some time since he enjoyed a hot drink, and indeed it felt like forever since he just *sat down*. But something told him there was much more ahead, and little time to relax. Shaking his head, the Warden drained his cup, grimacing slightly as the heat made his belly ache. Then, he cleansed the cup and headed back to the Tent of Station, just as The Moot readied to reconvene.

Within the tent, things had settled. Karos had his tunic, chainmail, and overtunic on once more, much to his pleasure and the tasks ahead were being laid out. This was interrupted, however, by the beating of massive wings and the throaty call that could only come from one bird. *Carwaan*, the raven of the Rangers. Turning to leave the tent, Karos threw his cloak back onto his shoulders and fastened it, before pushing open the flap. The Rangers cleared a sizeable area as a massive raven back-winged for landing. Many Tenderfeet backed away, intimidated by the size of the bird, as more senior rangers stepped towards it. Karos headed them off, looking the creature over to find what had brought him here. It hopped towards him and extended a leg, upon which was tied a small scroll. As he reached down to remove the item, the raven pecked at his belt-pouch, obviously expecting some compensation for his flight. "Of course, you greedy beast." These words annoyed the crow, who beaked the loop holding the pouch closed, tugging it down and away from the toggle it was slipped around. That done, he began rummaging through the pouch, before being stopped by Karos, who pushed the creature back, off balancing the half-spear length tall creature, and placed a hand over the pouch. "Duty first, scorch you Carwaan!" In protest, the raven squawked and pecked savagely at his hand. Only after removing the raven's cargo did Karos reach into the pouch and present him with a handful of highberries. Gleefully, the raven began snacking, following the berries as Karos placed them on the ground. He stretched his wings out for a moment, unfurling to their full span, just over a spear's length. From there, he extended most of his feathers long enough to stretch, before folding the great wings against his body.

A few senior Rangers dragged their Tenderfeet over to Carwaan as Karos removed himself to the Tent of Station with the letter. It was sealed in red wax with the sigil of the Kingmage, marking it as an important missive. As soon as he had entered the tent, he broke the seal and inspected the letter. To his great surprise, the letter was not written in the formal, careful hand of the Kingmage's usual scribe, but the tight and angular scrawl of the Kingmage himself. It even lacked the gilding and normal calligraphy associated with such a noble of high station. In Karos' mind, this was evidence of a situation of great severity. Clearing his throat, he read the letter aloud.

"TO MY DUTIFUL ALLIES, THE STALWART AND HONORED RANGERS OF SERAN

I, Harthos Alvor Harrolsen, Kingmage and Imperator of Seran and the Indeka Islands, issue forth this warning and request for investigation.

An unknown plague has struck the city of Cúledan, in the Province of Dragonmoor, known also as the City of Knights. Therefore, the city is to be quarantined, with the help of the Knights of The Brotherhood of Dres'lan, the Paladins of The Temple of The Ancestors, as well as the Mages of the Shining Star. No one will be permitted to make entry or leave the city, save for your Rangers.

My advisor, the Just and Fair King Mykil Dalviin of Dragonmoor, tells of the horrors of this sickness, indicating that, "the flesh of the victims is rotting to the bone, verily. Even the organs of the afflicted are rotting away, until they die." Whatever plague this is, magic affects it not and potions only slow the progression of the rot. The venerable Silver family, as my trusted advisors and executors, have begun their work of trying to understand and stop this plague. However, they admit their efforts may not bear fruit in a timely fashion without further information."

Therefore, I beg of you, as protectors of Seran and her people, to find the nature of this sickness and begin wielding your considerable skills towards formulating a cure, that we may save lives. This duty is to be placed above even my decree of averting and removing the threat of war from the Scala'Dun of Nevian and cleaved to with all haste and vigor.

Written by my hand upon this 4th day of Firstgreen in the year Fifty-Five of the Thirty-Fifth Empire of the Lands of Seran. May the High Ancestors see us through this trial.

Harthos Alvor Harrolsen."

Karos stared at the bindrune of the Kingmage's name for a moment. *This must be important if the Mages were getting involved. And for a plague to strike in Cúledan, a city which has long held the favor of the Ancestors... This was strange.* Something else was at work here and none wanted to say it. Karos broke the silence then, popping his neck.

"I shall take Rangers Pjotr Aegmunt and Alaya Wandering-Bow. They are fresh-blooded but show great promise. As well, I will take the Talons." The Moot nodded in agreement. The Talons were hand-picked by the Warden Ranger as the best of the Rangers and were nearly unstoppable, even against insurmountable odds. Given the situation, it would be foolish for them to be left to the wayside. Karos glanced up once more after he made notes in the runic Sk'av'A alphabet and nodded. "Before I leave, I shall visit the *wol'jalar*. Her advice has never led us wrong." The nodding of heads marked his words true. Turning to leave, Karos thought for a moment. "May the Ancestors watch over us all and Veljra guide our steps and arrows. *Kalatozi jevka wotik, Tengarii litik'ki.*" The farewell was echoed by the Moot and Karos pushed the tent flap open.

"Karos! Are we to prepare for a journey, *kala'taj?*" The familiar voice of Wastan Kivanis, the Ranger Loremaster, issued forth from the old man. Idly, Karos nodded, before turning his attention to the elder. Smiling slightly behind his mask, he could tell that the old man was ready for a new adventure, something to shake the dust off his bones. For a moment, he thought back to the time he had first met Wastan, in a battle near Dagon's Hill in Khataar. Many foes advanced upon him, believing his advanced age to be their advantage, only to be beaten down by the skillfully wielded quarterstaff carried by the deceptively agile man. His reputation was a legend among the Rangers, as was his skill at opening recalcitrant locks.

"Aye, Wastan. Gather Aegmunt and Wandering-Bow. As well, get the word out to the Talons. *Zenaz sul ta, la ca'e kiji.*" With that, he placed his hand upon the older man's shoulder. Being one of his Talons, Wastan would gather the others at their normal place of meeting, where they would receive their instructions from the crown. Idly, Karos plucked a rock from the ground and slung it at the bulky form of Carwaan, angling it so it would skip under the raven. This elicited a caw from the bird's throat and it dove after the rock, thinking it to be a treat or some prey. However, it realized its error after pecking the rock and let out an annoyed squawk, before turning to eye Karos. "Come on, *kardo kijini ska!* We must away!"

The bird's head bobbed for a moment, before it spread great wings and took to the air in a light puff of dust and powdered snow. Karos watched Carwaan's ascent for a moment, even through the nearly blinding snowfall, and smiled beneath his mask. That truly was a valuable ally they had in the magnificent bird. This reflection lasted only a moment, and he turned his attention to a tent set at the edge of the camp. Towards it he strode, steeling his mind for the immediate task of speaking to the Seer, or *wol'jalar*. Her advice was always useful, even if it was for a task that had not presented itself yet. But she was a little... unsettling at the best of times.

No sooner had he opened the flap than the blind Ranger spoke. "In, in, Karos. In you must come, for there are things to be seen." Karos investigated the dark tent to find the flame-haired woman. Up her face turned, milky, dead eyes looking at the Warden Ranger. It was said that as a trade for the gift of foresight, the Ancestors had taken her corporeal sight away as recompense. Others said it was her sanity that she lost her vision after she rubbed Basilisk Vine in them to ward off the Sight. Regardless, blind she was and clearer than most were her visions. Entering the tent and allowing the flap to close, Karos took a seat across from her when beckoned.

"*Wol'jalar*, I require guidance and foresight. What lies ahead on the road I walk?" Karos' had decided the question before he even approached her tent, as it should be. He cleared his mind of all other distractions as quickly as he could. Into a bag she reached, removing six small, carefully carved slabs of stone. At first, she placed them face down, her eyes never straying from his.

"Guidance you ask for this task alone, but your aura betrays your thoughts. You wish to know as well what the future holds for you in other things." Karos nodded slowly, though he knew she could not see it. Even blind, she had an uncanny ability to sense the emotions of others. What was on Karos' mind may not have been obvious to other Rangers, but to her, it was clear as daylight. "Turn over the stones and tell me what you see, Warden Ranger. And we shall know what the Fate-Weavers hold in store for you."

Karos nodded slowly and reached out towards the stones upon the table. She spoke again, her voice failing to hide an inner craftiness. "But know, of course, that the wills of the Ancestors change day by day. Know that it is not always best to know what lies ahead." The Warden Ranger nodded slowly and overturned the first rune. With a calm voice, he spoke aloud the name of the rune.

"Niruuz. The rune of the Wildmother." It never failed to

occur when getting a Runecast. He always found Niruuz, the rune of Veljra, the matron of the Rangers. For the Rangers, it meant safety in travels and that no test would defeat them. Heartening, but not that helpful to him currently.

"Veljra blesses you as she does all of us. You will never lose your way and you shall always arrive where people need you most. No task shall be too great for you." The woman waved at him to overturn another of the six runes that lay on the table. As he reached out, Karos cleared his mind once more to ensure the message would not fall astray. Gently, he flipped the next rune and read the symbol, naming it first in his head.

"Lufnat." The rune of loyalty. This puzzled Karos for a time, for he never faltered in his loyalty and his Rangers never faltered in theirs. What could it possibly mean? He took a breath and looked up at the *wol'jalar*. She raised an eyebrow in response to his reading and nodded slightly, as if impressed. When she spoke, her voice seemed oddly chipper.

"The Rune of Loyalty... you will forge a new friendship to last the ages, or perhaps many. Never will bond-brothers and -sisters fail each other and always will they stand together. The Sight is cloudy upon this rune and I cannot see *who*... But I see two forms, one great in stature, its aura majestic and dangerous, yet friendly. The other the size of a man brave and true. Never has he faced a test such as he finds ahead. But never has he let himself fail. There are more, but they are too far away... they are but wisps to my eyes." Karos nodded, still confused, but willing to trust the Ancestors. Even the *wol'jalar*'s sight had its limits after all, and she was one of the most powerful. Reaching out, he overturned another runestone and blinked at the one he found. At first, he did not believe it, but there it was, as plain as the day is bright.

"Paili..." Karos sat there for a moment, astonished. At least one runecast per year he had had for as long as he was a Ranger and somehow, *never* had this rune come up. He shook his head in bewilderment as he turned his eyes up to the *wol'jalar*. She smiled rather oddly and waited a moment before speaking. Karos took a breath before her voice issued forth, steeling himself for the knowledge to come. This was one instance where he allowed himself to doubt the Ancestors.

"The rune of love. Poulla's rune. My sight is foggy on this as well, but I see two forms- that of a woman, perhaps a man alongside. Time shall tell, but the message is clear- Poulla herself has deemed that your self-induced isolation is about to end and the other Ancestors agree. When and where your *Po'ul'lar* will reveal themselves is in the hands of the Ancestors. The most you can do is keep an open mind and a watchful eye. You shall know when they find you." She was still smiling in that rather frightening way. Disquieting, even, and Karos felt a shudder roll up his spine. She had expected this, to be sure. Often, she claimed that runecasts were one thing she did not know in advance, but in Karos' mind, she just said that to allay fears and questions regarding free will and other such things. She always knew more than she let on and it was difficult to let that alone.

Reaching out, he turned the fourth rune. Another odd thought to his mind. What could it possibly mean? To Karos, this rune casting was raising more questions than it had answered, and that troubled him. Usually, the Ancestors were far more direct when dealing with him. Of course, the only one he had ever encountered face-to-face was Veljra herself and even then, it was an oddity. But still, he thought, it was a sign of things to come. "Wulza."

The *wol'jalar* shook her head slightly and clicked her tongue. "Strife, confusion and chaos. Not just for you, but for all of Seran. Wulza speaks of a coming war... and far worse things. You will make choices that will dictate the lives of all... and end the lives of some. But through it all, victory will come for all." This disconcerted Karos- chaos he could deal with. But choices that may end lives? Of whom, his Rangers? Innocents? Victory for *all*? What on Seran could that possibly mean? Shaking his head, he cleared his thoughts once more. Again, he reached out to flip another rune.

The image on the stone comforted him slightly; Muhdan, the rune of strength and fortitude. He nodded slightly and his eyes moved up once more. He spoke, his voice less afraid now, as if the rune had already influenced him. "Muhdan." The *wol'jalar* nodded slightly and placed her hands against each other in thought. Karos could feel her focus reaching out to the Ties That Bind, that imperative force that links all life. Almost on instinct, he closed his eyes as well and after some time, the woman spoke again.

"Great tests lie ahead, but through them all, you and those around you will stand, like a mountain against the raging hurricane. You will not fail in your duties, nor will you ever give up. The same I can say about those with whom you will travel, Rangers or otherwise. Whatever the tests ahead, Warden Ranger, you shall see it through. Though there is darkness in the Sight, there is a greater light to behold. The pyres will burn many times and many Rangers shall pass into Veljra's Hunting Grounds. But we will not fail and we will not falter. We will forge new alliances in the absolute depths of adversity and hardship- alliances that will last many lifetimes." She sounded much surer of herself than usual, as if the rune were affecting her as well. Karos' eyes opened slowly, and he saw hers flutter open, the milky orbs regarding him severely. "Know this, though. Your voice may fail and your body may weaken. But you will endure and you will become stronger for it."

Karos nodded, his heart lightened somewhat by that revelation. After all, knowing that the people alongside him would not fail him was a boon. He sighed and looked up to the woman, before reaching out for the final runestone. Closing his eyes at first, he cleared his mind, focusing on the feel of the stone, the texture and warmth against his hand. His heartbeat became a deafening drumroll in his head. When the time felt right, he overturned the rune to reveal the symbol. His eyes flew open, and he released the held breath as he looked down upon the rune. *Otzal*, the rune of mercy and forgiveness. Karos nodded slightly at this and spoke the name. "Otzal."

The *wol'jalar* was silent for a moment as she searched with the Sight, wondering where this rune would come up. Folding her hands in front of her, lost herself in contemplation- or was about to collapse. At length, she spoke once more, her voice slightly quieted. "A choice will stand before you and you will know the hour. No matter your anger, it is imperative that you not strike the killing blow, else an event will never happen that should move the foundations of the world. Every fiber of your being will scream retribution... But you must not obey. Elyrea's command is explicit and she will make known the moment your blade must not taste blood. Enkar and dal'Kiyr affirm it and Veljra and Ybril both defend it." Karos nodded slowly, curious after this one. With one last look around the cluttered tent, he rose to his feet and turned to leave.

A thought struck him and his head turned slightly to speak

to the *wol'jalar* once more. His voice issued forth, like a stream across rocks, and he felt sure of what he was asking. It was one thing he must know; he felt and for all he knew, it may play into things more heavily than expected. "These *po'ul'lar* of whom you prophesy... what color is their hair?" The *wol'jalar* laughed for a moment, before closing her eyes and focusing in on that vision once more. Slowly, the ghostly forms made sense to her. Bit by bit, she poured her energy into it, gaining more and more details, some of which she would never tell Karos- after all, too much foreknowledge was dangerous.

At first, it was difficult to place the color of the hair. She was not used to such requests, and the focus needed drained her. But she felt it was necessary to allay the Warden's concerns. Finally, she had the answer. Opening her eyes, she turned the sightless orbs up to the man and spoke. "The question is difficult, for the Sight is not always that specific, Warden Ranger. But at long last, I have your answer. The first color you seek is as red as the fires that keep us warm, the other the silver of coin." Her normally tanned face was pale, evidence of the strain that she had taken on. She took a breath, reaching out to gather the runestones and place them in a black sack. Karos nodded slowly and turned once more, pressing the flap of the tent open and exiting into the frigid clearing. Taking a breath, he looked around for a moment, before slipping away to the edge of the Moot-lands. He needed to catch up to the Talons; they would already have a lead on him.

"Hail! Warden Ranger!" Or they had disobeyed and waited for him, reason unknown. He turned to face the one speaking and sure enough, there assembled were Wastan the Loremaster, Kiri the Long-Eye, among others. A bipedal lupine form, rather young and excitable, eyed Karos with a mixture of excitement and total awe. This was the newest Talon, of course, Sardra Wood-Strider. A young Snow-Dokk she was and a recent Ranger. But she had proven herself many times to be among the most stalwart and skilled. Only ones who knew what to look for could see why she fought so hard to prove herself. She was a survivor of many horrible things and had used the pain it had caused to rise above and against. She gave few her trust and fewer still numbered her *rak'an'opa'kaval*. To them alone, she confided her fears, her sleepless nights and her self-doubts. To them alone, she listened when they gave advice and pushed her through her dark times. Upon the fields of battle, she focused this pain into a fury, becoming a whirlwind of death with sword and axe or a flurry of arrows, each striking exactly where she wanted them to. She had a strange ability to know where she would be the most helpful- which line was about to collapse, which position about to be overrun and there she would be, wielding blade and voice or bow and arrow to turn the tide. When stripped of weapons, she would unleash her fearsome claws and teeth, letting her primal side take control- just enough to fight. She never succumbed to the bloodlust that often defined her race.

Karos was glad of her company, for the young dokk, though muted in emotion, often brought much cheer to travels. Her voice sang clearer than most, with energy few could match. Reaching out, Karos embraced her gently, patting her back. He spoke, his voice kind and collected. "*Skala'zan*, Sardra Wood-Strider! It is wonderful to see you." The dokk ducked her head, slightly embarrassed, but pleasantly so. To her, Karos was an Ancestor walking among them, though he refuted this as often as he could. She had seen him in battle though and thought more of him the more she saw. It saddened her that he was so lonely, but she knew his time would come. Just as hers would and she would find happiness.

"As ever the snow falls, Warden Ranger, it is an honor to see you." Karos smiled beneath his mask as he looked into the icy blue eyes of the dokk, and examining the colors of her markings. She was wolf sable, with a single gold stripe running the center of her forehead. For the longest time, he had felt like he needed to protect her, that she was someone who needed aid and comfort. It had taken them drawing each other's blood in a spar for him to learn that she was *not* defenseless and that he was *not* the one her distrust needed to focus on. Truly, during their battle, they had become *kaval'dagaan and* had learned each other on a level few would ever know. She had seen the depths of isolation that he knew, and he had seen the pain she hid so skillfully, and they had made a compact, unwritten and unspoken, to help each other through the Dark Days each faced.

As they stepped back from each other, Kiri stepped forth and placed a hand upon Karos' shoulder. He smiled and placed a hand upon hers and they touched their foreheads, much gentler than most would. She had been a mother to him and a mother twice before. But her story had taken a dark turn when her children fell defending her from bandits and in desperation, she had turned to the Rangers. At first for retribution and then for family, she joined and learned the ways of the woodland warriors, becoming one of their best. Still grieving for her children, she turned that grief into sympathy and a caring heart, knowing that many Rangers were orphans or unwanted children. She became mother to all she could, seeing to their basic needs, ensuring they had food, drink, and fresh clothing. In battle, she was a precise shot from afar, landing arrows in places none thought possible and slaying foes before they could become dangerous. When pressed, she was competent with daggers and incredible at *ljas'atuk*.

Her presence was quite welcome, and she knew it. Even Rangers many years her elder viewed her as a kindly mother to them, for she never ignored pleas for aid. When a Ranger celebrated their birth, she would be the first to bring them some small treat and the last to tease them. Truly, she was the Ranger-Mother, though many knew her as the Long-Eye. She could see farther than most Rangers even could and helped to identify persons wanted by the Crown or by the locals for crimes. Merciful though she was, she held a hatred for slavers and was often the first to enact the most brutal of deaths for each one they came across.

Karos released his grip on her shoulder and turned to the elder of the group. Wastan nodded to Karos, looking the younger man over for a moment. *He seemed to be in good health*, thought the Loremaster, *but something in his eyes... Something disquiets him.* There was, of course, the isolation the man always felt, but even that felt different this time. "You have been to the *wol'jalar*, have you not?" When Karos nodded, Wastan knew then that the young man had had a runecast for himself and the results were what had him shaken. It puzzled the older man, almost worrying him, for if something could shake the Warden Ranger, it must be quite fell or strange indeed.

He was already old when the Rangers found him. His wife had passed into the afterworld and he sought to give back as only he could- telling stories. Over his life, he had collected many and had intended to write them all down, but never found the time. Then, his wife sickened and passed. Saddened, he declined himself, until an opportunity presented itself. His Jarl gave him a sum of gold and told to travel for a time, to collect more stories. In this time, he had found the Rangers and his home. Given the life blessing early because of his advanced age, the man soon found himself hard at work measuring up to folk in their prime. At first outmatched in endurance and speed, he soon found his way to the top, becoming an avid runner and fighter. With his preferred quarterstaff, he was a force to be reckoned with - though many bandits and raiders thought him just an old man, much to their eventual dismay. After all, what they had thought to be an easy robbery would turn into chaos, with the supposedly frail old man throwing away his cloak and breaking skulls with a steel-and-wood staff.

With a mind full of lore and magic, Wastan was also the best lock-picker of the Rangers, although his preferred method was rather unconventional. Instead of crouching, which he vocally stated as being 'terrible on his knees' to pick a lock, he would simply speak a word of Sk'av'A to bolster his staff and slam it through the body of the lock with enough ferocity to shatter it completely. If they needed stealth and finesse though, he would whip out his tools and have the lock defeated in a manner of moments. For tougher or enchanted locks, he would delve into the well of knowledge stored in his mind to find either a charm or a curse that would unlock the door or blow the entire thing off its hinges.

He did not like to waste time.

There were, of course, Pjotr Aegmunt and Alaya Wandering-Bow, who had become friends through adventuring together.

When the opportunity came to join forces with the Rangers, they gladly showed up together and had learned to fight better together than most people could alone. With sword and shield in Aegmunt's hand, as well as a dagger and axe in Alaya's, they were a dangerous duo up close. At a distance, they would often compete with their arrow shots, striving to shoot further or more accurately. This often got them into trouble, for they would focus more on their competition than the task at hand and would forget their duties.

Aegmunt hailed from the northern reaches of Dragonmoor, where he had been a farm boy dreaming of greater things. His chance came to prove himself when a band of uroks stormed his village. Quickly picking up a discarded sword and a damaged shield, he charged head-on. Predictably, his charge did not last long, as he had no formal training, but it had given everyone else enough time to rally. He survived, fortunately, and became an adventurer, seeking danger where he could and pay when he chose. He was a dangerous foe and a fierce friend, willing to risk it all to ensure the safety of those he held dear.

Alaya Wandering-Bow was a wood elf from the Indeka Islands, which were, in her words, 'some of the most boring possible places to live'. At fifty, she paid her way across Se'he Tsalaemanka on the *Wave Minstrel* and had arrived in Elfshore. From there, she struck out, hoping her life's story would find her. One day upon the road, she found herself under attack from raiders and about to be overrun, when an adventuring company came to her aid. Gratefully, she joined up with them and learned quickly that adventuring was not as romantic as she had originally surmised. It was dirty, dangerous work- and that suited her fine.

Chuckling, a deep elf, from the lands under the ground, sat at the rear of the party, watching everyone. This was the Shadow-Walker, Kizarian Poloa. Quite a tough fellow to befriend, he was a master assassin in his younger years. When a contract came up that forced his blade against the neck of a child, he ddecided to re-evaluate his choices- and destroy his employers. He gave the child to a safe home, and wandered for many decades, trying to find his purpose. It was at the end of this that he, in a drunken stupor, pledged himself to the Rangers in a choice that, though he cannot remember, he has never regretted.

Karos waved them to follow him and began trudging out of the camp and into the depths of the snowy forest. One hand rested upon the hilt of his sword and the other hung loose at his side, ready to move at an instant's notice. After he took the first step out of the Mootgrounds, the man reached up to his pace-counting beads, and pulled down the first on the lower nine beads. Normally, he would only do this after his hundredth step, but today, well, he felt it appropriate. As with the rest of the Talons, he was ready for anything.

Or so he thought.

2: Hanmaer Tower, Eversnow Forest, Northrealm

"**A**gain! Try it again, Mirenel! Ashvathi may have an excuse to laze about and grow armor, but you cannot! You are far too slow when fighting!" An elf, well over a thousand years old, stood watching as the fresh blood under his command practiced their hand-to-hand fighting. Idly, he glanced to the sky, wondering just where their beasts were– *likely stuffing themselves*, he thought wryly to himself. "You are a wood elf from Dragonmoor, Mirenel. You should be right at home."

"B-but... Sir... it is far, far too cold here. Even Ashvathi is complaining." The girl shivered violently as she breathed her words. She had *never* seen this much snow in her life and had never been this cold. "Even though I am a wood elf, I have never been in woods such as these. How do the creatures here survive this cold?" The senior rider smirked slightly, but the young one had a point. Glancing over the other riders-in-training, he noted Joram seemed to care not about the cold. After a moment, though, he remembered why.

"Joram, you are from Northrealm, are you not?" Nodding, the large blonde-haired man dropped from his perch and strode over to the shivering she-elf. In one motion, he removed his own winter cloak to drape it around her shoulders.

"Aye, so I am. The cold bothers me not and Hjalgroþ is eager for more work. Please, Master Thäoldr, six hours have we been at this. I need not rest, but the others are freezing to the bone." Even the normally silent and stalwart Tel'varael was complaining, his body racked with shivers. It *was* their first day ever in the Forest of Eversnow, one of the coldest places of all Seran. To the uninitiated, it was a brutal experience, the bitter cold permeating fire-warmed huts and even the great Hanmaer Tower, to where the thickest of furs were necessary just to survive the night. Over time, though, the body would grow accustomed, acclimating to the cold and allowing the person to become tougher.

For some, it took a blessing from the Ancestors to survive the first night.

"Fine, fine. Into the tower, fresh bloods. Joram, you shall pull first–" He paused in the middle of the sentence as a storm of wings came overhead. At first expecting an attack, Thäoldr threw back his cloak and charged his pathway nerves, tracing one hand down the opposite arm to send magical energy pulsing through, readying it to be released as a powerful spell. When he saw the source, he blinked. *We were not expecting hawks... especially not this many!*

"Joram. You are on first watch." The powerful Nolvern nodded slightly and positioned himself accordingly. Planting his feet into the snow, he took a deep breath, bringing his bulk to bear as a deterrent against any who would try to assault the stronghold of the Riders of Gelvrentael. As the others trailed inside, he felt the door close behind him as he steeled himself for a few hours of boredom.

Thäoldr stood for a moment as the multitude of hawks landed nearby, crying out to have their burdens removed. One by one, they presented themselves to the grizzled elf until he had a massive collection of parchment letters, some with official-looking seals. When he'd gathered the last one, Thäoldr took his prizes inside, not watching as the hawks took to the skies once more, bound for places unknown.

Opening the most important-looking of the letters, Thäoldr sucked in a breath. *That bodes poorly.* It was from Kingmage Harthos, the head of the Empire of Seran, and the de-facto supreme commander of the Order. Reading the letter to himself, the elf found his stomach turning topsy-turvy with each new line.

"Honored Thäoldr, Sage of Wind of the Order of Gelvrentael.

This letter, whether or not it finds you in fine spirits, is of dire import. A plague has struck our lands, beginning with the city of Cúledan in Dragonmoor, the likes of which has never been seen. My counsel from King Dalviin is thus; verily, the flesh is rotting from the bone, organs turning into foul sludge, muscles wasting into puddles. As such, I require the services of the Order of Gelvrentael forthwith to assess the extent of this outbreak, and contain it as best you are able. I ask that you go immediately to your superiors in the Order, and know that I have sent them official instruction. This I write informally as a request from one leader to another; Do not let my empire fall.

Signed, Harthos Alvor Harrolsen."

Thäoldr stared at the letter for a few minutes, unsure of what to think. *Flesh rotting off? Organs to sludge? Muscles into puddles?* Surely this was in jest, but when the elf looked over the stacks of letters, his gut told him they would contain the same portents of doom. Sighing, he placed the letter face down and opened the next.

"Sagewind, I will forgo formality, as this is a crisis. Several of my riders have taken sick with an unknown illness. Strange pustules form on their bodies, and it progresses until they are quite literally rotting flesh from bone. I have never seen anything like this. Healing magic is completely ineffective, and I am running out of time. I need guidance.

Signed, Vloran."

Opening another letter, then another, Thäoldr found more of the same. For once, he was not tempted to complain about the utter lack of formality, as it seemed there was a deeper, more urgent need facing him. Sighing, he went through the stack of letters, reading through them to find other people facing the same doom, all asking him the same question; what is going on? Rubbing his temples, the elf shifted his focus, trying to think. Hanmaer Tower had limited archives, but perhaps something could be found? Putting thought to action, he slipped away from the desk and made his way down into the archive room and began searching for any clues as to what the dastardly sickness may be.

Is this punishment, or just recognition of a needed skill? The voice came unbidden, a deep echo of Joram's own. A wry smile crossed his face as he spoke to his dragon, using the latent telepathy that manifested with a pairing.

The coldest part of the day is nigh, so it is best that we be the ones to weather it unprotected, Hjalgroþ. This earned him a deep-throated rumble of amusement from his beast. *Where are you, Hjalgroþ?* He was curious, not just for the location of his own partner, but to know where the other dragons were as well.

Near. Cryptic, for sure. Then again, the great dragons of Seran were not well known for being forthcoming with information, even when it was necessary. As he stood there, a statue glowering out into the wooded expanse, he thought himself ready for anything. After all, the dragons had chosen him, had they not? When he heard the rush of wings overhead, he looked for the familiar bulk of his dragon, instead finding a small and quick green. In short order, the beast touched down, its eyes radiating alarm and distress. Slumped upon its neck was a rider. Reaching up, Joram slammed his fist against the bell, causing the loud report to echo through the area. Again and again he rang the bell, before running towards the green. As he approached, it reared, sending a buffeting gale with its wings. Where he expected a pained shriek, or even a hateful scream, instead came a cautionary groan as the creature shifted, letting its cargo slide off and to the ground.

The young woman landed on her back, and Joram nearly vomited. With a force of will, he composed himself and shouted. "Master Thäoldr! Master Thäoldr, I need you!" Down the stairs and out the door barreled the millennium-old elf. He was in naught but his trousers and boots, revealing his muscled frame and various tattoos. As he approached the green, he placed his palms out, glancing to the young woman in the snow.

"Easy, Kitorath, easy. What evil has befallen Elsaia?" Daring a glance at the woman, his stomach churned. Her clothing was stained with red, showing that she was bleeding badly. But when he lifted her shirt to examine the wound, he found much worse. Her flesh was rotting away, cracking and weeping with pus. Gently, he pressed two fingers to her neck, searching for a pulse. *Was that... no... yes!* It was there. Weaker than that of a starved babe, but it was there. "Joram. Get her inside. Quickly. Keep her away from the others."

Joram nodded, carefully gathering the poor girl, carrying her inside and laying her on the table. All the way to her neck, her skin was discolored, weeping and rotting. Once more, he called out to Thäoldr. "Milord Thäoldr, a dastardly wound besets her, the likes of which I have ne'er seen!" As the elder entered the Tower, he shook his head.

"This is no wound, Joram. Hearken to my words. Gather the healing herbs. There should be some in the stores. Quickly, now!" Down the stairs came the other two newbloods, and Thäoldr waved them back. "Stay back! We know not if this is infectious. Up the stairs, both of you! Now!" The two slunk back up the stairs of the Tower as Joram stormed to the cavern below in search of the healing herbs.

Thäoldr grabbed his pack from the shelves next to the door and upended it, scattering the contents upon the table next to him. From there, he sifted through his belongings until he found a healing potion he had mixed earlier that week. Carefully, he gripped the back of her head, angling her up a little. Against her lips, he placed the opening of the potion, gently pouring it into her mouth. The woman sputtered and coughed, her eyes flying open. "Easy, Elsaia. What has befallen you?" The only response he received was a spurt of blood, as she fell into a fit of coughing. Blood went everywhere, and she choked. Doing his best, the elf rolled the woman onto her side before striking her back with the flat of his hand to expel the blood from her airway. It worked, at least for a moment, and the woman choked out two words.

"Cúledan....plague..." No sooner had she exposed the source of the issue than she collapsed into a fit, her body convulsing, causing her to spew more blood.

"JORAM! AS YOU LOVE LIFE, SPEED YOUR SEARCH! BE SWIFT, FOR TIME IS OF THE ESSENCE!" He was feeling the stirrings of panic now. This was entirely alien to him and he knew not what to do. Gripping the woman gently as she nearly fell from the table, he shouted again for the Nolvern. "SCORCHITALL, JORAM, I NEED YOU HERE NOW!" Which caused the man, cursing the darkness, to grab what little he had found and charge up the stairs. Shoving the herbs into Thäoldr's hand, he took up holding the woman so she would not fall. "Get her teeth open. We must get this into her mouth." Nodding, Joram freed one hand and grabbed a nearby knife, pressing the blunt end between the woman's clenched teeth. When her mouth gave, he pried, opening her convulsing jaws long enough for Thäoldr to place the herbs in her maw.

"Quickly, bind her. We must take her to Mount Wounds-End. Hurry." Nodding, the bulkier man quickly bound the still-writhing woman, unsure of what would happen. "Summon Hjalgroþ. Take her and Kitorath, fly as fast as the winds will carry you." Joram nodded, easily carrying the woman out to where the ice-blue dragon already waited. Carefully, he placed the woman and lashed her to the saddle, before seating himself and spurring his beast into the air, hardly noticing the sickly green dragon next to them.

With speed, Hjalgroþ. We must take her to the healers. The dragon was silent as they ascended. Then, when they reached their flight altitude, he shot a gout of flame into the dying light.

No! Her only chance is with the Rangers. Thäoldr knows not what is happening. We must find a Ranger! Joram was taken aback. The Rangers kept to themselves and avoided all. It was impossible to think they would aid a Rider. Especially with the bad blood and millennia of frosty relations, which had occasionally blossomed into bloodshed.

You are not making sense! The Rangers can do nothing for us! But the dragon's mind was already made up. Dragging a wing, he looped, seeking out his prey with keen eyes. Certainly, a Ranger on foot could avoid being seen on the ground. But to the eyes of the dragon, flying hundreds of feet in the air, even the most delicate of movements were visible. Of course, this dragon was not just searching the ground, but also looking for a familiar creature. One his forefathers had known, before the rift between Ranger and Rider had grown.

Onward! We must push onward! The dragon ignored the commands sent by his rider. Had he gone mad? Or was something affecting his mind?

No. I know my actions! I am in command of my faculties! Circling wide, the dragon winged, tasting the air and occasionally letting out a brilliant gout of flame as he searched high and low for signs of those who could aid him. Fighting exhaustion, the dragon kept searching, hoping it would not be in vain as he winged into the distance, searching, questing, for one who might bring the girl back to herself.

Thäoldr, thinking the worst had passed, cleaned himself up. *At least no blood entered my mouth or nose...* As a test of this theory, he spat on the floor. Sure enough, there was no red tinge, no sign that he was in danger. Little did he know the work was already beginning and his time to reckon with the evil that was loose would come.

Outside, a dragon gurgled in pain, collapsing onto the ground and heaving, choking for breath and panicking as it could not move air. Its mouth opened and closed soundlessly, drooling ichor as it attempted to save itself. But the end must come for all things and soon enough, the young green dragon Kitorath moved her last, becoming still and cold, a macabre image of what was to come.

Thäoldr thought he heard a strange noise. It lasted just for a second and sounded like someone trying to catch their breath after water went down the wrong tube. Shaking his head, he put the thought out of his mind. After all, the dragon had followed Joram and Hjalgroþ, correct? As he sat, he felt a drop strike his head. Just one. He looked up, remembering the horror he had just witnessed. *Blood. Everywhere...* He shook his head, not thinking anything of it as he drew water from the cellar's well into a pan and set it over the fire to warm so he could clean the mess up.

Near the top of the tower, the two newbloods sat, trying to figure out between them what had transpired. Annoyed, Mirenel strode to the window, staring out across the expanse and wondering what new evil had awoken in the land. Tel'varael arched an eyebrow and shook his head. "I cannot just wait while things happen. I am a Rider, scorch it, not some child!"

"But you are still new, as am I, Tel'varael. And we must do what we have been told by our senior." To this, the deep elf shook his head and stood.

"Stay here and rot if you wish. I am going to find out what is going on." With that, he strode out the door and began descending the stairwell, heading down to the main area. As he reached the lower steps, he tripped over his own feet and fell to the bottom of the stairs, landing heavily. Thäoldr turned, surprised at first at the sound. Quickly, though, his brows knitted in annoyance.

"Stay away! A rider has fallen ill with some devilish sickness, and she vomited blood everywhere. If you must leave, do so from the top of the Tower! Come no further down the stairway!" He had thrown his hand up in a warning gesture, also indicating the blood trickling down the wall from the vomit. Shaking his head, Thäoldr continued cleaning. When his sponge was soaked in crimson, he wrung it out and rinsed it before cleaning again. Tel'varael's eyes widened at the sight of the blood and he backed up the stairs a way, only to be nearly bowled over by the young elf.

"Master Thäoldr! There is a dragon dead in the snow outside!" Thäoldr cursed his luck. Why were things going to the wolves now? Was it not just a week ago he made an offering to the Ancestors? Did he not do his duty to the lands, to the Riders and to his ancestors? This was insanity, pure insanity. Little did he know, the things he had witnessed were just a symptom of a far greater sickness plaguing the lands. It was taking hold rapidly and soon enough, all corners of the world would feel its effects.

3

3: Oakheart's Forest, Westerspring

In another part of the world, a wood elf was beginning her day. At first, she attempted to ignore the raucous cries of her familiar, as the large red fox repeatedly attempted to awaken her mistress. Playfully, she tugged at her blanket for a few minutes before latching onto her hair. Predictably, this got an instant shriek of pain and the elf sat up quickly. She regretted that instantly, as it sent poor the poor creature flying and with her came a clump of the elf's hair. This was quite a painful experience, which led her to scream loudly. Her head bloodied and her adrenaline pumping, the elf decided it was about time to wake up as the fox expertly caught herself, landing in the corner of the small hut they shared. With a yip and a tail shake, she dropped the clump of hair and darted out into the sun, followed by the now quite awake elf.

Stepping over to a basin, the woman quickly splashed cool water onto her face, as well as onto the fresh wound. It stung a bit, but after the initial pain, she could focus. The rest of her hair was in a catastrophic mess and she fought to get it out of her face. As expected, the mass of fire-red curls did not want to cooperate and finally, she stopped trying to work with it. Taking a breath, she looked around for her clothing and nodded. A pair of well-crafted suede trousers had cost her many a silver, but they were the best she had found in a while. Quickly, she pulled herself into them and removed her nightgown. In the same motion, she pulled on a loose shirt before she slipped her boots on. They were certainly not the most comfortable she had ever worn, but they withstood the tests of time and travel better than any. Next came her corset, slipped on and carefully tied into place, though the elf felt like she almost had to dislocate her arms to tie it on. Shaking her head mirthfully, she finished tying the laces and reached for her armor. She was heading into town today for some supplies and to check and see if there were any bounties on the board, so she felt it was necessary to have her full ensemble.

Quickly, she slipped the leather breastplate over her head and into place and then tied on her belt, with sword hanging from it on her left side. Then came her quiver, carefully made from hard leather and full of arrows, as well as straps which held her precious bow. Carefully, she looped the sling over her shoulder and pulled it tight across her chest, before pushing open the door to her hut and leaving. Once in the sunlight, she winced slightly, as her eyes had not adjusted to the glare of the sun. Nodding slightly, she grabbed the pack that always sat by her door and whistled at her fox before heading off.

Blue eyes regarded the road ahead, and she began singing one of her favorite songs to keep her spirits up. The road ahead was long, but she was in no hurry and the day was just dawning. The red fox caught up to her quickly, padding alongside her mistress happily as the two made their way towards the edge of the forest.

On the way, a person neither friendly nor hostile regarded the duo's passage for some time. This being had seen them before and knew they were a peaceful dweller in the forest. In fact, the elf had a Writ of Grant going back to before Karos became Warden Ranger, if their memory still served well. It was signed by the previous Warden, Thorvan Koza. Quite a wise man he had been, the being mused. As they moved, so too did the watcher, moving along until they felt ready to reveal themselves. Dropping from the tree, they sidled towards the woman. Speaking in a pleasant tone, they addressed her calmly.

"Well met, milady Elf. Where art thou bound?" The girl nearly jumped through her skin, letting out a shriek that echoed rather well through the forest... The fox, however, remained calm, as if she had expected the Ranger to come from nowhere. The Ranger chuckled slightly and removed her hood, revealing long black hair and a skin far tanner than what most elves could accomplish. But there were definite signs of Elven heritage, even if the only visible one was the ears. She smiled warmly beneath the black cloth mask obscuring her face. A quick bow and she identified herself to the woman she'd been keeping tabs on for safety. "I am Nelya Ardivari and you have lived in my forest with the permission of the past Warden Ranger for two and a half centuries. Never have you raised your sword in anger in my forest and never have you failed to heed the call of those around you. But for now, I must ask; might I travel with you for a time?"

"Veldan's Wounds! Warn a person before you just jump out of nowhere, Ranger!" Her hand had found its way to her sword the instant the Ranger had leapt from the trees. After the initial shock wore off, the woman looked at the Ranger striding alongside her. Smiling, she spoke, much calmer now that she knew the quality of her new companion. "Of course, Master Ranger. Your company is most welcome. I am Fae cos'Criux and it is a pleasure to meet you. But I must ask that you keep your best pace, for I shall not slow mine." This elicited a chuckle from the Ranger, who then began singing a different song, one of loss and heroism, one known mainly to Rangers, though it was gaining popularity with other folk. She was keeping up with the other elf and even set a faster pace. Her voice was proud as she sang a tale from long ago.

"As I came 'cross the river Wythe and
down into the clear,
there I saw three-hundred strong,
the slavers of the Tear."
Wi' a sword in hand,
an' behind a bow,
Coldforge must fight today!
The town had been surrounded long
the fight looked a'ready won
when ou' of forge came a beastly man
and two dragons on the run!
Wi' a hammer in hand
and dragons behind
defend us all today!"

Fae looked in awe as they recounted the tale. She knew about the Coldforge Massacre that happened all those years ago, but people rarely sang about it. Many thought the song itself was a bad omen and would bring about pain. Others ignored that and sang it anyway, stating that 'history forgotten is history relived.' The Rangers sided with the latter and included it in their own teaching ballads, as part of the basic education for a Tenderfoot. Nelya knew it well because she was *there.* She had fought the fight and seen it through and she could remember the names of every Ranger who fell that day.

"'To arms,' he cried,
his voice rang loud
and out the townsmen came
the battle joined, but fifty–five
stood against the strength
Wi'sword'n'hammer
and bows behind,
'tis fight or die today!
The first attacked was House Lyvan,
their child sent away.
Proud and strong did Myran stand
but fell to numbers great
wi' sword in hand,
and a foe in front
many brave ones died that day!"

Fae racked her brain for a moment, for the name Lyvan sounded rather familiar to her. She wanted to ask the Ranger, but felt it would be rude to interrupt, so she kept listening as they went plodding along through the forest. The question nagged at her for some time and grew as the Ranger continued the rather fast-paced song. It was mesmerizing, to be truthful, and fascinating. The history seemed to come alive in front of her as the battle played out in her mind. In the back of her mind, she wished she could be present at a battle like that, that she could be the one to turn the tide.

"Eldira stood with her magics
'tween husband and the throng

*with her power and courage
many fell around
wi'spell in hand
husband behind
Eldira stood her ground...
But fall they did,
as all men must
when faced with their own death
as the Dragonsmith came, he cradled them
as they gave their last breath.
Wi'a body in hand
and vengeance in mind
the Dragonsmith rejoined the fray!"*

This Dragonsmith sounds like one it would be unwise to cross, thought Fae as she listened. Nelya smirked inwardly as she remembered what the Dragonsmith was like back then. Brash, but loyal to the definition. A colossal man he was, a trait shared with only minor change by his son and grandson. They said that the line of the Dragonsmith descended from giants and Nelya heartily believed that. She had seen what Ulfric was capable of, as well as his father, Calem. The current Dragonsmith, however, was unknown to her, and she had no reason to make the trek to Coldforge. She continued singing, not missing a beat as they walked along.

*"Wi'a mighty blow of his hammer,
He scattered five and ten
As he stood strong,
against the throng
he swung the hammer again!
Wi' hammer in hand
and anger behind,*

the Dragonsmith joined the fray!
The fight was bloody,
And the bodies numbered many
after days went by
upon the third
the townsmen left
they heard a raucous cry!
In the sky above,
a raven cried,
Wi' the Rangers on the way!"

The Dragonsmith had scattered fifteen with a single swing of his hammer. Few indeed could boast the same prowess in strength, but then again, almost none had giants in their lineage. He had lost himself to something deeper within that day, something primal had broken within him as he looked upon the bodies of the townsfolk he called friends. Instead of succumbing, he had focused that rage, that pain, into crushing blows and sundering strikes. Even better, the very reason his title was the 'Dragonsmith' were the two dragons who aided him in forging his gear. They joined in the battle as well and helped to hold the line until the Rangers arrived. Never with such vengeance had their might been wielded to bear and since then, slavers and bandits alike had given the town quite a wide berth.

This was also the first time that Carwaan, the raven of the Rangers, had seen action. That day had been his first as a scout and he had performed with admirable skill, cementing his position in the ranks of the Rangers, even to the point of being given the Life Blessing. It thus improved his lineage dramatically, and he became a legend both among people and animals. His coming heralded terrible wrath upon fell folk and incredible hope for the good. On his own, the raven was terrifying enough, with a *standing* height just over half a spearlength, not to mention a weight of forty pounds. His wings brought forth powerful gusts and his talons had drunk deeply that day. Many arrows had sought him and none had found him. He truly was a sight to behold.

"Many a questing arrow,
Loosed forth from bows unseen,
And many a foe did scatter
As they heard the ravens scream,
Wi'bow in hand,
And arrows fine
The Rangers joined the fray!
'We fight,' one cried,
His sword ready in hand
The Rangers charged
And many died
As they bled for those around!
wi'sword in hand
And bow behind
The Rangers joined the fray!"

This told of the skill of stealth the Rangers employed, as they had encircled most of the town and the incoming enemies with fewer numbers. Through their tactics, they had placed themselves as a block between their foe and escape, though the foe did not know it. When the arrows began flying, the Slavers of the Bleeding Tear at first thought they were getting reinforced. It was only when the arrows began striking their numbers that they realized their mistake, and by then it was too late. Surprise as their ally, the Rangers split into three groups– one firing arrows to keep their enemies' heads down and the other charging in to get up close and personal. The third broke off and stormed into the town, rallying the townsfolk and routing the enemies within. Then, with their forces increased, they began pushing outwards as the dragons and Raven circled overhead, searching for targets.

"Many a questing arrow,
were loosed from bows taut-strung
Many a sword drank deep that day
As the Rangers fought and won!
Wi'sword in hand
And bow behind
the Rangers joined the fray!
But thirty-five were Rangers
Descending to the fray
the courage of the Rangers
Still rings out to this day!
Wi'sword in hand
and bow behind
the Rangers saved the day!"

The Rangers had numbered rather few indeed, but through smarter tactics and fighting, as well as the aid of the towns-folk, had routed the Slavers of the Tear. Though they had won the battle, however, the Rangers did not stop. A group stayed behind to carry the dead to their resting places, but the majority had broken off to give chase. By the week's end, the remainders of the Slavers of the Bleeding Tear had been annihilated, and the Rangers set their slaves free.

"Twenty-three fell that day
Rangers and townsmen too
But crushed their enemies were
they ran the bandits through!

Wi'sword in hand
and bow behind
we sing victory today!
Sadly buried were the fallen,
The survivors left to mourn
As the Rangers slipped into the night,
Wi' the bodies of their own!
Pyres were lit
And tears we cried
Victorious we were that day!"

After assuring the safety of the town, the Rangers who had not chosen to chase down the Tear had stayed with the townsfolk, working through the fields of the dead. The slavers ended up piled and burned unceremoniously and for the townsfolk who died, their friends and surviving family cremated them and held a memorial in the ways of the Nolvern. For the Rangers who had passed into Veljra's care, however, had their rites given and their bodies carried to the Mootgrounds and given a proper funeral. Among them was a proud elf by the name of Elruviel Caladon, who had gone to his death willingly, keeping the foemen from breaking through the town's defenses. With his death came a chance for a pair of adventurers to rally the beleaguered townsfolk into a fearsome band of defenders. After the bloodshed was over, an eerie stillness descended as the Rangers tallied the dead. Giving their dead their last rites, the Rangers moved on- though a few stayed in Coldforge, both to honor the fallen and protect the town, even if just to let the people know they would not leave them to fend for themselves.

They had made a fair distance in a short time and though Fae was in top shape, her chest was heaving and her legs were aching. Her fox seemed to do okay and the Ranger, infuriatingly enough, was not even breathing heavy. She stretched slightly, before shifting and popping her neck. Looking at the other elf, Nelya spoke, a grin playing across her lips. "Come now, we have only traveled but a league. Surely you are up for more?" Taking a breath, Fae shot a glare at the other elf. There were many tales about the endurance of Rangers, but to see it up close, Fae at first did not know what to think. After a moment, though, the thought came to her; it was quite annoying. How were they so fresh and chipper? Most people would collapse after a mile in armor and yet this Ranger seemed like she had not even hit her stride.

"How can you not need rest?" To this, the Ranger shrugged. It would take a while to explain, but she had the time. Clearing her throat, she patted Fae on the back and urged her on. As she did, she began recounting the ways the Rangers trained their endurance to the levels they did. It was quite impressive and daunting to hear of. Fae could only imagine how it must have felt to be called upon to cross such a distance with little rest and listened intently. Why anyone would want to be a Ranger, she could not fathom. But fortunate for Seran that many still did.

"From the first day a Ranger picks a Tenderfoot up, they train their body to go vast distances without rest. Beginning at ten miles a day and moving upwards, soon enough the Tenderfoot earns their name; their feet blister and their legs ache desperately. But still they press on, until by the end of the first month, you have walked one-hundred-sixty miles. By the second, three-hundred-twenty. When the year finally comes to pass, you are moving one thousand, nine-hundred twenty miles in a month. By the end of your first decade of training, you have doubled, or even tripled, that. And then you divide your time by crossing that distance with weight on your back and learning. Sometimes doing both at the same time." Fae scoffed. Even for an urok, that would be murderous. Surely it was impossible.

"How is that possible? Surely the body would collapse under such strain." To this, Nelya shook her head. Perhaps Fae had heard wrong? But when Nelya spoke again, her shock increased. The Ranger went in depth about how it was possible and Fae's jaw dropped. It sounded like a quick path to an early grave, but here was at least one Ranger as evidence that it was possible.

"The body adapts to the stresses placed upon it. It also helps that we carry these." Reaching into her pouch, the Ranger removed a handful of highberries, offering them to the other elf, "They make the distance bearable. Highberries, you know them as. Apothecaries prize them for potions and Rangers prize them for their effects. They restore energy to our bodies and allow us to continue along our way." Carefully taking a few, the woman looked them over. She did not think that the Ranger would poison her, but it always helped to be cautious. Around them, the green of the wood stretched for many miles. She noticed the leaves, twigs, and dirt under her feet. The uncomfortable stillness of the air around her and how close it felt in the forest. Taking a chance, she placed the berries in her mouth and chewed. At first, she could not place the effects, but soon, she could feel the weariness slough away from her form, as if it were a great weight she was leaving behind. Soon enough, she was ready for more.

"But how, pray tell, Ranger. How do these berries work?" The Ranger smiled slightly. This was a question people had asked her many times and always had she answered with knowledge collected over many years. Every Ranger knew how the highberries worked and they had even had help from the apothecaries in understanding. When she spoke, it was with the authority of generations.

"They are filled with juices that restore your body's stamina and rejuvenate you. The exact method is unknown, but what we know is that several sugars exist within both your body and the berries. When you partake of the berries, it replenishes those sugars in your body, as well as other essences your body requires. It is the reason highberries increase the potency of healing potions to the level they do and why they are valuable to alchemists and Rangers alike." She nodded and reached to her belt, grasping a brown leather waterskin. Quickly, she uncapped it and offered it to the adventurer, who waved it away with a look of thanks as she grabbed her own. Quickly uncorking it, she took a deep draught from the water within. Slowing her pace, she crouched to give water to Box, nodding as she drank happily from the stream. Nelya nodded, quite happy that she did not forget her familiar when drinking water. She took a drink of her own water and continued along.

"The road is long and the nearest town is ten leagues away. How fast were you planning to get there?" To this, Fae did not have a suitable answer. At her own pace, it would take a day or so, maybe longer, with stops for resting. She allowed herself a shrug and kept moving, doing her best to keep up with the Ranger. As they trekked along, Nelya kept speaking to Fae, her voice urging the other elf on, either with obvious compliments and motivations, or by enticing her with bits of information. Fae had enjoyed the experience as she was pushing her limits and given bits of knowledge to keep her tantalized as she pushed ahead. She wondered about the Rangers and what role they played in the world at large. Even with these questions, she kept silent, instead choosing to listen to the Ranger walking with her. "These woods are quite old and contain many spirits... But of course, you being a fellow wood elf, you know this." Fae nodded slightly. Of course, she could feel the forest spirits. It was almost second nature to her. "The spirits are all around us. The trees have spirits of their own. Sometimes, they walk among us, to teach and protect, as twylan. They are dangerous and sometimes quite harsh. But to those who protect the woodlands and live at peace, they are friendly enough."

"A twylan, you call them? What do they look like?" She was genuinely curious about these creatures. She had often felt tremors while she was trying to sleep, oddly enough. There were sounds of stomping feet as well, which frightened her slightly. Many strange creatures she had seen, but these twylan were new to her. Glancing up, she took a quick glance to read the position of the sun, wondering what hour it was. As if she knew what Fae was wondering, Nelya glanced up for a moment, closed her eyes and looked down at the ground, before opening her eyes once more. Quickly reading the shadows, she glanced over to Fae.

"It is a little after morning. And the twylan look akin to trees, though they can move. They stride through the forest, watching over it and ensuring no fell folk find their way inside the borders. In the more dangerous forests, such as the Eversnow of Northrealm, they warn travelers away from entering the forest less they come to grief within. As well, they deal swift justice to those who harm the forest or the innocent souls within." She took a breath and raised an eyebrow.

Putting an arm out, she stopped her companion. The ground was rumbling gently, and the Ranger began looking around carefully. With her keen eyes, she saw the source from a distance. Crouching and waving at Fae to crouch, she moved behind a fallen tree, carefully pointing out the creature. It was easily twenty feet tall, with a stride to match. Waving to Fae, Nelya moved closer, watching as the twylan turned to the east. Something in the way it walked warned Nelya that something was wrong, and she moved quicker towards it.

Her caution outweighed by curiosity, Fae followed the Ranger, hoping that no harm would find them. As they drew closer through the woods, she could feel the ground rumbling a bit more obviously, and it put her a little off balance. Taking a breath, she steeled herself for what was to come, expecting bad things. When the Ranger popped up and cupped her hands around her mouth, Fae felt that her coming along was a mistake.

"Skala'zan, undaraar anca'e drolsenya!" The effect was immediate, with the massive form swinging around to face the source of the voice. Upon seeing the Ranger, the stern image lightened into a smile and the creature crouched, bringing its body down slightly to speak. Fae approached warily, with her familiar seeming a bit more courageous than her at this point. Fearlessly, the small fox bounded up to the twylan and began yipping and barking at him. This elicited a deep chortle from the great tree-man and he dangled a thin branch just above the fox's head. After a short time, he turned his attention first to the Ranger and then to the adventurer hiding behind, before returning it to the Ranger.

"Elves... Two of you, in fact... *hoom-a-hoom*... What busi-ness have you this day? An awful hurry you seem to be in, Ranger. Is there trouble afoot?" Nelya shook her head, smiling beneath the face-covering she and indeed all Rangers wore. Dropping her form onto a stump, she looked up at the great carved face. It reminded her of many folks she had seen over her life and none at the same moment. As a Ranger, she knew all twylan were carven in the image of Ybril, who planted the forests and carved the twylan to look after them. This she echoed quietly to Fae and watched the great face before her.

"There is no trouble, great treeherd. I was escorting this one on her way to the town for supplies. In this forest has she made her home; you have likely seen it." The twylan shifted his focus from Fae to Nelya once more. He, as with all his race, shared a rather close relationship to the Rangers of the land, aiding, protecting, and teaching them, just as the Rangers did for others. Of course, it was not a one-sided relationship, with the treeherds learning much from the Rangers of the world outside the woods, as well as secret places the great ones could not reach. When slavers came into their woods, often the twylans would be the first to know, by reaching out through their tree-kin, root by root, until they had found the offending group. Sent then would be the Rangers to flush them out, as well as wilder, more angry and unkind trees. It was rare for a twylan to directly involve themselves, but not unheard of. They tried to stay neutral and unless the Rangers called for aid or the situation became a threat to the forest itself, they would not seek conflict.

"*Room-a-hoom*, I have indeed. As I have seen you, Nelya Ardivari, Ranger of The Forest of Summerdusk. Normally, I would not ask for your help, but for the trouble a pesky group of goblins has caused. We must find them before their mischief harms my forest!" Nelya nodded and looked as well to Fae, who nodded gingerly. Things were spinning out of control for her, but she felt like her blood bound her to provide some aid. After all, she lived in this forest as they did, so it would only be right to protect it. Nodding, the twylan stood up once more. Nelya spoke once more and motioned for Fae to come along as she followed the twylan.

"Tell us, great treeherd. What is your name?" This elicited another deep chuckle from the twylan as he walked, measuring his steps to avoid outrunning the smaller folk, as well as taking care to avoid accidentally trodding upon them. They kept a brisk pace and his deep intonations helped liven up the journey a little.

"*Burahuraruum...* In the Old Tongue, my name would take many days to speak and only you would understand it, Ranger. But in Common Tongue, it is much easier to say. I am Oakheart of Summerdusk. A friend of mine, Kindpine the Great, lives to the south of here and watches o'er that part of the forest. He is not as friendly as his name suggests, but he is not a foe to elves or Rangers. To the north, there is Gnarled-Root, an old and angry bloodwood tree. Take care when dealing with him, young elf-lass. He holds no love in his heart for any but the Rangers and druids. But he is wise beyond the age of many elves, *hoom-a-hoom* and if one is patient, he will tell fantastic histories. To the east lives Black-Acorn, whose acorn fell from the same grandfather as I. Whatever you do, mistake not his kindness for weakness, for he is dangerous beyond anger. He is a primal, as we call those who can awaken other trees to rage. When roused, his part of the forest can act and think as one, with devastating purpose." Nelya listened intently as the treeherd rambled on. In part, she was taking in his advice, as well as keeping her ears sharp for any hint of danger. Idly, she reached into a pouch and removed a lump of *pul'gra'an*, before bringing it up to her mouth and taking a bite.

The food brought back a bit of her vigor, not that it was needed, and it calmed the hunger pangs that had been growing over the past week. It was nearly time for her to have a meal, so she would string herself along with bites of *pul'gra'an* till then, gnawing on the flavorful dried meat to keep the hunger at bay. At length, they came to the destination sought by Oakheart. One glance and both elves could easily tell why the twylan wanted action. A massive swath of the forest was burning, obviously kindled by the diminutive, dangerous goblins running around. Some parts had obviously been burning for several days and others were freshly burning. They cackled as they set flame in the forest and only when the twylan called out in anger did they stop. It was only to ready themselves for attack, however, and they drew cruel, crude swords and axes as they barked and chittered in their guttural language. Wasting no time, Nelya nocked an arrow upon the string of her bow, drew the string back, took aim and loosed as she stepped out from behind Oakheart to reveal herself.

The arrow flew true, striking the heart of a goblin who stood in the center of the blackened, smoldering ruins that were part of the forest. As he fell, gurgling his last, his companions growled and positioned themselves to give chase to the Ranger, forgetting about the titanic twylan in their anger. As they soon found out, this was in error, as a massive limb came down upon three of them, crushing them instantly. From somewhere in the twylan's branches came Fae, her sword at the ready. Not necessarily a well-crafted sword it was, but it had not been poorly made, either. Surprise on her side, she descended into a small group of goblins, quickly launching one away with an expert kick to the chest. Another jumped at her, only to end up impaled upon her sword and then discarded. The Ranger seemed almost impressed until she remembered Fae was an adventurer by trade. Trivial creatures such as goblins would pose no threat. As she drew back another arrow, she heard a whoosh and instinctively ducked- none too soon, she realized, as a clumsily thrown spear arced past where her head had been moments ago. Redirecting herself, she slung her bow and lashed out with the arrow, catching a goblin unlucky enough to get near her between the eyes. Removing the arrow and replacing it in her quiver, she unsheathed her blade and went to work. With a single strike, she felled three, before throwing the blade and catching two more, pinning them together. Noting that goblins were grabbing torches and charging Oakheart, she gave chase, pausing just long enough to dislodge her sword from the small frames it had pierced. With a swift kick, she knocked one forward and down, before swiping her blade in the reverse direction, splitting him from rear to neck.

As the flames grew close, Oakheart grew angry. With a mighty kick, he sent one goblin away into the distance, flailing and screaming. Another he simply crushed underfoot, its torch smothered by the unyielding mass above and soft ground below. He cast a third into a tree, its body shattering upon impact with the trunk. Out of a group of twenty, there now remained but four, and the trio quickly cut them down. When the last had fallen, the warriors gathered. The fox's fur was smoking and her eyes afire, eager for more fighting. Fae looked bewildered, and Nelya was already checking everyone over. Only Oakheart's face screwed up with sadness by what had transpired, though it was hard to tell if it upset him more for the need for bloodshed or the burning of his forest. Sappy tears made their way down his carved face and he let out a great sigh. Reaching out, Nelya placed a gentle hand upon the knee of the twylan. "Many voices have been lost, but their seeds will regrow. This area shall be beautiful once more, great Oakheart. The Rangers will see it so."

"*Room-ara-hoom.* Your words are most kind, young one. I know in time this land shall be green again, but for now, the stench of death is too thick and I fear that the blood of those infernal creatures will make this land barren." Nelya nodded at the wisdom of these words. Immediately and without regard for the heat still radiating from the ashes, she plunged her hands into the dirt and began chanting in the Sk'av'A. Focusing her energies into the land and concentrating, she began praying– to Ybril, to Veljra, the Ancestor and Ancestress of wildland and woods and to Ynrasil, Ancestress of life. Through her, energy from them flowed, soothing the burned land. One by one, the still-burning fires flickered out, leaving smoking embers which soon died.

High above, the clouds swirled, and the sky darkened. Fae yelped as a deafening crackle of thunder tore through the heavens, as if Vese'He had boiled the skies with her anger to anger and Mydborh had struck his anvil as hard as he could in response. Sure enough, there came the sound of falling rain. Faint at first but growing in intensity as the rains approached. Even Oakheart looked rather worried and turned to the praying Ranger. "*Bura-ralla-hoom!* You must stop this, Ranger! The Sowers are angry!" When Nelya responded, the wise twylan realized it was not *her* speaking, rather her being *spoken through.* It was the first time in many an age he had heard that voice and all he could do was listen. Fae felt like it should have terrified her, but the voice had a more calming effect than she had expected.

"We... are angry, yes... But not at you, Oakheart the Great. Nor Fae the Timid, or Nelya the Stalwart. They angered us for the forest. And by our Ranger's hands we will set it right." Again, the thunder boomed, crackling over the valley, as if marking the words as truth. The rains fell over the area, cooling the hot, parched soil. Oakheart felt it in his leaves, the tickle of raindrops as they rolled along and dripped down to his branches and to the ground. Fae looked up and smiled as the raindrops fell, washing away the sweat that had accumulated upon her face. The fox wondered what had caused this rain and where it came from. Nelya, in the storm's epicenter, remained still and praying. She could feel the thirst in this forest, for it had been many weeks since last it rained. By her energy would she set it right. This was *her* forest, just as it was Oakheart's and Fae's. *They had desecrated it. They had desolated it.* A different sort of fire sprung up around the bodies of the felled goblins. It touched not plant and scorched not the soil, but one by one, it rendered their foul bodies into ash. *They harmed the forest. So, the forest they shall become!* The rainfall increased, enough that the ashes of goblin body and plant mixed, their nutrients beginning to wash into the soil. Trees at the edges of the forest raised their thirsty branches and wilting leaves to the sky, catching what they could and letting the rest fall to the smaller plants they protected. Nearer and nearer the epicenter, the storm grew, until it was alike to the massive rains of the coast. Where normally the soil in the burned area would wash away, the energy within kept the ground strong and sought surviving seeds and sparked them. Truly, it would be many months before green would return, but the process had at least started. Finally, rising from her knees, Nelya stumbled, nearly collapsing after the strain. Her voice was weak and when she coughed, drops of red spattered upon the ground, only to be washed away.

"How... did you do that?" Fae's incredulous voice called out to the weakened Ranger, even as Oakheart reached out to steady her. "I did not think such magic existed within the world..." Nelya shook her head. True enough, that sort of magic was beyond sages and mages. But to the Ancestors, it was but child's play to focus it through a vessel. The effects upon the Ranger were plain to see, though- she was pale and shivering. Carefully, Oakheart picked her and Fae from the ground and even allowed Box to scramble up his trunk. Once all were safely aboard, he turned towards the town, feeling which direction it was in through the roots of the plants of the region. With great strides, he began his walk towards the town. Weakly, Nelya reached to her pouches, fumbling for a handful of highberries. Fae, ever helpful, grabbed them for her and began feeding them to the Ranger, wishing to get her back on her feet.

"*Room-a-hoom-a...* The Ancestors must have been angry indeed to allow you to wield their magics..." the great twylan mused as he strode along. It was rare, even in the Elder Days, for the Ancestors to give their magic to one of their children. The last he could remember was Nevian deil'Andros, while he was Kingmage of Seran, and that had been at least a thousand years ago. Impressed would be a weak description of his astonishment, and he thought on this for a good many leagues. As time went on, the rain lightened up, becoming nothing more than a sprinkle and finally ceasing all together. The forest was healthier again, green already returning to parched leaves and trees, as well as becoming a bit more vibrant than before. The clouds vanished just as quickly as they had come and the sun's blue light once more filtered down through the sky.

Shaking gently to rid himself of the remaining raindrops, Oakheart nodded as the edge of the forest drew near. Near enough, in fact, that he spoke to his charges once more. Nelya was awake, with color in her face once more, but Fae was dozing gently. "*Room-a-hoom*, it seems we have arrived, my friends. Here I must leave you, for the forest ever needs watching." Slowly, the majestic treeherd crouched before reaching up into his branches and allowing the three to step into his hands. Gently were they taken and placed upon the ground and, with a wave, Oakheart turned to depart. "Hunt well, Ranger. May your eyes never fail."

"May your forest never wither and you never become sleepy." Nelya bowed to the great twylan as he bowed before leaving. Her attention then shifted back to her companion, and she nodded. "Let us continue. We are much closer to our destination. Nodding, Fae wrung a bit of water from her hair and gave a chuckle as her familiar shook, trying to rid herself of the water that soaked her fur. Nelya seemed not to care about her soaked clothes, instead choosing to continue along merrily. The town was but a league now, close enough to see if she concentrated. Nodding, she waved her companions along and took the lead.

As they broke out of the forest, the sun's bright blue light beat down upon them, they began feeling warmer. Their clothes and fur dried as they went, improving their spirits greatly. Around an hour and a half later, the town was near enough indeed that Nelya could hear the guardsmen call. "Who goes there?! In the name of the Grand Mayor, identify yourselves!" Chuckling, the Ranger raised her hands into the air and spoke. Her voice, which until now had been quite soft and friendly, took on an air of incredible authority and grace. The guardsmen were quite awestruck and the effect it had upon Fae was unmistakable.

"I am Ranger Nelya Ardivari, friend to the Grand Mayor, as well as the guards of this town! I come in friendship, as does Fae cos'Criux!" She could see the scramble of activity her words caused. As they drew closer, out of the guardhouse came three to meet them. Clad in the finest armor that could smiths could make for their diminutive race, the halfling guards of the town of Littlebrook were not the most imposing sight. The Ranger knew better than to judge by their looks, and Fae had dealt with them often enough to know that they could effectively deal with any threat that presented itself. Upon closing the distance between them and the guards, the Ranger immediately bowed, crossing her arms in a gesture of peace. The lead guard, who judging by the gaudiness of his armor and the attached tassels, was a Captain of the Guard, nodded in return, before removing his helmet to speak.

"Idorick Prith at your service, Ranger. The city is closed, but how might my men and I assist you?" His voice was gruff but not unfriendly. Similarly, he looked a little ragged around the edges, with evidence of a beard growing on his face, as well as unkempt hair. Evidently, he had been quite busy as of late and had not had time to take care of himself. Even his men seemed a bit strung out and the Ranger perked an eyebrow. She was suddenly quite worried about this town.

Where normally by now she was close enough to hear the merry sounds of the market, there was a somber silence. She took a breath and realized that there was something off about the air.

"Idorick, what is going on here? You have not slept in days, if your eyes tell truth." The halfling shook his head. Gesturing behind him, he indicated the town before speaking again.

"Five days ago, a caravan from Cúledan arrived, bearing many we thought drunk. We took them to the healer's home... It gets worse from there, Ranger. The town has sickened. Where normally you would smell the sweet scent of baking and gardening, only the smell of death will fill your nose." One guard coughed and Idorick rounded upon him in horror. "Perry, are you sickened?"

The halfling shook his head and blurted. "Nay, Captain, 'tis just a cough. I am fine, truly." Regardless, Idorick eyed him with suspicion from then. After a moment, he continued, looking back at the Ranger.

"Ranger Kar'Maerae is at work inside the town and seems unaffected. If you wish, you may converse with her, but I must ask you, Fae cos'Criux, to go back whence you came, with all haste for your own safety. It seems as of now that only the Rangers are unaffected, but who knows if that will change." Nodding, Nelya glanced to Fae and placed a hand upon her shoulder.

"My friend, you would be best advised to find your way back and hunt for the food you would need inside the forest. Something bodes ill in the town of Littlebrook-Once-Besieged." When Fae turned to leave, Nelya waved at the guards to lead her into the city itself. As soon as they'd passed the first line of houses, the Ranger wished she had not come to the city.

There was the unmistakable stench of rotting and burning flesh, mixed in with the metallic smell of rust. Blood was visible, clotting in the streets, and there were bodies piled and burning everywhere. Blinking, the Ranger grabbed a small sky-fusion flower from her pouch and tucked it under her mask to ward off the noxious air. "Tell me, Idorick, where might I find Kar'Maerae?"

Rather than answer, the Captain pointed at the House of Healing. Then, he and his men headed off towards a fight that was brewing between a sickening shopkeeper and a thief. Taking that as a dismissal, Nelya quickly made her way up to the House of Healing and opened the door. When she did, she regretted it instantly, as the aroma of death nearly overcame her. Sputtering, she worked up the breath to let out a shout for the other Ranger in the town. "Ayara Kar'Maerae!" From within the Hall came a shout.

"Who calls?" A frustrated voice called from within, most likely exhausted from trying to save the doomed. "I have taken on all I can!" Nelya became keenly aware of wailing families and, worst of all, the silence and stillness of death. Into the hall she strode and shook her head. Not even the sky-fusion flower was helping against this and she was having a hard time not gagging.

"Nelya Ardivari!" As soon as the words left her lips, Nelya heard something clatter to the floor. Ayara attempted an apology, but they lost it in the din and Nelya could make out a scuffle as the other Ranger made her way out to where Nelya waited. Her face brightened substantially, and she greeted her comrade with a clasping of the arm. "What has happened here, *kiri'taj*?" It was only then she noticed the blood and other, probably worse liquids covering Ayara's clothing and soaking into her hair. Nearly gagging once more, she waved the Ranger to step outside with her.

Following along, Ayara shook her head. "'tis terrible, Nelya. I have been doing what I can, but... most of these folk shall not survive." Nelya raised an eyebrow and blinked.

"But... what is it?" The young Wood Elf was incredulous. Nothing she had ever seen could match this, and it left her dumbstruck.

"It is a plague. The likes of which have never been seen in the land, not even during the time of Kingmage Las'Sa'Reeth! Behold!" Pushing the wood elf into the Hall, she forced her to look upon the bodies of the dead, dying and sick. Flesh was rotting away, maggots not even daring to crawl within. Pools of blood and liquidized flesh were *everywhere*, and filth covered the deep elf. Even her mask stuck against her face with blood and still worse turned her hair into a mess of mats and gore. "I do what I can to make them comfortable, but... I fear there is nothing I can do. We must get word to Karos and the Moot." There were people desperately clutching at their innards, trying to keep them from spilling and there were the gray, stiff bodies of those who had died, their torso rotted open, revealing what flesh it had left within. Lungs and hearts melted and intestines draining out. Strong-willed and strong-stomached as she was, Nelya felt faint. Shaking her head, she stepped back outside with Ayara.

"Do what you can... I will find a raven, a Rider, whatever I have to find Karos. Do you know of any other places where this is happening?" To this, Ayara shook her head once more. She did not know if there were other towns hit, but then again, she had no way to communicate with other Rangers.

"I do not... But I have no way to speak with anyone. Do

what you can, Nelya Ardivari. Word must get out. The town of Littlebrook-Once-Besieged is again under siege. We must have aid, or we will lose the town by the end of the month." Nelya nodded, understanding the Ranger's worry. Stepping away, she ran to the edge of the town, moving as fast as her feet would take her. At every corner, there was another pile of bodies, both of townsfolk and of travelers who had come and fallen. It was overwhelming, but she had a task to focus on. When she was free of the stench and rot, she took a breath, settling to the ground, both to clear her head and to concentrate. Slowly letting go of her form, she reached out to any Rangers near. She was not skilled enough in the arts of the mind to bespeak them, but she could at least give them a warning, a feeling of unease strong enough to put them on their guard. Soon enough, she found a bird on the wing who would listen and was smart enough to communicate the message being sent. A raven, what luck indeed. Filling its mind with images of the Warden Ranger and what had transpired in Littlebrook, she urged it on with all haste to the North.

Away it flew, carrying a message of doom, giving it to any near mind that could and indeed would listen. Rangers, mages and others began doubling over, their minds attacked with gut-wrenching images. All began trying to find out the meaning and the source. Rangers alone could decipher the message, though mages could gather what was going on. Soon enough, errant Rangers who otherwise needed a task mapped a course to Littlebrook and began moving with all speed. But still it was not enough. The raven winged on, day and night, searching for both the Warden Ranger and the greatest of its kind, Carwaan. Only then could he be sure that the message would arrive.

Working against wind and weather, the black-feathered messenger continued along, before touching down just south of the Eversnow Forest for rest. A nest of his kin welcomed him and he explained to them that something was very wrong in their world. As with all creatures who could recognize danger, they called out to Ara, the Sky-mother and Ynrasil, she-who-gave-life, as well as Veldan, he-who-learns. They asked for knowledge and how they could help. Confusion was their answer, for the Ancestors had yet no knowledge of what was happening. The conspiracy of ravens settled in for the night and prepared, juvenile and elder, to take to wing in the morn, to spread their message to the walking-men who befriended them closest. They and Carwaan, the gold-painted-king, would know what to do. They *had to*.

In Littlebrook, Nelya finally returned to herself, hoping that they would spread her message to the right people. Standing once more, she steeled herself to reenter the blighted town and headed to the Hall of Healing. Upon entering, she made her way towards the statuettes of Ynrasil and Elyrea, bowing and asking their aid for the coming tasks. Then, with a soft sigh, she turned, quickly rolling her sleeves, to help Ayara as she could. Potions, herbs and skill all came into play, but it rapidly became apparent that the best they could do was slow the spread of the rot.

As night fell, the sickening glow of burning bodies lit the town. Within the Hall of Healing stood the two Rangers, working back and forth, cutting away rotting flesh where they had to hoping to slow the demise of the afflicted. In the guardhouse, men began coughing, and a few broke away, stumbling towards the Hall of Healing, convinced they were only sick with a head cold. Idorick knew better, though, and his heart cried for his men, knowing they would soon join the fallen.

"Fire to flesh, this is no way for us to die. We are men of action. Surely there must be something we can do..." Idorick's thoughts echoed Parali's complaint. Steadying himself, he took a moment to turn to the men still assembled.

"Aye, lads. There is. Parali, take Will and Otho. Ride as hard as you can, stop for nothing. Get word to the Grand Mayor and tell him to send no one out and allow no one in. If you must, shout it to the gate-guards, but do not enter the city, lest you spread this. I send you because you have not fell sick so you are our best hope. The rest of the lads," He gestured to the others. A few had sickened and fewer still were unafflicted. "will do what we can here. Mayhap help will come... We will have to see." They met this with a fair bit of grumbling, but the guards knew any aid they could give would likely mean the difference between life or death for their families.

"Ebert, Rollo, Samned and Batam... Find all you can who live around, search rick, cot and tree if you must. Warn them away. I rescind all restrictions upon the hunting of game until we have a handle upon this. Our people must fend for themselves as best they can, lest they end up like the poor sods around the town. Go now and fear not death, for we walk through the shadow of plague!" The seven he had selected stormed out, three heading for the stables, four of them taking flight through field and on the road to find their way to the outlying houses.

As she made her way to the forest, the imagery given to the Raven assaulted Fae. Stopping short, she doubled over, dry heaving at the sights. Thankfully, she could not guess the smell, but she knew that right now, they needed her somewhere other than her home. Turning on her heel, she called out. "Box! My beloved familiar, we need to find some way to help!" She turned and took off after her friend as she took flight towards the town, legs pumping as hard as they could. The adventurer knew not what help she could give, but she knew for a fact that Indeka would never forgive her for hiding the crisis away in her forest. If she didn't help, she knew she could face no one again. In her mind, that just would not do.

4: Coldforge, Eversnow Forest, Northrealm

Deep within the forest of Eversnow, there sat a small town that, despite being attacked many times through its history, withstood the tests of time proudly. It was home to many people and the birthplace of several who had grown to greatness. One of these was already hard at work inside a forge, speaking to a pair of dragons who followed him effectively everywhere. A red dragon named Vu'Locav, and a white named Alvarath sat lazily, occasionally spouting gouts of flame or ice to heat or cool metal carefully, resulting in harder metal than most forges could ever hope to create. The man was rather tall, easily standing at nearly two spearlengths and obviously of half-giant lineage. This then was Viktor, son of Ulfric, son of Calem, the current of the line of Dragonsmiths of Coldforge, the gargantuan men who shaped steel, aided by the two dragons. One befriended, the other pledged to his bloodline. As he wiped away sweat, the man burst forth into a loud song, audible over even the din of his apprentices beating steel.

"Pump the bellows and work the wheel!
Heat the metal and bend the steel!
Make it steam and make it shine,
Sharpen it up across the line!"

His great hammer striking the plate of armor he was working on in time with his singing, and the great man nodded in appreciation as the dragons rumbled to provide a melody. After a few strikes, he raised the plate into the air and on cue, the red dragon blew a careful gout of flame, moderated to heat the metal to a searing straw color, rather than melt it as dragons are used to doing. As soon as it was hot enough, the man, clad in nothing but heavy hide boots, a fur kilt and a pair of obviously heat-resistant gloves, brought the metal down to his anvil. He looked at his gloves with pride as he continued hammering the metal, remembering fondly how he had got them. Someone had specially crafted them for him from the scales shed by Vu'Locav the Red, carefully being cut to the correct size to allow for dexterity.

"Straighten the sword and curve the axe
to stop our enemies in their tracks!
Beat the plate, edge the shield,
To protect our comrades upon the field!"

Alvarath's father had befriended both the father of Vu'Locav and the father of Viktor after a spirited series of battles. Having never met his match in combat before, the white dragon made a similar pledge as the one made by Vu'Locav's ancestors many years ago, that his bloodline would forever be friends to descendants of the Bludstyn clan. After learning to control his icy emissions, he quickly took a liking to forge-work and helped temper the steel, as well as carefully tend to burns that apprentices or Viktor would earn. The latter, of course, would hardly notice anything less than a deep burn and would indeed feel no ill effects from said burns. They said that he could plunge his bare hand into the hottest of fires to remove the metal he was working with and bring it back nearly unscathed.

"Weld the crack and temper the rest,
Make sure it withstands the test!
Shape the bar and spin the rod,
Say a prayer to the Forging God!"

It was no secret that Mydborh favored the Bludstyn clan. Legends said that Mydborh had placed the giants that make up the Bludstyn lineage in the mountains himself, after being crafted from the steel of his own forge and tempered by the sweat from his brow. Powerful they were, and they had a beyond-dwarven understanding of how metal worked and how best to shape it. This, combined with a massive fallen star that had struck in this area many thousands of years ago, cemented the Dragonsmith as the most influential of all metal-shapers, giving them quite a literal edge over the competition. Known far and wide for making star-steel weapons and armor for the more influential persons of Seran, though they were not without the occasional gift. For instance, when Karos had been selected as the Warden Ranger in recognition of his leadership and service, the Dragonsmith at the time created the sword of Northrage, especially for him. Heated entirely by Vu'Locav's father and cooled entirely by the sire of Alvarath, it had a strange ability to wield the magic of both, seeming to represent the raging fire within the Warden Ranger, and the icy winds of his homeland. When struck against another sword, some places would heat and warp, while others would freeze until they cracked. Against flesh, the outside of the cut would sizzle and burn, the damage of incredible heat spreading slowly across the skin as the inside of the cut froze, chilling the enemy to the bone.

"Fold the layers and drive the nails
Stronger than the foe that assails!
Fill the pitting and grind the rust,
leave our foes dead in the dust!"

The hammer slammed down once more and sparks were spat across the floor. Glancing up, the Forgemaster looked at a crude clay torso that had he had made to represent the person he was forging this armor for. It was in this moment that his skill became apparent, as he could replicate the curves perfectly just from a few moment's glance. Quickly, he returned to shaping the metal, carefully and almost lovingly ensuring that it would be a perfect fit, with just enough room to allow for necessary padding. He grinned as he slammed the hammer against the anvil, once more keeping time with his song.

"Dragon's fire heats the steel,
quenched it is by icy breath
Protecting wearer from gruesome death!
That is the way we seal the deal
As we shape the Coldforge steel!"

With an air of finality, he slammed the hammer down, finishing the last bend. As the steel was still red hot, he raised it. With incredible care, an icy wind came from the mouth of Alvarath, cooling the metal at the correct speed to ensure that it was the right blend of hard and malleable, to avoid shattering upon first contact, but still be effective as armor. When the metal was sufficiently cool, the giant of a man brought the breastplate back down, looking it over. After a moment and an inspection by the dragons, all three nodded, and he grabbed a new plate to shape the back. Again, he began the song and again the metal pounded, heated and pounded again, until it was in the correct shape. Then, he placed it next to the breastplate. Carefully, he bound leather straps to the plate, before adding padding beneath. Part by part, he made the breastplate as apprentices, all quite skilled, worked on other pieces of the armor. One on the gauntlets and another on the pauldrons, one on the greaves and another for the sabatons.

"Vu'Locav! Alvarath! Come, it is time for lunch. Wulunt, Arri, Skuld, Nils, Einar! Finish your most pressing work and get some food. We shall return." The massive man made his way to the dragon-sized door and pushed it open, stamping through the portal to allow the dragons through as well. One after the other, they made their way out into the crisp forest air, quickly arranging themselves and taking to wing as soon as they had room. Off they went then, to hunt for their meal, as their friend found his way to The Dragon's Drink, the only inn in town. Pressing a large hand to the door and crossing the precipice, he looked around as his eyes adjusted to the dimmer light.

"Well met, Viktor! The usual, I presume?" The voice was friendly enough, being that of the inn's owner, Martin. A portly fellow, he had inherited the inn from his father, Ralian, and his father before him. It was his longfather, several generations removed, that had originally built the Inn when Coldforge was first settled, many hundreds (or was it thousands?) of years ago. He was a friendly fellow, though in the way of Coldforge, always ready with a weapon. His preference was an axe, though he only used it in the absolute depths of need. He prided himself on the fact that he never had raised his hands in anger and had always, in fact, had a hand ready with a hot meal or cold drink to offer traveler or townsfolk alike.

"Aye, Martin, though with less snakeroot, please. My stomach has been feeling strange for a few days." Nodding, Martin spoke to the cook and waved the Dragonsmith to his normal seat. It was not out of preference so much as it was out of necessity. The first owner, many years ago, had built the place for the Bludstyn line, to account for their... generous height. The eldest of that line, Calem, had easily stood twenty feet and the successive generations had brought that height lower and lower.

As normal, Viktor ordered a small keg of ale to go with his meal, Martin crushed some dentry seeds into one. Enough that the effect would be noticeable, but few enough that it would not affect the taste of the ale, at least in his mind. Then, he poured a large quantity of his finest ale into the keg and stirred it. Once he felt it was properly mixed, he placed the keg before Viktor. "Most kind, Martin. Many thanks." Taking a great swig almost immediately, Viktor nodded. "I take it you added in dentry seed?" Martin nodded sheepishly.

"What gave it away, Viktor?" To this, the giant chuckled slightly.

"I have drunk your ale for over sixty years, Martin. By now, I can taste if the farmers changed the grain itself." He was not angry, by any stretch of the imagination. Rather, he was quite thankful. It was rare that others tried to help him with his ailments. "But of course, you have my thanks. Hopefully, this will settle whatever is wrong in my stomach." This elicited a hopeful nod from the proprietor, who then busied himself about the Inn while the cook prepared food for the man.

"So, what think you of the weather as of late, Viktor?" A grunt came forth from the monstrous man. Truth be told, he had thought little of the weather, being cooped up in his forge for the better part of the day.

"What mean you, Martin? The weather seemed fine when I made my way over here." He shook his head at the odd question, though his normally saturnine countenance lit up as a pair of servers brought out a plentiful tray of food. Hastily, he fumbled for his coin purse, carefully extracting a handful of silver and copper coins, thrusting them into the hand of the proprietor. Martin accepted them readily, smiling his thanks for Viktor's generosity. As the latter began eating, he bustled away, nodding at the cooks to head back to their duties.

"Well, the snows have let up, at least here, and I could swear I heard voices upon the air not two nights past. Odd words they were indeed." Martin shook his head slightly and reached for a broom. "There have also been whispers of sickness in Cúledan and bandit attacks along the Skyvale pass. The world is getting stranger by the day and hopefully it shall not touch Coldforge." Viktor laughed slightly. *Whispers*, he thought, *do not put food upon one's table. Hard work does.* Even so, he could feel that something was wrong. Not here, for the feeling was too vague and distant. But near and powerful enough that it was cause for concern.

To Viktor's great pleasure, the dentry seed in the ale had done the trick for at least the physical discomfort in his belly, and his brow relaxed. The unease, though, was another matter entirely, persisting through his best efforts to ignore it. As he ate, he thought on matters far and away, wondering when he should start the forging of a weapon for the Kingmage and her brother. He was one of the few who knew the truth of their station and had done well in keeping the secret. Yawning as he finished his meal, the great man looked once more to Martin and spoke his thanks before slipping out. The afternoon sun was warm on his shoulders and the sky delightfully blue. As he looked around the sleepy town and out into the snow-covered forest, he thought for a moment about what it must have been like for Calem, his longfather, to see it burning. He shook his head and followed the path to the memorial, where names had were etched onto stone to remember those who had fallen in the Coldforge Massacre, so many years ago. Most of the names he knew or had been told of and some he even knew the descendants of.

The ones he did not recognize, he read to himself, wondering what life they would've led. "Elruviel Caladon..." Following that name were several more, quite foreign to him. He surmised that these must have been the Rangers who had fallen in defense of the town, who had given their lives for ones they never knew. His thoughts trailed to the Rangers who currently guarded the town- Olin, Sunji, Skalla and Da'Shanaer. They were the town's most hardy guardsmen and many a time had protected the town against fell beasts and bandits.

Of course, you forget your own deeds in the town's defense, old friend. The voice was deeper than most drums could ever reach, a reflection of his own voice, even. It was the voice of Vu'Locav, the Red Dragon of the Dragonforge. Viktor shook his head and replied, his mind speaking back to the noble creature.

Deeds, Vu'Locav? The most deeds I do in defense of the town are swing a hammer and create the tools others use to deal with the threats. I am not one to cross distances or fight foes, for my need is here. My deeds are not so great as those of the Rangers. This earned him a chuckle from the magnificent beast. Clearly, they disagreed upon this matter and it was apparent that the dragons both thought quite different from the man. Another voice chimed in, this one lighter in tone, though still a whisper.

But what makes your deeds so much less than those of the Rangers? They, like you, merely send minions against a foe. The only difference is their minions are unknowing and unfeeling, being of obsyd and wood. And you forget, dear friend. There was a time when you tromped the wilds and roads in search of adventure. True enough, though, it was odd for the dragons to be so insistent on that point. Normally, they were the first to deny any attempt to liken themselves to the arrows sent by the Rangers. Not that they held any grief towards the Rangers, nor the Rangers towards them. They just felt the distinction necessary.

You have a point, Alvarath. I just feel they do far more than I, or we usually do. That was the distinction, though. *Usually.* For Viktor, a bad day involved bringing his hammer against someone's head. For a Ranger, that was more a way of life. They were the often-frightening rough folk who would visit with violence in the night on behalf of folk like him. He wondered for a moment about how hard it must be to live life as a Ranger. *How difficult it must be to face insurmountable odds and incredible distances as the norm,* he thought. Compared to such things, he was quite happy with his forge work in the dull little town.

How would you feel if I told you that the Rangers feel the same way about your profession as you do about theirs? This threw

Viktor for a loop. The Rangers, masters of all tasks, viewed *his* life as difficult? How so? He thought on this for a while, musing as he walked through the town. As he approached the forking of the River Wythe, he shook his head for a moment.

My life is simple. How could a Ranger have difficulty with it? It seemed unlikely for a Ranger to find a task difficult or impossible. It just was not who they were. But then again, he had never been a Ranger. Tasked though he was with repairing their weapons and armor, he was just a smith. Truth be told, he still held that romanticized view of the Rangers, seeing them as something beyond the capabilities of most. He grounded it slightly when he saw some Rangers coming into his shop, especially the old man, Wastan Kivanis, as well as the blind Seeress. He wondered how they and others like them had made it through the tests, and part of him wondered if he would ever be capable of something like that. Maybe someday, when he could no longer tend to the Forge, they would teach him? He shook his head. Thoughts such as that served no purpose. He doubted he could ever be a Ranger, and he doubted further that he would ever *want* to be a Ranger. He enjoyed eating often and plentifully and his bed was quite comfortable.

"Dragonsmith, are you well?" The voice sounded rather concerned and markedly feminine. Turning, the half-giant (quarter-giant, perhaps?) looked at the source of the voice. A young girl of merely eighteen winters stood there, looking up at him. She had been crying, the tear-streaks obvious on her face, and she was in pain. What kind of pain Viktor could only guess at.

"I am well, Varyna. It would take a blind man, however, to not see that you are troubled. Come, speak to me." The girl seemed hesitant at first. Someone as important as the Dragonsmith could not care for her troubles. She bit her lip for a moment and sighed, trying to keep the tears from welling up again. It was a touchy subject, even on the best of days, and she was afraid that it was silly.

"Ever since my mother died... my father has not been himself. He has taken to the ale every night... and he is distant. Unwell, though he denies it. He is killing himself, Forgemaster, and I know not what to do." She broke down into ragged sobs, her chest heaving with pain. Shaking his head, Viktor took a seat next to her and spoke, with his voice gentle.

"Young Varyna, you know as well as I this is something beyond my skill. You need to speak to the Rangers, or someone your father trusts." She shook her head at this. She was afraid the Rangers would see things much worse, and she did not really know her father's friends.

"My da's friends are... strange. I get a sick feeling whene'er I see them. They never remove their hoods, and they look at me with a strange light in their eyes. I have even seen them give my father gold and ale, but in exchange for what, I know not." Viktor, who many thought to be as slow of wit as he was deliberate in his movements, felt a new knot in his stomach. Standing, he extended a hand to the girl.

"Come with me, Varyna. You must." His voice held authority, authority she could not deny. Taking his hand shakily, it nearly bowled the girl off her feet as he bounded along towards the Tower. Within the stone walls, the Rangers of the town sat and ate their meals between shifts guarding the town.

No sooner had Viktor reached the door than his fist crashed

down upon it powerfully, shaking not just the door, but just about everything within. "One moment! Impatience will get you no-"

"If you love life and freedom, open this door, Ranger!" This caught the attention of the Rangers inside. Moments after Viktor shouted, the door flew open, to reveal two Rangers. One, a deep elf, was resting against a large spear. That would be Da'Shanaer, the rather unsettling warrior. He had a keen knowledge of the body and could find the weakest points on anyone. Next to him, hand resting on the haft of an enormous axe, was Skalla Woodrunner, a tall catlike creature called a Khataan'zhe, her lineage clear in fur colored as the snows and rocks of Northrealm.

"Forgemaster! How may we-" Upon noticing the crying girl, the Rangers both stopped. Nodding to Skalla, Da'Shanaer stepped out of the way. The cat-woman released her grip on her axe and stepped out, quickly brushing Viktor aside to guide the girl into the Tower. As soon as she was out of earshot, Da'Shanaer stepped out to Viktor.

"What is the problem? What has she confided in you, Forgemaster? What has you so worried?" With perfect recollection, Viktor relayed the information, what she had said to him, and even how she said it. With each word, the Ranger's expression turned darker and finally he nodded.

Viktor spoke, his voice hushed and quite tense. "Milord Ranger, I must ask you to look into this with all due haste. Question the girl's father and be on the watch for these people she hath identified." He knew he was overstepping his authority by quite a distance, but right now he cared not. A girl was in danger and he was afraid her father's purpose was to sell her. This was one thing he would not allow to stand.

Nodding, Da'Shanaer patted the massive shoulder nearest him and spoke.

"Fear not, Forgemaster. As your faithful servants, the Rangers shall sort this sordid affair out." Within the tower, the sobs were quite clear, and it was apparent that Skalla was having quite a time speaking to the girl. Though she was making progress, the Khataan felt sorrow because she could not help the girl further. Da'Shanaer slipped away from Viktor and headed out into the light of day, his steps silent even against the cobbled stone of the road.

Closing the door carefully, Viktor made his way back to the Forge, when he heard the furtive whispers of hushed, cruel voices. Hiding himself behind a pair of trees (no easy task for a man his size, especially during the day), he held as still as he could, in order to eavesdrop upon the conversation. What he heard chilled him to the bone and he felt the knot in his stomach grow.

"How fortunate it must be to know all things, Razh. It was your error that sent the girl to where that oaf was walking. If we do not find her and bring her to the chief, it shall be your head, not mine." A hiss preceded the others reply, followed by an almost panicked tone.

"We saw her go this way, yes we did. With that foolish oaf towards the Tower she went, Skel'za. If you want the money so badly, you go in and get her." This was met with some alarm by both the one called Skel'za, and Viktor. The Rangers within the tower had no way of knowing what was going to happen. He knew not how many were lurking on this side of the town and why they were being so brazen, coming this close to the Tower. But he knew he had to do something.

"Fool! Those Rangers is within the tower. It is likely the

chattel is as well!" *Chattel.* So, the girl was to become a slave. The knot in Viktor's stomach loosened and his vision clouded with rage. *Slavers? HERE?* Forgoing the fact that he was trying to hear whence they had come, the great man let out a cry of anger. Before the two forms could react, the great man was upon them. It was strange, Viktor would realize later, that the two had not seen him although it was *midday.* Their loss, however, as he crashed down towards them.

"Ay-ah! Razh you fool! It is the Dragonsmith!" Razh turned and his hand went for a sword. The pommel against his hand would be the last feeling he would have in this life, as a massive hand gripped his lower jaw and yanked abruptly up and to the right. This caused an immediate reaction in the dokk's body, causing clawed hands to attempt at first to free the head from the man's grasp. Then they dropped limp, twitching as the bones in the creature's neck shattered and his spinal cord snapped like sinew, severing the connection between brain and body. The Dragonsmith cast him aside and towards his fellow.

Having had a moment to prepare while the great man was killing his comrade, Skel'za had his sword at the ready when Viktor came for him. However, it was about the time that the sword was yanked away from him by the Forgemaster's gloved hands that he realized just how grave his error had been. At first, the cowardly dal'Korin attempted to plead for his life, offering treasures beyond count to the half-giant. When he found no purchase there, he went for a dagger hidden on his side and plunged it into the man's arm. This would be his last mistake as a mortal and would cause him great pain before he died. The arm twisted in pain and yanked forward, while the other gripped the creature. He didn't plan it, it was just a fact of reflex. Unfortunately for the dal'Korin, his grip was tighter than he had thought and the blade deeper than he would ever know. With a mighty yank, the Forgemaster tore Skel'za's arm from his body, eliciting a shriek from the lizard-man. To the door came many a person, armed with axes, swords, pitchforks, and hoes. What they beheld had them calling both for the Rangers and the local knight, as they witnessed a gravely injured dal'Korin get his skull crushed by a wrathful Viktor.

He gripped the skull, his thumbs resting just below the eyebrow-plates of the dal'Korin's head and squeezed inwards, putting down incredible pressure until the entire skull collapsed. This caused a rush of fluids, some of which would likely stain his forge-gloves, to spray out. That gruesome task done, he discarded the body onto the other, watching as its lifeblood ran onto the snowy ground.

"Viktor, what happened?" The voice was that of Nils, one of the town's bakers. To him, violence was a far-off thing, a threat for other people. To see blood on the snow of his hometown shocked him. Even more so, when he realized that the Dragonsmith not only had a dagger in his arm, but an arm hanging from that dagger. "Nevermind that, we must get you to a healer! ADRIC! ADRIC COS'ERICK!" Viktor glanced at his arm and noted the dagger. It was in deep and the arm hanging from it was quite comical to him. With a firm pull, he released the arm from the dagger and then gripped the handle. A shout stopped him and he glanced up to see the face of Adric, the town's masterhealer.

"Viktor, I do hope you will at least come to the Hall before trying to remove a dal'Korin dagger from your arm!" Sheepishly, Viktor removed his hand from the dagger and followed

Adric to the Hall of Healing. The healer was shaking his head, but honestly, this sort of thing from the Dragonsmith did not surprise him. "Come on then, Viktor. Off with your forge-gloves, they need to be cleansed." As soon as the great gloves were off his hands, the healer handed them off to an assistant, who took them to cleanse them in water. Then, the Healer looked over the dagger, musing on how best to remove it from the man's arm. "Well, we could try-" With little finesse, Viktor reached up, grasped the dagger and yanked straight out. A spurt of blood came with it and the Healer shook his head. "Of course you would take that route. Hold still, Viktor, this may sting a little."

It was a few moments before he noticed Viktor's look. "May sting a little?" He smirked at the Healer and then gestured to the dagger. In response, Adric merely shook his head. He had forgotten that the man had nerves of steel. Carefully and quickly preparing a salve, he slathered it onto the wound, placed a square of gauze before wrapping a bit of clean, dry cloth around Viktor's arm. Carefully, he tied the bandage into place and nodded. Grabbing a potion from his table, he handed it to the Forgemaster.

"Drink this, it shall help the wound heal faster." Nodding, Viktor uncorked the bottle and downed the liquid within. That done, he placed the empty bottle upon the table and glanced back to the Healer with a grateful expression. "That should be it, Viktor. You can go, but please try to avoid any more confrontation today."

"No promises, Master Adric." With that, Viktor stood. Making his way first to the statuettes of Ynrasil, Veljra and Elyrea, he respectfully bowed and said a short prayer to each of them. That task done, he turned and strode for the door.

The assistant who had taken his gloves stopped him, offering up the items. He took them, looking them over to ensure they were clean and clear of blood or other fluids that had sloshed over them. Slipping them back on, he made his way to the door, before carefully opening it and stepping back out into the sunlight. What greeted him there was a rather unimpressed Da'Shanaer. He waved at Viktor to follow him and sighed.

"You know, Viktor, you are like the clouds that herald a storm. I sought the house of Varyna and her father, Ulfgar. No less than six bandits were waiting there, expecting that I was bringing Varyna to them. They plied me with gold, jewels and finally threats to learn where she was." Viktor smirked. He couldn't see through the black cloth mask the Ranger wore, but he knew the deep elf was likewise smirking.

"I wager they did not live long enough to rue that course of action." Da'Shanaer shook his head slightly and chuckled. After a moment, though, that chuckle died on his lips. He looked to the two bodies in the snow a few yards away and then back to Viktor.

The deep elf's voice betrayed his thoughts as he spoke. "If something like this is happening, I fear that a slaver band has taken up residence nearby." Viktor nodded slowly. "Not a very smart slaver band, of course... but a brazen one."

"Why would you tell me this, Ranger?" Da'Shanaer gave him a knowing glance before speaking again.

"Because, Forgemaster, I know that you see yourself as a protector to Varyna. And that you would relish the chance to safeguard her future." That hit Viktor deeply. He was protective of everyone in the town, Ranger and commoner alike. They looked to him as a pillar of their community, and he did his best to deliver. There was no way he could resist the challenge when the Ranger worded it like that. He nodded slowly and grinned abruptly.

"Of course, you do realize that I simply *must* involve Vu'Locav and Alvarath, else they will be quite cross." The Ranger could not help but laugh at that. What a sight it would be, the Rangers and Forgemaster descending upon a slaver band with dragons in tow. They deserved nothing less than death and by the hands of those protectors of Coldforge would it come. Reaching out, Viktor grasped Da'Shanaer's forearm and Da'Shanaer returned the gesture. "Tell me when and where to come and I shall be there, Dragons, hammer and all."

The Ranger nodded his thanks and slapped Viktor's shoulder in a friendly manner. "If that is the case, Viktor, I shall put forth my efforts and locate the enemy. When we come upon them, it shall be as an avalanche in the mountains and we shall sweep away them before our might." *Quite a way with words hath this Ranger*, thought Viktor as he parted company with the deep elf. Calmly, he made his way back to the Dragonforge, where Vu'locav and Alvarath awaited him. Now was as good a time as any to work on a weapon for the Kingmage and her brother, he realized, and nodded. She preferred a spear and he a sword, he remembered from his brief talk with them at the Coronation. The first would be easy and he had an idea in mind already for the shape of the blade. The sword would be trickier, as he had not yet thought out the shape and look. He was not sure why this was suddenly a priority, but something just felt right about the time. As if there would never be a better moment to begin this work.

Grasping a small bar of star-steel, he placed it upon the

anvil, regarding it for a moment. The pattern of swirls within the metal itself seemed to speak to him, telling him how best to hammer and heat, to cool and to beat. Glancing at his gloves, he picked the bar up and raised it high, as if making an offering to Mydborh himself. Then, two gouts of flames, one yellowish-red, the other bright white, lit up the forge's dim interior. Taking slow breaths, his face turned to avoid the heat, Viktor counted slowly. Second by second, until the metal felt correctly heated. Then, the flames stopped, as the dragons both took deep breaths. Bringing the now straw-colored, searing hot metal down, he dropped it onto the anvil. His free hand, which until now had been idle, grasped the haft of the massive forge-hammer that had come down through the generations of his family. With a mighty swing, he slammed the face of his hammer onto the metal, sending a shower of sparks all over the place, including onto him. Where normally this would be quite dangerous (and at the least, incredibly uncomfortable), the sparks seemed to just fizzle and die upon contact with his flesh, neither burning nor harming the great man.

"Pump the bellows and work the wheel!
Heat the metal and shape the steel!
Make it steam and make it shine,
Sharpen it up across the line!"

With almost every word punctuated by the slam of a hammer, Viktor carefully turned and shaped as he went. When the metal cooled, he raised it and bathed it in a raging inferno as the two dragons let loose their fires once more. Again, they seared the metal to a fine straw color, and Viktor brought it down to the anvil once more. The clanging of metal upon metal became a rhythm that focused Viktor's mind on the task ahead. *Clang! Clang!* The hammer struck the glowing-hot metal, beating it towards the final shape. Little by little, the star-steel flattened. *Clang! Clang!*

"Straighten the sword and curve the axe
to stop our enemies in their tracks!
Beat the plate, edge the shield,
To protect our comrades upon the field!"

Clang! Plink! The third sound came not from Viktor's anvil, which caused him to glance upwards. He did not miss a beat of his work, continuing to slam the hammer down in a pleasant rhythm. When his eyes adjusted against the glow of the metal, Viktor saw the source of the interruption; one of his other Smiths had returned to the forge and was resuming his work on a pair of gauntlets to go with the cuirass he'd finished earlier. Nodding, the massive man returned to his work. *Clang! Plink!* The rhythm began anew, the heavy strikes of Viktor's hammer joined by the more delicate taps of Wulunt. Likewise, the younger man's voice joined the Forge-Song, adding a throaty baritone to Viktor's deep bass.

"Curl the socket, hammer the tip
Ensure the metal will not crack or chip!
Shape the bar and spin the rod,
Say a prayer to the Forging God!"

Clang! Plink! Ting! Another delicate sound, likely from the young dwarf working on the greaves. Her voice joined the choir as well, lending a bit rougher tone with a friendlier sound. Together, the three continued the song of forging and with it their work. Once more, dragon fire heated the metal in Viktor's hand, as the other smithies used bellows and coals. Carefully, the dwarf looked over her work before heating her metal once more. Wulunt swiftly bent the hand-plate of the gauntlets, ensuring a proper fit.

"Fold the layers and drive the nails
Stronger than the foe that assails!
Fill the pitting and grind the rust,
leave our foes dead in the dust!"

Clang! Plink! Ting! Clink! Another hammer's song joined the orchestra as Nerya the dokk picked up where she had left off on the helmet. Her harsh bark aligned itself in pitch and timbre, and the song continued. The work became more and more raucous and joyful as the friends slaved away to create weapon and armor, hoping neither would ever need to be used. Of course, that was a hollow hope, they knew. After all, with slave-raids and bandit attacks upon the roads, as well as assaults within the forests, none were safe. So, they did what they could to mitigate the risk for others and earn some coin for themselves.

"Dragon's fire heats the steel, quenched it is by icy breath
Harder than the prongs of death!
That is the way we seal the deal
As we shape the Coldforge steel!"

With finality, Viktor swung his hammer in a powerful blow to finish the basic shape of the spearhead. The metal was still hot enough to sear into flesh and he had the answer to that. Raising it high, the white dragon rewarded him with a carefully controlled rush of icy wind to quench the star-steel. Cooling it down carefully and at a good rate, Alvarath kept his breath flowing strong, using his second windpipe to continue fueling the freezing breath. After some time, the metal was cool and hard, expertly quenched. Viktor brought the spearhead down and looked it over, nodding at the handiwork of himself and his friends.

"Well done, lads. I shall sharpen this up and prepare it to be mounted for the Kingmage." With that, he gripped a pole and carried both over to a smaller workbench. Using careful hands and a steady pedal rate, he spun the wheel and brought the spearhead against it. Sparks flew as he ground the edge into the metal with great care, as the importance of the project caused a methodical approach. Then again, he had no choice but to take his time, for the metal was quite hard. Hard enough, in fact, that the sharpening would take at least an hour. He had planned for this, though, having worked the star-steel countless times before.

When at last the blade's edge was complete, he looked at the sketch that he had drawn based on the Kingmage's preferences. Nodding, he dipped the spearhead into a wax, carefully ensuring even distribution to protect the blade and socket. Then, with a steady hand and careful eye, he carved symbols out from the wax. The mark of his forge was first to come, followed by delicate traces leading down along the socket and the edge of the blade. Sk'av'A runes came later to denote the owner of the weapon, as well as the sign of the Kingmage, the wings surrounding the image of Kjetta, displayed proudly in the center on both sides. When he had finished carving the wax, he scrutinized it, looking over the work. Nodding slowly, he prepared a bath of acid. He was extremely careful not only to avoid spilling on himself or the surrounding things, but as well to avoid wasting any of the acid he had. Placing the basin carefully, he dipped the spearhead into the bath. One side sat face down for some time as the acid worked its way into the metal. In normal steel, it would not take long, he knew. But with the star-steel, it would take almost an hour for each side and that counted not the minute alterations that would need to be done afterwards. Of course, he could do nothing but monitor and occasionally check progress by lifting the spear out of the acid.

When one side finished etching, it he carefully dried and brushed it to remove any remaining acid. He cast a careful eye over the etched side and went over it inch by inch to ensure that met his standards. After a moment, the man nodded and placed the other side to the acid and began waiting once more. In his mind, he was already planning out the next stages of his project. He could see in his mind what needed to be done and how he would do it. It was simply a matter of waiting. Checking every so often, he nodded when the etching was finally complete. Carefully removing the spearhead from the acid, he cleansed and inspected until it satisfied him with the results. Bringing over a torch, he carefully melted the wax away into a bowl and set it aside. Once done with that, he placed the spearhead on the table and brought out a section of a gold wire, as well as a small hammer and rod. As he placed the wire, he delicately tapped at it with the hammer and rod, forcing it into the bites left by the acid. First came the wings and some of the scrollwork, carefully filled little by little. Then came a length of silver, placed and hammered in various areas. A bit of platinum joined as well, accenting here and there.

When he finished working on the facing side of the spear-head, Viktor took a small chisel and meticulously carved away at the excess. Little by little, he cleaned up the lines, and they became apparent, revealing a beautiful patterning and design. He allowed himself a small smile as he inspected his work. He inlaid the runes with gold, as well as parts of the scrollwork. Silver adorned some spots as well, joined by platinum at the sign of the Kingmage. Watchfully, he gripped the socket and brought it around to the shaft. He had crafted it well, and fire-hardened the wood to be stronger than steel. It would serve well; he knew as a certainty. Quickly, he slotted the head onto the shaft before punching the pin through the socket and into the wood. This he did no less than twice, to ensure that the blade would never come off. Nodding happily, he placed the completed weapon in a case that one of his workers crafted for the spear itself.

It was a few more moments before he realized that his Forge-Second, Helve, was already hard at work on another weapon; the Script Blade. Something uniquely suited her to work on this blade, as she had rather intimate knowledge of both the Sk'av'A runes and the Indekari script, both of which were going to be used on this weapon. It was a massive blade, causing both her and Viktor to wonder if anyone could use it effectively, let alone its intended recipient.

"By the steel, Helve, have you eaten today?"

The woman merely shook her head and kept working.

5

5: Eversnow Forest, Northrealm

"Onward! Fifty-five leagues in a day is a good start, but we have a thousand or more to go before we reach journey's end." Karos' words were discomforting to the younger rangers, Aegmunt and Alaya. They were used to distances, yes, but they were still fresh enough that they occasionally enjoyed resting. Even worse, Karos had plucked them from the Wild Nights' celebrations to trudge into the distance for reasons unknown. Sighing, Aegmunt shouldered his pack once more and steeled himself for the tasks to come. Alaya, who traveled much lighter than her friend, looked off into the distance, wondering when the forest would end, let alone the journey. All she saw was the white of snow, blue of the sky and the endless brown and green trees who had lived here long before her bloodline even existed.

As they continued along the hidden paths of the snowy forest, Karos reached up for his pace-counting beads. His hand went to the top stack of beads, five in total, and pulled the second one down to signify another thousand steps. A moment later, he did a quick mental tally. He'd pulled the

98

beads in the stack of five down and up 67 times. 67. He'd nearly lost count at this point, but knew it was critical to keep track of the distance. *Soon enough, I may have to change how I count the distance.* Glancing to his fellow Rangers, Karos put a hand up, signifying a halt.

They had been on foot for many hours now without stopping. For many of them, it was a warmup, getting them stretched out and ready to face the distances ahead. This would be nothing more than a food stop to give them enough time to down a small meal. For the senior Rangers, they knew it would also be a chance for Karos to explain just what was going on. It was only the most pressing of matters that would take Karos from the Wild Nights celebrations at the Mootgrounds. It would take something *beyond* critical for him to pull the Talons away. Especially after the year they had. Three deaths in the last months alone, not to mention the stirrings of war from Nevian.

The next to speak was the eldest of the group as he sought in his pouches for a lump of *pul'gra'an*, the long-lasting meat snack the Rangers enjoyed. It could keep for months, even years, if cooked correctly and could keep a man on his feet for days. "So, Karos. What is the reason for this journey?" Emphasizing his words, he took a bite of the food. It had the consistency of wet sawdust, but the flavor was always good. Largely, this was because of the berries and spices used in its creation, as well as the meat used. Wastan used river fish and pheasant, which he felt was most effective for his body. There was likely something to that, as most men his age had to deal with weakened bones and thinner skin. But he was strong and often contended that his body was stronger now than it had been in youth.

Karos made his *pul'gra'an* mostly from venison and wild sheep. Occasionally, he would use the meat of predators, but this was an extreme rarity, born of need only. While the Rangers widely accepted that the meat of predatory animals would give one strength when they most needed it, overconsumption would cause the loss of grip on who you were. It was a risk many had to take, for they lived in some of the harsher places of Seran, where fighting was common. Those who lived in such places and regularly ate predator-flesh became *ten'gar'ii vol'noren*, or 'rangers of terror'. While not evil, they forgot things such as mercy, especially on the battlefield. They became incredible fighters, carrying on despite mortal wounds until the battle was over. But at what cost? There were many who had gone down that path and few could ever return from it. Too often, they ended up becoming *actractus*; traitors to everything the Rangers stood for.

As he chewed on a lump of *pul'gra'an* contemplatively, the man focused through the thoughts crowding his mind. After a few moments, he swallowed the food in his mouth and spoke. "When Carwaan arrived at the Mootgrounds, he bore a message from the Kingmage. The letter contained a warning of a plague striking Cúledan in Dragonmoor. He asked that we investigate and intervene, hoping-" Karos stopped short as images of death and pain assaulted his mind. Bodies in the streets, the condition of the dead. But the topology was off. In no way did this resemble Cúledan, City of Knights. It was much too small.

The other Rangers watched Karos, curious as to what stopped him. In short order, though, they knew, as the sights in the town of Littlebrook-Once-Besieged assaulted their minds. Wastan spoke, having taken a moment to collect his thoughts. The town was familiar enough to him that even in this sorry state, he could recognize it. When he spoke, his voice was almost silent, for he could see nothing but sorrow in the visions given. "L–Littlebrook. The town of Littlebrook." Karos nodded, affirming Wastan's words. Quickly finishing their rest and meals, the sobered Rangers gathered their things and marched on. But there were no more songs for the day.

As time wound on, Karos found himself constantly afflicted by visions of torment, death, and rot. It was hard to nail down the source, as there were *so many visions* coming from so many sources. A few had a distinct corvid inflections to the vision, as well as queries about what they could do to help. There were also the confused jumbles from lesser birds, as well as the judgement of greater. Eagles offered themselves up to perform sweeps of the affected cities, hawks to warn off travelers heading to those cities. Carwaan, always taking the initiative, began rallying Rangers, his throaty cry calling out to ones far and near.

"Warden Ranger, against what is happening. What are we to do?" Alaya's voice rose in worry. She still had family in Dragonmoor, as well as kin in Khataar. In her mind, there was every reason to be worried, and right now, she felt as if she needed to be with them more than anything. Karos knew it was often hard for a new Ranger, when their family was in peril, to put things aside for the betterment of Seran.

"Everything we can, Alaya. We have knowledge of herbs and medicines not seen for hundreds of years. We shall find out this plague and the other Rangers shall sally forth, armed with knowledge and herb alike, to stem the tide." Somehow, the words did not feel as hopeful as he wished they would sound. It was as if he did not believe it, either. What could hold back a plague that had perplexed the Healers? *If none can solve this, then solve it, the Rangers must.* True enough thoughts, but *how?* That gave rise to an even bigger question; *at what pace* must it happen? How long does this plague take to kill?

As the miles wore on, Karos began closing his mind off to the images being relayed from other Rangers via the birds of the land. Again and again, he tracked his pace with the beads dangling from his shoulder. He knew what he must do, but not how to do it... At least, not yet. Spurring himself on, he took off at a sprint, his Rangers trailing behind. While they could travel directly south for a few days to reach the southern edge of the Eversnow Forest, he surmised it would serve better to make for the Skyvale Pass and ward off anyone from entering Northrealm. He knew not if the land was in the grip of this terror, but they could hope that it was not.

As they crossed into Frostnuin, Karos waved to the Talons to form up into a single line. A few more miles and they came to a halt, with Karos at the head of the column, listening. Abruptly, he dropped into a crouch, his hand laying upon the snow. There was crimson staining the ground, small amounts though, as if a forced march had occurred here. "Blood upon the snows. Small droplets, as if from manacles cutting into someone's wrists and ankles. Slavers are near." His voice dropped to a dangerous whisper, one that every Ranger knew by heart, for they often spoke in it as well. His breath steamed through his mask and he glanced ahead.

"I see. Talons fan out. Tread lightly and keep a keen eye." Wastan's words were nearly silent as he stood upright, his quarterstaff held at the ready. When Karos rose and dashed ahead, he was swift to follow. The other Talons looped around wide, readying themselves to flank an unseen enemy. Up ahead, Karos darted from shadow to shadow, following the sporadic blood trail. Soon enough, it rewarded him with the flicker of a fire and the sounds of slavers. Arguing over prices and people as if they were cattle, drinking and joking. A quick whistle alerted Karos to the numbers. Ten with three slaves huddled in a cage atop a cart, tied together and barely clothed. Nodding, Karos whistled back, relaying his position. It was a move he had used before, offering himself up as bait and causing chaos in the ranks to allow his flankers to close in from the sides.

The first vanguard fell without even knowing what struck him. His head fell, separated from his body with a single fell stroke. A second turned, blood warning him that something was wrong. His hand went for his sword, but he did not have enough time before a knife found its way between his ribs and up into his heart. A shriek tore its way out of the dying man as blood flowed from the newly opened gash. Karos tore the knife out diagonally, ripping a jagged hole down to his side. The man fell quickly as Karos turned to face the rest. His targets had been the ones guarding the slaves. Placing himself between the rest of the slavers and their chattel, Karos readied his sword Northrage. A voice cried from the crowd, harsh and merciless. "KILL THAT BASTARD RANGER!"

On cue, the other Talons broke into the camp, and chaos followed. Wastan struck first, leveling one with a powerful blow to the skull. Two blades came towards him, intent on slicing neck and midriff. Expertly he blocked them, and the quarterstaff pushed out, twirling to redirect the blades. One end struck an enemy in the chest with more than enough force to stop his heart. The second received a solid punch to the throat, and he brought the quarterstaff round as he fell, to be planted in his neck. With one strike, he slammed it down with enough force to pierce flesh and shatter the delicate vertebrae protected by the fleshy neck.

Sardra swung wide, her deadly axe coming around into the neck of one slaver. Her jagged blade came next, driving up and into the stomach of another. Spinning, she brutally bisected both her targets. One let out a gurgling scream, the other fell in silence, his lifeblood flowing out upon the snow. Karos readied his blade as three came for him. He closed his eyes, a dangerous move. Focusing, he felt his targets, reaching out with his instincts. His heartbeat was a deafening roar in his head, and he spun his blade. Left to parry a sword meant for his chest. Right in a slash, opening the chest of an enemy. His eyes snapped open, giving him a vision of what he had wrought. One falling, one knocked back. A third coming for him. Dropping low, he ducked the blade and kicked out a leg, sweeping his opponent off his feet. Down came an elbow, into the back of the slaver's neck. Not enough to cause death, but to overbalance and slam him into the ground face-first. A swift kick rolled the man onto his back and Karos' blade went to his throat. "Explain where you were going and your freedom is assured."

An agonized gasp, as well as a gush of blood, escaped the mouth of the top half of a slaver. Desperately, he fumbled for his wayward intestines, trying to keep his lifeblood within him. "P-please... a potion... Anything..." Sardra hissed, a hand going for her axe once more. Kizarian reached out swiftly, gripping her arm. His whisper was soft, barely audible, and almost merciless. *Was* this a Ranger speaking? Or something different?

"Use his pain, Sardra. Look at how the will of his fellow weakens." Sure enough, the slaver at whose neck Karos' blade sat, eyes darting back and forth, breathing coming in gasps. Even more so as his gravely wounded fellow reached out to him. His eyes begging for aid or a merciful blow. His blood, so much of it staining the ground, seeping into the snow and into the dirt. After a moment, he let out a horrified shriek. For the first time in his life, the slaver was at the mercy of one he would love nothing more to see in chains. His friends were dying gruesomely a few meters away, some begging for mercy.

"Spare me... and I will tell you anything." A terrified plea for mercy. For another chance. Sardra stepped forward, an angry growl escaping her lips. Surely the Warden Ranger would not allow this scum to survive? How much had those slaves suffered? How long had they been captives, torn from family, hearth and home?

"Think of what they have endured at his hands, Warden!" Sardra's voice was shrill as she gestured to the caged beings, emotion washing over her. Anger and terror overcame her. Terror that Karos would let something like this continue. She had known the pain of those in the cage and that was not something she wanted others to live through. Taking a step forward, she readied her blade. *To the Pits with it, if the Warden Ranger will not end this, then I must!* A hand stopped her before she could take another step as Kizarian shook his head. The Warden Ranger had some plan for sure, and patience was the only way to ensure it would work.

"Tell us what you know. Now." Slowly, the Warden Ranger drove his hunting knife into the man's shoulder, eliciting a scream. Carefully, Karos angled the blade, ensuring it would miss the vital arteries. Then, he twisted the blade roughly and the scream intensified. *This was all wrong*, thought the slaver. *The Rangers had no idea where we were!* Confusion, terror, pain and hate clouded his mind. Before he could react, he started talking. He had not had enough time to plan lies and his brain was too cloudy to think up any on the fly.

"We work for.... nnghh! Berol... Hyrwn." Karos scoffed. The Rangers knew that name well from long ago, as well as the grave. He twisted the knife further, allowing the serrations on the back to rip at muscle tissue once more. The man shrieked again; his eyes wild at this point. Sweat dripped from his brow and he was close to losing consciousness.

"Berol Hyrwyn has been dead for over a decade and my patience is running thin quite quickly." Out came the hunting knife, only to bite deeply into his knee. Up through the bottom of the kneecap and then twisted upwards and driven through the joint itself. It would cripple the man for the near future and it would be difficult, even with a skilled healer, to restore his full mobility. "Just how long do you think you could last with only one functioning leg in the Eversnow Forest, one of the most hostile areas of Seran?"

The man's defenses crumbled around him. Soon enough, he began talking, giving every piece of information the Rangers wanted. Too distraught and agonized to make up a competent lie. He had nothing left up his sleeve. "Korzi Tezh... he is our... boss." Sardra growled in anger. Korzi Tezh was the scum who slaughtered her parents, stole her from the life she knew and sold her into worse things than any should have to endure.

"Let me end him, Warden Ranger. He is of no further use

to us!" The man swallowed in terror. His voice came as a terrified whine, akin to the sound a stuck pig makes when it realizes its fate. He began clawing at the Warden Ranger's trousers, eyes begging for protection against the obviously crazed dokk.

"Do not allow her to slay me, please! You promised leniency! I have given you informa-" His next words came out as a gurgle of death as Karos' knife found its way into his throat. He shuddered and twitched his last, eyes fixed and staring into the sky in shock. His last thoughts wondered about the betrayal he had faced and regret at having gotten caught. But nowhere was there remorse for the evils he caused upon innocents, nowhere was there sorrow for the death he so freely dealt to defenseless persons. Karos twisted his knife and slashed the man's throat out, spilling his blood across the snows. Already, he could hear the forest-wolves gathering, the howls drawing near. They had slain many and the wolves would take care of the remains.

"Wastan. *Vez kurt al'da ca'e kadíyik... Ia, ekejta kurt'ak dú'wol.*" The old man nodded at the instruction before swiftly stepping over to the cage. His mighty quarterstaff rose above his head before lancing down with more than enough force to shatter the shank of the lock, sending it careening into the distance. Once he accomplished the breaking of the lock, the man pried open the door and offered his hand to the first slave within. Warily, the young woman took his hand, and he carefully hauled her from the cage, followed by her bond-mates. With a practiced hand, Wastan picked the locks securing the manacles, sending them falling away into the snow.

Karos wondered why Wastan had waited until he was told

to remove their bindings. Usually, the old man was swift to end the captivity of those around. Then he remembered the howling. Wolves would not attack Rangers, seeing them as kin... But he could not say the same for a weak and shivering person. Until attended to and protected by a Ranger, they would be vulnerable. Looking them over, Wastan clicked his tongue, both in disapproval and an attempt to get Karos' attention. It worked and the Warden Ranger gathered the Talons around the slaves, forming a protective cordon.

Karos' voice cut through the patient silence, swift and careful. If they were from Northrealm, he could likely send them back to their village to be cared for by family and friends. Otherwise, he would task a Ranger (or two) to guard and guide them to Tejg Sungetiigd, far to the east, where they would find a warm hearth, medicines, and any other aid they would need to find their way home. "Whence come you?" The eldest of the trio, a boy that could not be over 16 summers old, reacted quickly to place himself between the Rangers and the girls as best he could. His hands came up in a fighting pose and he faced Karos, his eyes afire.

"I am Tomas and if you mean harm to these girls, I will kill you all or die trying." Karos studied the young man's stance. Hardly that of a fighter, but there was no fear in his eyes, though armed persons surrounded him. There was no doubt in Karos' mind that he would resist bravely and the bruises and scars upon his back were evidence that he had already done so. Raising one hand slowly, Karos spoke, his mask hiding the smile upon his face.

"I am Karos, Warden Ranger of Seran. You have nothing to fear, stalwart Tomas. I have no doubts that you have and would put up a valiant resistance. But I must know, whence come you?" A sigh of relief escaped one girl and Tomas' eyes quavered. He did his best to keep a brave face, but in the face of this impossible rescue, he could not help but break down. He fell forward, grasping the Ranger's cloak and sobbing.

"I-I am from Kordanai Village... They... are from Clan Suteri of the gah'Drin wanderers... They are the only survivors." The Ranger nodded grimly. This meant that the girls had no family to return to, as their entire clan of wanderers had met their end. He mulled over his next words for a moment, wondering how best to phrase them to avoid behind seen as heartless.

"And you, Tomas? Are you the only one left of your clan?" Trust Wastan to broach the sensitive subjects. The boy took a breath and clung tighter to Karos' cloak. His sobs were beyond pitiful, to where every Ranger knew. He was the sole survivor, the last of his name. Karos nodded slightly and looked at the other Talons. A silent nod was all they gave, and Karos spoke once more.

"You have a choice then, Tomas. You and your bond-sisters may either make the trek to Tejg Sungetiigd protected by a Ranger... Or, since you have nowhere else to go, no family to return to... Become Rangers. Strike out against those who did you wrong and protect the defenseless." Grim his voice sounded, as if the life of a Ranger was fraught with peril and hardship. True enough, it was, for they fought and died in lands far and away, often alone. "I leave it to you to decide. When you know, a Ranger will take you to the Mootgrounds. There your life will begin anew." Gently, Karos pried Tomas' fingers away from his cloak. Once more, their life was in their own hands and it was up to them what to do. Go to Fytturterjag and Tejg Sungetiigd and live as paupers, homeless until they find fortune and move on, or become Rangers and dictate their own lives once more.

"I... can only answer for myself... But I would like the chance to fight back, Master Ranger." Karos eyed the child and spoke once more, his voice gentle, but firm.

"You have no master, Tomas, but yourself. I am simply Warden Ranger, or Karos." He smiled beneath his mask and looked up in slight surprise as the elder of the girls stepped forward.

"We will join the Rangers. The slavers have thrust many evils upon us and no longer will we accept that. I am Anna and my younger sister is Sara." The Warden Ranger looked to the much younger girl. Concern colored his face as he realized she could not be older than ten and he wondered how long she had been a slave. As well, a darker portion of his mind wondered just how long they had passed her around campfires. Looking up, he sought the only one among the Talons who knew such evil- Sardra Wood-Strider.

"I shall escort them, Warden Ranger." As expected, she spoke up before Karos even asked. She knew the pain and she would help them through it. Nodding, Karos spoke to the trio. His voice assumed the tone of a command, the first of many they would hear. But there was kindliness within as well, for Karos was not one to domineer his Rangers. He expected each to think and act differently for the same cause. Those who would not or could not adapt given safer duties. Those who could adapt, power through and toughen up would earn the title and become fighters.

"Very well. Take them before the Moot, Sardra Wood-Strider, and may Veljra guide both blade and arrow." Sardra responded with a goodbye in the Sk'av'A, then she ushered the trio to follow her. Their road would be long and arduous, but Karos was certain they would succeed. They had survived against all odds thus far, so what honestly could beat them? Whistling to the remaining Talons, Karos took off into the waning light, his feet swift across the snow. Soon enough, they joined in behind him, Wastan, Kizarian, Aegmunt, and Alaya. Kiri, who had trailed ahead to take down an advance party, joined back in with the Talons as well, nodding.

"You fought well, Warden Ranger."

"Did you find much trouble, Kiri?"

"Only the usual, Karos. Three had gone ahead towards the Hanmaer Road with intent to attack the caravans supplying the Riders. They did not last long." Her voice was dangerous, prompting Karos to remember the ferocity the diminutive elf fought with. Few could withstand her unbridled fury and fewer still would dare try. As they continued along, the Rangers of the Talon darted from shadow to shadow, over snow-covered hill and under tunnels of white. Along frozen rivers and through unknown caves. They had far to go but were still making good time.

A day gone by and they had crossed almost a hundred leagues. More than most people could do in a week. They were not holding back now, for their purpose was twofold. During their infrequent rest stops, Karos detailed how he would split his forces. Aegmunt and Alaya, under the lead of Wastan, would hunt for news of Korzi Tezh and end his empire of slavery. The others would proceed to the closest plague-afflicted town and begin planning, connecting with other Rangers, and aiding the Healers. From there, Karos alone would continue without rest until he reached Cúledan, City of Knights. Once there, he would search through the city until he found the source of this infestation.

If they had to, Wastan and his team would comb the entire Eversnow until they found their prey. Should he elude them there, they would at least root out every holdout of slavers and bandits they came across, hoping to make the forest a safer place.

The miles melted away under their feet, and the hours blended into days. Their pace-counting beads were arranged, counted, arranged again, going up and down on the leather cord as they passed threshold after threshold. Then, they broke out into the cold clear light. Below them, about five hundred yards, lay the Skyvale Pass, the only safe way into Northrealm. Hundreds, if not thousands, of caravans traveled along it. Most made it, thanks to the vigilance of the forty Rangers, who watched over the nearly two-hundred-ninety-league stretch. Each was hand-picked by Karos as the fastest runners and most competent navigators of the Rangers, able to race over each of their seven-and-a-quarter-league areas to get help or track a vulnerable caravan. This responsibility they shared with the honored few families of the Grey Wardens, who had been the protectors of the Skyvale Pass since the first records came to be written.

As the Talons broke out of the forest and onto the slope, a whistle caught Karos' attention and he glanced southwards. Sure enough, there was one of the uroks who had sworn their lives to the service of Veljra. A Ranger through and through, though much less diplomatic than most of his peers, the keen-eyed and long-legged urok was an ideal sentry for this area. "Well met, Warden Ranger!"

"Hail, Lognuk ugh'Darsk! What news from the Pass?!" His voice carried quite far in the clear air, echoing over the Pass itself from slope to slope. Lognuk waved for him to approach, before taking another glance down the slope, to where a few carriages rolled. As the Talons closed the distance, he pointed into the pass, showing the movement.

"They are fleeing from some unknown calamity. And about a week ago, I was assaulted by images of sickness and death, which bore the unmistakable tinge of one of our own. Sights followed it beyond count, all retelling the same tale. Warden Ranger, in the name of the people of Seran, I demand of you; what evil has befallen the land? What is going on?" Karos smirked as he eyed the masked urok. He was an Urok'ni of devastating intellect, and he also had never met an enemy he could not conquer. As a Ranger, he was heavy-handed in dealing with fell folk, but kinder than most when dealing with the regular peoples of the land. In battle, he was relentless and brutal and could pursue a horse-riding enemy until they spent their horse to overtake them. Out of the forty Rangers patrolling the Skyvale Pass, they regarded him as the fastest and most enduring, which was a feat among folk who could cross nations in weeks without rest.

"I speak the truth of what I know, Lognuk, when I say that honestly I know not. I received word from the Kingmage to gather who I could and proceed to Cúledan with all haste. When you received those visions, so too did I, *kala'taj*. Since then, we have been on the move, with few stops." The urok'ni nodded slightly. *If something had called the Warden away from the Wild Nights' celebrations at the Mootgrounds*, the urok mused, *it must be beyond imperative. Especially for him to drag away his Talons, but where is young Sardra?* As if he had read the Ranger's mind, Karos spoke. "We encountered a slaver band in the depths of our forest... They had three slaves with them, who, when freed, pledged their service to the Rangers. I felt

Sardra Wood-Strider to be the most appropriate of *saal'kwen* for them." Another nod. With what happened to slaves most often, it would be good for them to have a sympathetic face training and teaching them. That was a well-known fact.

"We can only hope she knows not to go soft on them."

"I have faith in her. She has failed in no test that I have given, and she has learned much in her years." His voice further reinforced the truth of his words, for not lightly did Karos trust Rangers so green with tasks such as that. "She knows her limits and will not fail to request help from older and wiser heads." A grunt was the response he got to this, signaling that they were near the end of the urok'ni's talkative mood. It was not unseen, for most Rangers preferred to speak less, so they had more time to contemplate the tasks ahead.

"In that case, *ten'gar'ii kuz'no'litik*, if you would accept my demand," A nod from Karos told him to continue, and he spoke candidly, "see that you do not fail in this test, for too many lives hang in the balance."

"And keep your eyes and blade sharp, Lognuk ugh'Darsk. For you *must* keep open the pass." The urok nodded and placed a hand upon Karos' shoulder. The man did likewise and in a flash, their foreheads met with a small amount of force. Not enough to be painful or dangerous, but both felt the impact, and their companions heard it.

"Until our paths cross again, Rangers-Most-Honored! Wander freely and fight with the rage of the just!"

"*And you! Sharp blades and keen eyes! Until our paths cross again!*" The exchange sounded strange, and the translation was difficult for any but a Ranger. In effect, they were words of parting and a blessing upon each other, that one may wander freely and fight with the fury of the just and the other that they may have keen eyes and light burdens. With those goodbyes said, the Talons were off, careening down the slope with sure feet and swift movements towards the road below. They were merely five leagues from the nearest way-stop and hopefully that would house people with information they needed.

Moving over the cobblestone road, which kept itself clear of snow by magic unknown, the Rangers set a blistering pace. Around caravans they flowed, seeming to have the form of water. When at last they approached the way-stop, their frantic speed slowed and Karos approached the door. Inside the tavern, there were the sounds of weary travelers celebrating that they had made it. Certainly, they still had quite a long way to go, but for now, they were in a place of safety and could eat and relax by a roaring fire.

The sound stopped momentarily when the grim Rangers entered, and a shadow seemed to pass over the interior. Soon enough, though, the Way-Keeper recognized the folks. "Rangers! As well, the Warden Ranger himself! How might I be of aid, masters?" Thus identified, the mystery faded from the men and the patrons went about their feasting, drinking and reveling. The Talons took a seat in a dark corner, save for Karos, who spoke to the Keeper.

"Tyrell Hearth-Tender. Well met, my friend. How fare you?" The man had visibly aged since last Karos had seen him, which had been only half a year ago. It was strange to behold, but not unexpected. Besides the stress he undertook in keeping a Way-Stop open, as well was the fact that he was a human approaching his sixtieth winter. Not all were ageless like the Rangers and that often became a wound deeper than many as they watched friends wither and die because of the ravages of time.

"Ahh, Karos, you have not aged a day. I trust you are well? Though, by looking at your companions, I wager it shall not be long ere trouble descends somewhere." The Ranger's mouth crinkled into a smirk. It was not his way to pass idle words, nor to let on what could cause a panic. Tyrell was a wise man, in his own way, though his wisdom most often came from what draught the many travelers he saw would prefer. After a moment, Karos nodded, leaning closer.

"Word has come of a fell sickness besieging many towns, including Cúledan. The Kingmage has tasked my Rangers with finding the source of this fell enchantment and to remove it with all haste. You *must* tell me if any coming through your way-stop exhibit the signs of illness."

"Of course, my lord. I shall inform you the instant I know of any but- how. Karos, pray tell- what am I to do against such? What am I to look for?" Tyrell grew slightly frustrated. The Ranger had hardly given him enough information to observe, let alone act on. He *had* to know more if he were to help the Rangers.

"I will teach you direct- for such things as this would cause hysteria if heard and there are far too many prying ears." The man nodded gently and took a breath. All too familiar he was with the ways the Rangers shared thoughts without words and many times it had put him off his feed. When Karos reached out, he gave no resistance and nodded as the Ranger gripped his head, before allowing his own hands to do the same. The men closed their eyes and the first thought that came to Tyrell's mind was one of how much he would rue his curiosity.

His mind's eye immediately filled with images of rotting flesh. Blood dripping from wounds that would neither clot nor close, no matter the healing potion poured within. Grotesquely pot-bellied adults and children stumbling blindly in pain as their bodies ate themselves from within, only to collapse to the ground, struggling to breathe, their last gasps coming out as a rush of sickly fluid. All wise creatures he saw, their bodies contorting with pain as the flesh sloughed from their bodies, landing in wet piles. Yet, despite all this, he did his best to hold his stomach- but nothing could prepare him for what was to come.

When the smell hit, he tore away from Karos, doubling over as if to vomit- but nothing came. He heaved, trying to push the rotten stench from his mind- but the more he tried to force it away, the more present it became. A poison for his mind and he stood there, heaving for a time. *Everything* now had the stench of such a horrific death about it- even his precious home. "Kiri. Let us take master Tyrell outside. He has a great need for fresh air." The voice was not from Karos, who stood watching the man react; but from Kizarian, the swarthy elf by Kiri's side. Nodding, the two positioned themselves, ever so gently carrying the dumbstruck man to the door. Snapping away from his reflection, Karos closed the distance as they struggled with the heavy portal and opened it himself. A blast of cold hit, and Tyrell's color seemed to return for a moment. Once outside, his recovery came swift, and he took a deep, gasping breath of the freezing air. A few more and he steadied himself on his own feet and return to a standing position.

"Karos, that tells me little. If I am to help, I need to know what to look for at the beginning, for scarcely will people travel when that ill." To this, the Warden Ranger nodded and shrugged.

"Alas, that I know nothing of the early stages, Tyrell. Only the end and even then, only what I have seen from other Rangers. If I am to know more, I must make Littlebrook-Once-Besieged soon. There two of my Rangers labor to save what lives they can." Tyrell nodded slightly, as the gravity of the situation became clear to his eyes.

"Very well, master Karos. Whatever supplies I can make available to you; I would have you tell me." He had few possessions and his wife had gone to the Afterworld many years before. In this way, he could honor her memory, even if his supplies were unnecessary. The look in the Rangers' eyes, though– that told him what needed to be done.

"Should you find anyone you think infected– guard them but keep them away from the others and, for Veldan's sake, keep yourself safe. There is no telling how this sickness spreads. I wish I could give you more to go by, but I am a babe lost in the woods. If you have potions, please make them ready. Strengthen your body however you need to and take great care. Kiri! Kizarian. Gather our things– we have disturbed master Tyrell long enough for the day." The two nodded and released the Tender, who was now braced against the visions swimming through his head.

"Karos, I was not asking for instruction– I was asking if you," he began, accentuating his point with a finger jabbing into the Ranger's sternum, "or your Rangers required any supplies of me. A night's rest, full bellies, anything– this disease I fear far beyond anything I could hope to muster– but I can at least give you respite until you must face this evil once more."

"Master Tyrell, I thank you, but we must away. The more we delay hastens the death of too many innocent people. We cannot let this stand, so we mus–"

"Yet if you do not delay, you shall arrive too weary to work. Ranger, I know this well- your companions and you have been long upon the trails already. I am no longer asking you- I am telling you. Rest, even if just long enough to fill your bellies and your packs. My stores are always open to your kind, Ranger. Without you and yours, I would have died long ago." Karos opened his mouth to protest, but after a glance at his two companions, who were already seating themselves once more, he closed his mouth and thought better of it. Nodding, he allowed himself to be escorted back to the seat he had claimed, before propping his back against the wall. When next Tyrell spoke, it was to Kiri, the chipper elf-maid who sat toying with a pair of raven feathers atop her bow. "My lady, if you wish, I can prepare a green sal-" a cheerful, but dismissive wave cut him off.

"Actually, milord, I would much rather a hunter's stew." This brought a soft chuckle from Kizarian's lips. *How often*, he wondered, *does poor Kiri have to contend with the fixed notion she eats only greens because of her race?* Tyrell prepared to stammer an apology, only for a wave of Kiri's hand to silence him. "Think nothing of it, Master Tyrell- I am quite used to it." The twinkle in her eyes was genuine, and she was not half as bothered as the man was afraid of.

"Do you often contend with that, Kiri?" came the thought in Kizarian's subtle murmur as he gave it voice. Glancing over at him, the elf-maid shrugged slightly.

"Many a day do I have to face such subtle bias," the woman began. Tyrell withered under her kindly gaze, as if she had just struck him through with her daggers. Evidently embarrassment was not something he tasted often and having made an incorrect judgement and being corrected on, it was not on his planned list of activities for the day. "But I do not let it affect me, for I am most definitely an oddity among my kin."

"For you milord?" The deep elf chuckled gently as the man spoke to him now. Idly, his thumb ranged across his knuckles, seeking those old scars he had earned over his life. It took him a moment to respond, making it seem as if he were losing himself to thought- soon enough though, his answer came.

"A hunter's stew as well- that would find me best. I daresay we are quite boring, Master Tyrell, for it is a safe guess that Karos will ask for the same." Karos, having heard his name, snapped back from his watchful inattentiveness. Glancing towards the deep elf and the wild elf, the man shrugged. He clearly had not given thought to his own needs- as was usual. Sighing, Kiri spoke up.

"Aye, he shall have the same as us." Tyrell nodded and slipped away, moving off to prepare the meals. He caught more of the wild elf's speech and could not help but chuckle. "Karos, you are impossible. I swear, you must find a lover just so they can remind you when to eat and drink." This conversation struck a nerve quickly and the Warden Ranger bowed his head, hiding behind his mask.

"See how he withdraws, Kiri! For shame, your words have struck him through!" The deep elf chided his friend, needling her gently. Playfully, her hands swatted at him.

"Begone, pesky fly. Allow me to take care of my student, for he is still in some ways a *valtagt*." That was quite a hefty thing to say about the Warden Ranger in his presence. Comparing him to a Tenderfoot? Unheard of- save for those who knew of his relationship to Kiri.

"Long-Eye, I would keep such comments to yourself. Love

is a taste I will ne'er again know." His voice was not angry- but saddened, and that had more impact. Kiri immediately cast her eyes down. She had gone a bit too far this time, telling him such.

"I-I apologi-" He cut her off with a wave of his hand. It was an easy enough mistake to make.

"Long-Eye, you know as well as I the reckonings- that if a Ranger has not found love by their second century, they never will." She shook her head, taking back her contrition.

"Karos, you know as well as I that there is no way for that to be true. For certain it is rare- but you have shown your proclivity to break the mold." Was that hope in her voice? Before Karos could speak, she continued. "Your sadness is known- and well I understand your *prúnsaal*. Many nights have you confided your fears to me, Karos. Many nights have you thought yourself broken. You are *not* broken, Karos- you simply have not found the right time. Remember the tales of Alfyrd the Hopeless? Nigh to 1000 was he when love found him, sweeping him off his feet thanks to Lord Tyrn." Again, Karos waved.

"This is simply not a constructive point of conversation, Kiri. I do not discount the things you have taught me; I just ask that we not discuss my shortcomings."

Kiri stopped for a moment. *Shortcomings*, she thought to herself, looking over the Warden Ranger, *that none but you can see.* She opened her mouth to speak once more, but a warning glance from Kizarian caught her. Sighing, she lapsed back into silence for a moment, before shifting the topic to something he would find more agreeable.

"So, what path will we take to Littlebrook? The highroad is likely to be filled with travelers this time of year and if our thoughts are true, there may be victims among them." Her companions nodded assent– careful they would need to be to avoid any exposure before it was necessary.

"I was thinking we would travel along the Borderwood and then drop from the north into the Summerdusk forest. In that way, we would avoid the main roads and should any bandits be waiting to raid; we could head them off." A nod came from the deep elf and the wild elf. Karos nodded his thanks to Kiri for the change of topic as well, before continuing. "We would, in that way, be able to visit the Waystop in that region and see what Ranger Ardivari, the Watcher of that area, has in store." Kiri thought this a grand idea– long had it been since she had seen the girl.

"Ah! This plan I like. Come then, let us feast. No, not just feast– let us have some merriment. Smile Karos and let us have a song! I remember that you have quite the voice." Again, the Ranger blushed– off key he thought he was, but the challenge was direct. Shaking his head, he took a breath and began.

"*Úþa ca'e rölkh un'tak,*" began the old Waysong. The commotion of the tavern stopped as they heard the man's sad baritone singing in the Sk'av'A,

"Úþa ca'e rölkh un'tak,
Kejg desht lor skújn lof'zi tejr!
Úþa ca'e rölkh kezk,
Kejg stra kaði kura lor'vin!"

Kiri and Kizarian tapped their feet in time, setting the beat for the song. Karos smiled and likewise beat his foot against the ground, a gentle drum for the explorer's song. The Rangers with him felt the urge rise in their chests and soon they joined in, Kizarian singing a powerful bass and Kiri with a gentle soprano.

The people within the Waystop cheered and picked up the beat as well. A minstrel struck up his vielle, taking a moment to get the beat in his head before playing along, the instrument adding a wonderful tune.

"Aze, aze!
Endure the road but one step more!
Stra'kejg hav'a
ca'e zen'ii vin'zat!
Aze Aze!
Endure the road but two steps more!
Kejg stra ia invec'da
Zen'ii hjld zat'ost lläs!"

These words, none but the Rangers knew– regardless, the Waystop patrons listened intently. The song spoke of the wandering of the Rangers, their self-assigned tasks as the pathfinders of the land and their role as protectors, standing between those who had need of their blades and the foes they faced.

Soon enough, their singing ended as Tyrell brought their meals to them. Having worked up a bit of an appetite, they dug in happily, though not before Karos gave several gold Aureim to the Stoptender in thanks. At first, he attempted to decline the money, though a glance from all three Rangers changed his mind quickly. Leaving them to their meal, he went about checking on his other patrons, ensuring all had what they needed.

Soon enough, the time came, and the Rangers were on their way with renewed vigor and heightened urgency. Down through the great stone border-gate they came and watched with mirth as the permanent winter of the North gave way to the greens, golds and blues of the farm country of Wester-spring. The scene lay before them, the trees and cliff giving way to the verdant hilly country as they crossed down from the icy winds of the Skyvale Pass and the great stone Caljen Gate, the great stone archway, easily six spearlengths wide and ten tall. Constructed long ago by a now-forgotten architect, it was the sentinel of Northrealm, standing a silent vigil. On either side of it were the grand statues of two of the High Kings of Northrealm, from back when the Pass was first cut through the mountains and the Gate created. Two eminent men of marble, standing with arms outstretched in the welcoming way of the Nolvern. "Long may the gate stand and may the Old Kings welcome us home soon." Karos intoned the old goodbye to Northrealm, traditionally said when leaving on adventures. He did not believe in the luck the statement would bring, but it felt comforting to say.

6: Hanmaer Tower, Eversnow Forest, Northrealm

"Very well, Mirenel. Do not come any further down the stairs, upon your life. I fear there is a sickness stirring and it may be spreading. Leave the tower- you both know the way to Ormere Keep, make your way there with all haste." Thäoldr had calmed, but only slightly. "Only fly from the top of the tower- but one dragon can land at a time. I will follow as soon as I can." He had to get them out of here- they were his students and his priority. Everything else came second and until he had washed himself, he had to be isolated. There was no way to protect them otherwise. He only hoped it was not too late for his own health.

Shaking his head, the elder rider hurried with his cleaning. The faster he could get this place free of blood, the better. If they had to abandon Hanmaer Tower, it would be much harder to project their strength here in the North. Such thoughts lingered in his mind not by choice but by the necessity of his station, forcing him to wonder if it may be better to sear the tower itself- burn everything out and rebuild. Perhaps then they would be safe? He knew not what was going on-why things were turning this way and again his thoughts drifted to the offering he had given the Ancestors. Surely, it'd been pleasing. There was no rotten meat, no wilted greens... "Scorchitall... Taog and his influence have doomed us all!" he screamed at no one in particular, wondering what was to become of his world.

High above, the mighty Hjalgroþ and his rider winged lower over the forest. He was tiring, his wings straining to keep him aloft. Inwardly, the mighty dragon wondered if he had doomed the girl with this gamble- he knew who he would need to find and he knew his rider would not be pleased with that idea. Finally, a spark of hope! Calling out, the mighty dragon angled into a dive, letting out a throaty roar, which was echoed by a warbling howl.

"Hjalgroþ, why are we searching for a wolf? What possible help can come from," he trailed off as they cleared the canopy of trees, coming upon a dokk who walked with three children. "A Ranger?" Surely the great dragon had gone mad! What use could one of the ground-walking Rangers be to a mighty Rider?

"Hail, Rider! Your dragon speaks of one beset with illness! Come, bring her to me and I will do what I can!" Making a note to berate Hjalgroþ over speaking to a *Ranger* of all people, he eyed the dokk warily.

"And for what reason should I trust you?" A perfectly reasonable question- or so he thought. As he gave voice to the thought, he could feel his dragon stir in annoyance, crouching low enough that the woman could see the plight of the injured. She was still alive- barely. Surely the only reason she had not drowned in her own blood was the position she was in and with a cry, the Ranger advanced quickly, ignoring the blade the man waved at her.

"If you want her to survive, use your blade helpfully and *cut her bindings*, curse you!" Already her hands had produced multiple healing potions, and she tightened her mask down. Whispering a prayer to the wild Ancestor and Ancestress, she grabbed the woman's head as the Rider reluctantly let her loose. "She is fading fast- I may save her, but you will have to follow my instructions *to the very letter*, Rider." A growl rose from his throat, only to be silenced by a glare from his dragon. They placed the woman on the ground and the Ranger began her work. "Tenderfeet, from my bag- I require highberries and sky-fusion." Luckily, she had been teaching them the most useful of plants when the rider had arrived. As she forced open the woman's mouth, it nearly surprised the dokk as she vomited black blood. The stench was terrible indeed, but the dokk had encountered worse. Uncorking one of her potions, the woman forced it to the rider's lips. "Come on, drink, curse you. Even a sip..."

To her credit, the young Elsaia was holding on bravely and she managed a weak pull at the lifesaving potion. It would help... but not enough. Her body seemed to calm, her breathing became easy, and the bleeding stopped, at least for now. But already the Ranger could tell that it was not enough, and she flew into a frenzy. "What manner of illness is this? What plague is this?" Taking a breath, the dokk ripped open the girl's clothes- and all hope seemed to flee from her eyes. "Scorchitall, Rider, I was told your kind were wise in the ways of medicine!" A withering glare she shot to Joram, who threw his hands up in defense. Turning to her pack, the Ranger grabbed a green package, nodding thankfully as the young ones handed her the herbs she requested. Quickly, she mashed the highberries and sky fusion together, before opening the package to reveal woven cloths inside. Rubbing the sludge onto the first cloth, she laid it upon the woman's stomach before quickly binding the cloth in place. "Quickly, cut away her clothes. If she has any other wounds, we must know." The rider hesitated at first, wary of the woman who seemed to so easily flit between rage and care. This earned him yet another shout. "CURSE YOU, IF YOU LOVE LIFE, DO AS I SAY!"

"Very well! Scorchitall, you would get further in life without shouting at everyone!" The woman ignored this as he began cutting open Elsaia's clothing. Quickly enough, he sighed in relief, even if it were to be short-lived. "I see no other wounds, Ranger." The she-dokk nodded and took a breath, before reaching down to the girl's neck, pressing two fingers to a vital point. It was faint, but the flutter of a heartbeat was unmistakable.

"She yet lives. For how long, I could not say. Rider, listen-give these to your dragon and as you love life, make no more stops. Get her to *Tejg Sungetiigd*. As fast as you can." The Rider eyed the Ranger with near disgust before speaking, even as she pressed a handful of berries into his palm.

"It was on the insistence of my dragon that we stop-" His dragon interrupted him, choosing right then to be the voice of reason. *Because I knew the Ranger could at least enable her to survive the journey, Joram.* Taking a breath, the man nodded slowly. He was out of his altitude and he knew this. Best to let the Ranger dictate his course for now. The woman, of course, was already wrapping Elsaia in a Ranger cloak to keep her warm. A prayer she whispered as she did so, placing herbs along the woman's throat.

"Av qis dran sa elyrök. Av qis dran sa tylca." She then looked at the rider and spoke once more in the strange language. *"Av qis dran sa tylbalt. Hjld Yrbos skjk kaz'in oksii pe sa."* The Rider was about to ask for a translation, but a look from the woman clarified that the time to go was now. Nodding, he bound Elsaia to the dragon's back and spurred Hjalgroþ to great efforts, having given him the handful of berries, though wary of their effect.

She asked for mercy and strength for Elsaia, that we be stone-strong and that Yrbos close his eyes to us. A pleasant enough parting gift to ask death to not see us. Joram could not argue there and into the sky he let out a wild cry- for speed, for fair winds and for strength for all. Then they were off, climbing into the sky and winging to the east as fast as Hjalgroþ could take them.

The skies were clear and cold, which gave him hope. Hope that they would reward his efforts. After all, a corpse would make for a rather depressing conversation. Occasionally, he reached back, gently placing a hand up from the woman's lips to check her breathing- still, she drew breath. Still, she lived. What the Ranger had done, Joram knew not- for his skills were yet to be built as far as healing goes. She had sounded enraged, though, when she had revealed Elsaia's wounds. *Surely master Thäoldr had done all he could for her? Or perhaps the Rangers were always this angry?* He could not tell for now.

Far below, the Ranger looked over the blackened blood in the snow. Delicately dipping her fingers into the gore, she brought a drop up to her nose and took a whiff, steeling her stomach against what she had already smelled. There were the traces of death- but it made no sense, for she had felt the girl breathing- her heart beating and she had followed commands. Shaking her head, the Ranger wiped her fingers into the snow, cleansing them of the infected blood with cold. Then, she looked at her charges. "Come, we must continue with all haste to the Mootgrounds. There you will be safe and I will by necessity leave you." They looked slightly confused, but nodded regardless. Taking a breath, the Ranger slung her pack once more and sighed. "There is something wrong... everything feels... wrong." She shook her head, trying to dispel the feeling, before waving her charges to new efforts. "Come, we must hurry! There is food and drink to spare when we arrive." That gave Tomas a bit of hope- too long his belly had been empty.

"Milady Ranger... My feet hurt; I cannot go on..." The youngest, Sara, looked on the brink of tears. Stopping her frantic pace, Sardra turned, slipping to the girl. Sure enough, her feet were raw from running, for they had found no shoes. Clicking her tongue, the Ranger looked her charges over.

"Leave it to the boys to forget that you need shoes with all those clothes given." This earned her at least a few chuckles, enough to warm her heart. Quickly, the dokk unlaced her boots- but it was not the boots she was giving the girl. Quickly unpinning her leg wraps, the Ranger unraveled them, before waving at Tomas and Anna. "Lift her, that I may wrap her feet. I have extra leg wraps in my pack for each of you- thank the Ancestors I always pack plenty heavy." Nodding, the boy gently opened his hands to Sara, who accepted warily. When Sardra hoisted her into the air, she panicked- until the Ranger was at her feet, gently cleaning dirt and grime from her feet before wrapping the woolen strips around her feet and up her calves. Soon enough, Sardra wrapped the girl's raw, tired feet. They would have a better chance of attending to them when they arrived at the Mootgrounds.

"Tomas, set her down. Anna, come, let me wrap your feet next." The older girl nodded and stepped forward, allowing the Ranger to wrap her feet for the journey ahead. Last, it was Tomas' turn, but he shook his head.

"Milady Ranger, I am of the snows and the ice. My feet feel fine." Chuckling, the dokk returned the last pair of wraps to her pack, before donning her boots once more. Then, she divvied out her stash of highberries, giving each of her charges a handful. Popping one in his mouth and chewing it, Tomas could not help but speak. "Such an odd flavor. What is this?" As he swallowed the berry, he felt a gentle surge of energy, his body feeding upon the stamina-giving juices and dissipating the lethargy. He stretched for a moment before popping another few berries into his mouth experimentally. Nodding, he smiled and stood up straighter, ready to face the distance ahead.

"These are highberries- my clan used to pick them all the time... They are invaluable on the road." Anna spoke gently, her voice barely disguising the pain the thoughts brought her. Immediately, Sardra was at her side and placed a comforting paw on her shoulder.

"You carry their memory and their name, Anna *anrak'Suteri*. Through you and your sister- their deeds, their triumphs- they live on. You wield ultimate power o'er how they will be remembered." A gentle squeeze and Sardra released her to her thoughts, before waving them on. "Come, we have far to go."

And so, they set on, with renewed vigor, if not renewed spirits.

II

Distant Thunder

7: Littlebrook-Once-Besieged, Westerspring

Fae felt her mind twisting as she fought with herself– To run as far as she could was most likely the intelligent option, but could she ever look at herself in the mirror again? Sighing, she looked at her companion. "Box, you are ever so knowing... but what must I do?" The fox blinked at her ally before padding around in a circle for a moment. She offered no answer, though Fae felt it was normal. Usually when she asked such of Box, it was a question to herself. Sighing, she shook her head. "I will come back in the night with such food and supplies as I can gather for the guardsmen. After all, someone must keep them going." Box yipped happily and sped off towards a farm field, with Fae bounding after. Her legs were muscular, and she kept up a good pace, striding through the night back towards the forest. In her mind, she knew just where to get the right herbs and vegetables to make a wonderful stew.

Enough, she hoped, to keep the guardsmen on their feet against whatever the oncoming peril may be.

Back in Littlebrook, things were not well. The Rangers had both spent their supplies of healing herbs and potions. In a rather sickening stroke of luck, at least, their number of patients was dwindling as they passed into the halls of their ancestors. Nelya spoke, her voice a frantic shout. "Kar'Maerae! Another comes in- this one from a far cot." A man came in, carried by two sturdy lads who wore the garb of farmers, along with a cloth over their faces to ward off the plague. He was not too far for hope and the boys looked in good health.

Ayara spoke next, her voice calm. "Place him there on a table- and then make a hasty retreat before it claims you likewise!" Immediately, she set to work, cleansing the obvious pustules and open wounds with pure water. "Nelya, find the Keeper of the Healing House and inform him that if he does not open the stores to us, I will be forced to execute the authority of the Rangers and take them by force! We must stem the tide of this dastardly plague!" Nodding, the younger Ranger took a deep breath. It was a grave task that she was being saddled with, for never did a Ranger wish to employ that bit of brute force demanding for what they needed. Many found it distasteful- dishonorable, even. But even as young as she was, she could see the necessity.

Running to the back room, the young woman pounded her hand on the door. "In the name of the Ancestors and the Kingmage of Seran, you will open this door!" No response came. Nothing at all, not even a shout to leave. This disquieted her greatly, and she took a firm stance. With a powerful blow, the slender elf knocked the door inward- but it did not collapse. Cursing her meager frame, the woman closed her eyes and focused her energies. She was *angry, and* this door needed to give way. Before she could stop herself, her voice called out with a power arcane, that of the expressive magic of the Sk'av'A before slamming her full weight into the door. "*Kajaat ne elvyklar!*" Instantly, the door responded to the demands of the Life-song, the Elder Language, in the only way the old wood could– it shattered, ripped asunder at the very core. The dust settled and the scene within sickened the Ranger greatly.

Inside was the Keeper of the Healing-House, sprawled upon a table. He was, as many of the patients in the Healing House, stone-dead, his body rotted away in various stages. The stench was unbearable– perhaps worse than that of the rest of the House because it was even more enclosed. Coughing, she searched through the room, seeking the key and as she did, she shouted to her companion. "Ayara... I fear the Keeper is beyond cooperation... The Ancestors' blessings go with him." In the other room, the elder Ranger cursed her luck– *the town's healer is dead as well.* This was growing far worse than the Ranger had feared– after all, if the Healer, a man who undoubtedly had the favor of the Ancestors, could die in such a way... What hope had the rest of Seran?

"Say your prayers and find the key, Nelya. And be swift! We must stem the tide; else all is lost!" Ayara's voice came through the Hall loud and clear. To herself, she spoke a moment later as she tore open the farmer's tunic to expose his body, readying herself for the worst. "Ancestors, I can only hope that it does not besiege other towns in such a way..." Little did they know, this was not the case, for many towns already were facing the same fate, the same grotesque end. For now, though– what hope had any of them? The Rangers could nary stem the tide, as evidenced by the bodies turning to liquid around them. Looking down, Ayara sighed. The man was not showing the signs that the illness had advanced too far- at least not yet. Idly, she wondered if bringing the man here had sped his demise- regardless, she steeled herself to heal the man, to protect him from this end.

Searching every cabinet, Nelya shook her head- *was it a chest? There!* Desperately, she ran to a massive steel chest sitting in the corner. Upon it were many blankets, enchanted to keep the contents of the chest cool. *Thank the Ancestors.* Key in hand, the Ranger quickly opened the lock to look within, sighing thankfully as she found what she had been seeking. Quickly, she grabbed the ones that would help the most now- Elderberry, garlic, licorice root, ginger and a few others. From one of her own pouches, she removed a large pinch of *dralathel* before mixing them together. Quickly, she brought the items to the senior Ranger, who handed her a mortar and pestle. "Mix that, quick as you can, Nelya. He is not too far gone; we may yet have a chance."

Nodding, the younger woman quipped. "Would it be better to get him outside?" A glance the two exchanged confirmed her thoughts- that it may aid in protecting this man. Shouldering the farmer, who was weakening, the two Rangers bore him outdoors, before laying him upon the cold cobblestone of the road to work. At the very least, it would give the three of them some fresh air. The night sky was clear, the stars bright. Idly, the Rangers wondered just how many more spirit-lanterns would need to be given to the Ancestors at the end of the year.

But that would help them little. Steeling herself, Ayara brought her knife out- to a terrified look from the farmer. "This may hurt." Those were the only words she gave before taking a radical direction– excising the already rotten flesh as best she could with the man writhing under her blade. "Fuckitall, be still!" Her words came as a reprimanding bark as her blade drew a little too close to an artery in the man's wrist. Carefully, she worked the blade along the border of the massive pustule, avoiding by a mere hair's length the man's radial artery. He was screaming, of course, wondering what he had done to enrage the Ancestors and garner enough anger to merit this torture. All he knew was that his boys had carried him here to be healed from whatever sickness had begun and now he was being cut open!

"Please, Ranger. No more! I have done nothing wrong!" With his words, Ayara realized she had nary spoken a word to this poor man before bringing the knife upon him. Closing her eyes for a moment, she took a breath, before once more looking to her work and continuing her surgery.

"You are not in trouble, master Einar." The man was far enough into shock to not feel the pain but he could at least understand her words. "She is simply trying to remove a strange pustule from your arm. We fear that you have taken ill with a plague the likes of which Seran has ne'er seen and we are trying to save your life." A reasonable explanation of events, Nelya thought. The man still writhed, but at least he bit back his screams now. Finally, Ayara's blade moved from his skin and a pulsating mass lay on the ground next to him. Both women eyed it cautiously, before one woman grabbed a healing potion and poured it into the man's wound.

"Nelya, wait." Ayara grabbed the potion– sure enough, the man's wound was healing, but into a scarred, pitiful clump. Sure enough, they cut the sickness out from there... but there were still more pustules and there is no way the man would survive more surgery. Taking the potion and looking at the pulsating mass, the Ranger curiously tipped the bottle and allowed one or two drops to fall onto the tumor. Whatever she was expecting to find, it was not there. Instead of dying off, the clump merely slowed. But as with most things that infect others, it could not long survive outside the body and soon became still, melting into the ground. "So... our healing potion seems to do nothing..."

"What do you mean, Ayara? The thing died off?" Nelya's words were quizzical as she looked over to her compatriot, while feeding Einar a handful of highberries to restore his strength.

"Aye, it did– but not by the potion, Nelya. It died off because the man's body was not feeding it." Sometimes the younger ranger bored Ayara... But she was at least useful, if unlearned. "The healing potion did nothing more than to slow down its movement– and its death." She, however, was seeing something in the way the disease worked. The pulsating pustules seemed to be the first of the disease– from there, the pustules broke open and wherever the fluid within touched rotted. She half wondered if it were possible to stop the pustules from forming if they could save the life much easier; and then she wondered just how she would stop the pustules from forming.

The man's strength had come back by a little– enough that he was breathing easily, at least for now. She knew not if he would ever trust a Ranger again, but as of now that was not her concern. He would live, hopefully at least a while longer with one less problem to deal with. "Master Einar, it is important that you stay with us. We cannot keep you in the House of Healing without fear of speeding this rot along in your body, but–"

Einar stopped her, his face contorting with wonder and a small amount of anger. "How are you not affected, milady Ranger?" This gave Ayara a moment to consider things; sure enough, she was unaffected by the rot that had covered her for the past few days. Even Nelya was none the worse for wear, though her hair clung to her face with blood and her mask stuck to her face.

"I... that is quite a good question, master Einar. I know not how, but for now let us just count it as fortune." This was not a satisfactory answer to the man, but at least it gave him *something*. This made Ayara quite curious, though, and she was not sure what the answer was. Quickly rolling her sleeves away, she looked on herself and sure enough, there was nothing. No rot, no pustules, just the sludge of dead souls drying on her hands. Idly, she tried to remember when she had last bathed... perhaps that is what she needed right now. Shaking her head, she dispelled the thoughts; there were far more pressing concerns.

Soon enough, Fae had returned to the town. Shouting at once to the guards, she identified herself to avoid being slain by mistake. "Hail, guardsmen! I am Fae cos'Criux, companion to Nelya Ardivari!"

"Turn back, Fae cos'Criux, for your own safety! Twice now have I given this warning and I beg you to heed it!" Came the reply from within. Fae was undeterred, however, and once more raised her voice.

"I bring stew to keep you on your feet and drink to ward off chill!" She had figured their stores were plenty low and knew they were likely hurting tonight. With caravans being turned away and citizens living outside the walls being told to forage and hunt how they could, it was likely that no one had thought to resupply the guards before her.

"You have our thanks, but there is too great a risk to you. If you must, leave it and make a hasty retreat- one of us will come out to collect the food." Nodding, Fae thought this a reasonable compromise. She placed upon the ground the heavy cauldron and several wineskins next to it. The cauldron was still fairly hot, which she knew would be a welcome thing. Then she made her way back and away.

"I shall come again tomorrow with more; every night if I must." The guards could not really deny her kindness; after all, it was rare for any to remember that they too were people, not faceless statues. She backed away, before turning to the forest once more and taking off at a slow lope. Behind her, Idorick, the stern captain of the guard, came out from the tower to retrieve the items she had left. He sang many praises to her name as he gathered the goods and went back inside, carrying the cauldron easily, though it was nearly half his height.

Fae wandered the nearby forest for a time, wondering what to do with herself now. *Perhaps I should try to gather herbs for the Rangers? Their stores cannot be that great...* After a moment of self-searching, the adventurer nodded. She was good enough with alchemy to know the components of potions of healing, at least. Letting out a whistle, she called to her faithful familiar, nodding as the fox came running. "Well, Box. That went over well, but I still feel I must make myself useful. Come, let us find herbs of healing to give to the Rangers." The fox yipped happily and took off into the forest, sniffling along as she sought the delicate scents she knew to be helpful plants.

Suddenly, she stopped short, her ears flattening against her head and her hackles bristling. A low growl emanated from her throat, a warning to her companion. Fae glanced up from her own movements to see two rather large men. They looked to each other and then to the girl before laughing.

"Oi, this 'un 'ell be easy. She shan' put up a figh'." With those few words, Fae knew she was in trouble. However, she was not a starry-eyed girl on her first walk through the woods; she was an adventurer by trade and ready at all times. Her blade, a nimble elven rapier, came into her right hand and she smirked.

"You are going to have to bring your best if you hope to take me alive." The men looked a little perturbed. One even had the audacity to speak once more, his arrogance hiding the fact that he had not been expecting much resistance.

"Oh, li'l girl, do ye not know tha' swords are the way of men? We shall take wha' we wan' and leave you dyin'." Expecting her to be an easy target, he opened with a thrust; surprised he was when the woman seized his arm and his throat met the pommel of the woman's sword. From there, Fae flipped him onto his face and a foot planted firmly in his back. His friend attempted to act bravely in the face of this peril, but at one look from the steely eyed elf, took off running.

"It would seem your friend has abandoned you." Stepping from the prone man, she kicked him onto his back. An attempt he made to grab his sword, and she responded by simply stepping onto his wrist. When he shrieked, she chuckled and called over her faithful fox. "Box, what shall we do with him? Making threats against women in the night, I think he should not survive much longer, lest he bring his evil against another woman."

In response, the fox merely growled. Fae calmly put her sword to the man's neck, ending his struggling as he stared at her, eyes wide with fear and shock. Never had a woman protected herself with such ease from him. "CURSE YOU, ARTHAN YOU COWARD!" He shouted, hoping to spur his friend back to the fight. Little did he know the fate his friend would face.

Not missing her chance to taunt the man, Fae spoke once more. "No honor among rapists, is there?" Her words brought a growl from the man.

"You bitch. You would na' be talkin' so high an' mighty with me-" A warning nick from Fae's sword silenced the man. She could have just as easily taken his life. She was being merciful, as was her way.

"No, and I suspect many women have faced that fate. I can read it in your eyes. In their name and the name of the Krygan-Shawv Adventuring Company, I shall do what I must do." With that, she raised her sword. In the moment that passed, she saw the man's face contort with fear. *This had not gone as planned. Not at all!* But instead of feeling the kiss of the blade enter his neck, he instead let out a screech as Fae excised his precious manhood, his claim to fame, from his body. With a savage twist, the woman flicked his dishonored parts away from his body and stepped down off his wrist. His hands moved and Fae turned, ready to fight once more. But instead of the attempt at a fight she expected, she saw him reduced the man to pained sobs as he cradled his bleeding groin. "If you crawl now, you may make it to Littlebrook before you bleed out."

That grim task done, the woman wiped her sword clean and sheathed it, before returning to her original quest. A few hours and three leagues passed, she found herself back in the deeper parts of the Forest. As she was searching the forest and keeping her eyes low, the woman nearly bowled over a masked, darkly clad man hiding in the bushes. "And what are you doing there, hiding like you ha–" The man shushed her, before slowly pointing outward to another. She nearly shouted when she saw the other and her hand went to her sword. "That is Arthan! He and his friend attempted to–"

"He is a wanted man. His face I recognized from posters in a tavern a few leagues from here." Already, two people clad akin to the man, right down to the mask and cloak, were moving on Arthan. Their target was obviously lost, confused, and terrified. He saw the woman and let out a yell, thinking she was hunting him as well. But this was not a shriek of terror; it was a call of anger.

"So be it! If I am to get captured, I shall claim another victim!" He turned fully towards Fae before someone slammed into his side, dropping him to the ground like a sack of potatoes.

A harsh voice called out, the owner fighting with Arthan, wrestling him to the ground and pinning him on his chest. "Thinking her another easy conquest, Arthan?" Immediately, the one pinning Arthan bound his arms with rope and pulled him to his feet. "You are at the mercy of the Rangers now, boy." The captor, a swarthy elf who wore the garb of the Rangers proudly, looked to Fae. "Well, what have we here! Karos, lad, introduce your friend!"

"I have only just met her myself, Kizarian, shove off!" Karos shifted Fae aside and strode over to Arthan and Kizarian, chuckling gently. "She will probably introduce herself if she feels the need. Right now, though; where is your accomplice,

Arthan?" For his question, Karos received spittle to the face. He sighed gently before letting out a soft chuckle; then, he struck Arthan in the stomach with his fist, doubling the man over. "I was being merciful. I have a feeling that the fine young one there would hardly have been as kind. So, I shall give you one chance more, where is Kalan? Where is your accomplice?"

Fae spoke up, her voice calm and cautious; after all, she had no reason to trust these Rangers, at least not yet. Perhaps they were going to gather the men and gang up on her. "If Kalan is a larger man, armed with a sword and dressed in gray... then he is bleeding from his groin and possibly crawling towards Littlebrook." This news struck Karos as odd and he looked Fae over curiously.

His next words were an order to one of his compatriots, and they were quick to obey. "Kiri, investigate. I do not doubt the veracity of the good lady's words, but we had best confirm this." Nodding, the wild elf took off at a dead run, heading through the forest and up the hidden paths towards Littlebrook.

A weak voice came from the side of the road as Kiri approached. "Help... please." Kiri snapped her eyes onto the source of the voice, a rather sickly colored man who was desperately holding onto his groin. "I was... attacked from nowhere..." Kiri smirked beneath her mask and stepped over to the man, watching as he writhed on the ground, trying to stem the flow of blood from his crotch. Glancing back, Kiri examined the trail that led to this point; he had not made it extremely far at all. Crouching, the woman looked into the man's eyes.

"I could heal you- but what would be the point? Scum

like you will only disgrace your ancestors and anger the Ancestress." The man's eyes widened in terror as he realized she had seen through his attempt at a lifesaving lie. Raising a horn to her lips, the elf let out a loud blast, one that echoed far and wide. Turning from the man, she glanced to the town, a fair distance away. "I wonder... we did not encounter the watcher of the way at their cave... Something must be amiss."

"Please... Ranger... have you no mercy?" Again, the pathetic voice came to her ears. Kiri wondered if it would be worth it to heal him or let him die. After all, he and his friend were both wanted for the same thing– rape and murder. Would it be so bad a thing to leave the world with one less rapist? She considered her options for a moment; she could be merciful and give him a potion... but then again, the blood loss was severe enough that he may not even survive then. Besides, she needed her potions for other things. Her mind made up; the Ranger walked toward the town of Littlebrook–Once–Besieged. It was high time for her to sort this out mess. As she walked towards the town, Kiri brought her winding horn to her lips and blew a powerful call.

Glancing up as the sound of the horn reached their ears, the Rangers nodded at each other. Karos gently took Fae's arm and Kizarian took control of his prisoner and the two began to march their charges out of the woods. Fae struggled and Karos shushed her, trying to keep her close. "I have many questions for you, milady. First off, what is your name?"

"My name is Fae cos'Criux of the Krygan–Shawv Company and I will thank you to unhand me, whoever you are." Karos chuckled as the woman wrenched from his grip, eyes afire, her hand on her sword. "I came to search for herbs to aid the Rangers in Littlebrook against some plague that has struck the town. That task I will accomplish without your interference. Unless, of course, you are not terribly attached to your life?"

This brought a hearty guffaw from Karos' chest. "Young Fae, you are indeed a wonder. I see it is no small assumption that you are the reason Kalan is dying on the road?" She offered nothing save for a grim nod and Karos patted her shoulder. She flinched and relaxed when she realized he meant no harm... at least, not now.

"And who are you who speaks of death so openly and stalks the woods as a shadow?" Her voice was defiant as she spoke. These strange people had still not identified themselves, though they wore the garb of Rangers. Oddly enough, Fae wondered where Box had gotten to, for she had not seen hide nor hair of the fox since this encounter began. Karos chuckled gently, a wise smile crossing his face.

"Sure enough, Fae, you are in the company of Rangers. I am *Karostrun anrak'Lyvan*, better known as Karos, Warden Ranger of Seran." Being that it was his first true introduction to the woman, the Ranger bowed slightly and smiled. When he came back up, he spoke once more. "The woods speak highly of you Fae cos'Criux. The trees and the breeze tell me you are a staunch defender of the land and thus a friend to my Rangers." When he identified himself by name and rank, Fae seemed to look at the man in a new light; it was as if she were seeing him properly for the first time. Now she walked eagerly, her steps much lighter as she fought to keep up with the tall man. Taking in every detail, she studied his clothes, from the brown calf-high boots and black trousers, to the black shock of hair and jagged scar. Upon his arms there were sleeves of green canvas and bracers of green and black. Chainmail and a heavy suede tunic covered his chest and nearly to his knees. Across came a bandoleer to secure his quiver, bow and pack to his back, not to mention the great long-knife that sat on his chest. His cloak fluttered out behind him, revealing a few pouches upon his hip, along with a bastard sword made in the Nolvern style. An axe there was as well, seemingly of fine make. He seemed clad for danger or journey, whichever came first.

Fae found her eyes strangely drawn to his bow and the strange runes that were etched into its surface. She studied the weapon as they walked, wondering just how he came by such a finely made bow. Without her permission, her mouth gave voice to her thoughts and she blurted out her curiosity. "How came you by that bow? I have seen nothing like it in my years."

"That is Ravensong, or *Carva'skav* in the Lifesong. It has been my companion since I first became a Ranger. Given by the great twylan, Eldest, the name came to me on the dust and the wind." She nodded, entranced by his tale. "When I need it, the bow's string pulls as if it had no weight; but should any but a Ranger get hold of it, they could never draw it back." Reaching up, he touched the two feathers tied to the top of the bow gently, running his fingers along the fine plumage. Then they came down to his quiver, and he quickly plucked a single arrow out.

Fae spoke up once more, this time much surer of her words. "I have encountered but one other Ranger, Nelya Ardivari, was her name and I notice you all seem to have unique patterns in the fletching of your arrows. If you will pardon my curiosity, why is this?" Karos smiled and brought the arrow around to examine it, as if it were the first chance he had had to see the projectile in a long time.

"Each Ranger picks a combination of colors for the fletching of their arrows. As I am the Warden Ranger, they gave me one of the most authority- black across the three. Those I travel with most closely, called the Talons, each pick one color to add. Kiri, for instance, wields arrows with black-green-black fletchings. Those belonging to Kizarian are black-red-black. It increases the ease with which we find our arrows after battle and should you not know any allies are around, it will tell you are not alone." Again, Fae nodded, wondering what happened if there were more than one Ranger with the same colors on their arrows. She saved her question though, for Karos held up a hand. There was a massive smear of blood on the ground, leading across the Great Road into a bush on the other side. Moving quickly, the Ranger dashed across the Road and shouted back. "Mistress Fae!"

When Karos summoned her, Fae came, her steps light. Quickly, she was by the Ranger's side and followed his hand to where a man lay dead. "Was this your doing?" Nodding stonily, the woman advanced until she could see the face of the supine cadaver.

"Aye, this is Kalan. I recognize his stench..." Her words were bitter and Karos thought that she had been one of his victims, or perhaps an intended victim? When she kicked the body, Karos focused his thoughts once more and gave voice to his question.

"I take it you were an intended victim?" She nodded slowly and spat on the body. A rather insulting thing to do, but the Ranger figured he could make an exception. "Well, the wolves will eat well of this fat bastard." To this, Fae chuckled; the sound was odd to Karos' ears, but pleasant. It was as the water of the stream, bubbling over the rocks. "Come then. We have other things to attend to." Turning and heading back to the road once more, Karos loped ahead, seeking to catch up to Kiri, who already had a league head start. In the east, the sky was brightening, and the day was soon to come. Fae kept up well, but tired after the second mile. Under her breath, she mirthfully cursed the Rangers and their seemingly limitless stamina, though with a much lighter heart than Arthan, who was being basically dragged along by the powerful deep elf, Kizarian.

8: Northrealm, Westerspring

"**N**amryll. Have I forgotten anything?" The man's voice echoed not just in the air but in his mind as well as he spoke to his great mount. Somewhere nearby, the great obsidian beast stirred, her great neck craning to see what all her rider was carrying. His thick riding leathers were not the best for holding things, and he'd packed as much as he could into his ruck. Time would tell if it would be worth it.

What of the Ledger? Asked the great dragon, extending her wings and stretching out. She had been sleeping comfortably nearby until the excitement had begun. When the other riders had fled, their dragons echoing their confusion, she had reassured them, instructing them to fly to the safety of Ormere Keep, the long-held stronghold of the Order of Gelvrentael.

"Of course. The Ledger, scorch it." Running back inside, the man grabbed a massive tome containing the records of the Hanmaer Tower, including supply trains, local trades and local disputes the Riders had been privy to. More importantly, though, it contained a list of all the comings and goings of the Riders in Northrealm. It was his duty to safeguard that information against all who might try to come for it.

Hjalgroþ states that he stopped and had a Ranger examine young Elsaia.

A Ranger? Why would a dragon and rider accept help from those tree worshipping fools? He opened his mouth to speak when a harsh glance from his dragon stopped him short.

Do not be so harsh to the Rangers in your thoughts, Thäoldr. Odd they may be, they are important, and their help may very well have saved her.

Not likely, Thäoldr thought to himself, *for they care nothing for anything besides their trees.*

Blind you are, my rider, if you think they are indifferent to the suffering of those around them. Did the dragon sound angry? His dragon? Perhaps he was misjudging the Rangers, but they had never come to give tribute to the great dragons and never had they come to ask the Riders for aid. It was insulting. *They ask for no aid because they feel they must solve all problems themselves. A noble, if rather foolish, thought. I can think of many in the Riders who think the same way, and many more who would ignore the plight of those not elevated in status or wealth. The Rangers at least give freely.* Thäoldr could not deny the noble beast's wisdom. After all, some of his riders had found themselves in dire straits and before they could summon another rider, out of the nearest woods came a mass of Rangers, fighting their way to wounded men and beasts, despite the millennia-long hatred between the two groups. Death they had faced on many a rider's behalf without so much as a thought to asking for reward. It was admirable, really. But admiration would not serve him right now.

"Namryll, speak to the lesser beasts. Find what information you can about thi-" He stopped short, his gut heaving as images of death and decay far worse than he had seen in his worst battles suddenly assaulted his mind. *Done. You may wish to steel- oh, nevermind.* As the rider swallowed down a mouthful of bile, he put the Ledger in his pack and clambered up into his saddle. "A warning next time, please."

To be fair, you did not ask for a warning. Where are we going? She waited patiently for the answer as she began arranging herself to launch into the cloudy sky. Her powerful hind legs folded beneath her great body and with a mighty leap, she launched herself skyward, her wings unfurling to their full span as she broke through the treetops. With her wings pushing gale-force winds to propel her further, she climbed higher and higher, breaking through the near-permanent cloud-cover of the Eversnow Forest to the crystal-blue sky above. Evening out, she glided for a time, still waiting on Thäoldr for instruction. Finally, it came, the man deciding his course of action.

"Take us to the source of these images. Take us to whatever town has this fate has befallen."

There are many, dear Thäoldr. The life-mind of the world is in turmoil and many places are afflicted. Sighing, the Rider tuned his thoughts . It would not do to lose himself in the future if there was a chance of helping in the present.

"To the source of the images, then. It has a familiar taste to it- baked goods, tilled earth and cheerful fires. Cold it is, but not terribly and there is the distinct smell of water... Littlebrook! The source is Littlebrook-Once-Besieged!" He nearly shouted when he realized the town's name. Sadness overtook elation, however, as he realized that the once friendly town was likely desolate and dead. He shifted and shivered slightly, realizing that they were at cruising altitude and sighed as he pulled up his riding-scarf. It would not do to catch a cold out here.

Are you proud of yourself for working that out, Thäoldr? The dragon's words shut any more excitement down quite quickly. If he had worked it out, it was doubtless that the dragon had figured it sooner. Crossing his arms over his chest, the Rider sighed in annoyance and shook his head, before laughing and slapping the beast's neck affectionately.

"Alright then, wise old lizard. Take us to Littlebrook. There we will–" He nearly lost his grip as the dragon bucked hard. At first, he thought there to be some emergency, some reason the dragon would react so violently. As he went over the possibilities, including charging some spells tattooed upon his arms, he heard the dragon's voice in his head.

The next time you call me a lizard, you are more than welcome to walk. Calmly enough, it reminded him of the height he was at. A creature like this would not be so ready to make a nice landing to drop him off, either. Proud and fierce dragons were and not above tricks such as letting him fall a few hundred spear-lengths as a lesson. Taking a breath, Thäoldr nodded and once more patted the great neck between his legs.

"Easy, old friend. I meant no offense." When she oriented herself, the great dragon began beating her wings once more, pushing massive currents of air down and behind them to propel her rider and herself through the sky towards the south. It would not be a long journey, for a dragon flew fast, but they would be in the sky at least a few hours. It gave the rider time enough to consider just what was going on. A plague like this, the visions in his head. As a thought, he spoke to his dragon.

"Could this be the work of the Disgraced?"

It seems possible. He was dabbling in many things considered unnatural. From what I was told, he always had a loose grip on the real world. Thäoldr nodded. They both knew well that the elf, long ago called the Paragon of War, was quite mad indeed.

But something of this level? Could it be possible? Surely, he had no resources to his name to attempt something such as this. After all, when the Council of Elders had deemed him too dangerous to be trusted as a Dragonrider, they put a warning out to all the nobility of the land. It seemed likely that a man such as him could not recover from that. *What is worse,* Thäoldr thought privately, *the talk of the Disgraced seems familiar.* Everything he knew pointed to the Disgraced being someone important.

After musing on this a while, Thäoldr resigned himself to think more of it later. They had not taught him enough of the Disgraced to know if this was his handiwork and all he had to go on were guesses. The extent of his education on the subject had been that the elf was an albino deep elf, cast out from his own hometown for murder. He had somehow gotten in with the riders and bonded with a black dragon, but that was the least concerning part. He took no interest in learning to refine his grasp of magic- only in enhancing its power. A dangerous man, the Disgraced had been cast out after he murdered a caravaneer he thought had been harboring slavers. Oddly, it was about that time that Thäoldr's teacher, an albino deep elf by the name of Vaelyn, had vanished. The potential connection had bothered him greatly, but he had never questioned it- for he had more important things to attend to.

As they winged to the south, Thäoldr felt the air warm

and sighed. It was pleasantly warm even at night and by his calendar at Hanmaer Tower it was the 18th of Harshheat, one of the summer months of Seran. Many around the world were basking in the heat, swimming in rivers, or relaxing. Most still worked their days away, though occasionally took time for themselves. But the Riders... they were always watchful, protecting the peace through the strength and abilities of themselves and their magnificent beasts. The Rangers likewise were protecting the vital peace, he admitted to himself, though at a slower pace. He wondered what life must be like for those souls in the Rangers, going about their wars on the ground, with little in the way of aerial support.

We approach. Thäoldr broke from his musings and nodded as the great dragon began her descent. At first, she used a speedy drop, tucking her wings in and letting gravity do the work for her, knowing she was more than strong enough to take the strain when she unfurled them once more. Down, down, down they went, faster and faster from the dizzying height. Feeling his lunch crawl up into his throat (along with his stomach), the Rider patted his dragon's neck and nodded.

His voice called out, both in mind and clear air, and Namryll unfurled her great wings, slowing their descent rapidly. "That will do, old friend!" They slowed to a much safer rate, and the dragon kept herself angled down, circling lower and lower. After a few moments, they were close enough to see the city, and Thäoldr's heart sank. It was empty, where the streets were usually full of life, there was nothing; wait, no... there were piles of the dead. The elf's heart sank even further. This town would never be the same- should it ever come back to life, that is. He was near tears when he saw the movement outside the gates and whispered thanks for the keenness of his eyes, honed by many weeks aloft and searching for foes. "Call to them. They look friendly enough."

As requested, the dragon let out a raucous cry, stopping the figure in its tracks. Then, with Namryll swooping in low, Thäoldr saw who she had called to and groaned. *A Ranger. Fantastic, this was the last thing I needed, one of these tree-worshipping–*

That is quite enough. You have not even met them, and you already are cursing their names. For shame, Thäoldr. The magnificent beast was not afraid to voice her displeasure. Bringing herself down to the ground, the creature made an impressively delicate landing for something her size. Craning her neck, the dragon affected a bow to the Ranger below, who gave one in return.

"*Skala'zan*, noble dragon! I am Kiri Topalin of the Rangers. I welcome you and your rider to Littlebrook-Once-Besieged, but I caution you to keep your distance. There is a plague the nature of which–"

"We are well aware of the plague, lady Ranger. That is what has brought us here. Now be off. This is now the duty of the Riders." He dismounted, and the Ranger regarded him coldly for a time. As always, he had dressed for altitude in the traditional riding leathers of the Order; thick enough to ward off even the chill of the heights the dragons traditionally rode at, yet supple enough to allow effortless movement. But already he was stripping his layers, to reveal chainmail armor beneath leather plates. His face was severe, as if he had had a hard life and his arm... if Kiri found his face interesting, she showed no sign of it. But the arm fascinated her– it seemed to be made of steel and yet moved like it was his own. She nearly lost track of what she was doing before remembering that she had a quest. Behind her, the rest of her party arrived. Karos, with Fae staggering along behind him, gasping for air, was the first to approach. Then came Kizarian and his captive, who looked worse for wear than Fae did. Finally, joining back together with his mentor, Karos glanced at the dragon ahead.

He spoke, his voice carrying an edge. "I see our betters have joined us. Bow, everyone, before the great dragonrider Thäoldr." He affected a rather insulting bow before bringing his eyes back up. "What are you here for, Rider? This scarcely concerns your people."

"This disease took one of my riders ill, so it is in my best interests to investigate the cause. You are familiar with my name, yet I do not remember your mask or voice. Who are you?" He was on edge already and could not help but wonder if he would win should they go hostile.

"ENOUGH!" Came the bellow not from man or elf, but from dragon, silencing all. Six pairs of eyes focused on Namryll and she grumbled. After a moment, she spoke once more, her voice carrying an edge of annoyance. "This pettiness will get us nowhere. Rangers, you have information that could aid my rider. Thäoldr, you are in the presence of Rangers. Curb your tongue." Reluctantly, Thäoldr allowed himself to calm down. His dragon's eyes whirled in an annoyed shade of red as she regarded the small creatures around her. Their antics were growing old, but she had to thank her ancestors that there were no dwarves nearby- with the number of elves, the confrontation would continue with no hope of calming.

"Great dragon, I beg your pardon. I will work with Thäoldr as best I can." Karos spoke, before realizing he still had not given his name. "I am Karos of clan Lyvan. I am the Warden Ranger of Seran and I am at your service." He bowed- this time a respectful one, though there was the hint of his roguish insolence. The meeting seemed to go better, when out of the guard post came a cry.

"STAY BACK IF YOU VALUE YOUR LIVES! THIS WARNING I HAVE GIVEN BEFORE!" The voice belonged to none other than Idorick, who was at his wit's end with people trying to come to his town. He stormed out, spear at the ready, only to stop at the sight of three Rangers, Fae, a strange man, as well as the rider Thäoldr and his dragon. "Fae, again I must warn you, thrice this time. Stay away if you value your life. Rangers, your kind seem to be unaffected by this plague- two there are within my city, Nelya Ardivari and Ayara Kar'Maerae." Karos nodded at this news and waved Kizarian forward.

"We would also like to turn this bastard over to your custody. A bounty notice there was, but the gold we care not about." Idorick scoffed- surely the deep elf was doing the right thing, but-

"Master Kizarian, my apologies... but is now really the time for that?" To Idorick's surprise, it was not his own voice giving life to the words. It was Thäoldr's. The rider looked from the Rangers to the Guard Captain and smirked. "I can respect your devotion to duty, but perhaps he is the least of our concern?" Though Idorick's eyebrows arched in confusion as well, he spoke up, this time in Kizarian's defense.

"Normally, I would agree with you, Rider. But at a time like this, people such as Arthan should be brought in and jailed." He made his way down from the guard tower, much calmer now that he knew who he was dealing with. As he descended, a fit overtook him, nearly doubling him over as he hacked and coughed, trying to clear his airway from something unknown.

"Master Idorick, are you well?" Fae spoke up but held her

ground. Karos and Kiri ran ahead to the man, quickly assisting him to a seat on the steps.

"Ancestors, man, you would think your armor unnecessary at this time." Putting thought to action, Karos quickly unstrapped the halfling's helmet and breastplate, giving him some room to breathe. This allowed poor Idorick to take in a deep breath, his face red from exertion as he continued to cough. Weakly, he waved away their assistance, trying to form words once more. He was not well, as was obvious to the two Rangers.

When finally he could catch his breath, the man spoke once more. "'tis but a cough, Rangers, fear not for me." Karos shook his head, knowing the man's tone to hide a lie. "Take your captive to the jail. It is by the guardhouse. Warden Ranger, have you any water?" Nodding to Kiri, Karos unstrapped his waterskin, bringing it around and uncapping it, before pressing it against Idorick's lips. Kiri stood and waved at Kizarian, silently commanding him to bring the prisoner forward.

"Take him to the jail; 'tis near the guardhouse, Kizarian." Nodding, the deep elf dragged his prisoner along, forcing the man to walk to his doom. Thäoldr closed the distance as well, stepping over to the two Rangers and the halfling. Following close was Fae, somewhat emboldened by the other's movements. Idorick took a long drink of water, swallowing hard and sputtering for a moment. This seemed to settle him, though, and he could speak soon after.

When he was able, the man again gave caution, speaking first to the elf girl from the forest nearby. "Fae, please go no further into the town, lest this illness take you too. The Rangers seem unaffected and the Riders I do not know." His words worried Thäoldr and the man looked to his dragon.

He speaks wisdom. With Elsaia taken by something similar to what we have seen, I would suggest you stay away from the town itself. Let the Rangers risk their peril. Nodding, Thäoldr looked now to Karos, wondering just what he could do.

"Karos, what would you have me do?" It was the first time he would willingly aid the Rangers and, unbeknownst to him, would pave the way for the two disparate groups to work together and forge bonds of kinship.

The Warden Ranger closed his eyes for a moment, considering his options. Fae seemed familiar with the forest nearby, and he wondered if she was from the land around. Thäoldr could spot much from the air, lending him utility as a scout- he doubted the Rider would willingly bear him to the City of Kings. Kiri and Kizarian would stay this town and do their best to help the two Rangers already here. He simply had to use his forces wisely.

"Thäoldr- take mistress Fae. Search the forests for healing supplies. I suspect you know which ones." When Thäoldr nodded, he continued, this time speaking to Kiri and Kizarian, who had just returned from incarcerating Arthan. "Kizarian, Kiri, I beg of you- aid the Rangers within the town as best you can. Give them your stores, meager though they are. Mistress Fae will hunt more supplies up and bring them to you." He was not sure if Fae would accept being commissioned with such a task and looked at her. Already, she was digging through her pack and extracting bundle after bundle of what she had already bought.

"Will these help, Warden Ranger?" Many herbs she produced, and Karos nodded appreciatively. In the back of his mind, he made a note to keep troth with her. She would be a valuable ally and a good friend in the times to come.

"*Za, ka'kozaro...*" Upon speaking, the Ranger did not realize he had said anything strange. The quizzical look from both Thäoldr and Fae soon righted him, and he realized that once again, he had slipped into the Sk'av'A without realizing it. Ducking his head bashfully, he spoke, this time in common tongue. "Yes, my thanks, lady Fae. You are quite wise to carry these with you. Do I see elderberry and olive-leaf in your possessions?" It was the woman's turn to nod and Karos smiled widely. "It would seem your uses are many to this task."

Fae was not sure if that was a compliment or an insult; so she took it in stride, wondering just how people put up with the Ranger for long.

Thäoldr was of a unique mind. It impressed him that the Ranger had taken command of the situation so readily but was a little incensed that no one had asked his opinion. After all, he was the Sage of Wind, knowledgeable in many things that might be helpful in this situation- yet he was being relegated to *transport and scouting*, like an Uninitiated. He was better than this- and he intended to say something. Before he could open his mouth, though, the voice of Namryll echoed in his mind. *We do not yet know the situation, dear Thäoldr. As insulting as this task may be, it may prove crucial to the survival of the Riders, not just Elsaia. Grit your teeth and carry on.* Thäoldr did just that, though he made a mental note to have words with the Ranger. Unconsciously, he scratched at the back of his neck- too late realizing that he was using the wrong arm. All eyes were upon him and Kiri spoke first.

"Were you not planning on revealing your magical arm?" Her words brought him back to reality, and he looked up. A moment passed, and he spoke curtly. It annoyed him that his arm was now being made a spectacle by these Rangers... though he supposed they had a reason for all they did.

"Would it affect anything if I did?" An honest question was on his lips at that point, though worded with annoyance. Karos looked to him then and then back to Kiri for a moment, before nodding.

"Actually, it might. The amount of energy required to make an artifice arm function may have a purpose beyond your knowledge. The amount of pure energy running through your body may protect you from the disease. *May.*" Useful enough information, thought Karos, though had his doubts as to its reception by the ancient elf.

This impressed Thäoldr greatly, and he bobbed his head in agreement. This was something that the Healers had hinted at when he was first fitted with the arm, but scarce information there was in the Archives of the Riders. Oddly, it didn't surprise him that the Rangers knew– they seemed to know an aggravating amount about him, though his knowledge of them was quite stunted.

"And how do you know this, Ranger?" He bristled slightly as he spoke. This was getting out of hand, and they needed to come back to the task ahead. But curiosity kept him following their bait.

"Oh, many times have I encountered tales of such devices." *An answer that boils down to, 'shut up and let me know things', if the Ranger's tone was anything to go by,* thought Thäoldr.

"Fine then, keep your hoarded knowledge. May we return now to the task at hand? Or were you planning on talking the plague out?" He could feel the surge in annoyance from his dragon, but Ancestors, did that one feel good. Karos looked appropriately contrite and nodded grimly.

"Well put, I apologize for my distraction." Cracking his knuckles, the Ranger looked to the city. "Should you feel like it, Rider, you could chance the city- find all survivors you can and get them out and as far away as possible." He hoped the Rider would accept this new tasking with more gusto. After all, the Riders, Karos knew, were not above helping where they could, for which he was quite grateful.

Thäoldr nodded grimly. This was more in line with his skills, and he would even accept being used as a ferry to get people to safety. Without another word, the stalwart Rider took to the city, his footsteps cautious and his hand staying near his sword- after all, there could by many kinds of ruffians about with the guardsmen depleted. It would not do to be caught unawares. His movements were careful and quick as he went from door to door, down narrow streets and through the outer causeways.

As he delved into the city, the Rider first noticed the sickly sweet smell of burning flesh. Then ahead he saw the bodies, and he felt his stomach turn. Men, women, children alike were in haphazard piles, and their families and friends had put flame to their flesh to destroy the plague. Most still had clothes and some even still had jewelry, though much had was missing, whether being placed in their homes or claimed by looters, Thäoldr did not know. As he rounded the corner, his answer would come quicker than expected, as he nearly ran over three young men who were sifting through ashes and bodies to find gold, squabbling over what they found. He cleared his throat loudly, and the squabbling stopped as three pairs of eyes turned to him.

The oldest, a man of 27 and undoubtedly the ringleader,

kicked a rock and shouted at the Rider, not knowing who he was or thought he was. "Look 'ere, git lost! This is our loot!" Thäoldr sighed as the man showed himself a fool. Without a word, he drew his sword and stood, preparing himself to attack. The three men, realizing that he had caught them red-handed, drew knives and hatchets, ready to defend their ill-gotten treasures.

"Stealing from the dead is rather low. 'tis an activity fit only for the clanless." His words sparked an immediate rise from the three, and they moved in closer, intending to rush him. The old elf mused on this and wondered if they were wicked at heart, or just desperate? Either way, they needed a lesson. The first of the men closed the distance, took a clumsy swing, and stumbled past. As he did, Thäoldr stretched a leg out and tripped him, effortlessly bearing the man to the ground and turning to his friends. "I will give you this one warning. Leave. Drop what treasures you have stolen from the departed and leave. You risk your health by staying and not just from me." The second stabbed wildly, and the Rider lashed out with his artifice arm, striking him in the gut. Predictably, he doubled over and Thäoldr aided his descent to the ground with a hearty clout to the back of the neck, sending him quickly to his knees. He hoped the Rangers would appreciate his restraint in this matter, though he half-wondered if they might have been harsher. They did not strike him as an understanding bunch with crime.

The ringleader decided that discretion would be better in this situation. Dropping what was in his hands, he took off at a dead run, abandoning his compatriots in his hurry to flee. Satisfied, Thäoldr stepped over the two he had felled and continued his mission, going house to house to seek survivors. So far, this was it. Three looters and countless bodies. He hoped there would be better news as he got into the more residential areas and he stopped when he heard movement outside the Hall of Healing. As he held fast, he listened, hearing womanly tones interspersed with a man's growling.

"Master Einar, if you wish for a drink, there is clean water on my pack. The waterskin remains ever full, thanks to the magic of the Salacen Glacier. By my reckoning, that would do you better than alcohol." The Rider knew right well that voice, for he had encountered its owner many a time. Ayara Kar'Maerae was nearby and for that, he was glad. Her company would be preferable to that of Karos and he hoped she would be up for the tasking ahead. He rounded the corner and stopped, barely recognizing her for the gore that covered her and another Ranger. Between them sat a man who looked none the worse for wear, at least.

"Rider! Did Idorick not warn you away? Fire and flesh, I told him that none should enter the town!" This, of course, came from Ayara, and it took her a moment to recognize who she spoke to. "Oh! Master Thäoldr. It is good to see you, but my inquiry remains." She cocked an eye at him, not realizing how terrible she must look... or not caring. Thäoldr worked through his mind for a response, coming up quickly.

"Milady Kar'Maerae, it is your Warden Ranger that sent me thus. By his thoughts, some magic may protect me- the same magic, he says, that allows me to use my arm." He nodded as if this was common knowledge and crossed his arms over his chest, ensuring that his artifice arm was visible. Ranger Kar'Maerae looked quite unimpressed, blunting the man's pride for a moment. Then he realized that through the things she had recently seen, a magical arm would be of little import. To be fair, the Rider wondered if her disinterest had roots in the expectation that he too would fall ill. "Warden Ranger Karos sent me to evacuate any who remained in the town," he continued after a moment, correctly guessing that she may wonder about his presence, "and I feel it would be wise to instruct you to do the same. You look like you could use a cleansing. Your fellow as well." Finally, addressing the other Ranger, he bowed. Nelya offered a curt nod in response, as if her mind were elsewhere. The man between them stood slowly and offered his hand to the Rider.

"I will take my leave, then. Rider, it is nice to meet you." They shook hands, and the farmer made his way out of the town. Thäoldr then turned his attention back to the Rangers there, examining them once more. They both looked a fright, like something out of his worst nightmares.

Nelya sighed gently and spat onto the ground. "Come then, Ayara. Let us inform Karos of what we have seen. Leave Master Thäoldr to his task." Ayara nodded and both women stood, with Nelya taking the lead. Ayara waited for a moment to follow her friend and offered words of warning to Thäoldr.

Her voice came as a harsh, nearly worried whisper, and her words shocked Thäoldr. "Be warned, if further into the town you go, only death will you find. Fair certain I am that this plague extinguished all life from the town."

9: Cúledan, Dragonmoor

In the stately city of Cúledan, one can normally find many attractions to keep their interest. The great Castle Vigilance, home to the king of Dragonmoor, boasts a reputation as the only castle in all Seran to have never felt the yoke of enemy oppression; The Spring Of Enkar, where they say that Enkar, the Ancestor of Justice himself, watches and judges the decisions of tribunals; They say that if a decision is unjust, the spring will run jet-black. Some say it is the work of Enkar. Others are unsure, but at least for now, we side with the Ancestors, as we do in all things. Other notable places in Cúledan include The Temple of Enkar, where Paladins train and receive their Blessing of Station. The Temple itself is a massive structure, capable of housing no less than 50 aspirants. There were more, but those are the most notable.

The town, however, was currently in a state of crisis. The healthy hid away while the dead and dying were everywhere. Sequestered, they were in the grand Castle Vigilance, hidden and protected. Among them, passing from person to person with water, food and blankets, walked a woman with fiery red hair and skin in hues of burnished gold. This was Khula, of the noble family of Tallam, a woman of seemingly limitless compassion and grace. Many of her kin saw these traits as weakness, as unbecoming of the great Tallam family and were callous, harsh people, leading many to wonder if Khula truly was a child of her mother's loins, for she was all they were not. Gentle in dealings, slow to anger and always compassionate. Inside her head there was a brilliance that few could match, limited only by her lack of speech. Voice to her was as alien as a fish to land and she communicated solely through a silent hand-code taught to her by the Rangers, the same sign language taught to all children. Most forget it over time, being used to speaking their minds, but to those unable to form words, it was a perfect way to communicate.

Touching a young woman's shoulder gently, Khula gestured to her, indicating that she had food and drink. Nodding, the woman turned and looked to Khula, speaking slowly and clearly that the woman could read her lips. With a chuckle that echoes the sound of water bubbling over small stones, Khula brought her finger up to her lips, rolling the finger over them twice- she could hear, the woman realized, and this brought on more questions. "If you can hear, why can you not speak?"

To this, Khula shrugged and touched her throat gently, pointing out that her voice-organs had not formed correctly. To emphasize this, she attempted to say her name, and what came out was a hiss of air and nothing more. That demonstration done, the woman signaled to the other that ever since learning she could not speak with her mouth, she instead learned to use hand-code. Nodding, the other woman spoke once more. "I am Ellyn, bard of the College. What is your name, milady?" Ellyn could tell the woman was a noble, but she did not recognize her face.

Tapping four fingers together in a cross, Khula spelled out her name in rapid finger-code, the letters clear for Ellyn to see. "K-H-U-L-A" she signed and followed it up with an emphatic hand chopping into her palm for pronunciation. Ellyn nodded and took a stab at the name, watching as Khula's face brightened when she got the name right. Then, Khula waved at her to follow and Ellyn stood, though with some weakness- she had not eaten in a week. Quickly by her side, Khula recognized her trouble, gently picking up the slack where the girl was having difficulty walking. Together, they made their way to the great hall, where many tables were prepared by the King's staff to accommodate those in need. At the serving-table stood the assistants to the King of Dragonmoor, though the regent himself was nowhere to be seen, serving stew and bread to nobility alongside his staff. Paladin-Healers milled about, checking the health of those within to ensure they were unafflicted. The knights of the city were out, sending warning to every corner of the land and the Rangers in the near area were busy in the city proper, attempting to care for the sick and dying.

"Food here. Eat, grow strong." The words came quickly from Khula's hands as she spoke to Ellyn, before moving off. Waving to one Paladin-Healer she knew, she showed her desire for him to approach. Quickly, the man clad in a white and blue tabard made his way over to her, nodding. "Ser Kigdan, How many dead?" Her hands asked him, her expression pained.

He shrugged, before speaking with both hands and voice. "Latest count is sixteen thousand."

This brought a near-silent gasp from the woman and a hand came up to cover her mouth. He nodded grimly before sighing and wringing his hands. "The Rangers do what they can, but more come in every day. I fear there is not enough time." They both nodded and Khula glanced away to a woman in obvious pain. Making her way over, the Lady tapped the woman's shoulder.

"Where is the pain?"

The woman did not respond for a moment and Khula was unsure of the reason. Deep, labored breaths pulled themselves from the poor woman's chest and soon enough, Khula recognized she was in the depths of labor. Quickly, she waved to a Paladin-Healer, though the man did not see her or was busy with other things, which annoyed her. Growing frustrated as the woman let out a cry of pain which was still ignored, she placed two fingers to her lips and let out a shrieking clarion call. Her piercing whistle caught the attention of all around and she frantically waved to two Paladin-Healers, who ran to her aid.

"She is in labor. Get her to a room." The two healers nodded and helped the woman to her feet, intending to walk her to a room. Seconds later, she doubled over as the force of a contraction struck her and the Paladins realized they needed to form a new strategy. The elder brought his arms down, one gripping the forearm of the other, and spoke.

"Tyern, grip your forearm with the other and then grip my forearm and I will grip yours. We will form a seat for her and take her quickly." Nodding, Tyern took the instruction and his place before the two sat the laboring woman in their arms for the brief trip, with a third Paladin behind to keep her from falling. Nodding, Khula made her way through the crowd to seek others who would need her.

As she wandered, Khula approached the door, guarded by no less than six Paladins, all heavily armed and fully armored. One stopped her with a hand and eyed her severely. "Milady, upon instruction from the King and his advisors, I cannot let you risk your life by exiting the castle." This stopped her for but a moment, and she eyed the Paladin severely. Raising her hands to speak, she kept her eyes locked on his before signing.

"The risks I own. There are people out there that I could help. Move aside." The man was unfazed by her speech and shook his head. Insistently, she moved to push past him, only to be shoved backwards- roughly, too.

"Ortan, that is Khula of Tallam, she could have your head!" Came a voice from behind the great armored man.

Again, Ortan was unfazed. "And the Exalted could put my soul in the Pits." He spat back. He was unwilling to let this foolish lady go outside to risk certain death and he was unwilling to displease the King and the Exalted, both incredibly powerful people in their influence over the Paladins of Seran. One did not go against such instructions, or indeed such power.

"The Pits you will probably find for not aiding those outside. You hide like a terrified child." Khula signed before shaking her head and walking away. If she could not go through the main door, she reasoned, she would have to try something far more dangerous. Pacing the corridors of the castle, she looked to each exit and found them blocked. Each window was too small, even for her meager frame. Each door guarded. A hand went up and combed through her brilliant red hair and she took a breath. Even the great Paladins of Seran allow none that could be helped in. Everywhere she looked, there were nobles, the gentry, the well-to-do... all of them had found their way into the castle in exclusion of those truly in need. The stink of privilege, even her own, filled her nose and she desperately sought an escape. She wondered what King Dalviin the Just must think as he watched everything going on in his castle. As the well-to-do hid away while the people they supposedly led died en masse in agony.

Trying to follow the noble was a rather frail looking servant woman who begged her to slow down, to see reason. "Milady Khula, please. Stop with your obsession with the poor-" The moment the woman had said those words, she realized her error. The mute woman rounded angrily, almost ready to swing on the woman.

Her voice came out as a hiss, the pain of trying to form words obvious on her face. "You will never tell me to forget my mercy." The words had scarcely left her mouth when she doubled over coughing. Drops of red spattered onto the floor and Khula's servant rushed to her side.

"Milady, please try not to speak. It harms you so." Khula shot her a silent death glare. Most of the time, she could forgive Cala for her callousness. After all, the woman was more a friend to her parents than to her and was hand-picked to serve as her voice. Someone they trusted to speak for her rather than let the brash girl speak her mind. It was an arrangement that benefited her family but drove Khula mad.

Signing frantically, Khula waved to someone, anyone, to get her some water to soothe her burning throat. When someone brought a waterskin, she waved her thanks and drank deep, sighing silently as the soreness subsided. Then she looked once more at her Voice and shook her head. Her hands came up to speak once more, and the message was not a pleased one. "Go. I do not want my parent's voice anywhere near me right now."

Cala shook her head and spoke to the girl. "Just because you do not know what to say..."

"Just because you say what my parents tell you." Khula shot back with her hands and looked at the one who gave her a waterskin. It took a moment to register in her mind what she was looking at, but the nights of sneaking out to the Ranger camps served her well. Brown boots, green shirt, black trousers and a brown tunic. There stood a Ranger from the camp outside the city, Otho Klimir.

"The Lady requested you remove yourself from her presence." Cala was stubborn- after all, money made people do things they normally would think foolish, but against a Ranger, she could do little more than walk away. Khula nodded her thanks, and the Ranger helped her to her feet before looking her over. "You wish to leave the safety of the castle?" His hands worked quickly, asking the woman his question. He was rather shocked that she would try to quit a safe place, especially with how the city was afflicted, but remembered that this was the same woman who often 'accidentally' spilled her coin purse all over the ground and walked away. Little did she do without reason and even less did she do that did not aid another.

"I thank you for your concern, Ranger... But there are people outside whom I could help." Her hands flew as she signed her words and the Ranger nodded. Where was he, she wondered, when the affliction hit? Was he hiding away inside, like the Knights and nobles? Or was he out working to provide succor to the ill and forgotten? A single glance at the Ranger told

Khula all she needed- he had found some secret passage. "I must find a way to aid them." She dropped her hands emphatically and nodded as if her words were the only truth in a world of lies.

The Ranger, a proud young-looking man from the tal-Edröhel clans of The Farlands, chuckled gently as he regarded Khula. Through deep blue eyes, he watched her motions, her hands as they spoke. He regarded his own form, the cloth he wore- was letting this noblewoman help worth the risk? A few moments of decision clouded his face, and Otho nodded. "So be it," he signed silently, "if that is your wish, I can do little to dissuade you." Waving at her to follow, the Ranger took off towards the Grand Hall. Confusion came to Khula's mind as an unwelcome visitor, but after a moment she saw he was not stopping. Passing behind the throne, Otho waited until she was close before he pressed his palm against the wall. Immediately, a secret passageway opened, and both entered. The door closed quietly behind them and Otho led Khula through an escape passage, one put in place by a king many centuries ago.

After a few yards, she grew worried- where was he taking her? Despite her own investigations, her parents' nagging warnings against the Rangers surfaced. Was he really going to lead her somewhere and slay her? Angrily, she shook her head and tapped the Ranger's shoulder. He turned to face her, and she signed impatiently. "When does this tunnel end? Where are we going?"

With a chuckle that sounded like the waters of a stream, the Ranger kicked his way through a tangle of vines, before pushing them aside and passing through. It was darker than Khula expected, having been inside for many days now, but she did not allow that to dissuade her. Otho kept the vines parted long enough for her to pass through the emerald portal and then replaced them, patting the plants back into place. Finally, Khula was outside the castle. Finally, she was free.

Quickly leading the woman into the city proper, Otho waved her close. "Go to the camp, Khula Tallam. You will be safer outside the city," his hands spoke, urging her to follow his instructions, "there one of my Rangers will find you. They will task you something they think will best suit your skills." Nodding reluctantly, Khula picked her way through the city- the city that normally felt so comfortingly alive, the city of her birth, of her childhood. Now, there was only death everywhere. Corpses piled high upon wagons to be taken and burned, their lives forgotten and washed away in fire. It grew on her, overwhelming her senses, and soon she ran as fast as she could to get out of the city.

As the Ranger observed Khula's retreat, he lapsed into his thoughts. What could I do? *She wishes to help. Who am I to deny her?* He shook his head, trying to dispel the thoughts, but they lingered at the back of his mind. Sighing, he made his way into the city as well and tightened his bracers. *What lies ahead of her,* he reasoned, *will be shown to her in time. For now, I must attend to my fate.* Slipping into a comfortable jog, the Ranger headed to where his compatriots were attempting to keep people alive- with little success. Here and there, there were many folks who seemed resistant to the ravages of the disease. To them, the cú Rangers either pled to flee, or asked their aid, running messages back and forth at their best speed, or supplies to help those afflicted.

"Hail Otho, son of Kinym!" a voice called from an alleyway, and Otho knew the source almost immediately.

"Hail Siddi, daughter of Kamat!" The Ranger turned down the alley towards the voice and found one of his companions there. A spritely maiden called Siddi, one of his Rangers, stood over two dying people, a man and a woman. She had done all she could and had resorted to dosing them with Tyngfir potion until they could no longer feel pain. Little else could she do, and she knew this in her heart, but it still pained her. "What need you, Siddi?"

"I have dosed these two with Tyngfir wine... they will feel no more pain, but I must go to camp please, I am wearied by sadness and doubt." She looked at the elder Ranger, her eyes pleading with him to let her abandon this hopeless post, even if for a time. There was nothing more they could do. All that were healthy had been sent out of the town to camp and stay safe. Within the town, there was naught but the dead. Sighing, Otho looked to the younger Ranger with pity and remorse. While they were still alive, there was still hope he had been told and to that he clung.

"Stay with them until they pass, Siddi. You cannot abandon them while hope still fills their eyes." Quite a lucky thing that they are unconscious, he thought to himself, as we discuss their fate. He pitied the forms laying there on the ground— he felt their pain a thousand times over. Siddi's next words caught him off guard.

"Will you stay with me until then?" She looked terrified, like she expected their passing to claim her life as well. But as he looked deeper into the young Ranger's eyes, Otho realized it was a deep sadness— did she know these two? Did she share some connection with the bodies at her feet? Taken aback by such a question, Otho did not know how to respond at first. After a moment, though, he found his voice.

"I will. And we shall do what we can. Come, hand me whatever potions you have left." He crouched next to the bodies and pulled his own bottles from their pouches. Quickly, he began mixing them and worked in a bit of highberry juice from one of his bottles. He hoped this would give the people's enough energy to pull through, but somehow, he knew it would not do much. He had to try though- every fiber of his being demanded that he exhaust his supplies as well in the attempt to save even one life from this plague.

An hour they sat, listening as the two victims spoke in slurred, confused words. Slowly, the first one's words turned into drowning gurgles and then the other's followed suit and Siddi looked away. Shaking his head, Otho sighed and looked at the faces- there was no pain written in the dying eyes- only dismay, fear. He knelt next to the first person's head as their eyes went dim and their spirit went to be with their ancestors.

"Valk lor sak rakjivkii sa lirk." The words came from his lips almost silently, as if they were a whispered prayer. Reaching out, Otho's hand brushed over the dead man's face, gently applying pressure to close his eyelids. The woman gurgled out three words, barely recognizable through the fluid in her throat.

"I am home..." With these words, the light faded from her eyes. She released one last gasp and was still. Otho said the same prayer over her and closed her eyes before standing and turning to Siddi.

"Come, let us bear them to the pyres. Then we can leave this place for now." Nodding, Siddi took a deep breath to steel herself for the task. But she could not bear to even look at the two bodies that moments ago had been people- people she had known.

Unbidden, words came to her lips, and she spoke to Otho. Her voice quavered, and she had to fight to keep from bursting into tears- this was the first time she had seen death this close- the first time she had sat and watched people die, helpless to save them. She was a young Ranger yet and Otho knew that with time she would come to view death as a passing into a greater world. "Their names... should anyone care after all this... Ysarl and Rijna."

Otho nodded and waved her over to the bodies. "In time, their story will be remembered. For now, help me bear them, Siddi. The best we can do for them is to ensure their bodies are nobly burnt-instead of being claimed by rats." Siddi, through her grief, could not deny the wisdom of his words. It was regarded as a great personal insult for one's body, even if they were the lowliest of paupers, to be consumed by carrion eaters such as rats. Some had a funeral by birds, but that was felt to be different, as it took them to the sky. Shouldering the larger body of Ysarl, Otho waited until Siddi had gently picked up the smaller frame of Rijna and together they carried them to the nearest pyre. They placed the bodies side by side, and Otho stoked the flames of the pyre to new heights, adding more fuel to consume the bodies. "Come, Siddi. Let us away."

Siddi was all too glad to turn her back on the town.

Khula's lungs burned as she fled the town, stumbling over loose paving-stones and other things in the way. Was it two turns? Three? She could hardly remember the way out of the town in her panic and everywhere she turned seemed to lead her to more pyres covered in charred or burning bodies. Taking a left past the Marketplace she ran onto the main road- there! The gate! It was finally in sight and she took off, ignoring the protests of her legs and lungs. *Just a few more spear lengths*, she thought to herself, and *I am out of this nightmare*. Then she stepped on part of her dress. The ground came up fast and slammed into her face with a viciousness she only knew when she was with her parents and Sir Magus Kefarion, her husband. She felt a cracking in her nose and immediately her eyes teared up. Blood flowed freely down her face, and she struggled to get back up and keep going.

If there was one thing to be said about her, it was that she was rather stubborn. Fighting through the tears that flowed in rivers down her face, she pulled herself to her feet. She had scraped her hands up terribly and could feel the same pain in her knees. Resolutely, she plodded towards the Gate, trying to see through the tears of pain. Everything seemed to close in and she wanted to sink to the ground; then she saw a form in the distance waving to her. Finding a well of strength to move on, she scrambled towards the form.

"Ancestors above, but you look a fright, lady Khula."

A Ranger, thought Khula, *I am saved*. Gasping out another breath, she collapsed to the flagstones and lay there panting before the feet of another Ranger. Looking her over for obvious signs of the plague sweeping through the city, the Ranger gently hauled her to a sitting position before offering a potion. Barely able to see the potion through the tears that still flowed from her eyes, she grabbed at the bottle, nearly dropping it. The Ranger was quicker though and caught her hands before securing them around the bottle and bringing it to her lips. His words had the gentle force of a kindly command and he tipped the bottle upwards. "Drink deep, lady Khula. You have exerted yourself beyond your body's skill."

As the drink poured down her throat, the woman gasped

and fell into the Ranger's arms. She was breathing, but barely. The man nodded slowly and rolled himself under her, placing the near-insensate woman on his shoulder and pushing to his feet. Thank the Ancestors, he thought, that I have strength in me. Making his way out of town with his charge, the Ranger strode triumphantly out of the city gate and made his way into the wilds outside Cúledan. Upon arrival, he waved one of his fellows over, and the two of them brought Khula to the ground next to the fire. "Let her rest, but watch her closely, Knal. We know not if she is afflicted." The much younger Ranger nodded and busied himself with the camp.

"Master Var, if I may ask... what is happening inside the city?" The Ranger turned, though not quickly enough to scare his young ally.

"Knal, again I must remind you, none are your master and I am just your *saal'kwen*. You are a Tenderfoot Ranger. Think less of me as a superior and more than your elder brother," he said, his voice soothing, "and that will serve you better. As for your question... It is difficult to say. The city has been afflicted with some form of sickness the likes of which have never been recorded. The Archivist is likely working herself to death trying to find something and we must stem the tide. Unfortunately, our best magicks and potions seem to do nothing. We hope that Warden Ranger Karos arrives swiftly." Suddenly, the Ranger moved, turning his back to his charges and placing his hand upon his sword. "Two approach. Knal, just like I taught you. Protect those who cannot protect themselves."

Already, the Tenderfoot had readied himself, his short sword gleaming in the firelight. If this was to be his first fight, so be it. He was ready, or so he thought. But when his teacher called out, the young man was confused. "Advance and be known! If you have fell intent, begone with you!"

The response came as a clarion call, sounding cleanly through the night. "*Tengarii! Lovik kejg!*" A cry for aid in the Sk'av'A. Immediately, Var ran towards the source of the voice, his swords ready. The voice called out again, and Var realized it was something worse than a threat. "Flesh and steel, Var, put your blades away and help me!" It was Otho and Siddi, bearing a severely wounded child.

"Is the child afflicted? Have you alread-" He was cut off with a wave and Otho limped towards the camp, nearly dropping his cargo. Var moved quicker, pushing his lack of knowledge aside and realizing that there was a grave threat here. The child had been beaten- badly. "Otho, curse it man, tell me! What happened?" He was becoming impatient and as they came to the camp, he helped Siddi place the child near the fire. Then he tore open the rags the child wore, desperately seeking any sign of affliction. What he found instead lit a raging fire within him and he looked at Siddi. Otho was already sitting down, grasping the shaft of an arrow that protruded from his leg. With a single grunt of pain and a quick jerk of his hand, the arrow came out and was cast aside. The Ranger then attended to his wound, quickly packing it with a clean woven cloth, before wrapping his leg and testing it. "Are you badly injured, Otho?"

"Nay. I will recover quickly. Thank Veljra that I resupplied from the *tengjäv* before we came back." Nodding, Var brought out one of his own healing potions and went to offer it to Otho, who waved him to attend to the child. "She was found clad in rags and being tracked by two men. Already in dire straits, she was, having been beaten and likely worse. I do not know if she escaped or was turned loose, but we slew all following her." Var stopped short- *turned loose*, he thought to himself. *I dislike that.*

"Siddi, use your magic- check her for spells."

"I have already begun." True to her word, Siddi was already performing the incantations and hand motions that foretold a clarifying spell. Pressing her hands to the unconscious child, the Ranger looked up, her face grim. "She is being tracked." The Rangers sprang into action. The child was covered in a heavy blanket, to be attended to by Siddi. Otho and Var took positions, beginning their own chants in Sk'av'A rather than the language of magic. Soon enough, bulwarks formed from the ground itself and the Rangers readied their bows and took cover. Knal, ever eager to help, drew forth some of the magic he had learned from his saal'kwen and placed his hands in the fire fearlessly. When the flames had jumped from the branches to his hands, the man stood and drew intricate patterns in the air. Var nodded, impressed, and watched as the man readied himself.

"From the east!" Silence fell upon the camp. A barrier that would shield them from unfriendly eyes already protected it, but against a tracking spell, it was pointless. The casters would know some magic was against them when they neared the point of their spell with no sign. Undaunted, six forms approached. Peeking over the earthen rampart, Otho focused his senses. Closing his eyes, the Ranger sought the Ties That Bind, grasping onto the thin trails that linked all beings. Finding those connected to the girl, he felt their position in the forest and spoke to the creatures around. The first to see them was a squirrel, and the images that came to Otho's mind included feelings of terror and apprehension. Then, a raven saw them and the wise bird judged their garb and speech to be that of foes. Cawing out an alarm, the raven leapt from his perch and winged to the west, towards the Ranger camp, as instructed by Otho. This encouraged the approaching figures, and they drew their blades.

"I want that meat back, you maggots!" hissed the first, a dal'Korin. He was graying in the scales and quite large even for his species and had the scars to prove that he had fought his way out of many battles. "We found Tagik and Klun dead a distance from the gates. Then our toy goes missing. Mark my words, 'ere's Rangers about."

"I smell them." Came the voice of an orc nearby. He gripped his cruel blade and pressed forward, following the lines that the dal'Korin had magically drawn. They all converged on one point ahead of the group- but there was nothing to be seen.

"Aww come now. This is just another dead end, Ful'sa'taan! You are lost and leading us on another wild goose chase!" His words angered the dal'Korin and his friends, but he did not have time to regret his words as a blade found its way into his spine.

"Do not question Ful'sa'taan. He is wiser than you know." They ripped the sword out and the man fell dead before he even struck the ground.

Up ahead, the Rangers watched as their foes approached. Glancing to the man with the flaming hands, Var waved him forward, and he followed the instruction silently. Holding out three fingers, Otho folded one, then two, before dropping his hand- Ranger code for 'attack'.

The first hint Ugtah had that something had gone hor- ribly wrong was when he faced an abrupt inferno. Flames consumed him in a moment and he fled, shrieking as he tried to ditch his flaming clothing. A moment later, his mind overloaded, and he dropped, suffering in silence as the blackness of death took him.

Having seen their friend immolated, the rest of the group knew they were facing a mage. That alone was cause for concern, but if Rangers backed him up, things would get even more difficult. "FECK! Someone get a bow! I want that mage's head!" Ful'sa'taan took the lead, his blades at the ready. He heard the whistling and narrowly avoided an arrow that instead found itself in his unlucky compatriot. *Curse it all,* he thought, *three men down and I have not even found the foes!* He strode forward and felt himself push against an invisible force. He realized his error as a sword lanced out from the hidden area and through his gut. Another crossed over his neck and his head fell free. Following this, two Rangers strode out, placing themselves between the hunters and their prey. As a rather burly Nolvern raised a great-axe, Otho readied himself to take the strike- but it never came. Glancing up, he saw three flame-crested daggers protruding from the man's chest and neck. Glancing back to Var expecting answers, the Ranger instead found the man busied with the last two foes. Evidently, the knives had come from elsewhere and it rewarded his curiosity as Knal came bounding out of the barrier, hands still aflame.

"It worked! I thought the heat would be too great to bear, but it worked!" In his jubilation, the man started a small brush fire as the fames continued dripping from his hands.

As he finished his two opponents with a quick succession of parries, slices, and stabs, Var shook his head at his student. "Control yourself! Do not harm the wilds!" He leapt past Otho and began stomping out the fire that threatened the precious lands. Knal extinguished his hands sheepishly and looked at the ground.

"I did not think-"

"No, you did, just the wrong thought. Remember that you have to keep control of the flames, else they will run away from you." His expression shifted into one of mirth and Var clapped Knal on the shoulder. "Come now, hear of what happens when the Warden Ranger tries to use magic."

This caught Knal off guard- The Warden Ranger has trouble with magic? Such a thing had to be in jest, for it were impossible. "But Var... If the Warden Ranger has trouble with magic, how is he the Warden Ranger? I thought skill in all areas was necessary?"

Otho picked this moment to speak, his voice calm as he regarded Knal's words. When he spoke, it was out of an experience he had had before the other man was even born and a rather painful one at that. "When I was a Tenderfoot, I was traveling with the Warden Ranger for a time. We ambushed a slaver caravan somewhere in the Farlands and during the fighting, they flayed my arm open." Quickly, he unlaced his bracer and sleeve, before pulling it up to reveal the long, ragged scar and the many branching scars from it. "I asked Karos to heal me, begged him really because this was my first real wound. He tried to get someone else to take care of me and I realize now he was trying to spare me. But when he realized no others were available and his potions were with his pack, he made the choice to use pathway magic."

"What happened? How did those other scars form?" Knal asked, impatient to hear the end of the story. Var made a mental note to have a word about that- he was trying to make the man better at listening rather than jumping in at the first sign of boredom.

"Karos performed the incantation- word for word, it was perfect. But when the magic tried to flow from his body to mine, something went wrong and my arm was... Rent into many pieces." It was clear the memory still pained him and he flexed his fingers slowly, convinced there was still some lasting damage. "As I was in a worse way, he called another Ranger over... Mother Kiri, if memory serves... While he sutured my arm back into its original shape, she mended the bones and flesh within. His skills at medicine are flawless- you could not hope for a better healer... but on your life do not get him to use magic."

This puzzled Knal even more and still his question remained. If the Warden Ranger was so terrible with magic to destroy an arm he was attempting to heal, why was he trusted with such an influential position? "But Otho... that does nothing to answer my question... If the Warden Ranger is terrible with magic... why is he the Warden Ranger? Why would he have been picked over by someone who had skills in that area?"

This brought a rather concerned look from Var, who was Knal's *saal'kwen*. He chose to speak this time, cutting off Otho with a gentle wave. "You should remember well what I have told you of the station of Warden Ranger, Knal. It is not just skill that leads one to be noticed by *Ca'e Mör*. He showed incredible resolve and courage with an outnumbered force during the Battle of Salrin Hills. This story I was hoping he could someday tell you, so you would understand just who he is. But if it must be told, so be it."

He grabbed an arrow from his pack and waved the younger man close. Otho, having heard the tale at least a hundred times, slipped away, moving to check on Siddi and Khula, as well as the child they had saved. Khula was sitting up on a stump, staring into the fire, silent and pale. At first, he wondered if that was her normal skin tone, before realizing that she was in some sort of shock.

"Come, Khula, tell me what ails you." He looked into the woman's eyes- they were distant, the gaze of someone who had seen far more death than they were prepared for.

"I... had aiding those ill and injured by the plague... but coming out of the castle I see nothing but death. Has anyone survived?" The red-haired lady's voice trembled as she whispered, causing Otho to grab a mug of tea from the table; They had prepared many for Rangers coming back, but he felt it would do her some good. With his free hand, he lifted hers and wrapped them around the mug before pressing it to her lips. It surprised him that she did not hurt herself worse than before with the exertion of those words.

"Drink." His words were a command, but a gentle one. Khula did as instructed and the life-giving elixir passed between her lips. She took a hearty drink and swallowed, her eyes almost immediately focusing in on everything around her. Quickly, Khula placed the cup next to her and looked at Otho, her hands coming up to sign to him.

"How many survive?" She gestured, always concerned about others. There was still a great pain in her nose and her throat burned once more, but the tea had soothed that well.

"Few inside the city. We have been warning all to stay away, and it will take some time to get a clear account of the dead. We do what we can, but we can only make them comfortable. I hope that when Warden Ranger Karos arrives, he can shed some light on the situation. Now come, listen to the tale of Salrin Hills, take your mind off the day's horrors." Khula wondered inwardly if the distraction would work, but soon found herself rather enthralled by the masterful storytelling of Var.

"Seventy-six years ago, in the month of Harshheat, the town of Salrin and the hills surrounding, a group of Raiders were lurking. They had been, until then, just a nuisance, sacking caravans and causing havoc. But they slew no one. Of course, that was before Ug'Tahash took control. Then, the force of 300 halted caravans, demand tribute and slay those who would not hand over gold or goods. The town of Salrin sent out a force to quell this, and they were quickly defeated." He began drawing in the dirt with the tip of the arrow in his hand, illustrating his story as he told it. "The hilled area was perfect for them to set up their tollgate and they seemed uncontested. Few would willingly go up against such a force, but ah, Karos. He began scouting their lines, learning their numbers and paths. For they lulled themselves into a false sense of security, thinking they owned the area. But one man may pass a great host undetected if he knows his way and none know how to move with more care than a Ranger on a task."

He paused long enough to get a drink of tea and cleared his throat, continuing. "For three weeks, Karos harassed their forces by night and day. Picking off the odd sentry here, drawing a few men into a trap there. He whittled their numbers down to just 200 in 21 days. A well-placed arrow had wounded the leader of the gang, so they were becoming cautious. But the land they thought they owned began working against them at Karos' bidding. The odd hole here, tripping up someone who may have seen him. The odd rockfall there, taking out a number. By the time Karos called for aid, the force was down to 175. Then, he gathered 45 Rangers, including myself. Otho was there too, though he may not remember it quite as I am telling. Karos was out of arrows, his supplies were spent, and he was growing hungry. So, he rallied us, splitting us into three groups. Two would scale the high hills surrounding the raider camp, one on either side and a third, hand-picked by Karos, would demand an audience with Ug'Tahash. They came under the banner of peace, but when Ug'Tahash and his men drew sword, we cut them down. From above, arrows rained, nearly blackening the sun. From below, sword, dagger, spear, ax, all weapons of the Rangers came to bear on their foes. Whenever the raiders rallied, Karos let out a deafening call with his horn, terrifying them and bolstering his friends. He had hoped to be merciful, but when he found several children and women being caged, or having been passed around as playthings, he realized there was no hope. Resolutely, he tracked down the survivors and slew them without remorse, in the name of the people they had wronged." As he finished the tale, Var watched the reaction on Knal's face- it impressed him. A victory of that magnitude with inferior numbers was no small task. Nodding, Var turned his attention to Khula, wondering at her reaction.

She was asleep on the ground, having curled up next to the fire and drifted off listening to the tale. Her mind was made up; she would meet the Warden Ranger. He sounded interesting enough.

10

10: Northrealm, Westerspring

"Please, you cannot do this! I have a wife and child!" The pleas fell on deaf ears, however, and a blade soon silenced the cry of the catlike creature, a merchant from Khataar.

"You should have thought of that before you gave coin to a slaver." The response came late, for the life had already left the creature's eyes. Satisfied, the murderer examined his kill through blood-red eyes before turning away. He drew his cloak about him, shivering in the bitter cold and trying to reason what was keeping his dragon. His unnaturally white skin was good camouflage in the snows of Northrealm, but worthless against the bitter cold that filled this hateful land.

The dragon winged in, her eyes whirling in colors of distress as she examined the scene. Her thoughts flew to her rider, wondering what had possessed him to commit murder in the forest. Wisely, she kept such questions to herself, wondering just what the tattooed albino was thinking at the moment. It would not do to upset him, the great beast reasoned, especially if he was in a foul mood.

Looking around, the dragon saw another beast lying, half covered by the snow. Curiously, she moved over and swept some of the powder away. *A dragon!* She realized a moment later, and nearly let out a cry of alarm. Then she remembered her rider had told her it would affect dragons, too. He was hoping it would kill them *en masse* and rid the world of those who would protect it. Shaking her head at the brutality of it all, she shifted herself and waited to see her rider again.

As the rider came out of the Tower, he looked around to see what could be seen. A dragon, half-buried in the snows, evidently dead from... what he hoped was his plague. *That will bode well and show that I mean business.* Hoping that other dragons would soon face the same face, the elf cleared his throat and spoke to his dragon.

"Hanmaer tower held no clues for us and even the Ledger was gone. They have vacated completely." The voice was a discordant one, holding tones of evil in every breath. As boots crunched across the snow, the albino leapt to the back of his dragon and urged her skyward. "You are rather silent today. What thoughts are on your mind?" The voice asked, an edge of distrust coloring the curiosity.

If you wish to strike back at the Riders, why use such under-handed methods? Why not attack openly? You have the power, Vaelyn. The concerned voice rattled around in the albino's head for a moment and he raised a hand to push his hair back past his pointed ears before he remembered he had none. Truth be told, he was not sure why he did not just outright attack. He had more than enough power, at least in his mind, to take them on. But some urging in his mind told him that this way was better, that this way would prove more effective.

Effective, perhaps, but still underhanded. Still dishonorable.

She thought privately, keeping her thoughts separate from her rider's consciousness. It wouldn't be a good idea to let him hear her protests. At least, not yet. Shaking her head, the dragon looked around once more. The rider climbed up onto the dragon's neck and settled himself in the saddle. Then he linked his flight belts to the harness and pulled them taut.

Secure, he thought at the dragon. She echoed it in her mind after testing the give on the straps. There was very little. Nodding, she positioned herself and hopped upwards, taking to the top of the tower. Then she bunched her powerful legs beneath her, took a breath, and shot into the sky. At the apex of her leap, she unfurled her wings and began beating them. Once she was stable in the air, she began circling upwards, round, and round until she was at the proper altitude for flying.

"Fools. All of them. Soon, they will taste my wrath. And this world shall be mine." A deep rumble came from the dragon's belly as she climbed into the sky. That answer did not please the magnificent beast, but she was unwilling to speak more on the matter. Turning southward, the creature beat her great wings to gain speed, before leaving them spread to glide towards warmer climes.

The dragon was no fool. What they were doing was madness, and it was dawning upon her that her rider was not exactly stable. But she was bloodbound to do as her rider instructed, even if for her it was terrible. This was not the first time the black dragon had found her own thoughts at odds with that of her rider and the beast knew it would not be the last. Dropping to a lower altitude, the dragon brought herself and her rider into the more temperate air of Westerspring. Without realizing it, they were following the trail of Thäoldr, who had vacated days before.

As they crested the lower reaches of the Eversnow Forest, the elf felt himself warm, little by little. He had always liked the springtime. It felt renewing to him. The sacrilege of what he was doing seemed a perfect irony in the elf's mind and he urged his mount to greater efforts. "Come, take us home, Talakath. I long to rest as I plan our next move." He had grown tired of chasing down the ties to his old life. He knew not when the meeting would come, but he knew it would mean the end of someone. His gifts had told him nothing, and he was growing tired of fumbling in the dark.

As the dragon turned to fly to the southwest, the elf looked out below them. *Someday,* the thought crossed his mind, *I shall rule all that I can see. And all will bow to me.* His thoughts went from those to ones that made less sense, and the elf slapped himself gently. Such thoughts would serve him little right now. The miles melted away below them and the rider lost track after a while. He was used to letting his attention slip to other things as he rode, allowing his mind to explore other tasks.

Finally, the scenery looked familiar, and the elf knew he was in a safe enough area that they could descend. Down and down they went, dropping from the colder air of high altitudes to the more temperate air down below. As the dragon circled around to land, she looked over her spot, rumbling softly. She hoped her rider would sleep- that would give her time to think over the events of the past few weeks. She was unsure that she liked where Vaelyn's mental state was going, but she was careful to keep such thoughts to herself.

Finally, she backwinged, her feet touching the ground in unison. Lowering her shoulder, she allowed her rider to dismount, watching as the elf slipped into the small house he lived in. Once inside, Vaelyn looked around quickly to ensure everything was still there, and he nodded, stripping out of his riding gear and cloak, before laying on his bed and closing his eyes. He fell into a deep sleep, plagued by strange dreams.

The dragon outside stirred, restless. Many dark things passed with her rider and it was concerning her. Ever since the day he had been banished from the Order of Gelvrentael, he had been without purpose, wandering and raiding for food. Yet when he came across bandits and slavers, he killed them without hesitation, refusing to see the fact that he had become the same. Even the great black dragon had trouble with this. She felt that strength could be found in numbers. As for the ideals of the Order, she often felt them too restricting, too orderly. Chaos was strength in this world. But for the greater good, she was willing to bow to those rules. Vaelyn, however, was getting to where he could not recognize his own rules.

Poking her great onyx head through the window, the dragon examined the sleeping rider. The tattoos covering his skin, which said 'OPEN' in an ancient, mystical language. Where other dragonriders had words such as 'DEFEND' or 'ATTACK' in the old tongue, Vaelyn only had "OPEN", written roughly 460 times over his body. *This, he felt, gave him the greatest access to his power... but at what cost?* Thought the dragon. She could already see that Vaelyn's muscles, which had long been a point of pride to the albino deep elf, had begun to waste away. More and more, he relied upon his magic, only using his blades when he could not work up the energy for another spell. It was a dangerous way to fight.

When Vaelyn awoke, it was sixth watch, or midnight. He lay still for a time, wondering at the nightly noises. His mind wandered, and he wondered how the cities would sound once they had no people within them. *What about your plans to rule?* Came another thought to the elf's head and he shook it away. Why would he want to rule such an impure world? Why should his hands be dirtied to uplift the foolish creatures bumbling around on it? *Better that they all die.*

This thought rang painfully with Talakath. She was a black dragon, a creature known for sowing chaos for the fun of it. But always there was a balance to her dealings. Always there was a reason for cruelty or kindness. In this way, she was unlike many of her kin, who sought nothing but to bring pain to those below them. The creature sighed gently and shook her majestic head. Her discomfort went unnoticed by her rider, who seemed to be preoccupied with his daily rituals.

The elf grabbed a bucket, stepping out of his home to walk to a small spring nearby. Back and forth he went, dumping bucket after bucket into a large tub in his home. Once it was full to his liking, the elf dropped the bucket and moved his hands in front of him. Touching one of his tattoos, he let loose with a gentle stream of fire to a pile of logs below the tub, igniting them to heat his bathing water. That task done, he stripped his clothing away and stepped into the tub, sinking slowly up to his neck. He let out a content sigh and relaxed, soaking for a time as the water warmed beneath him. Methodically, he cleansed himself, attempting to remember the last time he had taken a bath- a proper bath, not a soak in the river. His thoughts quickly turned to darker things. Chaotic things flooded his mind and he let out a confused sound, trying to sort through the thoughts.

"Talakath. Where are we?" came the concerned question. Was the rider truly that far gone? Could he not recognize his own home? Or was this another question entirely?

We are home, Vaelyn. What troubles you? The dragon's eyes whirled in different colors of distress and the black head once more darkened the window of the small cabin. Vaelyn lounged in his bath and found himself suddenly cold. He was vulnerable, and it was an uncomfortable feeling to the elf. *Be calm. If there is danger, I will rout it.* Despite his dragon's reassurance, he could not shake the sudden fear that gripped him. Why was he afraid? He was the most powerful mage of all Seran, at least in his own mind. *None*, thought the elf, *can hold a candle to my raw power!*

This drew a confused sound from the dragon. She did not doubt her rider's power, but she doubted he was the most powerful. *Surely the Kingmage–* She began but regretted her words instantly. Wincing as her rider shrieked at her, the dragon recoiled as he lashed out mentally. He put pressure on her mind, thinking her lesser, and for now, she endured it silently. For now, at least. But the time was coming when there would be a reckoning, and she knew it in her bones.

"That pretender will fall before me. I will tear him from his skin as a fox rends a rabbit!" He glared at his dragon, daring her to contest the words he spoke. Daring her to offer any resistance to his plan. *I will rule this world!* Came the thought again, forgotten was the thought of impurities. Power was what he desired now. Power over those who had wronged him, the power to make things in his design.

Spotting movement out of the corner of his eye, the elf panicked. Immediately, a hand came up, and he pushed outward with his mind, forcing a column of lightning into a hapless rabbit. It blasted the creature across the room, sending it into a crumpled heap in the corner and twitching in death as the electricity coursed through its muscles. Vaelyn felt a smile curl his lips and soon let out a deep laugh; not just at the absurdity of having used so much energy on a rabbit, but also because he had slaughtered the creature. Talakath looked on in no small amount of horror, realizing that her rider was going far down a darker path than even she was willing to. Desperately, she spoke once more, trying to distract her rider. *Certainly, that was unnecessary. The creature posed no threat to you.*

"Eat it." Was all Vaelyn said as he used his magic to move the carcass out to where the dragon could consume it. Talakath did, though, with distaste filling her thoughts. This was not her way. This was not right, even for a creature that longed for bloodshed. There were creatures beneath her notice, creatures she would not bother to attack. Subtly, she tried to press at her rider's mind, trying to guide it away from the dark, confusing thoughts. What she found was a wall, impenetrable even to her. She recoiled mentally, wondering just what could happen inside of a Rider's head to cause them to put up a wall against their own dragon. Surely it was a bad sign? An omen of worse things to come, perhaps? There was no way she could tell with finality and so she waited it out.

As the elf went about his day, the dragon became more and more concerned with her rider's mental state. It was devolving quickly, she realized, and there was little she could do to prevent it. Sighing, the great Talakath paced around in front of the small cliffside cabin for a bit, before settling back down on her legs and lapsing into inattentiveness. Occasionally, she thought she heard a voice on the breeze, something calling to her. *What is that?* She wondered, looking off into the distance to see- nothing at all. Not even a hint of a phantom to bother her. It was almost more disconcerting than Vaelyn's mental state. To think that her own mind could be going? It bade poorly in her eyes. Settling her head on her forelegs once more, the dragon tried to doze, but every time she got close to sleep, something else would grab her attention. Something else would jar her back to wakefulness. Sighing, she gave up on sleep and instead launched to the sky, planning on taking a dip in the nearby Laghe Valori, the Lake of Valor.

Where are you off to? Came the voice of her rider, in an oddly pleasant tone.

Taking a dip in the Lake. She replied and was rewarded with a slight huff of approval. Evidently, Vaelyn had other things on his mind than her trying to relax.

Inside the cabin, Vaelyn waited a few more minutes to let the dragon get as far away as possible. Then he slipped into the cliff face and pulled a tapestry aside, revealing a hidden passageway. Quickly, he slipped along the passage until he came to his lab, where he was concocting something. Something awful. *Something beautiful.* Grinning, the elf began toying with some of the reagents, wondering exactly how his helper had known to create this thing, this... *virus.* It was the most devastating creation he'd thought up, and the Void-Sleeper had given it to him to soften up this pathetic world so they could conquer it easier. *And I will rule it all when the dust settles.* Another grin, and this time he bent to the task of mixing two of the reagents.

For all he knew, Vaelyn was dealing with a creature of limitless power. One that could never be conquered. In the back of his mind, though, he kept worrying about being betrayed at his moment of triumph. At his moment of victory, would he have to contest with one of these creatures? That much he couldn't know, at least not yet. Taking a breath, he kept mixing the reagents until it smelled right. Wincing at the odor, Vaelyn was, as always, relieved to know that he was immune to its effects. It wouldn't do to be sickened by his own creation, now would it?

Hours went by as the mad elf worked on his tasks. Outside, the dragon played in the water, pushing the thoughts of evil works out of her mind. At least for now. But she knew that all too soon, she would have to deal with it again. Blowing water from her nose, the dragon looked around herself. A quick glance skyward told her that there were other dragons in the sky, so she filled her lungs and dove deep to hide away from them for a little while. It wouldn't do to draw attention to herself. She knew as much right now. Keeping her eyes skyward, she watched until the shapes, which to her were as clear as could be, were far away, winging away from her, rather than towards. Sighing gently, the dragon surfaced and once more blew water from her nostrils before floating around for a little while, just letting the waves carry her massive body for a time. In her heart, the dragon wished for a change of winds, a chance to... *to what?* She wondered, trying to pin down the thought. It eluded her, however, as mist from one's hands in the morning.

When the time came to finally remove herself from the Lake, Talakath stepped up onto the beach and walked along towards the cabin once more. Looking up the cliffs, she thought about leaping upwards for a moment, just to relax on the sunny cliff for a while. Sadly, she knew that the moment she got comfortable, Vaelyn would call for her once more. So she let herself settle on the fields outside the cabin, stretching her wings to their full sixty spearlength span to dry. Then she settled her head on her forelegs once more and tried to nap.

You must rebel, came a voice into her mind. Glancing up and around, Talakath wondered where it had come from. For a moment, she wondered if someone was there. But she saw nothing at all. No hint of a person. So she settled again, only to be interrupted again. *His path is evil! He must be stopped!* Sighing, the dragon thought hard, trying to identify the voice in her mind. *You know who I am,* the voice said plainly.

But I do not, she retorted. *You are just a voice in my mind.* Her eyes began to whirl different colors of distress and annoyance as she tried to reason with the voice. But it was insistent. Persistent. It redoubled its efforts to convince her of... something or other.

You know who I am, Talakath. Though you may not know my voice. The voice came again. *You must listen, for time is short. You must find a way to stop Vaelyn's works. You must.*

But how? How can I stop something so insidious? Her voice was plaintive as she spoke to the being in her mind. *And how do you know Vaelyn is involved?* She became a little defensive at the voice, wondering just how it had sussed out what she and the elf knew. It wouldn't do to be found out before things fell into place.

Because I am you. I am your conscience, your inner light. You must find a way to undo what he has already done. To make right what was wrong. The voice pleaded with her, constantly trying to get her to rouse to action. But she knew more than she let on, and sighed.

There will be a time when I can. But as of now, that time has not come. We must be patient. She sighed, sending a gust of wind out to rustle leaves in a few trees nearby in the Forest of

Memory, and focused on what she knew. What she could do at the moment, which was not much. But she had a feeling, deep in her bones, that righting this wrong would claim her life. She couldn't tell how she knew, but there it was, burned into her thoughts. And she welcomed it. As she drifted off to sleep for the first time in a few days, the dragon's breathing calmed and eased out.

Uneasy dreams would trouble her throughout her respite.

Vaelyn cursed as he dropped a large book on his foot, nearly leaping into the table in his pain. He managed to calm himself, though, and took another look at the laboratory he was working in. *Things are coming along nicely.* Using a gift from the Void-Sleeper, the elf looked over Seran, gazing into the cities that'd already been infected with the virus he'd been creating. A few cities were quarantined, but that was to be expected. He knew it would take time to whittle the cattle down until they were conquerable, but it was good to know that progress was being made. *Most places.* Annoyed, he looked at Karnost, realizing that the virus hadn't taken root there. *Or in Northrealm.* There, too, the virus was simply dying out. Karnost had no excuse. The city was rife with commoners, commoners who likely knew nothing about hygiene. One would think that such a thing as a virus would take hold. But Vaelyn had been separated from the world for some time. He didn't know that they had made great strides in hygiene, or that people had such things as *running water* in public bathhouses and that they cleaned the public restrooms *daily.* As he watched over the city, a black rage threatened to overtake Vaelyn.

And why is Northrealm faring so well? Casting his gaze up to the frigid land, he realized too late that he would have to reformulate his virus to be resistant to cold. Cursing and screaming in impotent rage, the mad elf took to his lab and work once more, going over everything and trying to figure out a way to make his precious virus stronger. Hardier. But he could find nothing. At least, nothing *yet*. Scrubbing his face with his hands, the elf descended into a black pit of despair and doubt. Then he tried to shift his attention to other things, and ended up calling out to the Void in his desperation.

"Why do you summon me, Vaelyn?" As the creature spoke to Vaelyn, a great pressure felt like it would split his head in half. Groaning and holding his head, the mad elf did his best to compose himself.

"I... I need a way to make the virus survive in cold climates."

"You did not foresee this?" The voice sounded agitated. Angry, even. More pressure was applied to Vaelyn's mind, and the elf yelped gently. "I am not helping you fail. You *will* fix this oversight, and you will not contact me for petty concerns."

A sudden surge of indignity shot through Vaelyn, temporarily defeating the mental pressure the creature was exuding. "I *am* trying to fix it. I do not know how to make such a tiny creature survive the cold, hence why I am asking *you*."

The creature laughed, an eerie screeching noise, like a violin out of tune. Vaelyn felt a liquid run down his forehead and touched a hand to it. As soon as he brought it away, he could see that it was *blood*. Panicking for a moment, the elf winced as the mental pressure renewed itself and the creature spoke again. *"Fix this problem. However you must. I will not reward failure."* Then, all at once, the creature's presence was gone, leaving Vaelyn curled up in a ball on the floor, bleeding from his head and panting.

So he worked through the night, trying to find ways to make the virus more resilient against the cold of Northrealm, but every experiment ended in failure. Sighing, he wiped his face and kept working, until exhaustion nearly overtook him. Panting, he raised a vial to the sky and looked at it in the torchlight. It was a jet-black hue, and when he turned the vial over, it moved rather like sludge. But when he blasted it with his best cold spells, it seemed to survive. Or at least, he thought it did. *Time will tell, I wager.* Putting the vial down, he stumbled out of the laboratory and up the passageway into the main cabin. Barely making it to his bed, he collapsed onto the mattress and was soon sound asleep.

The next morning, Vaelyn was ready. Calling out to Talakath, he loaded up the precious vial into the strange device he'd been hiding. *An aerosolizer,* he thought the name to himself. *That is what this is.* Chuckling, he wondered about the inner machinations and magic that made this thing run, realizing that the Void-Sleeper had given him the idea and the patterns. He had simply followed the instruction. Setting the aerosolizer aside, he slid into his riding gear, tightening down the coat and helmet, adjusting his goggles, and boots, and tested his gloves. *All in order,* he thought to himself as he picked back up the device. Then he made his way out of the cabin, to where Talakath was waiting patiently.

As soon as he'd climbed to her neck and fastened his riding straps, Vaelyn chuckled and looked out over the land. *This is too small for me,* he thought, about his holdings. *It was always too small. I dream bigger.* After checking the tightness of the straps, he slapped Talakath's neck and gave her the go ahead to take to the sky. *Secure.*

She echoed the word back and bunched up her massive legs

beneath her, waited a moment, and then kicked off the ground with more than enough force to send her a few hundred feet skyward. Then she opened her wings as she began to fall back to the ground and began beating them, sending small tornadoes beneath her as she pushed herself into the sky and turned northward. Winging high, she caught an air current that pushed her even further into the sky, and she glided for some time. Occasionally, she would beat her wings to propel herself faster and higher, and other times she would simply glide along, letting the currents lift or lower her accordingly.

They flew for a few hours, and soon enough, their first goal was in sight. The southern border of Northrealm, and *that damnable gate*, Vaelyn suddenly thought. The dragon chuckled gently and soothed her rider's mind as best she could, but he was implacable. Something was agitating him again, and she didn't know what it could be. Regardless, she flew on, over the landscape and up into the higher reaches. For just a moment, she thought she saw a flash off in the distance, but when she turned her head, there was nothing. Huffing gently, she beat her great wings and continued on. *To Snowkeep!* The instruction came from Vaelyn, and she nodded her head gently and continued flying.

About twelve hours later, the city of Snowkeep was in sight. The castle, dead center in the city, stood proudly above the rest of the buildings. All around, she could see the people getting ready for the day. The guard shifts were changing, and people were beginning to bustle about. She felt Vaelyn shift, and turned her head as he commanded her to hover high above the city.

He was busy with his device, the *aerosolizer*, and was trying to get everything locked into place. Once he had, the elf grinned and activated it. A slight whirring caught Talakath's attention, and as she watched, the device extended out from her neck, far enough that she wouldn't be caught in whatever it was doing. Then, it began to spray a fine mist out, and Vaelyn commanded her to circle over the city. So she did, again and again, until Vaelyn gave a grunt of approval. Looking back, she saw him retract the device and tuck it under his arm once more. Then he spurred her on, and she winged towards Westerspring once more. Something caught her attention, and for twelve hours, she chased after it. Then twelve more. Vaelyn was curious, but not enough to interrupt her in her chase. *Certainly it must be important*, he thought to himself. Little did he know just how it would change the coming days.

As she winged along, Talakath felt the presence of another flying creature. Something small and fierce. Something that could easily take her on, and if she were not careful, win. Rising as high as she dared, Talakath flew above the clouds, masking herself in the mists. Then she lingered over the area, though she noticed the creature give a cry and dive into a cloud bank. Amused, she circled high and moved off- for now. It wouldn't do to give away the chase just yet.

A moment passed, and she realized what the creature was. A griffon. One that looked suspiciously like a Moriani Dart. Grimacing slightly, the dragon made a mental note to keep out of sight. The creature could easily outrun her, and if one of the two beings riding it sensed her purpose... Things would not go well. Alone, the griffon would be no match for the dragon- unless it was quite clever. Dragons may rule the sky, but griffons kept them in check. A smart griffon was more than enough to keep a black dragon at bay, long enough that they could call for reinforcements. And against a dragon, even wild griffons would aid a domestic of their kind. So Talakath knew that the smaller creatures would swarm her if she wasn't careful.

So she eased up the pressure, winging away to the east and dropping down out of the creature's range of sensing. Landing delicately, she craned her neck around to look at Vaelyn. He was fidgeting, annoyed almost, and stared at her in return. *Finished chasing whatever that was?* He asked impatiently, and she huffed gently.

It was a griffon. With two people astride it. I thought it prudent to track them for a time. She sounded unperturbed, though her words set off alarms within Vaelyn's mind. Immediately, he pressed her for details. Where they were bound, who they were. She answered as best she was able. *A dokk and a small man. Not sure who was the rider or who was the passenger. One looked like a Ranger, judging by the quiver and bow attached to their pack.* A Ranger. That thought alone gave the dragon pause to consider her options. If the Rangers were working with the Order... things would be difficult for Vaelyn. But she refused to let the elf know her thoughts. She felt it would be crucial to let things play out as they would, and to avoid interfering until she absolutely must.

Does the Order know what I am doing? Vaelyn thought to himself in a panic. *Are they doing reconnaissance to find my hideout? Impossible. None but that oaf Magus know where I am living. Perhaps it is just a random patrol?* The thoughts flooded his mind and he reeled, even as Talakath touched down on the soft ground. Abruptly, he realized just how desperately he needed to move around. Unlinking his flight belt, he slid from her neck and his boots hit the soft soil. His legs ached abominably, and he paced around and around until they started to feel normal again. Then he went back into his mental hole, trying to figure out what the griffon had been nearby for. *And a Ranger?* That thought soured his mood. He didn't know much about them, but he felt they could be an annoyance, to say the least. How little he knew was immaterial, and he shrugged the thought off as quickly as he could. Sighing gently, the elf resigned himself to meditation on the matter. *I had best not bother the Void-Sleeper.* The thought of engaging with the creature again tempered his manic worries, and he paced a bit more until he realized his pants were attempting to fall. Grunting, he tightened them back down. *I have been eating, have I not?* He wondered to himself.

Eventually, the thought fled from his mind and he grunted, realizing he wasn't hungry. At least, not at the moment. Sighing, he settled down into a cross-legged position on the ground and stared into his lap. Placing his hands palm up in his lap, he focused his energy into the point above his hands. Little by little, he pushed energy through himself, focusing on the feeling of the power surging through him. *This is all mine!* He thought to himself, grinning victoriously as he manifested a ball of lightning in front of him. It floated to his eye level and remained there, as if staring at him. *It is judging me!* Reaching out, he swatted at the orb, only to be rewarded with searing pain as the electricity surged through him. Yelping, he swatted at it again, with the same result. The third time, he was a bit wiser, and blasted it with more energy. But that only made it bigger.

Vaelyn, came the reproachful voice of his dragon. *You know how to dispose of it.* She was growing bored with his antics, and shook her head. Pouting, the elf reabsorbed the energy, unknowingly speeding himself towards the end. Towards an end that would consume him, mind and body. Towards an end that he wouldn't realize was his until it was too late. The dragon sighed gently and looked at Vaelyn. *I suppose we should get moving before the trail grows cold. We had best find that griffon and their riders again.* That thought soured Vaelyn's playful mood and he grunted before pushing himself to his feet and climbing back up to Talakath's neck. Once more, he secured his flight straps to her neck. Once more, he gave the word to signal his readiness.

Once more, the powerful legs bunched up beneath dragon and rider, and the beast sprang into the sky. At the height of her leap, she unfurled her wings and began beating them, pushing both her and her rider into the sky once more. As they rose, Talakath circled higher and higher, until she was at a comfortable cruising altitude. Then she took off, following the faint scent trail left by the griffon and the two riders.

Soon enough, they were closing on their quarry. Pushing herself ever higher, the dragon climbed as high as she dare. With little thought for her rider, she rose to the top of the clouds and simply watched from above as she cruised along. Blinking, she occasionally spotted the odd creature flitting by, but gave them no mind. For a moment, she locked her eyes on a Great Raven as it cruised along silently. It acknowledged her presence without a care, wondering if she was something important. But then it continued on, leaving her to her own thoughts.

Cruising along, the dragon continued looking around. A large bird rose to her altitude, gave one look at her, and fled in terror, beating its four wings rhythmically as it put distance between them. Vaelyn reached out and began charging his pathway nerves, evidently planning to blast the hapless creature into oblivion. So Talakath banked hard, jarring Vaelyn and taking his focus off of the creature as it vanished into the distance. He screamed at her, a thousand curses that she didn't listen to, but settled down quickly. *I must focus,* he realized, *and slaying a xalwyn will do nothing for me.* Shaking his head, he adjusted his focus back to the here and now, looking around above him for anything that might pose a threat.

They cruised into the night, only landing to rest for a few hours. Vaelyn took the time to stretch out his legs and arms once more, grunting as he wondered exactly *why* they were chasing a griffon and riders. A moment later, he chastised himself for letting his guard slip. *We are chasing them because they saw us.* It wouldn't do to let the three creatures live now that they'd seen Talakath, else they might raise the alarm about her. *So they must die!* Laughing to himself at the thought of outright attacking a griffon of the Order, the mad elf decided then and there that he would kill the griffon and rider, and take the Ranger hostage. After all, she *must* know something that would help him to his goal. She simply must.

On they flew for another day or so, following the scent trail the griffon had left in the sky, it rewarded her when she saw it again. It was racing along, evidently intent on some goal, but little did it know what awaited above it. Biding her time, Talakath rode along the air currents, a shadow unseen. Waiting for the moment to strike. Vaelyn was constantly putting pressure in her mind to tell him *what* she was chasing, or why she'd been on the wing so achingly long. But she kept silent. At least, until the time was right, and she folded her wings and dropped out of the sky onto the griffon.

11: Coldforge, Northrealm

"**D**ragonsmith!" The voice called from outside the forge, stirring the great man from his thoughts.

"Aye, what need you, friend?" Viktor's voice came deep as a great drumbeat as he spoke. He hardly looked up, wondering who would be bothering him at this hour. He did not have to wait long to solve that mystery, as a hooded and cloaked figure swept into his forge. Another Ranger, here on some important purpose, no doubt.

"Just a quick favor, Dragonsmith-most-honored." The Ranger held up a shirt of fine mail that looked more ragged than a pauper's clothes. Evidently it had not held up quite as well as one would hope, and the Dragonsmith whistled slightly.

"*Nel ca'e armä*, Ranger. What happened to this mail shirt? Are you injured? My skills are lesser with bodily harm." He looked from the tattered shirt to the Ranger, who seemed no worse for wear. The Ranger shook his head and Viktor nodded slowly. "It will take time to repair the mail. Give me a day or so and I should have it back together." When the Ranger offered his purse, Viktor shook his head. "Nay, you do so much to defend us- I would feel ill taking coin from you."

"By the steel indeed, good Viktor. Please, Dragonsmith-most-honored. Accept it, for it was a wager. My life on your craftsmanship- and you proved my wager correct." The Ranger gave a hidden smile beneath his mask. With a nod and a grumble, the great man took only a few coins from the Ranger and handed the purse back. Satisfied, the Ranger gave the mail shirt to the smith, turned on his heel and slipped out.

"*Nel ca'e armä...* brave they may be, but steel be witness, they are a foolish lot." Speaking to no one in particular, Viktor hung the mail shirt upon a stand, looking at each hole- judging how many new rings he would need to forget to get this shirt back to full strength. After a moment, he had his number and began crafting the rings one by one. It would take a few hours at his best speed, but he was sure he could do it in a day. "Mydborh bless me this day, for I defend the defender." He placed his great hammer aside and instead he reached for his pliers to shape the links. As he worked, he hummed one of the Teaching Songs to himself and smiled. It was rare he got such work, something methodical and relaxing, and he enjoyed it thoroughly.

"There is a strange taste on the breeze." The voice caused the normally unshakable Dragonsmith to nearly jump from his skin. He spun around, forge-hammer in his hand- an improper weapon, but his size he hoped would be enough of a deterrent that he need not use it. There was no one- no source to the voice, nothing for him to find. He turned back to his work; slowly, for he was disquieted. Reaching out with his thoughts, he stirred the sleeping dragons of the forge.

"Vu'locav. Did you speak to me?" The answer came quickly.

Nay, Viktor. I, like Alvarath, have been sleeping. That revelation only grew the unease within Viktor's stomach. Sighing, he went back to his work, threading the wire into his press and bringing the edge down, section after section, bending the thick wire and looping it into chain links. He paused as he worked, checking each link and testing them before carefully looping them back onto the shirt.

"I feel a change in the air. Something fell stirs." Again, a voice from nowhere. Viktor shrugged it off this time and took a breath. This was growing annoying, and he shifted slightly. He was just about to return to his work when the voice came again. "A fool ignores these warnings– and you are no fool." This gave the great man pause as he considered the words. *Warnings? Of what?* He thought to himself. Reaching out, he again touched the consciousness of his dragons, wondering what they may think of things.

"Vu'locav. Surely you heard the voice this time?" His voice sounded almost frightened to him. Surely this was just some trick, some jest to put him off his work. *Nay, Viktor. I have heard nothing. Perhaps you need fresh air?* The idea did not sound so bad. Perhaps it would be a good idea to get out of the Forge for a moment. Sighing, he stepped away from the bench he had been working on and rubbed his eyes. He felt exhausted, though just twelve minutes ago he felt fine. Quickly, he untied his apron and draped the heavy leather garment over one of his stools. Then he stepped out into the bitter cold and took a deep breath before exhaling a cloud of steam.

Winter again, Viktor. It was always winter here. In Coldforge, they were in the depths of the Eversnow Forest, a place blessed– or was it cursed? By the Ancestors to be eternally gripped by winter. The Loremasters had taught him the Old Tales- how a massive piece of the skies fell upon where Coldforge would be, throwing up a massive cloud of dust, burying itself into the land. This was the source of the star-steel Viktor used; he knew as much. But he was unsure of the rest of their tale- how the Ancestors pooled their power to keep the dust from spreading to choke the rest of the world. *But that was just stories*, thought the Dragonsmith.

Truth be told, he did not have a better explanation for the bitter cold that endured even in the summer months, or the snows that always seemed to come back to haunt the Forest and the towns within. But this he knew- Coldforge sat upon a rich source of star-steel and for as long as that endured, his line would work it. He took another breath and exhaled once more, watching the steam waft away. The cold hardly bothered him, but he could tell it was a bitter day. Shaking his head, he strode through the town, seeking- what, he was not sure. Soon enough, though, he found himself at the door of the local Fate-Watcher, one of the strange, blind old women who could read the Ties That Bind. Strange they were, but often had the best advice. Raising a hand to knock at the door, it startled him when he heard a raspy voice within.

"Enter, Viktor, son of Ulfric. I have been expecting you for some time." He blinked for a moment- he had told no one where he was going and had honestly did not know himself. *But this woman can tell one's fate*, he thought to himself, *so I had best not keep her waiting.* Opening the door slowly, he pushed his way into the dimly lit cottage. "Viktor, how wonderful to see you. Close the door please, you will let out the heat." Viktor rolled his eyes and closed the door behind him. She was right, of course, but he would not tell her that. When she waved for him to take a seat, the half-giant slowly lowered himself into the all-too-tiny chair. He could hear it creak beneath him and he wondered just how good the craftsman's skill really was. "You are troubled, Viktor. Speak your mind and the world will listen."

"Lady Trensa, I apologize for bothering you. 'Tis just... about half an hour ago I was sitting in my forge, working... when I heard a strange voice whispering ill omens." He spoke swiftly, his voice betraying the nervousness he felt in his mind. The woman clicked her tongue slightly and waved, urging him to tell more.

"Come now, speak up, I need more to go on. What did these voices say?" She was one of the more impatient Fate-Watchers. This was well known.

"The first time the voice spoke, it told of a 'strange taste on the breeze.' The second time I heard it, the words were different, saying, 'I feel a change in the air. Something fell stirs.' Thrice it spoke and finally it seemed directed to me, saying 'A fool ignores these warnings- and you are no fool.' Pray tell, wonderful lady Trensa. What is the meaning of this trickery?" He shook his head for a moment before looking into the milky-white eyes of the Fate-Watcher. "Have I gone mad?"

"Nay, lad. Your mind is boringly sound," she began, before bringing her hands to rest upon a ball of pure crystal. There they sat for a moment as the woman concentrated, her mind focusing in on what she had told him. Reaching out with her being, she touched the Ties That Bind and gasped when she found his thread. "Viktor Ulfricson... The voice you have heard- the voice that spoke to you belongs to one Ancestor... There is a scent... fire, metal, sweat and etching fluid. Leather in great thickness." Viktor scratched his chin for a moment. After what felt to him like too long, the thought popped into his head.

"Is it Mydborh?" His voice sounded like it was questioning even itself, and the Fate-Watcher clicked her tongue once more.

"I see no one else it could be... but the image is not clear in my mind. It is reasonable to think that Mydborh would speak to you, Dragonsmith, for you are among the most celebrated of metal-workers in Seran." Viktor nodded slowly, but there were still questions on his mind. What did the words spoken to him mean? What could Mydborh be telling him?

"Lady Trensa... What could it mean? What could Mydborh be telling me? Why would he be telling me this, in the stead of a Ranger who might act upon it?"

"Anyone can act upon words given from the Ancestors. They only give counsel to those they believe capable." The Fate-Watcher nodded slowly and shifted in her seat. She watched the man with milky, sightless eyes until he became uncomfortable. "There is more on your mind. Speak of it, Viktor, and I will tell you what I can."

"Erm... I have felt a strange presence as of late. As if someone is watching over my shoulder. At first, I thought it was an apprentice of mine, but it feels... ominous."

Trensa nodded slowly and rolled her eyes upwards. Looking, it seemed, to the ceiling and the sky through it. She focused her mind, taking deep, labored breaths as she reached out once more. This time, she was seeking something specific- something tangible to her. Minutes passed and all was silent in the home. Viktor became uneasy- there was a strange feeling in the air and even he, unaccustomed as he was to the arcane, could feel it. The energy around Trensa seemed to shift, and she opened her eyes at long last. Where Viktor expected to see her milky, sightless orbs once more, he found them glowing with otherworldly energy and authority.

"Viktor Ulfricson of clan Kavabalt. Hear my words and take warning. Fell deeds are awakening. Search you, your ancestors, find the Old Clans. Call for a moot."

"But... Why me? I am no Ranger; I am no adventurer. I am but a smith."

"You are greater than you know, more important than you realize, Dragonsmith of Coldforge. You are the Blood of the North. Your line holds the power of the Snow Guard and the tenacity of the frost drake. You are what they will seek to kill. Armor long discarded, you must don. Weapons long forgotten must find your hands again."

Viktor was taken aback. He had never raised a weapon in anger and now he was being told that he must? This was nonsense, and he could not fathom the need.

"Surely there are more capable warriors than I."

"Heed my words and obey, Dragonsmith, for the good of the many outweighs the comfort of the few. A great upheaval is coming and you must play your part." With that, the glow died from Trensa's eyes and she fell forward. Reaching out quickly, the great man caught her and steadied her.

"Lady Trensa?" His eyes held concern for the frail woman's health. She did not look well right now, her skin pale, her cheeks sunken. Her breath was coming in ragged gasps and a trickle of blood was running from her nose.

"Be... warned, Viktor... dark times... are coming. I must.... Rest now..." Unsteadily, the woman rose to her feet and felt her way back to her bed before collapsing onto the furs. Within moments, the sounds of snoring came from the small form, and Viktor shrugged. Making his way out of the home, he trod the path back to his forge, before stopping as he heard the voice of Vu'locav. *The Rangers are the greatest of loremasters. Perhaps they can unravel some of this tale?* He nodded slowly and turned, making his way to the grouping of tents that served as the home for the Rangers. Placed on the outermost edge of town to comfort those who felt too enclosed anywhere inside the village, the tents were carefully erected and kept by thankful townsfolk. Next to them was the guard tower where the Rangers kept watch over Coldforge, and it was here that Viktor found himself.

Raising his hand to the door of the watchtower, the great man debated his next actions. Was he really going to bother the Rangers with his odd tale of... visions? Would they even listen to his words? He hesitated long enough that a voice within the tower called out to him from above. "Come on, then! Do come in, in the stead of standing there like a scared doe!" The voice beckoned, carrying the dulcet tones of the Ranger Kalvuth Nydred, who had brought the chainmail shirt to him mere hours ago. "I had not expected you so soon, Dragonsmith. I hope you do not have bad news for me?" From his angle, he could not yet see the darkness crossing the Dragonsmith's face. When he descended the stairs and opened the great door, though, he saw the man's concern. The weight of it nearly stopped the animated Ranger in his tracks and he quickly ushered the smith in. "Dragonsmith, are you well? You look as if you have seen terrible things!"

"I... am unsure how to describe it, Kalvuth. I feel as if the Ancestors have addressed me through Lady Trensa, nearly killing her in the performance."

"Lady Trensa is quite able to take the strain. But pray tell, what did the Ancestors pass to you? Words of wisdom? Instruction?"

"Warnings. Fell deeds are awakening... instructions to gather armor long discarded and weapons long forgotten. That I must play my part in a great upheaval coming." The Ranger beckoned Viktor to take a seat, and the Smith reached out with his thoughts, asking Vu'locav to keep his apprentices on track- and have one rebuild the mail shirt on his bench. "What should I make of this? I must sound mad to you, Ranger..."

Kalvuth simply shook his head. "Nay, Viktor. Your mind is boringly sound." Viktor blinked. Trensa had used those same words when he asked if he was going mad. Was it another sign?

Without thinking, he gave voice to that thought. "Trensa said the same—"

"Oh?" began the Ranger, his eyes lighting up with interest. If Trensa had said the same words, perhaps their thoughts were connected at some level. This was strange- but more than likely it was just coincidence. "Now tell me, Viktor. What did you feel as the Ancestors were speaking to you? That alone may aid in deciphering their intent."

"I felt... apprehension. A warning in my heart, as if the Ancestors were wishing me to be vigilant. But what could this mean, Ranger?" Kalvuth smirked, looking the man over. He was growing tired of formality. It served little purpose at a time like this.

"Viktor. Call me Kalvuth. Enough with the Ranger non-sense. I am your friend, not your better." He chuckled gently at the sheepish glance from the Dragonsmith and patted the younger man on the shoulder. At 211, Kalvuth did not look his age- such was the blessing and curse of the Rangers. Years did not touch them at all, decades barely left a mark and only centuries showed on their faces. Kalvuth was an odd one, even among the enigmatic Rangers. A freeborn, he had been told, and that was different enough that some more conservative folk didn't like him. But true to his person, Kalvuth did not have a care for what people thought when he wore a dress or trousers. He only cared for what made him happy and for his oath-kin in the Rangers. Truth be told, Viktor had only told if Kalvuth was male or female when Kalvuth himself instructed the half-giant on what he preferred to be called many years ago.

Kalvuth shook his head slowly and sighed. "It sounds as if the Ancestors wish for you to uproot from your comfort. Uproot from what you know and take your dragons where they might change the course of coming troubles. You may be all that stands between an innocent life and terrible things." Shifting, the Ranger adjusted his tunic and popped his neck. He then looked at Viktor once more, his eyes growing severe. "But be warned, Dragonsmith. Once you leave your forge, your spirit will always wish to wander. That is the giant in your heritage." This Viktor knew already in his heart. He had often felt the call to adventure and wondered if he should leave the forge to his apprentices for a time.

Thanking the Ranger for his help, Viktor made his way back to the forge. It had been a few hours already, with him wandering and talking, and he felt he needed to get back to his work. Even if he left after this, he needed to get this Ranger's mail shirt repaired. So, with a calmer mind and renewed focus, he bent to his task. But always his mind wandered to the armor hidden away in a chest beneath piles and piles of old rags; to the great warhammer of his clan, sitting idle above his mantle.

In his heart, he knew it would soon be time to take them up, and he was not sure what would become of him when he did. He knew his family's ways, and he was not sure if, when the time came to shed blood, he would not lose himself in it. For now, though, he contented himself to work the steel before him to repair Kalvuth's mail shirt. He could find comfort in such tasks and he hoped that when he returned from whatever awaited him, that he would find such comfort again.

Sighing, Viktor found himself unable to focus on the task at hand. It was easy enough work for him, but his mind was just... not there. Shaking his head, he put his best effort into the mail shirt, forcing himself to focus. *Kalvuth needs this. I must help the Rangers.* So he pushed himself, winding each ring into place until he had the biggest holes in the shirt repaired. Then he focused on the smaller ones, replacing worn-out rings with new steel.

All in all, it took him a day of forcing himself to focus on the task before it was done to his satisfaction. As he sat in his chair, he heard what sounded like voices outside. Shaking his head once more, he set the shirt down. Stretching as he stood to his nearly two spearlength height, the half-giant felt his bones crackle and shift back into a more comfortable position. Then he shook himself back to wakefulness. Again the voices came, just at the edges of his hearing, so he made his way to the great wooden door and pushed it open. The hinges creaked as the massive portal was forced wide, and Viktor looked around. *No one. Strange.* Sighing, he wandered out into the town square, thinking that he just needed some of the fresh, chilly air. A few breaths later, he felt no change. He wasn't weary, or at least he didn't feel such, but neither was he fully awake. Looking around, he shrugged and headed back inside, this time avoiding his workstation and heading into the small home that was connected to his forge. *How long has it been?* He wondered as he stepped into the dimly-lit home and looked around. The torches were cold, marking that he'd not been back into his home in some time. Shaking his head, Viktor sighed and traced his pathway nerves, emitting just enough flames to light up the torches and lanterns anew, to bathe his home in the harsh orange light.

Moving to his hearth, the half-giant checked the pots. *Both empty. That will not do.* Quickly starting the hearth fire and grabbing the kettle, he filled it and set it next to the fire to heat up. As it did, he grabbed a bag of his favorite tea, a braceroot and highberry leaf mix, and placed it in the kettle to steep as the water warmed. That done, he looked around for what food he had left. His stores of meat were basically empty, as he usually ate at the Dragon's Drink more than he did at home. All he really had left was oat groats, so he grabbed a pot and filled it with water from his personal well. Placing the pot next to the fire, he poured a generous helping of groats into the water and left them to simmer and cook. Shifting himself a moment later, he looked at the chest in the corner, hidden under blankets and other oddments.

He tried not to think about it. Tried to avoid looking at it, and at the warhammer that sat above his mantle. But both seemed to be calling to him. Whispering his name. Finally, he cried out.

"Torment me not! My days of adventuring are long past, damn you! Torment me no longer!"

But the whispering continued, just incoherent enough to make him feel like he was going mad. Shaking his head, the half-giant sank into a chair and scrubbed at his face with his hands. He was beginning to panic, now, thinking he'd gone round the bend. He was halfway into a trance when the sound of a hammer caught his attention. Quickly, he strode to the doorway into the forge. *There is no work today, I told them to spend Family-Day with their loved ones.* But when he looked into the forge, he found not any of his apprentices or journeymen. He found instead a massive figure, bending over the hot forge and staring into the coals as if entranced. Shakily, Viktor grabbed his warhammer, thinking the figure held ill intent.

"You there!" He called out with the sternest voice he could muster. The figure turned to see him standing with a cruel-looking warhammer in hand, and raised an eyebrow. A moment later, the figure laughed, a deep, rumbling belly laugh.

"As if you could harm me with such a weapon. I am of the hammer, boy. Now tell me, how do you tend to this forge?"

"It is usually tended by my apprentices. I focus my work with my dragon companions. Who are you that addresses me with demands?"

"Not a good answer. You may have dragons, child, but you need to remember to care for your charcoal forge as well. It will not do to let the coals burn out. Come, tell me where you store your coal."

Raising an eyebrow at the calm demands the figure was making, Viktor slowly lowered the hammer and pointed to the coal pile. Nodding, the figure shoveled fresh coal into the forge and cast a fire into it with what looked like no effort at all. Then they spoke again. Where Viktor had been unable to place the tone of their voice before, he suddenly realized that it was incredibly masculine, a deep, confident bass that nearly shook the walls.

"Now then. What were you working on?"

"I... I was repairing a mail shirt for one of the local Rangers."

"Splendid! Show me."

Strange and stranger. Viktor thought to himself, but nonetheless showed the massive figure his work. He seized the mail shirt and looked it over with a masterly eye, making the occasional noise of either approval or disapproval. Then he pulled the shirt away from his eye and looked it over from afar.

"Good work. A few loose rings, but nothing that would compromise the integrity of the shirt. Just as I expected from you, Viktor Kavabalt."

"You seem familiar with my name, and yet I do not know you."

"Oh, lad. You know me, even if you do not know this face. I am the iron you work, the forge you tend, the weapons you shape. I am the blood in your veins and the steel in the ground."

The realization hit Viktor like a hammer to the head, and he found himself unable to speak for a few moments. When he did, his words were but a whisper.

"Mydborh."

"Yes. You stand before the Master of Crafts himself, and all you have to say is my name?"

"I... I apologize, oh great Master of Crafts. I am simply awestruck by your presence. To what do I owe the honor?"

"Lad, you know better than most that formality has no

place in a forge. Be sensible, now and speak as one smith to another."

Swallowing hard as if that would help him work up the courage to speak as Mydborh wished him to, Viktor steadied himself against a post and tried to make himself look relaxed. It wasn't working, he knew in his mind, but the effort was there.

"What do you need of me, Mydborh?"

"You seek to fight against destiny. You think that by hiding away in your forge, you can avoid the inevitable. But you alone must realize this; war is coming. Northrealm is going to fall under the heel of an evil never seen. She will require you to take up arms in her name, and bring your weapons against your countrymen. You cannot hide from this. You must go to the Clans. Call a moot. Prepare their minds for war."

"But... I am no one, Mydborh. I am but one snowflake in an endless winter."

"No, you fool. You are Viktor Kavabalt, currently the last of the Bloodstone line. It is imperative that you find a way to end the evil that will face your lands."

"I am no adventurer... I have not been for many decades."

"It is in your blood, boy. You will remember your old ways when the time is right. And, you will learn just how precious one of your Forge-Seconds is."

Blinking, Viktor shook his head. This was all too much. All too strange. Suddenly, he wished that he *were* truly nothing than a smith in Coldforge. That his family name wasn't so important. That Mydborh did not *choose* his family to be his avatars. It was overwhelming to live up to, especially now that Mydborh was staring him down.

"Do not deny the truth of your blood. You may be the most

celebrated smith of Seran, but you are half-giant in blood. You have let that blood sit idle *far too long.* This must end. Now, your oats and tea are boiling, you had best attend to them."

Nodding, Viktor blinked and the Ancestor was gone. Shaking his head and wondering if he'd just fallen asleep, the half-giant made his way back into his home, hung his warhammer back above the mantle, and checked his pot and kettle. Both were boiling, so he removed them from the heat to cool somewhat, and watched as the bubbling slowed and stopped. A few more minutes and he poured himself a mug of the tea. Taking a swig, he grimaced. It tasted far too medicinal for his liking. Sighing, he fixed himself a bowl of groats, adding honey and fruit to it, and began eating absently. Occasionally sipping the tea, he grew used to the taste after a while and found it more pleasant.

A moment later, he heard the sound of a hammer again and cursed silently. Placing his bowl of oats and cup of tea on the table, he stood and strode to the doorway. He was about to call out, to voice his annoyance at the interruption, when he found himself staring at Helve, his forge-second and most trusted worker. Bewildered, he entered the forge and walked over to see what she was working on. It was the spear for the Kingmage's sister, one of the projects they'd been given. She seemed not to notice him at first, simply focusing on her work and ignoring all else.

After a few minutes of him staring, Helve shook her head and spoke.

"Are you just going to stand there agog at what I am doing? Or are you going to say something, Viktor?"

"What are you doing here, Helve? It is Family-Day, you

should be with your loved ones."

The glance she gave him was somewhere between kindly exasperation and a withering glare. He immediately regretted his words, and that well deepened when she spoke next.

"You know it is just me, Viktor. I have no one else. No one to look after, no one to look after me. I am alone."

Viktor sighed gently and mumbled an apology, to which she offered a rueful smile and bent back to her task, working on the spearhead further. Hammering the shape out and preparing it to have the edge ground in, making the socket, all of it. She was consumed by work, and after a while, Viktor found himself back in his home, sitting down to eat once more. The sound of the hammer was music, though he regretted his words. Shaking his head, Viktor finished his meal, cleansed the bowl and cup, and slipped back into the forge.

"We should talk, Helve." He began, and winced as she struck the hammer down a little harder than necessary.

"I am not one for small talk, Viktor."

"I am aware. But I am not *trying* to make small talk. I am trying to learn more about you."

Sighing, the woman tossed her head back, throwing her long, braided hair over her back. Taking the spearhead, she dunked it in the quench tank and looked at Viktor.

"So what do you need to know, Viktor? I can name off those who taught me, and where I come from, if that interests you."

"I am interested in *you*, Helve. Even if you do not wish to talk about yourself. Damnit, woman, look at me!" He was growing annoyed at her constant deflection, and when she turned, he rued his harsh tone. Her silver eyes flashed dangerously as she regarded him.

"You and I both know that tone will *not* sit well with me,

Viktor Kavabalt. So tell me what you want from me or fuck off." She was clearly getting pissed, and it showed in the way she spoke, the gritting of her teeth, all of it. After a moment, she sighed and the kind smile came back over her face. She muttered something to herself and looked back up at him.

"Why do you push yourself like this?"

"How many women work in your forge?"

"Hmm?"

"I am asking you, Viktor Kavabalt, to tell me how many women work in your forge."

Doing a quick mental tally of his journeymen and apprentices, Viktor blinked.

"Just... you."

"Which means I must be good at what I do to be good enough for the legendary Dragonforge of Coldforge. So tell me. How am I your Forge-Second?"

"Because you proved yourself the most capable out of all my workers."

"Exactly. I did not get this far on my looks, I got this far on my work. Which is why I push myself. Because I, according to some of the *men* who work here, *do not belong.*"

"Who said that? I will remove them–"

"No one has had the balls to say it, Viktor, but I can see it in the glances they give me."

That makes some sense, thought Viktor. As much as he liked his apprentices, they weren't a particularly brave lot. Some of them were stuck in ancient ways of thinking, and saw a woman such as Helve as a threat to their masculinity. So they expressed it in little ways. Ways that a normal man would avoid and just outright declare. He'd seen a little of it and had always done his best to put out the fire before it could grow, but apparently... *Well, some things tend to happen that way.* Sighing, he nodded gently.

"A few," she continued a moment later, "have even begun whispering about *putting me in my place.* And I welcome them to try." Her eyes sparkled maliciously. She wasn't about to get ramrodded out of her profession by fragile men. Viktor knew she had worked too hard to walk away. She consistently out worked *every* man in the forge, save for himself, and had even managed to get the dragons to work with her. For someone outside the Bloodline, this was completely unheard of, even among the Dragonsmithy. So Helve was something special, to be sure.

"Maybe you should stay in my home a while, Helve. Just until they cool off."

"They *will not* cool off, Viktor. It will fester until they decide to try something stupid. And in that moment, I will lay them out, one by one, and teach them what it means to live *nel cae armä.* However, I appreciate the invitation." Again, the malicious sparkle. She meant business, and Viktor knew she would take no quarter. He wasn't sure what the men she was speaking of had planned, but evidently, Helve had caught wind of it. So she planned to be ready.

"Do you even have a softer side?" He asked, half-jokingly, some time later.

"Do you look for the softer side of steel? The pleasant side of iron? Or do you work it just the same, heating it to where it bends to your will? Working it with love and devotion, until it becomes what you want?" She retorted, and Viktor couldn't tell if her words were about steel or something else.

Something stirred in Viktor at that moment. Something he didn't have a name for. He didn't know in the slightest. But for some reason, as Helve had said that, he found himself looking at her in a different light. The way the torchlight caught her auburn braids. How she shone like a polished blade, even in the dim light of the forge. Inwardly, he wondered what she looked like with her hair down. The thoughts massed on him quickly, and he knew he would think of little else for some time. It wasn't the first time she'd had this effect on him. Something told him it wouldn't be the last.

He had to step away. His head was spinning, and he had dreadful collywobbles out of nowhere. Slipping outside, he took a breath and sighed, wondering why all these feelings, these realizations, were hitting him *now*, of all times. Screwing his courage to the sticking place, he made his way back into the forge and went back to the mail shirt. Mydborh had inspected it and approved of it, so he wagered it was good enough for his eye. But every so often, he would cast a shy glance towards Helve, wondering what was on her mind.

Wondering if she was as tormented as he was, right now.

III

The First Rains

12

12: Littlebrook-Once-Besieged, Westerspring

When he had finished his sweep of Littlebrook, Thäoldr had found little life and it was near twilight. In the last house, however, he heard the wailing of a child- not of sadness or despair, but of hunger and confusion. Quickly, he stormed to the door, but found it locked. Shaking his head in wonder, he braced himself before slamming his foot just to the side of the door latch, collapsing the door instantly. He made his entry quickly and began searching the house.

There, in a sleeping-basket lay a young child who, by Thäoldr's estimate, could not be older than a few months. His brow furrowed in concern, and he could smell the death in the house. In another room lay the adults, too far gone even for pity. Shaking his head, Thäoldr made his choice- grabbing the child and carrying them out of the home as quickly as he could. Once out, he secured the wailing infant to himself and took off at a dead run towards the main gate where he knew the Rangers would be waiting.

"Rangers! Rangers! I need aid! I have a small child, the only survivor of their family!" He shouted when he approached the gate.

Immediately, the Rangers dropped what they were doing. Ayara, who was now cleaned up, was the first to run to Thäoldr. "Quickly, give her." As he handed the crying child over, Thäoldr looked to Karos, who looked as if he were ready to head out elsewhere.

"What are you planning, Warden Ranger?"

"I trust by your pace that this child is the only survivor of the town– thus, there is nothing more we can do. My orders from the Kingmage were to head to Cúledan immediately and thus I shall– but my Rangers will move elsewhere to aid those they still can." Karos looked to Ayara, who was already shedding her tunic, mail, and shirt. Then, off came her chest binder. Thäoldr immediately turned, his cheeks assuming a shade of red. Karos and the other Rangers looked on as Ayara began to feed the child.

"She is starving. I give thanks to the Ancestors that my breasts seem to always produce milk." Nodding his appreciation, Karos allowed Ayara to take his seat. Thäoldr still refused to look and finally spoke.

"Would you cover yourself? This is indecency!" Ayara looked unconcerned, and Nelya seized the chance to speak.

"Come now, Master Thäoldr. She is merely feeding a child. It is no more indecent than you not wearing a shirt."

"But her breasts–"

"Have more use than yours and are thus more important than your comfort. You do not command the hunger of a child, nor a Ranger who has a way to help. If you are so distraught that you cannot look, find yourself of use elsewhere!"

Karos could only look on and chuckle at the sound thrashing that the Rider had just endured and how he looked properly contrite. He had never tasted the lashing of a tongue in such a manner and was now worried that he had done some great insult to the Rangers. "I apologize, milady Ranger. I am just unused to women taking such freedoms."

"Then you had best grow used to it if you are to travel with Rangers, Thäoldr. I pity the women who have to live under your thumb if this is how you view such things as nudity." Shaking her head, Nelya moved to seat herself next to Ayara, who seemed quite content. Thäoldr took a deep breath and shook his head, wondering at his own reaction. They had the right of it, but scorch him if it was not shocking. He had many things to learn about the Rangers, it seemed.

"Ayara." Karos' voice snapped Thäoldr back to reality, and he looked up at the Warden Ranger, even though he was not the one addressed. "When you are ready, take the child back to *Ca'e Möratuk*. Protect her and raise her as best you can." Ayara nodded, accepting the responsibility that she had saddled herself with.

"You have not answered my question, Warden Ranger," came the stern voice of Kiri. "What are the rest of us to do?" She stood there, hands on her hips, staring down the man she had helped raise. It was high time the Warden Ranger revealed his plan to the rest of the folk with him, and Karos nodded.

"I will continue to Cúledan with all my haste. Kiri, Kizarian, you must seek any who still live in the area. Warn them away from the town and keep them away from each other. Nelya, stay with Ayara and protect her. Fae cos'Criux, I beg you to take your leave and find safety, but if you must remain, aid who you can. Thäoldr, I feel you may need to bring word of what has transpired to your people. For that I hope you fly fast and with the winds."

Thäoldr nodded and looked to Namryll, who exhaled a deep breath. The Rangers nodded, immediately moving to their assigned tasks, and Fae blinked. "I came to help, Warden Ranger. Not to be cast aside and told I can do nothing. I am an adventurer and know the herbs of the land. Let me help."

Karos sighed gently and shook his head. "It is too dange-"

Fae's words had a mocking tone to them. "Too dangerous for you, young Fae. Is that what you were about to say?" Her anger grew until she felt a calming hand on her shoulder. Kiri looked her over and nodded for a moment.

"You will do nicely."

"Do what? What am I doing, instead of giving your Warden Ranger a much-deserved kick to the groin?"

This brought a chuckle from all around. Thäoldr because he felt the Ranger deserved it, Kiri and the other Rangers because they knew it would be quite difficult for the girl to strike Karos. After all, he had a distressing tendency to move around. When Kiri regained herself, she spoke again. "I will need your help, mistress Fae, in keeping up my stores of healing herbs. In return, I shall teach you more of hand-healing if you wish."

Calming down, Fae nodded slowly and smiled. She was being allowed to be helpful, which is what she wanted. At least the other Rangers could be agreeable. Why was Karos so rude?

Having settled things there, Karos made his way away from the rest of the group. He was heading south, back into the wilds once more, to make his way to the next town- and eventually to Cúledan. He knew his path would be difficult, and he was more than ready for it.

Ayara fed the child for quite some time- but she was not surprised. Given how long the child had likely been without food, it was a wonder she was still alive. When she was finally content, the Ranger quickly donned her clothing and tied her cloak into a sling to carry the young one. After a moment, she scratched her chin and watched as the child fussed about. Then, nodding to Nelya, the two headed off, planning to make their way to the Caljen Gate and from there into Northrealm. "With Ynrasil's blessing, this child will grow strong. Perhaps she will even become a Ranger. But that is for the future to tell."

"Let us raise a prayer to Veljra that we do not encounter any unsavory characters on our path. Thäoldr!" Nelya's voice caught Thäoldr as he began preparing for his own journey and he glanced over. "You have done well today. Our thanks go with you." Thäoldr merely nodded in return and tightened down his belt. He had not had time for a proper meal, what with all the excitement.

We can get a meal when we reach Jorun's Watch. Ara bless that they have not been already taken. Thäoldr nodded at Namryll's words- indeed, he hoped that the Ancestress had protected them from this pestilence.

In his heart, he was afraid that it had already come. He threw his saddlebags over Namryll's great neck as she obediently bent down and launched himself into his saddle, throwing a leg over to drop into the other stirrup. Then, he fastened his flight-belts to keep him from falling to his death. He chuckled as he did, remembering when he was just a newblood, how annoying it was to hook up all the straps and belts. But when he had seen a young elf fall thousands of feet, he learned quickly how critical it was. *One does not reach your age by taking shortcuts, Thäoldr. Make your belts tight.*

The thought rattled in his head and he double-checked the lifeline belts. *Secure.* The dragon flexed her neck muscles, testing the belts as well- they held firm.

Secure, she echoed into Thäoldr's mind. Nodding, he slapped the great beast's neck gently in the silent command to take to the sky. Unfurling her wings, Namryll the Black bore her rider upwards into the darkening sky.

As they rose, they could see Karos, his form making good headway to the south and east, moving over the countryside like water. Thäoldr chuckled and urged Namryll up to flying altitude, before the black dragon turned and made their way south and west, breaking away from the group. In the back of his mind, though, the Rider made a note to find Karos at a later time. His gut told him it would be crucial to join the man's company again.

On the ground, Karos was moving at his best speed. The fields were rather uneven, but that did not bother the Ranger any. He was used to moving over such problems with impunity. Such was the way of the Rangers, being able to feel any obstacles ahead. As he ran through the fields, the night seemed to melt away; the darkness growing until he, even with his eyes accustomed, could barely see for the clouds. Taking a moment to slow himself down, he looked for the telltale magical glow that foretold a *tengjäv*, or Ranger cave. They built these over time into comfortable homes-away-from-home for the Rangers and far from towns. Built into natural caverns, they sealed the entryway with the magic of the Sk'av'A. They did this for a few reasons, the chief among them being protection. Few had the tools to get through a seemingly unassuming stone, and fewer still would bother.

Finding a path, the Ranger pursued it until he reached a sheer rock wall. Grinning beneath his mask, the man pulled out his spearhead pendant. Carefully, he placed the pendant into a slot on the wall and pressed his hand against the seemingly unyielding stone's face. Shifting his weight, he rolled the slab to the side, revealing a tunnel down into the cave itself. Removing his pendant from the wall, he stepped inside and the door closed behind him, taking on the appearance of flat stone once more. Down and down he made his way, and it comforted him when he heard voices nearby. As he rounded a corner into the first of the caverns, there was the great bonfire burning and around it sat a few Rangers, as well as folk he could not recognize. He tapped the wall gently and one ranger, a rather dour looking Khataan, turned and spoke. "Hail to you... Warden Ranger! By the Ancestors, what brings you out this way?"

"Nothing good, Kivrasa. Perhaps you have not seen the events going on? That Littlebrook has ceased to exist?" Kivrasa nodded slowly and gestured to the thirty-regular folk, sitting around the fire.

"These are the lucky few left alive. We brought them here to give shelter and the protection of the Ancestors, and it seems to work." Karos nodded appreciatively. *So they were not unaware of the situation.* "Tell me, Warden Ranger, have you seen Nelya or Ayara?"

Karos chuckled. "I just broke company with them and my Talons. Nelya and Ayara are off to *Ca'e Möratuk* on important matters- an infant found by the Rider Thäoldr." Kivrasa sucked in a breath- that they had found a child alive was both a blessing and a curse.

"I must beg your forgiveness then, Warden Ranger, for I sought all I could through the town and found no one. I have failed you." He went to kneel in apology and Karos motioned for him to rise to his feet once more. Closing the distance and shaking his head, the Warden Ranger patted the Khataan on the shoulder.

"It was by pure luck that Thäoldr found the child. I would not doubt that you checked for her." Gently, he pushed the other Ranger back down into a seat. "Now, I must find myself in the bathing pool. My muscles are sore and I must ruminate on the day's events."

Nodding, the Khataan waved Karos to a cavern far to the rear of the one they were currently in. Clapping his shoulder in thanks, Karos made his way past the throng, nodding to the Rangers he knew and the folk he did not. Then he passed the threshold into the bathing room and pulled the curtain closed behind him. Quickly stripping his clothes, armor and gear, he stepped into the rock pool, sighing as he entered waters heated by some unknown magic. Moving quickly to the deepest end, he took in a breath and dove to sit at the bottom of the pool for a time. Little by little, he eased himself down and sat, feeling the current of the water as it pushed and pulled at him.

Slowly, the past few days came back to him, the events flashing through his mind. Thäoldr was unexpected, but welcome. Looking back, he realized he should have been more than ready to listen. His help was appreciated and without it, an innocent child would have died alone. Hopefully, the child would thrive, but it was far too early to tell. Fae was another unexpected variable, and he hoped she would stay in strong health– *tyl syrinta* he wished upon her.

Today had been a dire day- there were nearly no survivors in Littlebrook, merely corpses everywhere. He sent up a silent prayer to Veljra, hoping that it would not be the case everywhere else he went. Otherwise, things would become worse. As he sat thinking, he felt the twinges at the edges of his thoughts- his *þrúnsaal* was trying to resurface. The thoughts of self-harm, self-destruction. The negative self-talk, all trying to come back. He fought down the thoughts until his lungs starved and he kicked off the bottom of the rock pool and ascended, blowing what was in his lungs out.

He breached the surface and took a deep breath, thinking to descend again- until he saw someone standing before him. The reddest hair he had ever seen and garments of a noblewoman. He blinked hard and when his eyes opened; the figure was gone. The vision shook him for a time and he realized it was a sign to think on. Another deep breath and he dove back down to sit upon the floor of the rock pool, this time his thoughts focusing on the figure he had just seen. There was no visible face, for she had been turned away from him, but he could make out many details of her form. She was but a few inches shorter than he, with the obvious red hair and had reasonably tan skin. Her dress was fashioned from brilliant red and purple cloth, with a belt inlaid with gold. The dress was loose fitting, but not enough to get in the way. The sleeves were wide enough to allow free arm movement, and the bodice was tied up the back, likely tight. He mused on what this vision could mean until his lungs again starved and then he surfaced, his shoulder-length hair flowing all around him. Moving to the edge of the bathing pool, he reached for a handful of soap-sand and began scrubbing himself dutifully, removing layers of dirt that had accumulated over the last few weeks.

When that was done and he was clean once more, the Ranger hauled himself out of the water. The cooler air hit him, though he did not give it much thought. Quickly seeking out a fresh towel, he dried himself off and pulled his clothing back together, quickly clothing himself once more. Once he was dressed and garbed appropriately, he stepped out of the bathing-room and stretched. The fire was still roaring, though there were less people sitting around it and a quick glance to the sleeping-room told him why. Most of them had gone to get what rest they could, given the circumstances. The sleeping areas were not the most comfortable, but at least one could get a full night in.

When Karos returned to the fire, he dropped himself onto a chair to sit next to one of his Rangers. He recognized the half-elf well but could not in his life place her name. "Ranger, your name has slipped my mind. Please, refresh me." The woman chuckled gently and shook her head.

"Were it anyone else, I would be insulted, Warden Ranger. But you have lived and heard many more names than I. I am Aryil Runvakt." Karos nodded, the memory flooding back to him. She was an older Ranger and the last time he had seen her was the Wild Nights celebration- fifty, maybe sixty years ago? He could not remember right now.

Patting Aryil's shoulder, the Warden Ranger spoke once more. "Your pardon I beg, Aryil. It has been six decades since last I spoke to you." She nodded and chuckled, confirming for him the time. Then, the half-elf reached over and gripped the back of his neck, shaking him mirthfully.

"My pardon I give, Warden Ranger. It is rarely I get to enjoy your company." *Not often enough*, thought Karos, *for I had pledged to know the face and name of every Ranger.* Evidently, he was failing at that goal, and that thought soured his mood somewhat. Before he realized what he was doing, he had taken a large pinch of sand from a nearby table and cast it into the fire. Immediately, the colors of the fire changed to a brilliant purple. The other Rangers drew closer, interested, and Karos spoke.

"*Ikii ia rakyivk,*" he began, invoking the High Ancestors and the ancestors of his people, "*kejg ekvi pe tajfa.*" A call to commune with the Ancestors- a dangerous thing for the unaware, but these Rangers knew their places.

"Who summoned the Ancestors?" A voice echoed in the minds of the Rangers assembled. A powerful voice, resonating with the authority of eons.

"It is I, Warden Ranger Karostrun anrak'Lyvan, Guidestar of the Rangers and a dead clan." Karos intoned carefully, keeping his eyes to the ground. The voice came again, this time seeming much calmer.

"Speak, Karos of clan Lyvan. What troubles your mind?" A woman's voice- carrying the wisdom of ages long past. A familiar voice to Karos and the Rangers. It was Veljra, Ancestress of the wildlands. She was the matron of the Rangers and was said to speak through the great twylan Eldest.

"Ranger of Highest Station, I seek counsel on the gravest of happenings. A plague is tearing through Seran. Littlebrook-Once-Besieged lies empty, nearly all her people dead. I ask of you and the rest of the Ancestors. Where did this plague come from? What have we done that displeases the Ancestors so?"

Veljra went silent for a few moments as she spoke with the other Ancestors, seeking knowledge from them. Karos took in a breath, steeling himself against the worst possibility- that the Seranese had brought this upon themselves by displeasing the Ancestors. This must have been in response to something, he thought.

The voice of his Ancestress roused him from his musing, and her words did little to comfort him. "This is not the work of the Ancestors, Karos. The Path is fuller than ever before. We do not know the origins of this plague. Do you know if the Archivist has found anything?"

So, the Ancestors knew nothing. Somehow that was far more disquieting to know than the alternative- that the world was displeasing the Ancestors. "I do not know. I am certain if she found anything, she would send word."

"Dyzysus has given word. This plague is born from magic- it has the taste of energy born from anger." *So, this comes from Seran... but who could have such energy, such command of magic?* Karos wondered.

Nodding slowly, Karos spoke once more. "I thank you, Veljra and the others in your company... I will do my best to sort this out quickly. This news is... not as comforting as I had hoped." He wondered how pathetic he must sound to the Ancestress. How tiny he must seem, with his mortal troubles.

"We will continue to ponder this trouble. If I learn anything, you will be the first to know, Warden Ranger. Goodbye and we shall be with you." With that, the flames returned to the normal orange color one would expect. The Rangers gathered were silent for quite some time, as each pondered the ramifications if what they had been told.

Aldin Longfoot, the courageous halfling, spoke first. "If this is the way of things, so be it. Karos, when you learn more, please inform us."

Nodding, Karos answered his friend, his voice sounding alien to himself. "But of course, Aldin. I have my Talons seeking answers and trying to heal those they can. I hope in time they will find a cure. I ask you to aid them however you can. Kiri Topalin and Kizarian Poloa are the two I am leaving here. With them is the elf-maid Fae cos'Criux, aiding in the search for herbs that may prove of worth." Nodding, the Rangers continued to converse well into the morning.

When the dawn's light struck the diffusing-stones that had been worked through the cave, the Rangers had come up with a definite plan. The Waywatcher and one other would remain and tend to the people taking shelter in the waycave and the others would join up with the two Talons in the area. Karos would continue his journey with all haste and hopefully arrive in Dragonmoor by the week's end. Thus, they adjourned to go about their tasks, with renewed hope for the coming days, dark as they already seemed.

Karos began gathering the supplies he would need, namely dried meat and pul'graan, and refilled his waterskins from the cave stream. He checked his sword, axe, knife, and arrows for any nicks, noting any he found for later. He had not the time to fix them now, but it would be worth keeping an eye out. That done, he made his way up the cave and out into the sunlight, closing the door behind him.

Squinting against the harsh light cast by Kjetta, the Ranger began making his way to the southwest once more. He was at a dead run once again, moving over the land like water. Over hill and river, he went as fast as his feet would carry him.

As he ran, Karos had much to ponder. *Where did this plague come from?* That was the question foremost on his mind. He knew of no one, the Kingmage included, that had the ability to create sickness. Even the scholars knew they could not create such things, only hold them at bay. So for one to pop up, especially one that the Healers seemed to know nothing about, was doubly troubling. Sighing, he pushed himself to his limit, sprinting across the land at a blistering pace. As night fell, he slowed his gait to a walk, found his way onto the High Road, and kept to it. Occasionally, he passed a signpost, declaring the approximate distance and direction between different towns. He didn't pause to look, though, as he knew the way by heart.

Glancing backwards, Karos thought he saw a shape in the gloom. It shifted form before his eyes and he blinked hard. Then it was gone, and he cursed silently. *It is happening again.* The visions. The... *what do the healers call them?* He couldn't find the word, but turned his focus back to the road ahead. It wouldn't do to be caught unawares, especially at night. Taking a deep breath, the Ranger did his best to steady his mind. It was getting worse, and he knew it in his heart. Something had to give, had to give soon, and he wasn't sure how bad it would be when it did.

Hiking along, Karos stopped only when he managed to spot a small town off the road. Searching his memory, he sought the name of the town and soon came up with it. *Easbrook.* A pleasant enough town, he knew. Altering his course, he made his way toward the town and to the Inn and Tavern that was the closest to the edge of the town. *The Minotaan's Lodge.* He remembered coming here. *What was it, eighty years ago?* He wondered if the proprietor was the same as back then, and figured he would find out soon enough. The building towered above him, tall enough on each floor that a minotaan, or minotaur, would have plenty of room to avoid bashing their head and horns on the rafters.

Pushing the door open with some difficulty, the Ranger slipped around the jamb and into the main room of the Tavern. As his eyes adjusted, Karos could see the lively scene within. Minotaan young and old bustled about, carrying food or drink. One, a grizzled-looking old bull, glanced up as the entry bell tinkled gently. Upon seeing who was entering, his face broke into a grin.

"Karos Lyvan!"

All activity stopped in the Tavern portion of the building. Everything went silent, and all eyes were on the Ranger, causing him to wince slightly. He hated being the center of attention. Finally, he spoke, his heart pounding in his ears.

"Hullo, Turgon!"

Once Karos had identified the bartender and strode into the room proper, things went back to normal. The minotaan, standing at just over a spearlength, strode out from behind the bar, throwing a rag over his shoulder. He made his way through the mass of tables and people over to Karos and seized the man in a bear hug, lifting him off the ground for a moment and crushing the breath out of him. A moment later, the minotaan set the Ranger back on his feet, giving the man room to wheeze and catch his breath.

"By the Ancestors, Turgon! You almost broke my ribs!"

The bull let out a deep rumbling laugh and gently slapped the man on the shoulder.

"Come, come, let us sit and talk. You have missed much."

"I would find that helpful, Turgon. I have things to discuss with you." His voice dropped, and so did Turgon's expression. The bull looked suddenly quite rueful as the two made their way to a private booth and sat across from each other. One of the younger minotaan made their way over and spoke with a gentle, feminine voice.

"Good evening, Ranger. Father, your usual?"

The minotaan nodded and waved at Karos to speak.

"I would like a bowl of hunter's stew and mug of cider, please."

The young heifer nodded and scribbled down something before stepping away. As soon as she was away, Karos cleared his throat.

"I must press you for information before I hear any news."

"But you *need* to hear this news, mate. It is not good, either."

"Very well. Speak your piece, and then I shall inform you of the oncoming doom."

The minotaan shook his head gently and sighed. Steepling his fingers in front of him and thinking for a moment, he came up with what he needed to tell the Ranger.

"The town has sickened. Something has affected the people, and from what I have seen, it is quite gruesome. I have been trying to warn people away from the town, and have kept things civil. I dare not speak louder, lest I cause a panic, because the people in town who have not been affected have fled to your *tengjäv* places. There they hope for protection against this evil, but... well, as much faith as I have in your people, Karos... I do not think they can stem this tide."

Karos nodded slowly. *So he does know already. That takes that weight off my shoulders.* Sighing, he looked at the minotaan, his old friend, and spoke again.

"I am on my way to Cúledan, which by all word is the center of this plague. I make my best speed, but the night is moonless and too dark for even my eyes."

"Then you need a safe place to stay."

"I will make my way to the Ranger cabins outside town. I wished to stop here, though, to get a meal and press you for what you knew, and pass along a warning."

"What warning is that?"

"Beware of your own body. Do not let yourself be exposed to this grief, and keep your kin safe as well. We do not know yet who is unaffected, but so far, I have found only my *tengarii* immune."

Sucking in a breath, the minotaan nodded stonily. He'd already learned that much the hard way. But he had not sickened, at least, which gave him hope. *But how long can we rely on such?* A moment later, he reached out and grabbed Karos' hands.

"Listen to me, Ranger. Let nothing stop you from solving this puzzle. I call upon you as friend and comrade. Do not let our world fall. Make alliances with whomever you must, and spare not your pride."

Karos nodded slowly, wondering what the old bull knew. It was disconcerting how connected to the Tapestry such beings could be, but after a moment, he wagered it was simply because the bull-man had his ear to the ground at all times, being an innkeeper. As such, he was somewhat expected to be a collector and disseminator of information. The bull released his hands and scratched the back of his neck as his daughter brought the requested food. She set a hearty helping of salad and milk for him and a bowl of stew and hot cider for the Ranger before them, and both dug in ravenously. Turgon realized he'd gone his entire shift without eating, which he chastised himself for, and wondered just how long it'd been since Karos had eaten. *A week or more, if my wager is right.* He still wondered how the Rangers survived punishing themselves so. But it seemed to work for them, so he wasn't one to judge.

Flicking his ears a couple times, Turgon finished his meal and sat back in the large chair that'd been carved for him. Eyeing the Ranger, the bull went to speak again. But Karos' voice erupted quicker in the silence.

"You will, of course, keep track of comings and goings for me?"

"Of course, Karos. I will make sure to note down any that come by my inn and their character and number."

Nodding, Karos finished his meal and laid a handful of gold Aureim coins on the table. Turgon was about to protest when the Ranger shot him a glance, and he put his hands up in surrender. Then, the Ranger was out the door and headed to the edge of town where a pair of cabins sat. There was light coming from the windows of both cabins, and as the Warden Ranger made his way to the campfire out front of them, a voice hailed him.

"Oi! Fuck are you?"

Turning to spot a trio of street ruffians approaching, Karos raised an eyebrow. A gentle sigh escaped him and he mentally prepared himself for a scuffle.

"A Ranger. On business, so you should mind your own."

"Oh, a Ranger, eh? We do not like your kind around here."

"And you accost me so close to where other Rangers rest?"

"Ah, but you are alone. And we are more than a match for you, mate. So watch your manners. Now you best hand over all the coin you carry. We saw how much you dropped in the inn. Hand the rest over."

Sighing, Karos thought for a moment about unsheathing

Northrage, his precious sword. He thought better of it a moment later and simply dropped into a *ljas'atuk* stance. One foot to the side, slightly outward for balance. The other foot pointed towards the threat. Hands up, curled, not clenched, elbows in. Shoulders squared.

"Oh ho! You think you are enough to match us?"

"Let me say it plain. If you can last five minutes against me, I will gift you each a Sereim."

"By the time we are done with you, you shan't have need of your coin."

The man watched as the trio began to break apart, intent on circling around him. He took in a breath, let it out, and traced a line in the dirt. He wasn't planning on letting them overtake him, but he knew they were dangerous. One was carrying a large sax knife. Another carried a shortspear, and the third was wielding a bladed club. Out of the three weapons, the club was the most concerning to him, for even with his gear, a good thump would break bones. Luckily, it was the leader of the group that carried it, so that made him the primary target. *Take down the leader and the others will likely scramble*, he told himself. The leader closed in, and the two circling around dove for Karos, weapons coming at him.

Three things happened at once. Karos dove to the ground, causing the two coming from the sides to collide heavily. Then he rolled and came up too close for the club to be of any use. Grabbing the leader on both sides of his head, Karos slammed his forehead into the man's face. Once. Twice. Thrice. He crumpled, insensate. The Ranger turned to the others as they attempted to regain their footing.

He was about to go after them as they raised their weapons, when suddenly he heard the ever-so-fine twanging of bowstrings. The sax knife flew from its wielder's hand, landing point-first in the dirt. Then the spear carrier let out a cry as his hand became somewhat more permanently attached to his weapon, pierced through by a cruel shaft. The man turned in shock to see a Ranger standing there, eyes afire.

"Oh, do try something else. You three have been a thorn in my side for *months*."

The Ranger's eyes sparkled maliciously as she stood, an arrow nocked on a taut string.

"Or," said Karos placatingly, "you could carry your leader off and run like the scared little boys you are. If you do, she will not follow you."

The Ranger let out a soft growl, but at a warning glance from Karos, went silent. The men thought about their options for a minute, and the one with the spear reached up and yanked the arrow out of his hand. Then he turned the rest of his body around and grinned.

"A little girl thinks she can take me?"

Karos groaned. The other man was edging toward his sax knife, thinking he was sneaky. Their leader was on the ground, blood still trickling from his shattered nose. He was at least breathing, which is more than Karos could say would happen to the other two.

It happened in a flash. The man aimed his spear at the female Ranger, who stood at least two heads shorter than he, and charged. A moment later, he was sailing through the air *sans* his spear, and landed with a dull *thwack*. He didn't move after that. Either out of injury or fear, Karos couldn't tell. The woman hadn't even taken her hands off her bow and had thrown the man with just her shoulder and legs. The other man leapt at Karos, brandishing the sax knife, and Karos turned, moved around the incoming blade, and delivered a bone-crushing punch into the man's guts. He stayed there for a moment, hung up on Karos' fist, unable to breathe or even function, before the Ranger pulled his hand away and let the man drop to the ground.

"Gather their weapons." Came the command from the man, and the woman let out a shout of assent and immediately grabbed the spear, club, and sax.

"Bind their hands," she commanded Karos, and he nodded, quickly pulling a length of rope from his pack and dragging the three men together in a sitting position. Then he bound their hands together, leaving just enough room for blood flow to be maintained. But he made certain that any movement would cause shrieking agony.

"You are?" The woman asked a moment later, looking up at the towering man.

"Karos."

"Warden Ranger." She breathed, barely willing to believe it. As she went to take a knee, he seized her collar and hauled her back to her feet.

"Ranger, you do not kneel to me."

"But, Warden Ranger. It is an honor."

"The honor is mine, *tengar*. You struck like a viper, how did you manage that?" He gestured to the man she'd thrown. He'd seen her move, but still couldn't believe that she'd thrown him without using her hands.

"Oh... A little trick from my *saal'kwen*. You might know her. Sardra Wood-Strider."

Karos' eyes sparked at the mention of his *valtagt* and closest friend.

"Oh yes. I have a few tales I could tell you, *tengar*. But come, let us haul these three off to the guards. I have little time, and I must away at dawn."

The woman nodded and helped the Warden Ranger haul the unfortunate fools to the guardhouse and drop them off. Then, they walked back to the cabins together and sat for a time, with Karos regaling her with tales of Sardra in her Tenderfoot years, and how she became his most trusted of Talons and Rangers. She was in pure awe at what the she-wolf had accomplished in such a brief span of time, and how ferociously Karos applauded her. According to him, she fought like a beast cornered and routinely put more experienced Rangers in the dirt.

When dawn came, the Rangers parted company and Karos once more took off at a breakneck pace over the fields and meadows. As he crossed the border of the Easbrook farmlands into the fief of Jorlin, he heard a cry from above.

13

14: Westerspring, Dragonmoor

Thäoldr, meanwhile, had made Jorun's Watch and what greeted him was a scene of such strange tranquility it made him wary. There was no activity outside, no newbloods being trained and no winged beasts present- at least, not that he could see. Dismounting quickly, he ran to the door and slammed it open, to find the watchrider sitting by the fire. The door slamming open of course jarred him from what he was doing and he rounded, sword in hand.

"Peace, watchrider. I am Thäoldr, rider of Namryll. I come with grave news."

"More grave news? I am wearied by such things. Already I have heard much of death from the local towns, of pain and worse. If you have such news... please spare me."

"The Rangers have asked for our aid. Littlebrook is all but extinguished. Worse, it sounds, for the city of Cúledan."

"Scorchitall, man. I said spare me. Ill news is an unwelcome guest, for already we have had riders taken sick with some strange illness. They are upstairs in the resting rooms. I am the only one not afflicted as yet, so I tend to them. I long for battle, though, something worthy of a rider!" Thäoldr shook his head and strode across the room to seize and shake the man.

"Rider listen to me! We must inform the Council of Wind. I remember your face- you are the rider of the griffon Sahralos. He is far faster than my Namryll. You must go quickly."

"I cannot abandon my riders, Thäoldr!"

"They are already lost, you fool! Unless the Council of Winds is informed- unless we work with the Rangers, all will be lost!"

"Thäoldr, you may be the Paragon of Knowledge, but this is my watchtower. If you wish to involve the Council in your meddling with Rangers, that is your duty. Not mine. Now get out!"

Thäoldr sighed and stormed from Jorun's Watch. *That went... much worse than I expected,* he thought to himself, *but my mind remains settled.* Looking to Namryll, he spoke his mind. "If that fool will not aid us, then we will go to the Keep."

You will need supplies, the dragon spoke, *but it would help to have an ally in this.*

"Who would be our ally, Namryll? Surely none of the riders within can help."

He nearly leapt from his skin as a voice issued from behind him. He turned, his sword at the ready, and saw a lithe young woman. "I will help you, Thäoldr!"

The rider eyed the woman warily. He did not recognize her at all, but she was wearing rider garb. "Who are you? How can you possibly aid me?" He could not remember her face and was unsure if she was even a rider- he felt no other beasts nearby. "You are no rider. I feel no beast nearby other than

Namryll."

"I am a rider, Thäoldr! I am Trässa and my Iftra is the fastest of the Khataar griffons!"

As if on cue, a shadow blew overhead at an eye-popping speed. One circle around the tower and the beast landed. A small griffon she was, her feathers decorated in blue and gold with a black stripe down her back, but a griffon she was. Thäoldr nodded slowly, already impressed by how the woman had hid her beast. Normally he could quite sense riders and their beasts, however, both of them had slipped beneath his notice. "Very well, Trässa. You and Iftra will aid me. We must head to Ormere Keep with all haste. But I have not eaten in some time."

Trässa nodded and waved at Thäoldr to follow her. Quickly, she brought him to a small cave nearby. A supply cache, for any who needed to pack up in a hurry. Working quickly with her magic, she heated a small pot of soup after peeling the wax seal away. Then, she placed it on a stump for him. "It will not do to have you falling from your saddle from hunger, Thäoldr. We must ride far. I heard you mention Cúledan. Would it do for me to continue on to Ormere, while you see what you can do there?"

Thäoldr gave her words consideration. It was a good thought, and he nodded slowly. "If that is the case- then there is someone we could help who must get there as well." He ate quickly, speaking in between bites of food. When he had finished, he handed back the pot. The meager meal had done little to bed his appetite, but it was enough for the trip. Gulping down some water from his skin, he nodded to the girl. "Come then, let us be away. If the watchrider will not help us-"

"We shall do it ourselves!" Trässa jumped to her feet and clapped, before jogging briskly to where Iftra sat preening. She clapped again, and the beast jumped to the ready, slightly lowering her shoulder to allow her rider to climb aboard. Once she had seated herself, Trässa quickly linked up her belts, securing them down tight and slapping the back of the beast's neck. "Secure!" she called out to the night, and the beast let out a shrill cry in return. Coiling back on her haunches, Iftra folded her wings tight to avoid breaking them against the Watchtower or the trees. Then, half a breath later, she bolted into the sky, before Thäoldr had finished securing his own straps. Iftra unfurled her wings at the apex of her leap and began beating them to keep in place while they waited for the hulking dragon.

"Secure!" He cried out once he finished linking his belts and tightening them. Namryll felt the tension and bobbed her head slowly. *Secure,* she thought at Thäoldr, and *who are we assisting to Cúledan?* She was curious about this, for he had not discussed the thought with her. Far from being against it, she welcomed the idea of helping another, but all she could think of was Karos. *Is it Karos?* "Aye." He did not enjoy the idea of working with the difficult Warden Ranger- but his thinking had led him to only one solution: The Order of Gelvrentael working with the Rangers. It boggled his mind to think, especially after the feud lasting millennia. None were alive who could even remember the spilling of bad blood that led to this.

As they rose, he let out a cry to any who were listening. The ears it reached were not of Seran, but the High Ancestors themselves. "It is time to put aside the Order of Telhrahan. May this feud die today! This I swear by the Ancestors and the sky! That for the good of Seran- the Riders shall join forces with the Rangers, even if I am the only one to aid them."

Namryll let out a cry, as did Iftra. Trässa whooped, and the riders winged into the rising sun- towards dangers untold and towards the future. They winged hard to the south and east, with Trässa and Iftra ranging far ahead, trying to spot the Warden Ranger based on the mental image given by Thäoldr.

They had been flying for hours when Iftra let out a cry and dove. Namryll dove after her and Trässa let out a whoop of excitement. The cry that had issued forth was Iftra's hunting call, meaning she had spotted Karos. Or maybe a fat deer. Either was possible right now. They dropped like a stone and back-winged just in time to avoid colliding with the ground. The resultant burst of air knocked Karos flat and his first instinct told him he was under attack. Rolling to his back, he threw his feet under him and drew his sword in time to see Namryll drop from the sky. The griffon let out a smug cry and dropped to the ground, followed by the great black dragon. Karos' calm demeanor broke, and he spoke first. "Thäoldr, what is the meaning of this? I thought your goal was to inform your people of what had transpired?"

"I met with a fool at Jorun's Watch and it gave me think. The Riders trust the Rangers not, for an old feud exists, written in blood long ago. This I intend to correct, for the good of all, Karos." As Thäoldr spoke, he undid his belts and slid from the noble beast's neck. Following him, Trässa slid from her saddle and Karos sheathed his sword. His surprise doubled when Thäoldr closed the distance and drew his sword. Karos barely had time to react, thinking this was an attack. His sword already back in its sheath. He drew his long-knife and prepared his stance, ready to fight off both. To his shock,

Thäoldr placed the flat of his blade in the palm of his hand and drew a deep gash in his hand. "Warden Ranger Karos. I ask of thee now to forget old hatreds. To put aside your distrust of the Order of Gelvrentael as I put aside my distrust of the Rangers. That we work together for the betterment of all and use our considerable resources to help all of Seran. That the feud between Rider and Ranger be forgotten and a blood oath made."

Karos let out a yell of surprise and quickly drew his blade across the palm of his hand, inflicting his own deep gash. He regarded the old, scarred elf warily and extended his bleeding hand. Thäoldr gripped it and Karos spoke. "By the Warden Ranger, is your oath heard and witnessed."

From the powerful throat of Namryll came a cry in the common tongue, echoing far and wide. "HEARD AND WITNESSED!" At the same moment, Iftra let out a scream that pierced even the heavens- and the Ancestors bore witness. From the power of Thäoldr's oath, lightning erupted from a cloudless sky and was met with shields of light from the energy of Karos' answer. The noise was deafening as both forgot old grudges against each other's people and Trässa stood stunned. Never had she witnessed such a blood oath, one that shook the bonds of the world in such a way. There were millennia behind the feud between Ranger and Rider. This she knew and had been taught. But never in her wildest dreams would she have imagined she would see it cast aside. The energy from both man and beast was such that Trässa echoed the dragon's call, adding her own witness to the historic event. Both men sheathed their weapons, but kept their hands locked.

The storm settled, and both men looked at each other as if

they were seeing the other for the first time. Karos regarded the aged elf, an old but powerful man covered in scars. His piercing blue eyes seemed to stare directly through Karos and his smile was permanently curled up on the left side- a remnant of some ancient fight. Probably that had happened long before Karos was even born. His head was bald, not a trace of hair to be seen. He had a stern countenance partly hidden by the wisps of a beard and Karos could tell that it was from the weight of knowledge untold. Karos could feel the powerful way he stood, the way he moved with grace and dignity- the movements of a teacher who knew far more than he could ever let on. If he had to, he would almost describe him as intimidating. He had gained a great ally.

Thäoldr regarded the much younger man as Karos pulled down his mask, looking into his amber eyes. They were blood sworn brothers now, and he etched the man's face into his memory. The black hair atop his head, coming down onto his shoulder in a ponytail. The many scars and pockmarks from being out in the weather far too often. The confident way he held himself, as if he could face the world alone and outfight most of it. This was a man who was more dangerous than a legion of Riders but held himself in check for reasons unknown. He had gained a powerful ally, and he hoped a good friend.

"Now. We have wasted enough time, Karos. You move with impressive haste, but I have a way to move faster." He gestured to Namryll, who was already bending down to allow her rider and the passenger to climb aboard. "Mount up and let us fly with all the winds behind us." Karos nodded and released Thäoldr's hand, watching as the cut on his own healed. Likewise, Thäoldr looked to his palm, surprised as he felt the bisected flesh reknit itself. Turning, he led the Ranger to the magnificent beast and moved to offer him help to climb up to her neck, when he saw the Ranger had already gauged the distance and vaulted himself up behind the saddle. Namryll rumbled her approval and Thäoldr climbed aboard before handing one of the flight straps to Karos. "Pull it tight and secure yourself to Namryll's neck." Quickly, he looped the remaining flight strap through the appropriate buckle and pulled it taught. Karos thought quickly and looped the belt through his own belt buckle, wondering how this would end up. Mentally, he pictured himself dangling below the beast's neck and hanging there for most of the flight. He slapped Thäoldr's shoulder and Thäoldr bellowed out. "Secure!" Namryll tested the straps and nodded, echoing in both men's minds. Secure.

With that, the great dragon beat her wings, sending small tornadoes away as she rose into the sky once more. Iftra and Trässa followed soon after and the group took off to the southeast with renewed purpose. Wings beating strongly, Namryll bore the unfamiliar weight proudly. Karos was an inconsiderable weight compared to some things she had had to carry, but she would not deny the significance of what just happened. Her own rider, The Paragon of Knowledge, had thrown away a custom built before he was newblood.

Hours later, as they passed over Nevian, the group climbed higher into the sky, above the clouds. It would not do to be spotted in such a place, as the native people held a deep hatred for the Riders and the Rangers. They were wise to limit their time, though, and soon crossed the Wyrmspine Mountains, said to be the remains of a massive elemental dragon the likes of which the world has not seen since the World forging.

Karos, for one, was glad such a beast was only a legend and he doubted the combined might of all the armies could bring one down. He shook his head slightly and looked below as the group broke into Dragonmoor's sky. Already the air felt more energetic and Thäoldr could feel tingles thrill through his fingers. As they descended, the feeling only increased, causing a high in both the riders- Karos felt nothing, though. His senses were attuned, but the pathways of magic never formed correctly in his body, muting his response to such magic by a large degree. He would find no advantage here.

The flight continued until Karos let out a sharp cry. "Down! We must land!" Thäoldr wondered what had gotten into the Warden Ranger and reluctantly urged Namryll towards the ground. She was far more willing, having already seen what Karos was seeing. A Ranger, back-to-back with someone wearing the torn garb of a slave, against many foes. The riders chose this moment to show what their beasts were truly capable of and coordinated. Iftra dropped farther, furling her wings, and extending her talons. Three foes she grabbed in her first pass and as she did, Trässa felled one with a well-placed blast of flames. Namryll dropped close to the ground and let out a gout of terrible black flame, incinerating two. Karos quickly unloosed his belt and dropped from the beast's back, rolling as he hit the ground. What he saw enraged him, and his sword snapped from its sheath.

The Ranger was fighting on, despite wounds that looked grave. Something likewise had heavily injured the slave and she fighting for her life. As the Warden Ranger approached, he felled two of their foes. One with a simple thrust through the back and another ended as he sliced their head from their shoulders. The Ranger let out a cry of relief as she saw the Warden Ranger and urged him on. Above, the dragon and griffon continued their assault, burning and tearing at the foes until their numbers dwindled from 30 to two in a span of minutes. Karos wondered to himself how long the Riders would truly need the Rangers with such power at their command but was happy for the intercession.

One foe charged the slave, who was tiring and slowing from her wounds. Seizing the chance, Karos rushed in, putting his body between the two combatants. Up came his sword in a dazzling array of thrusts and slashes, meant to test his foe. They were expertly blocked, showing that this man was a cut above the usual reckless slaver. A glance over him confirmed why- this man was a knight, his sigil marked out by charcoal paint, showing that he no longer believed as his contemporaries did. He was clanless and extremely dangerous.

"Ranger! Speak! What brought you to this fight?" Karos shouted as he deflected a thrust intended for his heart. Drawing close, he intended to put the larger opponent off balance with attacks of speed. Putting thought to action, he pressed the attack in a dizzying fashion, his sword probing the enemy's defenses. Finding a weakness, he dove in, twisting to avoid the knight's blade as his own blade found purchase on the man's flesh. The former knight let out a squeal of pain that turned far worse, as the magic of Karos' blade Northrage worked. While the skin inside the wound sizzled and burn, while the outer edges froze to the point of agony. The knight let out a pained yelp and leapt back, bringing his blade in a downward arc. *Last mistake*, thought Karos as he deflected the clumsy attack. As his foe's sword slid outward, Karos brought his own sword in and slashed the man's chest, opening a gaping wound. Again, it froze and burned and the man cried out in pain. Pressing his advantage, Karos leapt in and rushed and ran him through, ending his pain and reign of terror.

"Protecting a slave when we were ambushed. I have fought as best I can, Warden Ranger... But I am spent." The last enemy fell and so too did the Ranger. Her breathing was labored and ragged as Karos ran to her side. When he arrived, he saw that a multitude of arrows pierced her and wondered how she had kept fighting- and for how long she had been protecting the slave girl.

"Elliana. Stay with me!" Karos cried out as he pulled a potion from his pack. The woman weakly pushed it away as he brought it around.

"I am sorry, Warden Ranger... I have nothing left... Protect the girl..." After choking her words out, Elliana cos'Halara, Ranger from the Farlands, breathed her last. His heart heavy, he reached forward and placed a hand on her forehead, gently applying pressure to close her eyes. The slave girl limped over and slumped next to her and spoke, her voice quiet.

"I am sorry... she fought well."

"She was a Ranger. She did what we expected and will live on in our memories." After a moment of thought, he spoke once more. "Veljra, Mother of Rangers. Take Elliana cos'Halara into your arms. Comfort her and give her peace. Let her join the Great Hunt by your side, I pray. She lived and died well and rests now forevermore." His voice resonated with energy during the prayer and Thäoldr, who had landed some time ago, spoke.

"She will be remembered, but what will be done with her body?"

Karos looked the man in the eye. "I would ask you or your

dragon to incinerate it. It is the way of our people."

Thäoldr nodded and spoke to his dragon, his face revealing no emotion. Immediately, the dragon began moving over and the two men bore the slave girl away. In a moment, Namryll reared back and unleashed the purest fire she could, aiming it toward the form of the Ranger. In a moment, the flames struck and Elliana cos'Halara became a memory in the minds of the Rangers, to be honored and sung forevermore. The slave girl wept, fearing that she would have no advocate, no voice now. Then the Warden Ranger turned to her.

Already, those around could hear wolves howling and Karos turned to the injured slave. "Come, girl, drink this. It will protect you from further harm and give us time to heal your wounds. Thäoldr, I trust you are skilled at healing with magic?" Thäoldr nodded as the girl drank the potion. Normally, she would be cautious of strange liquids handed to her, given what she had recently endured. But she had nothing left to lose, so why bother with fear?

Thäoldr reached out, pushing his sleeve out of the way. He then touched one of his many tattoos, causing it to glow. Extending his arm to touch the woman's shoulder, he pushed some of his life force into her. Her wounds glowed and closed, while the internal damage healed thanks to the magic in the potion. When the deed was done, her wounds had sealed into jagged scars- those would remain forever. "The scars will remain- but you are healed."

The girl looked from one man to the other, and she gave voice to a question. "What am I to do now?" Karos eyed her severely before looking to Thäoldr.

"She would not be safe in Cúledan. We must find a *tengjäv*."

"A what, Karos?"

"A Ranger waycave. Fortifications built into the ground itself. Homes. She will be safer there than with us."

"Agreed. So where is the nearest *tengjäv?*"

Karos removed a well-worn map from his belt and smiled beneath his mask. Quickly unrolling it, he focused his mind and thoughts on the things he sought- safety, warmth, food, healing and companionship. Slowly, the world's details faded from the map, to be replaced with an arrowhead representing Karos. The compass rose was still visible, and a path shimmered and show on the map. It flew from the arrowhead, going quite some distance to the north. Karos nodded and jabbed a finger at the end of the path. "Roughly six leagues to the north. On the edge of the Vadayen Forest. Thäoldr, I must ask you or your other Rider to bear us both to the tengjäv. Please."

Thäoldr growled somewhat. The man was his blood brother, but this was asking a bit much of the proud beast and her rider. "Karos, we are not a steed for your eas-" A sharp growl from his dragon interrupted him. Turning, he looked at the magnificent beast and nodded a moment later. "-but Namryll is happy to carry the burden for this purpose." He wondered for a moment if the dragon was embracing a more open outlook on things than he was. *That would not do,* thought Thäoldr, *so I must change as well.* He was not one to consider being left behind by changing times.

Karos raised an eyebrow before chuckling at the exchange between rider and dragon. He took a deep breath and looked at the woman. "Come. Rider Thäoldr has agreed to bear you to the tengjäv. Lady...?"

"I am no lady, master Ranger. I am Isilda, daughter of Piyra."

"And I am not your master. I am Karos, son of Myran. This is Thäoldr of the Order of Gelvrentael."

The woman nodded slowly and took a breath, steeling herself for what was to come. She did not enjoy the idea of flying, but if it meant safety, so be it. When directed, she took to the dragon's back, sitting between Karos and Thäoldr for safety. A signal from Thäoldr and Namryll was airborne once more, gladly carrying the woman to safety.

To the north, they flew as fast as they could. Iftra cruised ahead, keeping her eyes ranging from any threats or folk in need. Being a griffon, she could see quite a way further than a dragon, and that often helped the riders greatly. Soon enough, Iftra let out a screech and dropped as a Ranger was running below. One low pass to catch the Ranger's attention and her rider called out. "Ranger! Ranger!"

Hand on his sword, Etric Vansala stopped in his tracks, wondering if he was about to be assaulted. *This close to a tengjäv*, thought the man, *they must be desperate indeed for someone to assail.* It quite surprised him to see the massive black dragon wing down with– was that Karos on its back? He was about to demand an explanation as the dragon landed, when Karos and a rather ragged looking girl slid off the beast's neck. "Etric! Thank the Ancestors. Quickly, this woman needs shelter. She was with Elliana cos'Halara." Etric's face lit up for a moment at the mention of his friend's name; but when he saw the sadness in Karos' eyes, his heart sank.

"Where is she?" He asked, unsure if he wanted to hear the answer.

"She walks with Veljra." Etric sighed at that answer. Looking down for a moment, he nodded.

"Then I hope the foe that sent her there met a fighting

end." Karos nodded this time and reached out to pat the man's shoulder. He knew right well what it was like to lose a friend, for he had lost many over his years.

"A single arrow may fell the greatest warrior- and she fought though pierced by many. Sing her praises for as long as you have a voice, Etric, for she earned her rest well." Etric looked up, regarding Karos in a new light after those words. Then he nodded and placed his hand on Karos' arm, giving a thankful squeeze.

Then, he asked in his mind. "How are you in the company of Riders? I thought their animosity endless!"

Karos went to speak, but before he had the chance, Thäoldr seized the moment. "Karos and I made a blood pact that the old hatred dies. I have been working with him since we arrived at Littlebrook, and I hope that both Ranger and Rider forget the foolishness that led us to be so hateful to one another. It may take time, but my riders will be at your aid, Ranger." Etric nodded in astonishment. This was completely unexpected, but not unwelcome. Rangers and Riders united would prove a formidable force when wielded for the good of the people.

"Now, brave Etric. I leave this woman Isilda in your care. Protect her as you would your own blood." Etric nodded slowly, readying himself for the task ahead. He was the way-watcher and could not leave his post. What luck then that one of the itinerant Rangers was a guest at his cave and thus could take the woman where she would be best served.

"It shall be done, Warden Ranger. I have Ysatta Flooding-Waters with me. I shall ask her to escort lady Isilda to Tejg Sungetiigd." Karos nodded quickly. That would serve best and on the way, Ysatta could pose The Choice to the woman. Give her the chance to become a Ranger or be protected at

Mount Wounds-End. Waving a goodbye to the other Ranger, Karos saddled back up behind Thäoldr, who was eager to be back on task. Trässa was likewise ready to be on the move, as Iftra lazily hovered above. Thäoldr and Karos checked their straps and when they were satisfied, both men shouted.

"Secure!"

"Secure!"

When she had checked the feeling of the straps against her skin for the correct tension, Namryll let out a rumbled, "Secure." and began flapping her wings to gain altitude, pushing small tornadoes of dirt and dust away from her. Up and up she rose, her powerful form once more bearing the two men into the sky. When they rejoined the other rider, Thäoldr rose one hand as a signal to Trässa and she readied herself for Iftra's powerful start. Thäoldr dropped his hand and Iftra took the signal, her wings driving powerful winds behind her and pushing her forward. Namryll followed, making her way above the griffon to allow both free movement.

As the hours passed, the plains of Dragonmoor flew beneath the group. Midday had come and gone and twilight was coming soon when they reached their goal. There ahead of them lay the city of Cúledan. Immediately, the group could tell things were amiss. No watchrider to greet them, no banners flying. Even from afar, there should be some signs of life. "I dislike this. There should have been a watchrider to call out." Karos nodded slowly as the great dragon descended. As they began gliding down towards the city's gate, Thäoldr half wondered if they would find it as dead as Littlebrook. He mused on this for a moment, when Karos let out a cry.

"Thäoldr! Land over there!" He shouted, gesturing to a small campsite a way away from the gate. Nodding, Thäoldr urged Namryll to light where he was told, and he could see why Karos had chosen that site. A collection of Rangers awaited them there, as well as a few regular folk- and one noble? *One would think they would take shelter in the castle.* Scarcely had the great dragon's feet struck the ground and a moment later, before Karos slid from her back, running to meet the group. "Otho! Otho Klimir!" He shouted as he closed the distance. Stopping short, he looked over at those who met him. They looked tired, worn down, as well as sad and anxious.

"Warden Ranger Karos, your arrival is most welcome." Otho began, too exhausted to care that the Warden Ranger had arrived on dragonback. "What news have you?"

Karos chuckled grimly, and Otho nodded, having guessed just by that what the news would be. "Only dire news, Otho. Littlebrook-once-besieged is gone. Few survive. I can only think the worst for other affected towns. How have you fared here?"

"Not well, *ten'gar* most honored. Few have survived here and those that do have taken shelter in the castle- and refuse to come out. From what Lady Khula has told us, the air is of terror and cowardice, even among the Paladins." Karos' eyebrows raised at this news. For the Paladins to sequester themselves in terror was grave indeed. This meant that they thought the Ancestors were punishing them and all of Seran- though he was confused as to why the Order had not already convened and sought wisdom from the Ancestors. As he examined Khula, Karos felt something strange- a tugging in his soul the likes of which he had never felt before- it was enough to take his breath away. As he looked her over, the details from his vision in the pool came rushing back to him. The purple and red dress frayed here and there and covered with dirt and grime. The fiery red hair, which was pulled back in a sensible pony's tail, rather than being free as most noblewomen wore their hair. Her face was elegantly shaped and even with the now-crooked nose, she looked as though a man seeking to capture true beauty sculpted her. Her green eyes felt like they were staring right into Karos' soul, which normally would make him slightly uncomfortable. But right now, it seemed to soothe his weary soul- and calm the voices in his head.

Khula was likewise speechless as she looked over Karos and only half-noticed that her necklace was warm, the abryx shard within glowing strong. She felt the same tugging in her soul as he did, as if they were connected- but she was not about to give it voice. After all, her parents had given her to Magus, and she was rapidly learning there was more darkness in her husband than she realized. She studied the details in the Ranger's face- the kind brown eyes that hid a sadness so deep it intimidated her; the resolute brow, thin nose-bridge and the multitude of scars, the grandest of which was the large silver-threaded scar running the length of the left side of his head. The cloth covering his lower face made it difficult to see any details, but Khula could pick out the barest hint of a raised cheek. This subtle shift sparked an image of him smirking in her imagination, as if he knew some world-shaking secret. By just meeting this man, she could tell that he was someone of consequence. She felt as if she knew him- but the feeling was intangible, as if spiritual rather than mental and here and now. She tried to shake off the thoughts, but they persisted. After a length of time, she realized the man was speaking and his voice enthralled her.

"It is my wish, Otho, Var, and the rest of you in attendance. Let the old hatreds between our kin and the Order of Gelvrentael die. It is by my command that this be done. I have pledged a blood-oath to make it end." The Rangers nodded quickly and opened their ranks, waving at Thäoldr and Trässa, the latter of whom spoke up.

"While I thank you for your company, Rangers, there is a task I must attend to. To Ormere Keep I go to warn the Council of Winds of what has transpired." Trässa then bowed to the group and ran to her Iftra, quickly climbing to her back and securing her flight straps. Then, with a cry, she urged Iftra into the sky. Within moments, she had vanished, unfettered by the need to stay with Namryll now and thus allowed to ride as fast as she could go.

"Karos! Karos!" The Warden Ranger felt a sharp slap across his face and he blinked, focusing in on the source- Otho had struck him. "You drifted off, *ka teljt*. Tell me, what has you so flustered?" Tracing the man's eye-line, Otho found his own eyes drawn to Khula and he slapped himself. "*Aze!* I have not introduced you. Karos anrak'Lyvan, meet Lady Khula anrak'Tallam. Known it is that the Tallam clan are heartless cowards obsessed only with their coin and status, but I assure you- she is diffcrent. She is kind and aids others."

Karos bowed low, taking Khula's hand as he did. Gently kissing her on the back of the hand, the Warden Ranger then released her and rose back to his full height. Otho was rather shocked- none had ever seen Karos greet a lady in such a way. Slowly, Karos looked her over. "Hello, Lady Khula. As Otho said, I am Karostrun anrak'Lyvan. I am the Guidestar of the Rangers and a dead clan."

"Guidestar..." she whispered, her face screwing up with pain. Otho glanced at her, slightly alarmed by her whisper.

"Lady Khula, you mustn't try to speak. It harms your throat so." Gently, Otho patted her shoulder and looked at Karos. "If you speak to her, Karos, try to use hand-signs, so it does not tempt her to answer with her voice. To use her voice causes her great pain." Karos nodded distractedly and brought his hands up. Quickly, he signed to Khula, his words flowing from his hands just as easily as from his mouth. At times like this, he was glad that the Rangers taught hand-code until it was instinct, for it would not do to have this wonderful lady harm herself in speaking to him.

"How fare you, Khula?" He spelled out. She watched his hands, wondering just what secrets they held. How many battles had they seen? What deeds had they done? For now, only Karos and his Rangers knew the answer to that.

"I fare well, my thanks." She signed quickly. Reaching up, she touched her throat, before bringing her hand out to symbolize fire. Karos nodded and quickly grabbed his waterskin before anyone else could even react. Otho slowly realized what might happen and he backed away, letting the two have their time. Karos offered the waterskin and Khula took it, quickly taking a pull and feeling the water cool her burning throat.

"So, what must we do, Rangers?" Thäoldr's voice jarred Karos back to reality. He felt like he could watch Khula move, speak with her, be near her forever. It was a discomforting feeling for someone so used to being alone, and he wondered where it was coming from and what was causing it. *Why does she feel so familiar? Have I met her before?* His mind wandered from possibility to possibility and he snapped himself back to the here and now- with great effort.

"We must find some way to cure this plague before the

entire city dies." Otho's voice was matter of fact as he looked from his leader to the Rider. Nodding, Karos adjusted his pack before placing it down next to the fire. Khula had found herself a seat and watched the man wistfully. There was something about him she could not put her finger on- it was as if she knew him from... a previous life, perhaps? At times like this, she wished she could remember the other times she had walked The Path- if there were any. He was so maddeningly familiar and yet just out of reach of her memory.

"Aye, Otho. We must focus our efforts. I have Kiri and Kizarian helping who is left around Littlebrook. Thäoldr graciously offered to bear me here, and now I need to repay that debt." Karos glanced over at Thäoldr slyly, wondering if the man had already thought of repayment and how he would be compensated.

"You can repay me by saving our world, Karos." Thäoldr intoned grimly, crossing his arms over his chest. Clenching his artifice hand, he suddenly cried out. "Scorchitall, we are fumbling in the dark! We must find a solution."

"I concur, Thäoldr. I know one thing about the Riders- that you have a vault where grave secrets are kept." Thäoldr was taken aback- the existence of the Vault was a closely guarded secret, even among the Order of Gelvrentael. Few outside the Riders would know that it even existed as a legend. How then did Karos know of it?

Guessing his new friend's question, Karos spoke once more. "A rider I saved from death once told me that the key to saving Seran may very well be locked there. From what he would not say, but I assume that he may have known something we do not." Thäoldr was still processing the fact that Karos knew, but after a time, he accepted it and spoke once more.

"Very well, I guess there is no keeping secrets from you, Karos. The Order of Gelvrentael has long held a vault full of secrets and artifacts that could tip the balance of power in Seran. As the Paragon of Knowledge, I alone am privy to their secrets and I tell you now- there is nothing but death in those archives. But if poring through those old tomes once more is how I can best help for now, then so be it." He sighed and turned to leave, but Karos stopped him.

"Hold, Thäoldr. The time may come when we must unlock the secrets in that vault- but if, as you say, it is filled with naught but death, then let us follow another path." Thäoldr nodded, much relieved. The mere thought of using anything in the Vault horrified him. That Karos knew about it just added insult to injury, and he was not pleased. Shaking his head, Thäoldr looked to his dragon for some wisdom. *What aid can we give in the moment, Thäoldr? That is where we must focus for now.* Namryll's words were not the most reassuring, but they held wisdom. It would not do to get bogged down in what-ifs. He was about to say more when he noticed Khula frantically waving. Tapping Karos on the shoulder, he pointed to Khula, who signaled in hand-signs.

"Try dragon pipe. May slow progression." Karos nodded slowly, thinking it over in his head before replying.

"How know you?"

"Mother used when I was sick. Did not make me feel much better... but slowed infections." It was Karos' turn to be impressed. In a gesture of thanks, he squeezed Khula's shoulder, eliciting a momentary smile from the woman. It faded when Karos released her, but she still felt the touch. It was more comforting than the few shows of kindness her parents had ever done for her. She longed to feel it again- but knew there were more important matters.

"Know you where to find?" Karos asked, his hands working with excitement. If they could slow this rot- then he must take that road. Nodding, Khula hiked up her dress and took off running towards the nearby trees. Karos and Otho followed, and Thäoldr waited with Var and Knal. Var looked the rider over and nodded.

"If Karos trusts you enough to ride dragonback, that is good enough for me. What do you suggest we do, Ride-" a shriek interrupted him and he turned towards the source. His sword snapped from its sheath and he began looking for a threat- or some reason for the scream. Thäoldr touched three of his tattoos, opening his pathway nerves as quickly as he could.

They saw it moments later- a woman carrying a child and supporting a man, possibly her husband? Regardless, Var ran towards them, seeking to aid however he could. "

"Ranger! Please, some dire sickness has afflicted my husband and child! Help them, please!" The woman was sobbing as Var and Thäoldr, who had come running after, approached. Var took the child in his arms, and Thäoldr supported the man on the other side. Together, they carried them both to the fire and set them on stumps next to it. The man's condition looked grave to Var and Knal grew sick just looking at him. The child was in better condition physically, but Var could see the pustules manifesting on him. Inwardly, Var wondered if it would be better to give the man a merciful death and focus on the child while there was still hope.

Khula ran as fast as she could, nearly tripping herself several times. Finally, she stumbled into a hole and tumbled forward, only just managing to avoid breaking her ankle. As she fell, she threw her hands out, hoping to avoid an incident like the one before. The impact never came and she felt the touch again. Her heart leapt as she was pulled up- almost into Karos' arms. *So tantalizingly close*- she shook her head at the thoughts- as well as the burning sensation coming from her abryx shard. Why were they coming so quickly? She did not know this man at all, or at least, she didn't know him now. Why was the shard burning her? She pulled away from him, disgusted at her own thoughts, but not before signing to him. "Thank you." Then she hiked up her dress once more and was off. Karos chuckled at the girl's enthusiasm- as well as her resilience and bounded off to follow her. Var had not stopped at all and was quite a way ahead of the two. Khula grew more and more confused- the burning faded somewhat, but she could feel that her skin may have been scorched. Shaking her head, she continued running until she reached the edge of the woods. Spent, she leaned against a tree and gasped for air. Karos loped up not a minute later, not even bothered by the sprint.

"This copse is not a natural occurrence. 'Twas planted- twenty years ago, judging by the size of the trees." Karos began, only to be stopped as he noticed Khula, who was still struggling for breath, signing to him.

"I planted. When I was ten. Parents taking me to Magus for the first time." She shook her head angrily and Karos blinked. *Who is Magus?* He thought to himself.

Moments later, he pried. After all, if she was that disgusted by the man, he may need to be kept away from her. Signing distantly, he waited for her response. "Who is Magus?"

Her hand came up in a knife from her belly to her forehead. An easy enough sign to remember. "Bastard. Was not always, though." Karos nodded slowly. Not much to go on, but it would be enough for now.

"Where is the dragon's pipe?" He asked with both hand and voice, anxious to get back on task. Khula nodded and waved for the men to follow her into the copse. It was not large, but bushes and the trees themselves sheltered it well. Twenty years had brought quite proud trees and Karos was happy for it. When he passed through the bushes behind Khula, a spectacular sight lay before his eyes. Dragon's Pipe, which was usually relegated to being considered a pretty flower and hardly medicinal, grew in abundance. Everywhere he saw the branches and pitchers, forming the shapes of great smoking pipes. Nodding, he reached out to grab one, only to be stopped by Khula. Gently, she pulled his hand away and tugged him along to follow her. Her abryx was still burning, but she had much greater purpose now. Leading him to a group of Dragon's Pipe that seemed to fell off the branches while still fresh, she waved and signed.

"These have given themselves for the greater good."

Karos nodded slowly, impressed by Khula's connection to the world itself. She had a surprise at every turn; it seemed. Reverently, he took a knee and collected the Dragon's Pipe pitchers that had fallen from the branches before raising his gaze to the sky. "Wildmother Veljra. We thank you for your blessing and ask that you watch over us, that we may save lives or at least give them time for us to find better methods." Looking down at the plants in his hands, he whispered gently. "Thank you for your sacrifice. I pray it will be enough." Nodding to Khula, he stood once more and gently folded his hands over the plants in his hands. Then, he led the way out of Khula's grove. She walked behind him for a time, before reaching out to touch his shoulder. Mere inches shorter than he, she was impressive in her own right. Stopping to look at Khula, it surprised him when she pressed her hands against his, before bringing them up to her chest, where her abryx shard sat. It was a sign as old as the Northrealm Clans, a sign of trust. He could feel the heat of the crystal and blinked– it was burning her. Inwardly, Karos wondered why this woman, who had just met him, was giving such a sign. Why she was placing trust in him when she barely knew him.

As if answering his unspoken question, she reached up and touched her abryx shard. The surrounding skin was bright red and had no sign that it was going to calm down soon. *She is trusting in the abryx, perhaps? Perhaps she thinks I am to be important to her life.* For a noble to wear the abryx crystal without knowledge of its purpose was exceedingly rare, so Khula knew what it did; knew about its connection to the Ties That Bind. "Is the crystal causing pain?" He asked when she released his hands. She nodded slowly, and he arched an eyebrow. "Why not store it in a belt-pouch, then?" She shook her head, breathing easily through the pain.

After a moment and a concerned look from Karos, she signed once more. "Worse happens with Magus since..." As she trailed off, Karos nodded slowly, coming quickly to the realization that he hated Magus, without even meeting him. Khula drew one of her sleeves up as they walked, showing where she had defaced a brand. *A brand*, thought Karos, *shows that this Magus is little more than a slaver.* He shook his head and continued until they had reached the camp. Seeing the two victims, Karos went to work, with help from Var and Khula.

Quickly grabbing a pot of water and setting it on the hook to boil, Khula grabbed the healing herbs she knew– shepherd's purse, sky-fusion and Trollsbane stem. Nodding, Karos added in a strange-looking plant. She eyed him warily until he explained himself. "Tyngfir. It will ease their pain and put them in a dream. Hopefully, they will remember little of their pain." He then began to delicately mix in the Dragon's Pipe, as if he were putting someone to their last rest. When the water came to a boil, he let it sit for a time, stewing the plants until all their juices had mixed into the waters. He drew a vial of the fluid out and placed it a little way away from the fire. When it had cooled sufficiently, he brought it over to the man, who looked like he was turning for the worst. "Come, drink this, friend. It will help you."

The man managed a nod, and Karos uncorked the vial and tipped it into his mouth. He sputtered a little, but choked it down. Almost immediately, his breathing evened out, and he fell into a deep sleep. Quickly, Karos caught him as he fell and brought him close to the fire. Then, he exposed the man, looking over the various sores and pustules that had formed. Karos could feel that there was not much of a chance for the man- but as he closed his eyes and focused on the Ties That Bind, he could see the man's Strand lengthening. *So, there is hope*, thought Karos as he voyaged down to see if the man's Strand ended here, *and I must cling to it*. Beads of sweat formed on his face from the concentration required to see that far, and after a moment, he had his answer. Opening his eyes, Karos nodded slowly and popped his neck.

"What is it, Karos?" Var spoke, his words calm through the possibility of witnessing death yet again. He was accustomed to it, though not willingly so. Yrbos seemed to follow all Rangers as a constant companion, and he often wondered if this was by design. Clearing the thought from his head, he took to a new task. Drawing another vial of the life-prolonging liquid, he nearly dipped his finger into the mixture, but caught himself. *It would not do to potentially ruin something that could save lives. Or at least give us time to find a solution.* When the vial was full, he placed it away from the fire so it could cool and moved to find a seat that had not already been taken.

"His life is safe... for now." Karos sounded uncertain that the man would pull through, but they had at least given his family time to come to terms with whatever would happen. Sighing, he looked at the fire for a moment, trying to collect his thoughts. He could feel his *prúnsaal* encroaching again, those dark thoughts talking about ending it all. He rocked his head, trying to force them away, and sighed when they merely became louder. "I am going into the city- to the apothecary shop to look through any reagents that are left."

Otho spoke next, his mind made up- he could not go back into the city. "I will remain with the folk here. I grieve too much to return to Cúledan's gate. Your pardon, I beg, Warden Ranger. Too many friends now walk The Path and I have not the heart to tread their streets. I may never." Sighing, Karos patted Otho on the shoulder. The Ranger had seen much already, Karos realized, and it would be heartless to drag him into it again.

He felt a tap on his shoulder and turned to see Khula signing. "I will help. Let me show you where the apothecary is."

Immediately, Karos shook his head. He could not tell if she was infected, but the risk was far too great. "No, Lady Khula. It is not safe for you to be in the city." Otho sucked in a breath- this just got interesting.

One of Khula's hands clenched into a tight fist and she

stepped dangerously close to Karos. Her voice barely sounding above the fire, she hissed out. "You do not decide what is safe for me. I came to help. I am no less capable than you." When she finished spitting her words out, her body heaved, falling into a coughing fit. She could feel the burn in her throat and waved at Otho, who quickly brought a cup of the restorative tea. Khula downed it in one gulp and sighed as it cooled her throat back down. She could taste the blood already, but resolved to not let Karos see her cough it up.

Karos shook his head and went to speak again, before being cut off by Otho. "Karos, she will follow with your permission or without it. It would be best to just let her aid you. Besides, has it not been a century since you were last in Cúledan?"

A century began Khula's thoughts, *so this man must be at least seventy years my senior. I wonder how old he is.* Such thoughts would do her little good, she realized, and planted her hands firmly on her hips. She wanted to know more about this man; she was not about to let this chance slip her by. When Karos finally nodded, she clapped her hands together happily. *If he is in my life, I had best learn all I can of him. What better source than the man himself?* Var and Knal nodded to each other, and Var spoke. "Warden Ranger, with your permission, we will search the area and warn folk away from the city. It would be best to keep them from entering, no?"

"Aye, Var. That would be best. Let us ensure no others become afflicted." With that permission, Var and Knal made their way away from the camp. Thäoldr looked from Otho to Karos before raising his own query.

"Karos, what would you have me do? It seems your Rangers have plans of their own."

The Warden Ranger considered Thäoldr for a moment,

appreciating that he will help. He tried to think of a use, but nothing came at first. A glance to Otho gave him some inspiration, and he nodded. "Thäoldr, I ask you to aid Var and Knal- but differently. Fly out to any caravans that approach- warn them away as quickly as you can. Should you encounter any foes, give a report to Otho. Do not engage them unless they are a threat to you."

Thäoldr grinned- aerial reconnaissance was one of his favorite tasks. Namryll rumbled her approval, and the two went off to prepare themselves. Karos then turned to Otho once more, having realized that Siddi, who normally went everywhere with Otho, was absent.

"Otho, where is Siddi?"

"She is escorting a child to the *tengjäv*. We found a child that had been badly mistreated and brought her to safety. We slew her pursuers without mercy." *Good*, Karos thought, *that means fewer slavers to deal with.* He nodded to Otho, before waving at Khula to follow him. *Duty calls and we must away. I wonder what this will hold for us...* The thoughts rattled around in his head for a while, even as he began walking the path towards the city.

At first, Khula said nothing as they walked. She was still measuring Karos, watching his stride, the way he carried himself. Confidence radiated from him as warmth from the sun, but she could tell there was something hidden beneath, as if the confidence was an affectation rather than a fact. *Sorrow, perhaps, or maybe anger, but about what?* It was hard to tell, even though she was an empathic soul. Many things had happened, and the situation was alien to her, but that merely resolved her to see it all through. Perhaps she would even gain a friend in the Warden Ranger, which at the very least would anger Magus and her family. That would be a victory to Khula, and she would be happy to see it. After a time, she decided that talk was necessary and tapped Karos' shoulder to get his attention. Karos shifted his gaze to her, and she began speaking with her hands. "How did you become a Ranger?"

Karos chuckled dryly at the question. *How indeed?* He thought. He was supposed to have been a woodsman, eking out a meager existence in Northrealm. A simple life, but easier than this. But alas, fate was not always kind. He spoke, his voice sad as he recalled the things that had brought him to where he stood. "Hardship, loss and resilience. I learned things I never expected to know, and I have watched many friends and allies enter The Path. I lost my family at a young age. My parents were slain by bandits allied with the Bleeding Tear, roughly three-hundred-sixteen years ago. I was but a boy of ten." He sighed wistfully, unsure if he wished to relive that dark day for the sake of another. A glance to her had his answer- she was begging to know more. *If it must be so*, he said to himself, *then let the tale be told.*

He looked Khula over for a moment, as if gauging how worthy she was to know that much of his life. Truth be told, it was no more than his Rangers knew... but he had at least known them for almost his entire life. Her, he had just barely met. His reluctance was obvious, but after a moment, he swallowed it down. "My mother was an enchanter, weaving spells into tools or clothes for the folk of Coldforge and my father was a woodsman and hunter, felling logs to sell to the lumber mill and finding meat for my family. We were adopted into the wild elf clan Lyvan, after a chance meeting, where my mother protected one of their members."

He paused for a moment, remembering being brought out

to a fire deep in the Eversnow Forest. Scores of folk gathered in the flickering firelight. Hair twisted into long braids or shaven close, facial tattoos, arm tattoos, pale skin glowing with the fire. Dancing merrily as they welcomed his family into their circle. "We learned they had been watching over our town of Coldforge for some time and had been quite close with the Rangers. Through them, we learned of a slaver band, the Bleeding Tear, that was coming to claim Coldforge and Clan Lyvan. They had already struck one member of the clan down— Sayra Loud-Water. It is in her memory that I wear this," He sighed gently and blinked away the tears that threatened to introduce themselves as he rummaged under his garb for a pendant with an abryx shard of its own, glowing bright and searing hot. "She was the first person other than my parents that I... I believed I loved. I was the one who found her body, and she had been... mistreated by her captors."

Taking a breath, he continued. "The day dawned like any other, cold and clear. My parents did not indicate that anything was wrong— but I may have been too young to remember. I do not quite remember what I was told, just that it inspired me to leave town quickly. I wandered for hours and thought about going back. Then," The tears were coming on stronger now and Karos wasn't sure if he could fight them back this time. "I heard the sounds of distant battle and did what any child would do— I ran until I felt faint. Curling up under a tree, I stayed there until I was found by what I thought was just another Ranger— 'twas Veljra, who guided the Rangers to me. They took me back to Coldforge and the news of my parents' last stand was delivered. They gave me The Choice— become a Ranger or be taken in by folk in the town. The answer I felt in my soul. I was a Ranger." Khula nodded gently and reached out to pat his arm in sympathy. She could never know his pain, but she could at least be kind when he was revealing his life to her. He nodded slowly, blinking away tears he never expected to form, and adjusted his belt. "'Tis history now, told as one of the Teaching Songs in Northrealm- the Ballad of Coldforge. It was strange to hear the tale as a song- rather than having lived it as close as I came." He shook his head mirthfully at that revelation and looked at Khula. "And what of you? You asked much of me, so it is only right of me to ask- what path brought you here?"

She was about to answer when a commotion distracted her. Her heart sank as she saw the source- Magus. Shying away behind Karos, she tried to tug him away into the bushes- they were still far enough away from the gates that they could hide and that was her desire now. Karos, having pieced together what was going on from the urgency of her movement, pulled her into the brush and away from the gate. Rather than try to convey her thought through hand-signs, she took the risk and whispered. "I thought he would cower in the castle..." She began heaving as the words tore at her throat and Karos threw a hand over her mouth, silencing her hacking cough as best he could. He hoped they were far enough away for anyone to not hear them.

Luckily, Magus was far too immersed in his conversation to notice the sound of coughing. "Fucking peasant, you must have seen her! Tell me!" He roared at the Ranger near the gate, stepping forward with his hand on his sword.

"Magus, I would remove your hand from your hilt- I am in no mood for your games. I have just come from Taranith to the south- I know nothing of your runaway bride, so threatening me will do no good." The Ranger, a burly half-elf from one of the many gah'Drin clans of Dragonmoor, replied coolly. One hand rested behind him on the haft of a belt-knife- a poor weapon against a sword, but Magus had strayed close enough in his fury that he would have no time to bring up his spear. *It is true then*, the Ranger mused, *anger makes fools of all men.*

"Do you not know who I am, foolish pay-" His slur cut short by a stone colliding with the back of his head, the man yelped and spun on his heel. Karos stepped from the bush, already nocking an arrow back onto his bow. Magus turned, enraged beyond words at the audacity of whoever threw the stone. In the bushes, Khula laughed silently; it was rare she got a shot in at the bastard.

"I would suggest you stop pestering and threatening my Ranger. Unless you direly need to depart this life, go about your business." Karos was standing proudly, bow bent back in an obvious threat. Magus growled low, his sword still resting in its sheath. These Rangers were a meddlesome bunch, and he had no doubts they had something to do with the disappearance of his intended.

"And who are you who so casually threatens Magus, General of The Red Lance?" He called out, his voice sounding a hint of his supercilious nature. "I am here on purpose from the Lord and Lady Tallam, so it would be in your best interests to not get in my way." He sneered at Karos, daring him to loose the arrow and completely ignoring the Ranger he had put to his back.

"I am Karos, Warden Ranger of Seran. I advise you to go about your business without threatening my Rangers. No authority supersedes that of the Ancestors and the Kingmage of Seran. I call upon you, General of The Red Lance," the title came in a mocking tone that Karos hoped the man would notice, "to quit this area immediately and go about whatever task they assigned you in peace." His voice carried the authority of centuries and he judged the other man silently. He looked just over 60 or 70- he was showing some age, but still had his prime ahead of him. "I had thought none allowed to leave the Castle Vigilance. Tell me, how have you been allowed to leave when such a quarantine exists?"

This Ranger is prying far too much into matters of his betters, fumed Magus, *and I would do well to show him his place.* "Come and challenge me if you are to pry into my business. Otherwise, remain in the bush like a cowardly peasant- unfit to be in the presence of your betters, Karos Ranger." He spat the name and the term out as if an insult- when a heavy staff struck the back of his head. He fell forward, momentarily stunned, as he tried to figure out where the blow came from.

"Who dares?" He rounded angrily, sword in hand, ready to cut down whoever had the audacity to strike him. He faced a rather smug looking Ranger who had him at quite a disadvantage- a spear was already sitting near enough his throat to be rather uncomfortable. "Who do you think you are?" He nearly shouted at the Ranger, his face burning with anger and embarrassment. He tried pushing the spear aside with his sword, but it stubbornly stayed in position.

"I am Dalan of Kurost, Ranger and former Knight of the Red Lance. You have no authority over me and you will depart. If you offer any more resistance to myself or my Warden Ranger, I will not hesitate to slay you where you stand." He was standing in a defensive position, ready to deflect any blow that may come his way. Magus noted the aggravating grin on his face and felt like he should take this smug man down. Then he heard a calm voice behind him.

"I would suggest you leave- while you still have your head." He turned, startled beyond words at this point. *This is not going the way it should. I am a General, they should show respect!* He stared into the fiery topaz eyes of Karos, who had his sword at the ready. "We have not seen the woman you are chasing, and I would not speak of them as property. Now take your cowardly ass and get out of my sight, you impotent whore-son!" To drive home his point, he slammed his foot down on the top of Magus' own, causing the man to let out a pained yelp and leap to grab his damaged foot. Another stone flew from nowhere, striking the back of his head- and he had had enough. He took off running, desperate to put some distance between himself, the insane Rangers and whoever was throwing the stones. Stones rained down behind him and he ran as fast as his legs would carry.

When he was out of sight, both Karos and Dalan doubled over laughing, their mirth unchecked. Karos slipped over to the bush and gently took Khula's arm, leading her back to the road. She was smiling broadly and when Karos released her arm; she began signing. "Felt good to strike back at Magus. Many injuries have I suffered from him. Thank you." In a show of gratitude, she threw her arms around Karos and hugged him tight. Karos, unsure of what to do when hugged, stood there awkwardly before reaching up to pat her back. When she released him, he nodded for them to enter the gates of Cúledan.

"Dalan, many thanks. Your aid was invaluable. Good hunting!"

"My thanks to you, Warden Ranger. I am pleased to see you again." With his fighting arm, he reached up and Karos reached out and grasped the arm with his own sword arm- a gesture of trust, for neither could effectively draw weapons in such a compromising position. The two men released each other's arm, before Karos and Khula passed through the gate.

Khula grabbed Karos' shirt, clinging close to him- in a gesture of trust, perhaps, or as a gesture of fear. She pointed him down the first street on the left and Karos followed the instruction quickly. While wandering the streets, they encountered little signs of life and Karos began to grow worried, thinking the town already dead. Rounding a corner, they found a pair of knights- looting the houses and businesses left behind. Karos' sword snapped into his hand and he let out a shout. "Rather low to be stealing from the departed!"

One knight was quick with a retort. "Just a redistribution of wealth. None of your business, Ranger!" To this, Karos shook his head, getting ready to chastise the two men, when he spotted a rock sailing through the air. It struck the closer knight square between the eyes and he fell back, momentarily stunned. Another missile soon followed it and struck his companion just above the ear, leaving a large goose egg in its wake. The man turned angrily and shouted. "Watch where you are throwing stones, wench!" After a moment, he realized who he was seeing- and laughed. "Ho! Look at this, Cathani! Magus' little toy seems to have gotten away and gone with a Ranger! Looks like it is up to us to return her!" They both prepared their stances, bringing their swords out.

With unexpected force and volume, Khula cried out. "You will never take me!" As soon as the words had left her lips, another stone was sailing through the air to strike Cathani. In rapid succession, another stone bolted out to strike the other knight, Sir Holdrin. Karos glanced at Khula, noting the unrelenting fury in her eyes- and then the brand on her arm made sense. They saw her as a thing- as property. The Nolvern's eyes filled with anger and his sword snapped out of its sheath, ready for bloody work.

"I will give you one warning: leave or you will fall by my blade. You have this one chance to save your own life." He positioned himself between the knights and Khula, watching them. Again, another stone flew, striking with much more force than Khula had expected, and the crack was loud as it collided with Holdrin's skull. He fell to the ground, twitching in his death throes, and Cathani let out a cry.

"You will pay for that, you foolish cunt!" His sword came from its sheath and he advanced on Khula, disregarding Karos in his rage. This nearly cost him his life, but he was quicker than most. Remembering Karos in the last few feet, he snapped his sword to the side, trying to throw Karos away so he could grab Khula and leave. Karos was having none of it and easily deflected the poorly timed blow. Having a clearer head, he pressed his advantage against the burlier man, driving his sword towards the man's throat.

Cathani had expected such a move and slapped Karos' sword aside and leapt in to run him through- only to have his sword grate uselessly upon tightly woven mail. Growling, he leapt back and brought his sword in a wide slash.

Karos let out a breath at his luck. He had been expecting the sword to pierce, but evidently, the mail was made tighter than he remembered. *Pure luck*, Karos chastised himself, *that was a stupid move, Ranger.* Twirling his sword to deflect another slash, Karos dropped in close and delivered a stunning kick to Cathani's stomach. But it was nearly worthless, merely pushing the man back. He was quite strong or had just flexed his muscles at the right time. Karos would not make the same mistake twice. Dropping back, he planted his feet firmly beneath him and readied for another strike.

Cathani recoiled from the blow and thanked his stars he had seen the strike before it hit. *Lucky*, he thought, *this Ranger is persistent and quick. I should be more careful.* His sword lanced out, probing his foe's defenses, only to be slapped aside.

Karos stepped back in, unleashing a flurry of pokes and slashes, meant to put Cathani off-balance. In the time, he closed in and drove his foot once more towards the other man- this time to a more sensitive area. It rewarded him with a squeal of pain and Cathani fell back. "You bastard! That is not honorable combat!"

"What do you know of honor, referring to a woman as a plaything? Fool." Cathani struggled back to his feet as Karos was talking and readied himself for another strike. The last thing he saw was a rather large stone coming at his head- with no time to defend himself or dodge. It struck true, collapsing his face and the front part of his skull and he dropped like his friend, gurgling his last breath out through a destroyed mouth, before becoming still. Karos turned in shock to see Khula standing defiantly, another rock in hand. Her eyes were still afire and Karos shook his head in wonder. "Lady Khula, you are full of surprises." He also noticed what she was trying to hide- a thin trickle of blood coming from the left side of her mouth. She had avoided coughing so far, but when things calmed down, she fell into a fit.

Karos rushed over to her, quickly uncapping his waterskin and offering it to her. She nodded in thanks and took a long pull. The Ranger watched her carefully, making sure that she would be okay. When she handed the waterskin back to him, he capped it and tied it back to his belt.

Khula stood shakily at first, leaning against Karos for support. When she was steady on her feet, she waved him onwards and stepped over the dead men, moving along the road towards the apothecary's shop. They had lost too much time already.

Karos, now curious about his companion, spoke up. "Where did you learn to throw stones like that?" He was not ashamed to admit that he was quite amazed. Killing someone with a stone was no small feat, even for his Rangers.

"I learned from a halfling friend. I think his name was Tyled." The words flowed quickly from her hands as she spoke back to him. He nodded slowly, thinking that he may have to meet this friend and congratulate them. Nodding to each other in a new understanding, the two moved on up the street. Quickly, they found their way to the apothecary's shop and were quite glad to see someone within tending to the displays. Karos pushed the door open, and the bell rang as he entered, causing the old dal'Korin to turn.

"Hello and welcome! Hold still, hold still, I cannot see you well." The aged lizard-man reached onto the counter for a pair of dusty glasses. Quickly brushing them against his tunic, he dropped them onto his head and adjusted them. A moment later, he cried out in surprise. "A Ranger- and Lady Khula! Oh, happy days, happy days! Have you come to get healing herbs for your folk?" Karos, having read the apothecary's name off the creaking wooden sign that hung above the door, spoke first.

"Well met, Et'Ka'Saan! I am Karos, Warden Ranger of Seran." This caused an immediate reaction in the dal'Korin, his neck frills swooping out in surprise. He immediately moved to take a knee and Karos stopped him. "Please, good sir, there is no need to bow."

"But it is such an honor, Warden Ranger. For you to be in my humble shop- how may I aid you? Are you here about the strange goings on? They have been burning bodies in the street, but I have paid little attention. Not my tail to the fire, as my mum used to say! Goodness, but she has been gone all of 80 years now."

Khula let out a gentle chuckle and tapped Et'Ka'Saan on the shoulder. Then, when she had his attention away from rambling, she spoke quickly, her hands a blur of speech. As old as the dal'Korin was, he was still very fluent in hand-sign and picked it up quickly. "A plague has struck. Many are dead. We need all the herbs you can spare."

"Of course, of course, Lady Khula. Sad thing that a plague has hit- reminds me of learning about the Great Plague during Kingmage Las'Sa'Reeth's time. Goodness the things they told us about that and how it was averted when he found survivors and drew their humors down for the straw-colored fluid- called plasma, by the way." Karos was listening, but none of the information was of use to him- he knew it all by heart. *Woe that we do not have a great mind like Las'Sa'Reeth at a time like this,* he pondered, *for the wise one may have some ideas.* After a moment, he shook himself from his musing as Et'Ka'Saan continued rambling on. He had had no one to talk to since this complete debacle began, and it was quite distressing.

Karos reached out and tapped him on the shoulder gently. "I apologize, Et'Ka'Saan, but we are in haste. What herbs do you think would aid us in this task?"

The old dal'Korin looked surprised as they addressed him,

but after a moment, he regained himself. "Well, if memory serves, Dragon's Pipe may slow sicknesses from spreading." Karos nodded slowly, having already learned that from Khula. "Saritash may be a useful herb for this, helps the blood to clot. Ynalos is also helpful. But induces fever- one must be careful." He puttered about for a moment, almost as if he had forgotten about the two in his shop. Shaking his head and muttering, he gathered a few reagents into a sack, mumbling strange plant names to himself. Karos listened intently and, though the names were familiar, the dal'Korin's muttering was making it hard to distinguish the names he was speaking. Finally, Et'Ka'Saan turned, holding the bag proudly and gave a toothy grin. "I have gathered what medicines I know will aid you, Warden Ranger. Please- do not reach for your coin purse- consider this an old lizard's way of aiding those in need."

Karos nodded swiftly and accepted the offered bag. "Many thanks, good sir. May your scales never soften and your claws never dull!" Bowing, he made his way out of the shop. Khula likewise said a swift goodbye and slipped out to follow Karos.

"I like him. He has taught me many reagents," Khula began signing when she had Karos' attention, "including ones hard to find. He sometimes helps me make Magus sleep and has taught me many things."

Karos nodded slowly, eyeing the woman, and he realized she was not to be trifled with. If a dal'Korin had taught her how to put people to sleep- that was dangerous knowledge in the wrong hands. He would have to be careful with this one. "We must sweep the city and find any more survivors. You may see terrible things. Are you sure you want to proceed with me?" Karos looked Khula over as he waited for her answer.

She looked determined enough, but he knew the horrors they would see. She stood proudly, though her dress was getting worn down in some places. Her nose had healed into its engagingly crooked position- likely because of a potion, rather than nature. Suddenly, Karos stopped and wondered- *did I just consider her 'engaging'?* Already she was affecting the Ranger's mind. When she was near, his *þrúnsaal* seemed to quiet. His heart picked up its cadence, which normally he did not notice, and he felt his breathing deepen and his focus shifted often to her. *What is this effect she is having on me?* It terrified him wondering when this feeling would end- and how it would break his spirit when it did.

Khula was likewise considering him as she thought of her response. She had seen the burning bodies, smelled the cooked flesh- and could not shake the images from her head. But somehow- it did not matter when he was around. By his side, she felt like she could face whatever terrors they came against. He had already given her the courage to throw stones at Magus and slay two of the man's knights- no small feat. She wondered where that courage came from- or was it rage from the things they said? She knew normally she would have meekly gone with them, knowing that fighting back would be worthless. At best, it would delay the inevitable and, at worst, earn her a beating from Magus. Now, she did not want to think about his reaction- she wanted to think of other things, of what was going on. She was going to help people however she could- and she would do it alongside the Warden Ranger proudly. After a few moments, she signed once more, "I will stay with you." She looked defiantly at him, half expecting him to send her on her way.

"Very well, Khula Tallam. Let us face these horrors together." With that, he waved her to follow him and moved off quickly, searching building by building for any who remained in the city. He did not expect to find that many. But despite his *þrúnsaal*, he held onto hope.

14: Westerspring, Oakheart's Forest

As the Warden Ranger headed out into the distance and the dragonrider took to the skies once more, the Rangers who remained behind, as well as the adventurer Fae cos'Criux, gathered and began enacting their plans. Sketching out the area on the loose dirt of the road, Fae, a leader by profession, began speaking.

"Rangers, you will find the most luck in foraging between these two forests. Summerdusk and Moonglow, to the north and west. Kizarian, that is your name, yes? I wager if Karos is your captain, you may wish to stay near him, but that is your choice. If you remain, I am certain there is one of your Ranger-caves nearby. They may have more answers for you, sir. Kiri, you asked for my assistance, and I will in turn ask yours. While we forage, we must warn all we see away from Littlebrook. We must save them from this fate." Shifting herself, the spritely wood elf glanced at the much older Rangers. In the back of her mind, she guessed them to be only a century older than her, from their looks.

Kiri smirked beneath her mask and took on her usual

matronly tone. "Of course, young Fae, but you know more than we do about the area. There may be *tengjävii* nearby, but you may find them easier than we, though we know the magic to look for." *There is something about this young woman,* thought Kiri fondly. *She is going to shake the world... or she already has.* Getting a feel for the younger elf as she looked her over, Kiri etched the details of the adventurer into her memory. Jet black leather armor– well–fitted and polished, protecting her vital organs with harder plate, and thick suede under chainmail over her belly, allowing movement and providing decent protection. A rapier, which Kiri had seen in action long enough to know she didn't want to be on the wrong end of it. The way she held herself, though. That interested Kiri immensely. She stood with a quiet confidence and seemed to unwittingly position herself with far more intelligence than the normal adventurer. When speaking to Kiri, she seemed to hold at an angle that would allow her to defend from both Rangers, even though Kizarian was closer to being *behind* her. Her right hand remained cocked at the angle of a professional swordfighter, resting at her side while her other rested on the hilt of her rapier.

At first, Kiri had missed it, but the specific positioning of Fae's left hand was fascinating on further looks. Her hand gripped the scabbard itself, with her thumb tucked just under the top of the basket hilt. *Curious. She does not seem like a normal adventurer.* At length, the wild elf's gaze finished on the woman.

"Do you Rangers usually stare at someone before talking to them?" Fae finally asked, a little perturbed at the intense scrutiny.

Kiri popped up finally, grinning behind her mask, eyes

twinkling. "You are with Krygan-Shawv, and if I had to guess from the black armor... Dire Company!" She said with barely constrained glee.

"All of that from looking at me?" Fae asked.

"And more. The way you hold yourself. Your hands at your side, on your scabbard. You are not just an adventurer." Kiri said, glad to finally talk to someone other than another Ranger. "You are a Captain, or my mind is worthless."

"Not worthless at all. I am indeed Captain Fae cos'Criux of Dire Company." Grinning, the woman touched two fingers to her left eyebrow. Her blue eyes glowed, her red hair looked like the flames of a campfire, and her harvest-moon colored skin only showing the barest hint of her age. But her gaze was intense, as if she had faced things that would've conquered anyone else. "But you seem familiar with my crew, and I not with you." She said after a moment. "And you seem far too young to have met me before."

"Oh, do I?" Kiri grinned. "My dear girl, I remember the first seeds of the nearest forest. I remember Oakheart before you were even a dream in your bloodline. I am Kiri Topalin, and I am aged beyond the years of many. Kizarian is younger than I, and he numbers his years in millennia." As she spoke, the wild elf touched her face, causing the faded remains of intricate knotwork tattoos to burn faintly green, giving her an otherworldly look. The tattoos had faded with the centuries, but even now, what Fae could see reminded her of interlaced briar branches.

Suddenly, Fae felt miniscule before the two Rangers. Without much effort, they'd become ancient. Almost on the same level as the High Ancestors themselves. Taking a breath, the younger elf nodded. "I am but two centuries and fifty old, so

I beg your forgiveness." She said after a moment.

"And we both give it gladly, young Fae. You have given us no wounds." Kiri's eyes crinkled in a way that foretold a smile. Even with the kindness in her voice, the younger elf flinched at the older elf's words. The deep elf standing nearby chuckled gently.

"Well, Kiri, it would seem we have our assignments from the good Captain." He finally said, patting Fae on the shoulder before vanishing. Again, even with the cheer and kindness in his voice, she felt like she'd done something wrong. Insulted them on some crucial level.

Chuckling at the confusion written on the girl's face, Kiri waved at Fae to follow her away from the town. "Come then, young Fae, let us see what trouble awaits us!" She said with a bubbly voice, before loping off into the distance. Fae followed after, as quickly as she could catch up.

"What can you tell me of Karos?" Fae asked a while later, as the two began searching through the various plants and growth to find supplies, "He seems familiar to me, and yet, I know I have never met him. At least, not in this life," she finished, recalling what she'd learned of the Seranese view on life being endless and cyclical, with people finding faces familiar from past lives. Pulling out her belt knife, the woman crouched down near a rosemary bush. Saying a quiet prayer as was her people's custom, she whispered her thanks to the plant, promising that she would spread its seeds wherever she found herself next.

Looking on, Kiri smiled beneath her mask at the prayer. It wasn't unlike what the Rangers did. *Thank everything for the sacrifice it makes for you.* As she continued working through the underbrush, inspecting the blue and green leaves, she thought back to some of her younger days. Days when she'd been more bright-eyed and full of adventure. Now, millennia on from those days, she often found herself wishing for the quiet reading room in a *tengjäv* and a nice, piping hot cup of tea, kaffa, or cider. Perhaps a hot scone or two. But as a Ranger, she knew those comforts weren't guaranteed. Even her next hour, day, or month were precious. So she went on, checking berries against her ages of knowledge to ensure she wasn't collecting what would kill someone outright.

Fae was a seasoned adventurer, certainly. But she was nowhere near the knowledge the Ranger had stored up, and she knew it. Though, she knew these forests, these blue and green trees and plants, better than... than she'd known her parents, honestly. That line of thought distracted her for a while. *Mum and da.* She thought for a moment, trying to remember the faces of those that'd brought her into the world. It'd been nearly two hundred years since she'd seen them last. Smirking, she remembered part of why. Part of why she'd blocked them out of her memory. *Women, especially elf women, should not be adventurers. You are above such things.* Shaking her head, Fae remembered her answer to that. *We are wood elves. We are above no one.* And in that argument, she'd proven her point- her parents had thrown her out, disowned her. So she sailed to Seran and started making her way as an adventurer.

Less than a century, she was certified and licensed with Krygan-Shawv Adventuring Company. Had a reputation as a cool-headed leader, a volatile combatant, and a capable seeker. So capable, in fact, that the Scouts Conclave had posted her an offer. *But, the adventures are better with Krygan-Shawv than they are with the Empire.* With Krygan-Shawv, she was free to pick contracts, go where she wanted. With the Empire, she would have to follow rules and regulations. *Enough red tape to make a Ranger lose their way.*

Kiri wondered what the younger elf was thinking about. Again, her eyes drew back to Fae, watching how she worked. *I think she might,* the elf thought cryptically. Chuckling at the very thought, she shook her head and went back to her foraging. *Ouh! Wood-Chicken Mushrooms!* Carefully slicing the fungus away from the tree it was growing on, she whispered a prayer of thanks, as one should, before tucking the large mushroom in her foraging pouch. A happy find indeed, for she knew such mushrooms were prized for flavor, among other things.

As she worked, the Ranger pondered what she knew about Fae so far. She was a bit of a hot-head, at least when dealing with Karos, *which is what he needs. Someone unafraid to call him on his shit.* She smirked beneath her mask and continued foraging. She seemed skilled with her rapier, though Kiri hadn't a chance to test that assumption yet. *But why do I immediately feel like she needs to be around Karos?* The older elf wondered as she said a prayer and picked a handful of berries from a highberry bush. *Is there something special about her? She seems to be a normal adventurer.* Normal enough, at least, that Kiri was curious as to Fae's words. *Familiar with Karos, despite never meeting him.* Abruptly, a thought popped into her head.

"What is his favorite food?" Kiri asked without a trace of context or interest in her voice. As if she were asking about someone Fae had known all her life.

"Havaersk, but he has not had it since... huh." Fae said without a moment of hesitation before blinking a few times.

"Since when?" Kiri pressed, more curious now. This was something even *she* didn't know about her Tenderfoot.

"Since I..." A moment later, Fae shrugged. "I do not know how I know any of that. Or even who you were asking about." She said as a way of shutting down further questioning on the topic.

Kiri was more than wise enough to get the hint.

The truth was, though, the questioning had already begun. As they finished the first day of foraging and settled into a neat little camp in the forest, Fae threw together a lean-to shelter and fluffed her bedroll out under it. Lying on her back and staring up into the sky. *How did I know that?* She wondered to herself. *What else do I know about the man?* Scratching behind her left ear idly, Fae pondered asking Kiri a question, and a glance over to the wild elf told her she'd be receptive.

"Oi, Kiri?" She asked.

"Hm?" The ancient elf said.

"Who did he lose? When he was a child?" She asked, again unsure how she knew he'd lost someone. Perhaps it was just an assumption? Perhaps it was something more? Who knew?

"Well, his parents, the wild elves that adopted him, one of the first Rangers he had been friends with, several playmates and young friends." Kiri replied offhandedly as she pulled a whetstone from one of her pouches and examined the edge of one of her daggers. Bringing the stone to the steel, she began honing the weapon.

"Anyone specific?" Fae dug further.

Kiri scoffed gently. "Everyone he knew before the Rangers? Why, did you know any of them?" She said. *If you are going to dig, girl, you had best do better than that.* Rolling her eyes, the Ranger continued dragging the stone along the blade, the scraping sound almost comforting to both of them.

"I..." Fae sucked in a breath. The idea seemed so concrete, and yet so intangible at the same time. "I must sound mad, but I remember a name from... somewhere. Sayra? Is that name familiar?" Glancing over to the Ranger once more, Fae found Kiri's eyes staring into her. Piercing her very being.

"What did you say?" Kiri whispered.

"Sayra?" Fae asked again, confused by the Ranger's sudden reaction.

Kiri stared for a while longer, eyes boring into Fae's soul. Even as she searched the millennia of her memories, she knew exactly where that name belonged in Karos' personal history. And by extension, her own.

"Sayra Loud-Water was a child of the wild elf Lyvan Tribe of Northrealm. From what Karos could bear to tell me, she was one of his first real friends." The Ranger said, drifting through what the man had told her as she'd trained him. "He said a few times that her memory, even above his parents, is what kept him pushing on through his Tenderfoot years." She paused for a moment, fighting to remember the exact words he'd used back then.

"Because she told him to." Fae finished. "She told him that no matter how dark the night, no matter how he might feel, that he was never without hope." Again, she blinked a few times, wondering what had come over her. "Or something. I know not." She said, trying to seem as if she wasn't going completely mad.

"No, that is exactly it." Kiri said offhandedly. "Either way, girl. Get some rest. We continue on the morrow."

Fae shrugged, unwilling to argue the point. She *was* fairly tired, at least. So, she settled in, pulled the wool of her bedroll over herself, one hand beneath her head, the other near her knife hilt, just in case. Within a few minutes, she was off to the sea of night, sleep taking her.

Kiri just sat there, staring into the fire as she pondered the question she'd asked Fae, and what it had caused. *Everything is connected in some way, Kiri Topalin,* she thought to herself. *You must discover that connection. If it is the obvious answer, you need to be certain.* Placing her hands in her lap, Kiri focused on the sounds of the night, listening, watching, and maintaining her vigil as her companion slept.

As she drifted into her dreams, Fae continued questioning herself. Her world, now. Faces, both familiar and not, swam around her. Occasionally, one would speak to her, saying something in a language she'd never heard before. Writing words she'd never seen. And that was the easiest part of the dream to deal with.

His face. Somehow, she knew it even through the mask. The Warden Ranger, but at the same time, it wasn't the dour, tanned man she'd met earlier. Certainly the shape was the same, but the face, somehow she knew it, though he'd been wearing his mask. Far younger, fewer worry-lines, less concern weighing it down. Far less tan. But still, it was certainly him. Then, there was the face of a stripling, the same basic shape, but with a glint of... happiness? Cheer? Something she'd not seen in the man's eyes at all.

He seemed far too devoted to duty to be cheerful, though she could assume he'd smiled at some point. *But who fucking knows?* She wondered as she wandered through a hall of faces, each one slightly different until she reached the one she knew. Though, she didn't know how she knew it. He'd been wearing a mask of green linen. All she'd seen were his eyes and everything above, the shock of black hair topping his head, pulled back into a short warrior's tail. The scar on the left side of his head, threaded with silver through it. But somehow, she knew his face. Knew it as if she'd slept next to him every day of her life.

That. She realized. Somehow, she knew. That made no sense to her. *How is that feeling so familiar?* Suddenly, she was awake, staring up into the brightening blue sky. Tired, as if she'd not slept at all. *More questions than answers.* Sighing, she pulled herself up into a seated position, arms hugging her knees for a bit. A glance told her that Kiri was away, either already working, or off on some Rangery task. Her grumbling stomach pulled her attention back to herself, and she grabbed for her pack, little realizing she'd left the main part of it at home. *Right. Had only expected to run for some supplies. Not... whatever the fuck has happened since.* A growl alerted her to the return of her vulpine companion, as Box chose to make herself known again. The fluffy tail came into view as the red fox bounded out of the underbrush, yapping and chattering.

Pulling herself to her feet, Fae stretched a few different ways and shuddered away the worst of her exhaustion and looked around. The fire was crackling happily, as if it had been freshly fueled. *But where is the Ranger?* She wondered. Her mouth opened to call out before she heard a chipper voice somewhere behind her.

"Oi, Fae! Got a few things from the river. Hope you like fish!" Kiri said as she approached, a few decent-sized salmon in a bundle of leaves.

"I do not mind at all!" She replied, smiling brightly. Setting herself to work, the elf found her companion's tools and went right to work, gutting and filleting the fish before the Ranger started cooking them. Kiri broke out a small tin from her pack, though Fae couldn't see the contents, and soon the wondrous aroma of cooking spices and frying fish filled the area. Even Box began chattering with excitement.

When the fish was ready, Kiri waved at Fae to come over.

"There are two plates in my pack, Fae. You have one, I will have the other, and your friend here will have to deal with the ground." The elder elf offered a large piece of fish to the fox first, before dishing up Fae and then herself. Once that was done, the companions sat to their meal.

"I think," Fae began, quirking an eyebrow and looking off into the distance, "there is a bog a ways over the hill there. After I got a bit wounded hunting some bandits, I found it and used some of the bog moss to pack my wounds. Did a real treat, but scarred something awful." Chuckling, the younger elf pulled up her left sleeve, revealing the remains of what must've been a nasty gash.

"Well done, Fae. Rangers have used bog moss for centuries to aid in healing wounds. In fact, we used it even before mount Wounds-End knew of its properties." Kiri said pleasantly.

"That makes sense, certainly. You Rangers always have had your ear to the ground on many things." She grinned kindly at the elder woman. "So, if we gather moss, perhaps we can grow it at one of your Ranger-caves? Or is that already done?"

Kiri chuckled and tapped the side of her head. "Good thinking, Fae. But aye, we do have growing spaces in the *tengjävii,* but I know not if the nearest one has bog moss. So, how far do we need to go?"

IV

Lightning Crashes

15

15: Northrealm, Westerspring

It was nearing dusk when Sardra took to her feet once more, having sat with the Tenderfeet for quite some time to allow them to rest. They had made significant progress in crossing the Eversnow Forest to *Ca'e Möratuk*, and now it was time for the fresh blood to see the fruits of their torment. Calling out to the perimeter guard, Sardra approached slowly. "*Tengarii!* I have three Tenderfeet with me! They need to rest and have succor!" Immediately, three Rangers came from around the fire, each picking up one of the exhausted Tenderfeet and bringing them to a seat at the large table. Then, they were served food and their feet and legs rubbed by Rangers many years their senior.

"Flesh and steel, Sardra, how long have you had these poor dears on their feet? They are nearly dead from weariness!"

"We have been traveling three days non-stop. I wished to get them here before any harm could come to them. They have done well and I must leave them in your care, Aliyria cos'Tunarik." The swarthy tal'Edröhel nodded to Sardra and grinned.

"We will care for them well, Sardra Woodstrider. Now be off to your tasks. We will–"

Overhead, six dragons came into view, each bearing a Rider of Gelvrentael. With them rode no less than twelve griffons, each bearing their own rider. A Ranger's voice called out and every soul with a weapon threw up defenses. Mounds of dirt rose with words and hand motions, and weapons flashed into skilled hands. They readied bows, arrows nocked and drawn. They placed spears to cover swords, and the normally welcoming sight of *Ca'e Möratuk* became much less friendly.

They landed swiftly and all the Rangers came out of the tents, even the blind Fate-Watcher. As she exited her home, the woman cried aloud. "Dragons and griffons above the Moot-Ground! As the Ancestors foretold!" She raised her hands towards the sky and dropped them, signaling the riders to land. Immediately, the riders dropped in a loose formation, with the head of the delta landing first and sliding from his mount.

"Who is in command here?! I demand to speak with them!"

"Who addresses the Rangers of Seran so aggressively? Explain yourself now or be killed where you stand!" Her war-spear was at the ready and her neck frill was extended, rustling as each rider landed.

"I am Kessir, rider of Ethryll. This is my Lance of Riders. My Lance-Second, Elarac, rider of Kathryll. We have received word of a blood-pact that has been sworn between our Paragon of Knowledge, Thäoldr, and your Warden Ranger Karos Harsh-Eye. Long have our people been at odds, avoiding each other's company. By Thäoldr's command, it ends now. We are the first to honor this pledge. I– *we* are at your command, Rangers." In a show of trust, Kessir unsheathed his blade and stuck it into the dirt before him. His other Riders followed suit, and all looked to Tas'sa'Raath. The Rangers lowered their weapons as each processed the information in their own way.

Finally, Tas'sa'Raath spoke, her neck frill relaxing and shivering back into place. "It is with great joy that I, Tas'sa'Raath of the Ranger Moot, welcome this move. Welcome, riders of Gelvrentael to *Ca'e Möratuk*! We will uphold this blood pact with all our might!" She threw her arms wide in the accepted welcoming gesture and stuck her spear into the dirt.

Following suit, the other Rangers stuck their weapons into the dirt and all cried out at the same time. "HEARD AND WITNESSED!" Came the shout from many a Ranger and their hands raised above their heads, slapping together in dramatic thunderclaps. The Riders joined the cry and likewise the clapping and the fortifications went down.

Tas'sa'Raath closed the distance between her and Kessir. Reaching out, she put a hand on his shoulder before placing his hand on hers. Then she tapped her forehead against his in greeting and gave a grin, showing her fangs. "You are most welcome here, you and your Lance." The Rangers crossed the lines and began greeting the Riders. This went on for some time until Kessir spoke.

"What need have you of my Riders? How can we make ourselves of use?" He looked over at the Rangers for a moment before Sardra spoke up.

"I need to find the Warden Ranger. I am one of his Talons and must be ready to aid him at a moment's notice. If you have a rider willing to bear me to Cúledan, my gratitude would be great." Sardra spoke, shifting her position to join the throng.

A few riders shook their heads before a short man stepped

forward. "We can bear you to Cúledan. I am Porrik, rider of Tyfa." He gestured to his beast, who was currently preening.

Sardra nodded and approached. "I have but what I carry," she began, looking from rider to beast. *My, has the world changed*, she thought, *but I am glad for it.* "And I am quite light." She moved to the noble beast slowly, extending her hand so that it might see she meant no harm. The creature bowed its head and Sardra began petting it. "This is a powerful creature with a good heart and keen eye."

"My Tyfa is one of the greatest scouts of the Order of Gelvrentael. She can spot a ferret from the top of the clouds," he boasted. Sardra was unimpressed, knowing that eagles and Great Ravens could do the same. "Come, milady Ranger, let us ride."

Sardra nodded quickly, eager to be on the road and to see her best friend again. "I am Sardra Woodstrider, Porrik. Thanks be to you and Tyfa for bearing me as cargo." She patted the halfling's shoulder first and then patted the griffon on the head. When instructed, she saddled up behind the rider and secured herself as Porrik did likewise, walking her through all of it. Then they took off, the beast's wings beating strongly to carry her and her passengers into the darkening sky.

"We will ride all night if we must!" Porrik shouted above the howling wind to his companion. "Tyfa is willing, as am I. We will make our best speed to Cúledan and we will reunite you with your Warden Ranger as swiftly as we can arrange it!" His voice was still barely audible above the roar of air rushing past them.

Sardra nodded swiftly and leaned further forward, as did the rider. This helped the air rush over them, as opposed to into them, and was crucial to safe flight. At the top speeds a griffon could reach, leather straps would not hold well if they did not position themself appropriately.

They flew fast and far, and the land blazed by underneath them. Soon enough, they were clear of the wintry air of the Eversnow forest and breaking into the more pleasant air of Westerspring. Tyfa stretched her wings wide and glided for quite a distance, using thermals and a lucky tailwind to push herself as far as she could between flaps.

Sardra was ecstatic- she had experienced nothing like this, and it made her heart hammer in her chest. She doubted if she could ever travel the same way after this- as much as she loved walking through the woods. There was just such a free feeling about flying that one could not get from walking. Without thinking, she let out an exhilarated whoop.

Porrik chuckled to himself as he caught Sardra's whoop and let out his own jubilant cry. Riding the winds was always something that pleased him, and he was glad to share the experience with someone.

Suddenly, Tyfa let out a raucous cry and dove. Porrik let out a startled shout and looked to find what the griffon was chasing. His mind immediately leapt to terror as they saw a great black dragon- bigger than Namryll the High Mother. Immediately taking the reins, he hauled hard left into a bank of clouds. Tyfa followed the command quickly, moving herself to hide. Hopefully, the massive beast had not noticed them. Hopefully, it would go away.

Sardra was unsure of the problem- was it not a dragon, like the others? Reaching out with her thoughts, she felt the Strand the creature had- and it was immensely sinister- or something sinister had twisted it. She felt a shiver run up her spine as she felt the creature's presence. There was another nearby, many hundreds of feet down. A dark presence- an evil presence and Sardra could feel hatred coming off it. Reaching out to the birds of the surrounding skies, she watched the dragon as it lumbered on its way- searching for something- or someone. Soon enough, it was away, and she patted Porrik's shoulder. "It has moved off. We must leave before it returns."

Nodding, Porrik urged Tyfa to greater efforts- and pulled Sardra down until she buried her muzzle in the middle of the griffon's back. The air rushed over them, nearly tearing the breath from Sardra's lungs as they fled the behemoth. Faster and faster, Tyfa fled through the deepening gloom, until she was confident that she had put the enormous beast behind her. Then she descended- rather quickly.

"We have not yet made Dragonmoor- but Tyfa needs rest after that excitement. We will land near the town of Eldergrove. There we will rest- perhaps the Proud Lute is open and we can get a proper meal." Sardra could hardly disagree with the man as he spoke. Her belly was empty, and she did not like the idea of flying much further without food. Tyfa dropped through the clouds, landing gently just outside the town. Quickly, Sardra and Porrik unbelted from the back of Tyfa and slid to the ground. Porrik patted his beast's shoulder and sent her on the way to eat and rest. Then, the two headed towards the town, which was luckily bustling with life- *evidently the plague has not reached this far,* Sardra thought and was glad for it. Eldergrove was isolated, near the Nevian border, which normally was no trouble- but with the whispers she had heard of the Scala'Dun mobilizing their forces- trouble could soon come.

They approached the Inn, which was thankfully set on the edge of town- many an adventurer came through here, so the location was lucky. Striding to the door, Sardra pulled it open and smiled at the sight within. People were reveling and merry, drinking their cares away, or eating a meal. The activity stopped as she entered, followed by Porrik and all eyes were on them. No one spoke for a moment until the Innkeeper shouted.

"Ranger! Rider! You are most welcome in my Inn! Come in, find a seat and rest! You must be weary from the road!" Sardra merely nodded and strode to an empty table- far removed from the crowds, who had now gone back to their business. Porrik selected a chair across from her and sat easily, sighing as he took the load off his feet.

The Innkeeper, a portly halfling, made his way over to them and pushed a couple of people aside. "Tygan, Urvan, this cannot be the first time you have seen a Ranger and a Rider. Shove off and give them some room and some respite from your prying eyes!" Finally weaving through the throng in his Inn, he reached them at last. "Now then, honored guests! I am Werrick Riverton! It is my pleasure to serve you tonight! So, what will you be having, milady...?"

"I am Sardra Woodstrider- and my companion is Porrik, rider of Tyfa. I will have the hunter's stew if you would be so kind. As well, a large glass of cider would do me wonders." Sardra spoke quickly and succinctly, as there was no reason to be anything less right now. She eyed the man, and he watched her, taking in the sight of this Ranger. Her scarred muzzle, graceful arms and clawed hands. He dreaded to think of what must happen to those that found themselves on the wrong end of those claws, and he hoped he would never find out.

"And for you, master Porrik?" Werrick spoke, now looking to the diminutive Rider.

"I shall have the same, if you would be so kind, good sir." He nodded kindly to Werrick, who moved off to prepare their orders. He took a breath and turned to Sardra, speaking after a moment. "So, what does your Warden Ranger have awaiting him in Cúledan, Sardra?"

"Plague and worse. From what Carwaan told me, Little-brook is completely empty. I can only hope that the people there find peace in the embrace of the Ancestors." Sardra nodded gravely and was joined by Porrik in the motion. *Such a death does not look pleasant at all,* she thought to herself and *I fear it may come for more people if we are not swift.*

"What exactly does this plague look like?" He voiced his question a little louder than he expected, partly from fear. Regretting it instantly, he looked around to see if they had called any attention to them- thankfully, everyone was too busy or too drunk to care.

"Flesh sloughs off the bone. Rots away, pustules form- this I have seen from Carwaan's mind, but not much else. My Warden Ranger will know more. He will have likely seen it first-hand." She nodded sagely and dropped her voice. "The creatures of the land say it is spreading like wildfire. We have seen caravans of the dead being carried out of Hollyhead itself, and I fear the worst there. I have heard nothing from Dhol Kaszam or Daelath Ronson. But I have a fear that they may face the same troubles. Especially if Cúledan is already hard hit." She shook her head as she spoke- then continued. "But we have other concerns. Namely the skies ahead. How long does Tyfa need to rest before bearing us for the rest of the journey?"

Porrik sucked in a breath. He was doing a favor for this Ranger, and she was asking much. He had not seen what she had, so he did not quite share her sense of urgency. "Sardra, she is not as resilient as a great dragon. She cannot ferry us back and forth forever."

"I understand, Porrik, but our quest may change the fate of Seran for many a year. I sense she will give it all for this cause. I would not ask it of her if I did not believe it to be the most critical thing either of us has ever done." She watched Porrik for his reaction and failed to realize her own face was giving away her thoughts.

Porrik went to speak and stopped as he saw her expression. It struck him with the full force of a woman who had seen more pain and death than he could ever dread seeing. Of a woman who had suffered much and conquered it all to be who she wanted to be. A woman stronger than he knew. He took a breath as the feeling of being next to a giant receded and spoke. "We... will help anyway we can. If you asked us to go to the ends of Seran, we would. If you asked a blood-oath, I would do it without hesitation." He was becoming scared. *What have I gotten us into?* He wondered and had an odd feeling- a sadness the likes of which he had never encountered. He felt like this task would be his undoing.

"Hopefully, that will not be necessary- but your enthusiasm is comforting." *Enthusiasm,* Sardra mused, *may not be the right word. That was pure terror written on his face.* She smiled as Werrick brought them food and drink. He placed it before them and stepped away, smiling.

"Let me know if you need anything else!" He turned to leave, but was stopped by Sardra, who held out her coin purse. Nodding, the man removed a few gold- the cost of the meals and stepped away. Sardra returned the coin purse to her belt and began eating- with none of the fastidiousness of someone worried about manners, she dug into her stew and cider.

Porrik did the same a few moments later and reveled in the stew's taste. They seasoned it to perfection and seemed to get better with each bite. He grinned as he ate more carefully than his lupine companion, taking the time to taste his food. When he had finished, he pushed the bowl away and took a drink of his cider, though he wished he'd had mind to order an ale. Porrik called to Werrick, who made his way over, only to be stopped by a rather gruff adventurer- or perhaps a bandit? Porrik could hardly tell the difference.

"Instead of waiting on him, let us have you wait on a real man." The braggart growled at Werrick, intending to keep him and insult Porrik at the same time. "But perhaps if you give the boy there some milk, he will grow. Did you hear that, short one?"

Sardra moved for her sword, only to be stopped with a look by Porrik. He stood; his diminutive frame laughable compared to the burly heckler. He chuckled dryly and spoke, his words carefully measured. "When you call me 'shorty', put Rider ahead of it."

"Hah! You, a Rider of what, a goat?" He reached down to pick Porrik up. Then, several things happened at once. Porrik touched one of the tattoos on his arm, invoking the magic of the riders and causing it to glow. This sent a shockwave through the man, who stumbled backwards and landed against the bar. Then he touched another, and it likewise became luminous, and a ball of flame formed at his fingertips. Pressing the flame to his mouth, he blew outwards and engulfed the rude man in flames.

Werrick cried out, "Careful! Pray do not burn down my Inn!" as Porrik torched the bastard. The flaming man stumbled for the door and was helped along by another blast from Porrik's magic.

"And next time, mind your own, you crooked-nosed knave!" With a last blast from his tattoo, the man was out the door and on his face, only for a moment, before he began writhing to escape the flames. That unpleasant business done, Porrik returned to his seat- to find his companion doubled over laughing.

Werrick approached Porrik more warily this time and cleared his throat. "What need you, master Porrik?"

Porrik smiled genially and chuckled. "An ale if you would, please Master Werrick. I am quite parched after that... unfortunate business." Werrick nodded slowly and bustled off to get the requested drink. *Never has there been a fight in my Inn*, the halfling thought, *but I guess Kyon had it coming for his treatment of a Rider. The bastard is always causing trouble, but this is the first time blood has been shed. Maybe it is time to bar him from my Inn... if he survives.*

Werrick brought the ale to the table and Porrik handed over the price of the drink from his coin purse. Then he began sipping the ale, judging its taste and quality. He nodded after a moment and began drinking deep.

Sardra scoffed, "I will never understand how people can put such poison in their bodies." She shook her head for a moment, but after a glance from Porrik, quieted herself. She was being rude again, she realized, and needed to calm down. "But to each their own- a Ranger must always be on duty, which means hard drinks must never touch our lips."

"That is no way to live, Sardra. At what point do you realize you are going to go mad from lack of leisure time?" His words sounded genuinely concerned, and he shook his head before taking another drink. "Riders have leisure time, though it seems to only come when we are at our breaking points."

"Because we expect Rangers to aid others no matter what. Thus, we must have our heads always clear at all times. It is possible to survive in such a way; you just take your leisure time as you can." Sardra rolled her shoulders in a gentle shrug and shifted her stance on the chair. Then she drained her glass of cider and leaned back. A pipe came from one of her many pouches, as well as a smaller pouch of a smoking-weed the Rangers used to calm their nerves and focus their minds. *Dra'la'thel*, it they called it, or cold-smoke. It had a minty bouquet when smoked and caused the inner workings of the brain to even out and focus up.

Placing a pinch of the herb into the bowl of the pipe, Sardra struck a flame from one of her fingers and brought it to the herb and began smoking. Relaxing as she exhaled a cloud of smoke, she toyed with it for a moment. Using her magic, she shaped the smoke into the form of a wolf and watched it run through the Inn. The other patrons looked on in amusement and Porrik finished his ale.

Slowly, Porrik rose to his feet and there was no unsteadiness apparent in his gait as he walked to Werrick. "I would like a room, please. I must rest as my griffon rests."

Nodding, Werrick replied. "Of course, sir. Will your companion be needing a room?" He looked over at Sardra, who simply shook her head. Idly, she took another puff on her pipe before exhaling the smoke cloud. This one she did not turn into anything, just watched the smoke rise and fade away. She had too much to ponder to sleep and besides that, she knew what sleep would bring for her. Flashbacks, nightmares and worse would come to her if she tried to catch a night's repose, so she elected to remain awake- luckily, thanks to her training, there would be no ill effects.

She sat there for the longest part of the night, smoking and reflecting on her thoughts. Long after Werrick had gone to bed, there were few other patrons still awake and none were interested in bothering the Ranger for any news. Each had their own tasks and trials to deal with and knew not of the plague ravaging Seran.

When morning came, Sardra was to be found pacing in front of the fireplace like a caged animal, her thoughts focused to a razor's edge. Werrick, being the first sleeping person to awaken came down the stairs to find her there. "What troubles you, Ranger? You seem... disquieted." She sighed and shook her head, taking a moment to gather her thoughts before she spoke.

"Werrick, a plague has struck- the likes of which has never been seen. People die in the streets, their bodies rotting away. Thus far all I know of it is passed from beasts that have seen it, rather than firsthand." Her voice dropped gravely as she spoke. "I must ask of you to keep a log of all travelers to your Inn, that we may find any infected peoples. This is imperative, Werrick. I must know of all you see. Send a raven if you find anything troublesome about people."

"But what should I look for, Ranger? I cannot just stop each of my patrons and demand a bill of health. What must I ask for?" He was not sure what evil she was worried would land on his doorstep, but it concerned him greatly.

Taking a breath, Sardra nodded before speaking once more. "I am unsure of what to look for, Werrick. As I told you, I have not seen this first-hand, so I would not venture to guess. But I have a feeling you will know when you see it." With her piece said, she looked outside as the sun rose. Stepping quickly to the door, she passed through and stood on the porch of the Inn, watching Kjetta crest the hills, his vibrant blue light filling the sky with life and radiating warmth. She basked in the oncoming warmth for a moment and turned when she heard a voice behind her.

"A beautiful day to fly," began Porrik as he strode out to meet her. He had obviously taken the time to wash himself up and freshen his clothes as best he could. He nodded to Sardra and continued speaking. "If our luck holds, we should be in Dragonmoor by midday- and Cúledan by evening."

Sardra nodded, before giving voice to her concerns. "I fear that many more will die today. We must press on with all speed. If you need food, I would eat now. Otherwise, let us away as swiftly as possible." She stepped away from the door and stretched, arching her back as she bent to touch her toes. The lupine woman did not mind sitting, but waiting around made her restless and sometimes irritable.

"I concur most heartily. I had Werrick prepare us something small." As he spoke, he broke a small loaf of tavern bread in half, revealing the meat and eggs cooked within. Handing one half to her, he quickly ate the other. Refueled by food and rejuvenated by rest, the Rider leapt upwards. As he came back down, he slammed his fists together in excitement. His tattoos glowed bright for a few moments and he grinned at the Ranger, his eyes flashing. "Let the combined might of the Rangers and Riders see this through!" Cupping a hand to his mouth, he let out an ululating call, sending his voice echoing into the morning. They heard a rustling of wings, and a shadow blazed past, the owner turning sharply in the air and dropping towards the ground. Tyfa landed quickly and let out a screech, waking all in the Inn and any camping nearby. The guards in the watchtower leapt to, brandishing shields, swords and spears as they looked for some great threat- only to see the great griffon standing proudly.

Sardra mimicked Porrik's gesture, hopping into the air and slamming her fists together in excitement, before running after the short man to where Tyfa sat waiting. When instructed, she climbed aboard and secured herself to the beast's shoulders before patting her feathers. Porrik seated himself in the saddle and tightened his straps, before slapping Tyfa's neck affectionately. The griffon drew back on its powerful legs and pushed off with incredible force and speed, sending herself and her passengers careening into the sky. As she cleared the tops of the trees, Tyfa unfurled her wings and flapped them in powerful strokes, driving the trio through the air towards the rising sun.

Tyfa cruised leisurely, hitting updrafts here and there. Occasionally, the griffon's great wings stayed extended, and the creature glided along, enjoying the feel of air on her feathers. A happy scream tore its way from her beak and folded her wings for a sharp dive towards the ground. Both Porrik and Sardra cried out in jubilation as they dove, with Sardra clinging to the rider to keep her from flying off and away. Just before impacting the ground, the griffon extended her wings to catch them all, before sending herself back up into the sky. Taking a breath in, the griffon allowed her eyes to range far and wide, seeking anything that may pose a threat to herself or his riders.

She never noticed the great shadow above her.

Descending fast on their prey, Vaelyn and Talakath dropped from the clouds like a falling star. Talons extended, Talakath slammed into Tyfa, knocking her wings out of socket and knocking Porrik cold from the sudden change in direction. The griffon screamed out, her wings fluttering uselessly before she was seized by the shoulders, but when Vaelyn gave the command to rip her apart, Talakath refused– it was an ignoble death for a beautiful creature and she would not be part of it. Enraged, the albino elf mentally screamed at the beast, attempting to cause pain via their telepathic link. To force the dragon to his will. But some beasts are stronger than men and the great black dragon held firm. Any other time, the creature would not hesitate to have slain the smaller beast. But not now and not here.

Sardra reeled– there was hardly enough room to maneuver, but she would have to manage. Some massive black creature had assailed them and it was time to put her skills to the test. Twisting carefully, she grabbed the unconscious Porrik and secured him better in his straps, fearing that his neck might have been broken. Hoping this would not prove to be a fatal mistake, she unsheathed her sword and drove it into the underbelly of the beast as it brought the trio close enough to hold. Her frustration doubled when her sword snapped clean, unable to pierce the beast's hide. Cursing her luck and realizing her powerlessness in this situation, she resigned herself to wait for the right moment to strike. She could feel two presences that unknown means had hidden and surmised that the two must work together– so she would have to realize a plan to take down at least one of them. When it finally occurred to her that they were the prisoner of a massive black dragon, she called out to the ravens, hawks and eagles of the area to relay her peril to the Warden Ranger. They were quite far from Cúledan– but word travels fast with the birds of the land.

Taking a breath, Sardra positioned herself to check Porrik's neck for a pulse. She searched for a few moments before she could finally feel the subtle thudding that showed life continued in the man. Sighing, she resigned herself to inaction, as the dawning feeling of helplessness washed over her- not for the first time in her life. Steeling herself, the woman growled and shifted her patterns of thought- she was not helpless. It was simply the wrong time. This was not the first moment in her life she'd had to surrender to the currents carrying her and she knew it would not be the last.

When they neared the ground, Tyfa was rather unceremoniously dropped to the ground, landing in a crumpled heap with her riders still in their places. Sardra unlinked herself from the flight belts quickly and dropped to the ground, bringing her broken sword around in a fierce display. She would never stop fighting. The black dragon landed nearby and the beast's rider made their way to the ground, giving Sardra her first good view of her attackers. Tyfa groaned weakly and flexed one wing back into the socket, the pop resonating loudly, echoing in Sardra's skull. It was a distraction she sorely needed right now, but she kept her eyes fixed on the elf approaching her.

Vaelyn let out a laugh as he saw the Ranger before him- she clung to her broken weapon like it was her last hope. He would strip her of that soon enough, but first, he had to deal with the Rider and his beast. Touching the tattoos that blackened his arms and torso, he began an incantation that shook the surrounding ground. The sky grew dark above them, but no clouds were in sight. Then, the Void opened a gaping maw and out shot a burst of the brightest fires anyone had seen in ages. Tyfa let out a terrified squawk before she and Porrik were consumed in an inferno, the likes of which most mages could only dream of creating.

Sardra felt a heat more intense than any she had ever known on her back and, instinctively, she dropped to the ground and rolled away from it. When she chanced a glance behind her, she saw only the singed remains of Tyfa's wings, burned clean from the poor beast's body. Snarling, she leapt to her feet and charged at the elf who had just committed this atrocity. "Bastard!" Her intent was simple- rip the life from the man who had killed her newest friends. But such a victory would not be simple, as a force unseen slammed backward into her and sent her crashing to the ground. She studied the man's face, every detail, from the Two-Soul eyes, one amber, one azure. Face sculpted as if by someone trying to recreate an Ancestor. Flawless, snow-white skin and no hair to be seen- he was albino, but that made it difficult to tell what race produced him. Obviously, he was an elf, which was easy enough to judge by the ears. With dedication, Sardra inscribed every detail to memory, reminding herself to be patient.

Vaelyn chuckled, realizing he could get more than a few hours of enjoyment out of torturing this Ranger. Touching his tattoos again, he prepared to open the Void once more and offer to it her life energy- just a little of it, to give the Void a taste. A sudden, excruciating pain in his head distracted him as his dragon pressured him to take her prisoner- to render her defenseless before she butchered them. *Wisdom would be in declawing the beast before playing with her.* Nodding, Vaelyn focused his energies in a different direction- sending very precise bursts of Void-flame to destroy the Ranger's equipment and then to bind her. He wrapped her hands and muzzle in jet black fire, keeping her from being able to go on the offensive. Then, Vaelyn simply dragged her to Talakath and tied her to the seat before taking his place on the saddle. "Now then, I expect you to sit still. It is only due to my dragon that you are even alive." Once he was settled, the elf spurred Talakath to flight and away they went. Only later would Vaelyn realize the folly of not covering the dokk's head.

Sardra fumed- she had let herself be taken. This was not the first time a male had taken her in bonds toward a fate unknown. But she knew there were far more useful things to do than just sit and fume- with careful eyes, she watched the world below, mapping out the route being taken, noting landmarks and relaying them to all birds friendly to the Rangers. Within a day, she hoped, the news of her peril and the way to find her would reach her beloved Rangers- and they would come as an angry tide to destroy this bastard and his dragon.

They had been on the wing for more than a few hours and the sun was at its peak when Talakath dropped from the sky, circling downwards toward a large cave that had been carved out of the cliff face. It was not long before the magnificent beast touched the ground once more, lowering one shoulder to allow her rider to debark with his cargo.

Rather than bring her down carefully, Vaelyn dumped his unwilling companion onto the ground. He had had little interaction with the Rangers, so he wasn't sure what to expect of this one. She had already tried to lash out at him, so he made a mental note to be at least somewhat careful. Grabbing her by the shirt, Vaelyn hauled his prisoner to her feet. "Take in the view- it is the last you will see. You will die here, forgotten, lost, and broken." She snarled at him, wishing that her bindings would dissipate- just for a moment. "Oh? Fiery one, are you? I will enjoy making you beg for death's embrace."

Sardra had had enough of his sneering and his attempted threats. Focusing her mind on the natural magics she was skilled with, she forced the Void to retreat- a little at first, but as she pressured more energy through, the retreat quickened. When she was free of the bindings, she snarled. "You are not the first man to set his will against me, and you will not be the last."

Vaelyn laughed- not the rich laughter of happiness and cheer, but the deep disturbing laughter of a being whose mind was well and truly gone. "You do not comprehend the situation you are in, child. I am beyond your Ancestors. I am the most powerful being in all Seran! Your pathetic magic does not compare to mine. You are a drop of rain before a raging firestorm- you have nothing. I will be the last face you see." He smirked for a moment and his voice dropped into a dangerous tone- one that Sardra was all too familiar with. "You have nothing. No aid coming for you, no friends to rescue you. You have no hope." He thought those words enough to quench the fire he could see growing- but her actions showed the fire ran stronger than he could ever understand.

In a flash, Sardra lashed out, her hands gripping her precious pendant- the sign of the Rangers, a beacon of hope for all to see. One yank and the leather cord holding it around her neck snapped clean, and she lashed outward with it- burying the pendant in Vaelyn's azure eye. He recoiled, shrieking in pain and confusion; above it, her voice echoed in his mind, taunting him. "I am a Ranger. I am *never* without hope!"

Vaelyn stumbled back, clutching at his face, blood running

freely from his destroyed eye. Sardra used her time wisely, lashing out with her powerful claws to lacerate his arms multiple times. She kept up a vicious assault, intending to put an end to the foe that threatened her, tried to force his will upon her. She was having none of this. Realizing she still gripped her pendant, she made an important choice- and shattered her pendant, letting the crumbling shards cut into her hand and cause her to bleed- activating the last-ditch magic of the Ranger pendant. A flare, unseen but felt for hundreds, if not thousands, of miles, went into the sky. As far away as Northrealm, Rangers suddenly felt a stabbing pain in their heads, enough to knock even the most stalwart over. It passed like a flash of lightning, but all Rangers had a clear picture of Sardra's hand, bloodied and gashed, burned into their minds. Several began preparing to home in on the signs given and more acted as relays, sending the image towards their contemporaries hoping to reach Karos.

When his pain had died down enough to react, Vaelyn was livid. With a force of will, he blasted Sardra with a jet of black flame, intending to incinerate her. But she had already memorized his attacks and by the time the Void opened itself, she was prepared. She knew she would still get burned, but not as badly as Vaelyn was obviously hoping. Screaming his rage at her, he flexed his will, plucking her off the ground with his magic as one plucks a flower, before slamming her into the cavern wall, floor and roof. "Which will break first," Vaelyn screeched at her, "your spirit or your body?!"

In response, Sardra spit some of the blood that was flowing from her mouth into his face. She had survived far worse than what he could manage. "I defy you, bastard. I will defy you until you tear the last breath from my body."

Picking herself up off the floor, she dug her feet into the ground and rushed forward, claws extending. Her gear was gone, all that was left on her body was her clothing and fur. But to her, that was enough. She let out an annoyed yelp when her feet left the ground and a pained cry when she was slammed into another wall. Again and again, she was pummeled and thrashed for the better part of an hour. When Vaelyn finally lost interest, Sardra was sure she had at least one broken bone, as well as countless bruises. But she was alive, and that mattered. Lifting her once again, Vaelyn threw the dokk woman into a cage and slammed the door, locking it with his magic.

That will keep her contained so I can continue my work... he thought to himself, so sure that he would never fall, but unaware of the storm he had called down upon himself.

16

16: Northrealm

"**D**ragonsmith!" the voice cried as a powerful hand slammed down on the door to the Forge. Once, twice, thrice someone knocked on the portal, rousing all inside. First to move was the man addressed, the imposing Dragonsmith of Coldforge, Viktor of clan Bludstyn. He strode to the door, clearing the distance in just a few steps. Reaching out, he pulled the door open to reveal one of the town's Rangers.

"Aye, Ranger, what do you need?" The half-giant's voice was barely above a whisper; rarely did the Rangers like their business being spoken of loudly.

"It is time. Are you prepared?" Speaking softly, the Ranger gestured to his gathered force; twelve other Rangers and with the Dragonsmith, they would number 14, a lucky enough number.

"Prepared? Ranger, you must remind me." Viktor rumbled gently, searching his memory for what the other may talk about. As soon as the words left his lips, he realized what the Ranger wanted.

At the same time as the Dragonsmith realized the answer, the Ranger spoke. "You were interested in joining us on a raid against a bandit clan that had set up too near the town for comfort?"

Nodding, Viktor let out a call to his Forge-Second, the only other person he currently trusted to hold down the forge. Suddenly, he remembered the reason he had dressed in more normal clothes than he was comfortable in.

"Helve! Rouse the Dragons and bring me my hammer, as well as Kalvuth's mail shirt. Then, take to your tasks and see to the Forge. I will be out for a day at least."

Immediately, the shorter woman called out to the magnificent beasts as she searched for the great warhammer that Viktor kept above his mantle. In the back of her mind, the stout woman wondered if he would have need for his armor and moved to grab it as well. Rumbling a protest, the two Forge-Dragons began stomping towards the great door that stood between them and the world outside.

This had best be important, began the great Red, only to be interrupted by another voice.

"It is. We are hunting down a bandit clan. It has been far too long since your talons have seen use." The reply startled the dragon, for it came not from Viktor, but from the Ranger. Curiosity replaced astonishment, and he reached out to the mind of the Ranger, to find it was closed off; *Focused on the task ahead,* thought the dragon.

Finally, Helve brought the requested items; the repaired mail shirt, which Kalvuth took gratefully. Quickly, he dropped his sword-belt and his overtunic before working his way into the shirt. Then, he re-dressed and belted, looking much more comfortable in the armor; the great Warhammer of the

Bludstyn Clan, forged centuries ago by the first Half-Giant in the line. It was an imposing weapon, standing almost as tall as she did at five feet; and finally, Viktor noticed the other burden she bore, the chest in which his armor sat. He chuckled gently and relieved her of the burdens and placed them down.

"A chest? Pray tell Dragonsmith Viktor. What use do you have-" The Ranger's question was answered not by voice, but by deed. Opening the chest, the Dragonsmith removed a sizeable set of plate armor, obviously forged for him. It was richly decorated, with runes telling wonderful tales of exploits from his youth.

Evidently, this Dragonsmith is not as docile as he puts on, Kalvuth thought to himself. *This should be an interesting quest.*

As Kalvuth lost himself in reading the runes, Viktor tapped the Ranger on the shoulder. "If you do not mind, dear Ranger," he began, raising an eyebrow, "I would very much like to get dressed." He seemed oddly distraught as he looked at the armor the Ranger was holding as if it contained some painful memory.

Sheepishly, the Ranger nodded and stepped back, though words flowed quickly from his mouth. "Someday, or perhaps on the journey, you must tell some of your tales. I know you to be younger than our Warden Ranger, but you are definitely older than myself." Kalvuth grinned and reached up, slapping the half-giant's shoulder affectionately before turning to the assembled Rangers. Shifting his tone, he spoke in the ancient language they used. "*Tengarii!*" Immediately, they snapped to attention. "*We march on the Dragonsmith's command!*"

Viktor sighed as he donned his armor, his eyes growing misty as he remembered the last time he had put the gear on. He was just reaching the end of his Restless Years, the period when Giants and their kin could not physically settle down, and had joined up with an adventuring company for one last hurrah. The job was simple enough, go into some ancient ruins and retrieve a family's long forgotten relic. He could hardly remember what it was- perhaps a winding horn? Or an ancient casting-card deck? *It is pointless to remember, Viktor. That was decades ago,* he thought to himself. Still, the memory came flowing through him and reminding him of old wounds. He thought of many faces, but only one hurt him deeply, shook him to his very core. His beloved Seldred, taken too soon. Taken by illness, in fact, while he was on that last quest. Sighing sadly, Viktor steeled himself against the thoughts that invariably followed the mention of her. *What could have been? Where would I be?*

He shook his head after a moment and belted on his greaves. Then came the gambeson, which he noted was in good shape for spending at least six decades in a chest. After that came his cuirass, vambraces, and gauntlets. For a moment, he looked over his helmet, trying to decide whether to don it. He had fashioned it from the skull of a cleaverback he had slain, a beastly large and hateful creature. He chuckled slightly as he remembered how that creature had fought- hours and hours they tried to best each other before he finally gained the upper hand and smote its ruin. In its honor, he wore the beast's skull, as it was the only creature that had ever come close to besting him in combat. Sure, he had amassed his share of wounds, but if his hammer couldn't solve the problem, his great fists would. He was a terrifying sight, decked out in black armor with gold highlights and standing over eleven feet tall at the chest. There were few alive who could remember when he would last worn his armor and fewer still who wanted to remember those times.

When he had assembled himself, the Dragonsmith turned to the gathered force and took up his warhammer, raising it to the skies above that the Ancestors themselves would witness that The Dread Giant had once more risen. At his sign, the Rangers began making their way out of town. Viktor scooped up his traveling pack from Helve, who again had remembered something he needed. *How do I live without that girl,* he mused to himself, *were it not for her, I am sure I would forget my forge hammer.* He shook his head and gave a glance around as the townsfolk that had gathered looked on in pure awe. He was a terrifying sight in his armor for sure, and he could hear the whispers.

"What errand takes the Dragonsmith? Why is he clad in such terrifying armor?"

"Quiet yourself, Alara. He is obviously on a quest of some importance."

As they left town, the company made its way south and towards the town's wall. Viktor tried to remember how long it had been since he'd even gone with a woodsman group to gather firewood from the forest and he realized he was coming up blank. *Had it really been that long?* When they passed outside the wall of the city, Viktor heard the unmistakable sound of great wings laboring to hold massive beasts in the sky. Glancing upwards, he could make out the twin dragons as they cruised above the treetops, circling when necessary to keep pace with the folk on the ground.

"Just how far is this slaver camp, Kalvuth?"

"About three leagues. Close enough to be quite concerned."

Viktor nodded slowly and brought his warhammer up to rest on his shoulder as he walked. He was having a hard time keeping himself with the group because of his size. One would expect someone as calculating as he was with his thoughts to be slow of movement, but he was surprising his companions. Just as he was having trouble keeping himself back with them, they occasionally had to break into a brisk jog to keep up.

As the sun rose the next day, the leagues had melted under their feet and the head of the formation held up a fist just long enough for all to see and pass along behind them. Iridian, the lead scout, stepped from the brush, startling Viktor as he seemed to melt out of the scenery.

"Report, Iridian."

"Just over sixty bandits and they have captives. It is likely they plan to sell them at a slave market. Various weapons, ranging from swords and axes to warhammers. One battlemage, evidently under contract from someone else. Armor varies, as with all bandit clans. Heaviest seems to be a steel plate on their leader. From what it sounds like, his name is Korgrim. He is a half-dwarf and rules by utter terror."

Ducking down, the Dragonsmith looked to see what the others were doing.

"If I may, I would prefer a stand-up fight to what you folk usually do. I can likely kill their leader in my first attack, and it would take a very keen blade to bring me to ruin."

The Rangers nodded among each other, before Kalvuth glanced up at the giant-descendant.

"Of course, Viktor, but you will need help to reach him. There are sixty of them and they have captives here-"

Showing the outside of the camp, Kalvuth nodded as if that knowledge was of utmost importance. *It is critical,* thought Viktor. Nodding, he glanced up and saw five cloaked forms moving into position near the cages; he realized that just under half a dozen of the Rangers had vanished. Kalvuth continued speaking until Viktor tapped his shoulder.

"What is it, man? I am pla-"

His voice dropped when Viktor showed the cloaked forms. Kalvuth did a quick head count and realized that a group had broken off and sighed with no small amount of annoyance.

"Or we can just perform this on the wing. Viktor- go for the leader and destroy him. Sow terror in their ranks however you choose."

"Right."

Approaching the edge of the camp, Viktor let out a terrible cry; one that resonated through the clearing and roused the bandits from their revelry.

"Vu'Locav! Alvarath! The time is now! The time is now! Loose your great fires and bring vengeance with me!"

The closest bandit to him did not even have time to react as the great warhammer slammed into his back, shattering his spine. He fell forward, barely able to gasp from the impact. Then, his assailant was off as the man's friends began trying to rally from the sudden assault. Swords came from their sheathes as a cry went up throughout the camp, but there was no stopping the devastating momentum of the giant. When defenders stood in his way, he simply bowled them aside and continued towards their leader.

"Korgrim!" called the Dragonsmith, realizing that he recognized the man wearing the armor. The armor was ill-fitting, having been stolen from one of his many victims, but it bore the maker's mark of Viktor's own forge. His rage clouded his mind for a moment as he crossed the distance between them.

"And who are y-"

The words never finished their escape from his mouth as the powerful blow struck him, shattering the breastplate, his ribs and launching him into the sky. As he fell, gouts of flame lanced down into his camp and the screams of terror and pain filled the air.

"Dragon's fire! The giant commands dragon's fire!"

This shout caused utter chaos amongst the bandits as they began trying to run to evade the firestorm that was being brought down upon their heads. But everywhere they ran, they found another foe. From Rangers to the Giant, they could find no quarter. A group rallied, planning on rushing Viktor, but they realized their error as his great hammer swung down. With a mighty blow, all five were sent into the air, their bodies crushed and bleeding from various wounds. The lucky ones that survived the first blow slammed into snow and tree and lay there dying as a coordinated attack cut their comrades down.

Soon enough, the fighting died down and the Rangers took stock of their casualties. Thankfully, they were only minor, with one Tenderfoot having tripped over a corpse and another having had a body fall on them from the sky. Viktor made his apologies to the victim of the falling body and wagered that the Ranger would have an interesting story to tell their friends.

As the group sorted through the camp, Viktor knew something was dangerously wrong. *Was there not a battlemage when Iridian reported?* He was just about to voice his concern when he heard chanting. Instinct screamed at him, and he dove behind a large cart meant for transporting folk, but that thought exited his mind as a wave of heat passed over him. Glancing up, he saw a stream of fire aimed his direction. He yelped and ducked back down, wishing that he had skill with thrown weapons. He could hear the crackling flames striking the cart and it slightly surprised him that the thing was not moving. As the cart gave a loud crack, he remembered that he probably weighed as much, if not more, than the cart and the thought of being behind it was suddenly less comforting.

"Rangers! I could use help!"

His call prompted the Rangers nearby to glance over from their tending to the captives to see his predicament, and this caused an immediate scramble. One shouted to the rest in Sk'av'A and arrows began pelting the mage attacking Viktor. He had planned for this, though, and had erected a ward against physical attacks; but the Rangers were well-known for having skill across a spectrum of combat.

Iridian swore loudly as he realized what was going on; he had forgotten about the bastard battlemage. Quickly shifting from anger into calm, he readied a Sk'av'A phrase in his mind, focusing energy from the world itself through his body. His heterochromic eyes flashed from purple and gold to red and white, and he uttered his chosen phrase with the solemnity of someone putting a friend into the ground. His hands rose, and he circled one around the other, faster and faster as his expression shifted his words from conversation to an elemental assault.

"Rise snow; rise wind. Rise snow; rise wind. Rise and mix, become blizzard, become death."

The wind, which had been gentle and kind, sprang to a gale force and a howling pitch and the snow, which had been falling gently, became driven with deadly intent. At first, the only effect was that things became harder to see, but within the small camp the temperature soon dropped dramatically.

The newer Rangers fell back, relying on their enchanted clothing to protect them as the more senior Rangers stepped up, adding their own voices to the spell.

The battlemage was distracted from his attack on Viktor as his breath suddenly froze in his lungs. He was not from this land and where normally his enchantments would protect him, abruptly they lost effectiveness. He could hardly hear above the raging wind, but that was the least of his concerns. Shifting his focus from attack to survival, the battlemage began several incantations meant to warm himself up to protect from this sudden onslaught and in doing so; he let his wards falter.

Viktor could feel a change in the air and chose his moment to strike. The mage had been hovering high enough that the Rangers could not reach him, but he had not considered the Dragonsmith's generous height. Through the dense snow, he could hardly see the mage, but Viktor had been an adventurer long enough that instinct could guide him through. Taking a breath of the frigid air, he charged, putting the charred cart to his back. His hammer came around in a wide circle as he charged blindly and he felt the impact of steel on- something. There was a loud crunch and suddenly, the chanting stopped.

Afraid for a moment that he had accidentally killed a Ranger, Viktor looked around; was he far enough away from his companions? He pulled his hammer down after realizing that it was staying where it was fairly well and saw what he had hoped for. There was the battlemage, dead and frozen to his hammer. Reaching up to the dead man's head, he gave a mighty yank and separated man from metal with a meaty squelch and a rush of blood and gore onto the snow.

"The battlemage is dead," he called to his companions. "I

feel we have done well."

The blizzard subsided, and the air returned to normal; at least, normal for the Eversnow Forest, which was merely a few degrees above freezing, in sharp contrast to the depths of cold the artificial blizzard had reached. The Rangers seemed right pleased with themselves and Viktor made his way over to his companions.

"Kalvuth, tell me. What of the captives?"

"Already on their way to *Tejg Sungetiigd* with part of my detachment, milord. They have a long road ahead, as do we, to get back to Coldforge."

"Aye. Well, let us be off then, master Ranger."

The Ranger grinned at the title he had given him and shook his head. *I will never understand some folk. Time and time again, we ask not to be called masters and time and time again, we are called such.* No Ranger held mastery over another sapient. Masters of Nature they could be considered, but even then, their skills and abilities were a single flake or flurry in a great blizzard compared to the skills of, say, the Druids. Kalvuth shook his head at the thought of such folk. He had only seen perhaps one tribe in his lifetime, and they were welcoming enough to his kind because of their shared hope of protecting the wilds, but they were an odd sort.

Snapping back to his senses as another Ranger tapped his shoulder, Kalvuth turned to see Iridian standing before him.

"Aye, Iridian? What need you, my friend?"

"All accounted for, Kalvuth."

"*Skúlt.*"

With a sharp cry, Kalvuth rallied the remaining Rangers and pointed toward Coldforge. It would be at least a few hours' journey at Viktor's speed and the Rangers were glad to be in the giant's company. Even the largest, most implacable of creatures would weigh their options against a giant. So, when they left the camp, the tailing Ranger gave a wolf-like howl to signal to any wolves nearby that there was a tasty treat awaiting them. One must always return the dead to the world; hungry wolves were the easiest way of this.

The road was long and the Rangers cheerful as they escorted the Dragonsmith home, though one might wonder as to the necessity of escorting a half-giant clad in plate armor. After all, they were a scant ten miles from Coldforge and with dragons cruising overhead, one would be forgiven to think the Rangers unnecessary.

Reaching out to Vu'Locav and Alvarath, Viktor spoke privately, trying to see what the two dragons were thinking. *What say you to that adventure?*

The response was immediate, causing Viktor to be surprised by the terseness of the two dragons.

Not enough to do, came the reply from Vu'Locav, who seemed awfully ready to wing and watch as the battlemage made a cinder of the cart Viktor had been behind.

It was dull, was Alvarath's response, and it seemed easy for the dragon to say when flying above the scene as the folk on ground fought against greater numbers.

Viktor chuckled gently and shook his head. It took him a moment to form his thoughts, but when he gave them to the dragons, he did not hold back. *You know, you two were awfully silent while I ducked behind a cart with fire being blasted at me.*

Immediately, there was a plethora of mental apologies and defensive excuses, but the one that stood out to Viktor the most was simply, *you seemed to have things under control.* For a moment, the ridiculousness of the statement struck him dumb, and he fought to find more words.

That does not mean I would not appreciate the help. The words sounded almost hurt in his mind and in truth, they were. Just because he "had the situation under control", he reasoned, *does not mean that a dragon spewing fire wouldn't have made things easier. Though the Rangers had done well with their application of the Old Tongue, we could have handled simpler it. Be off home, noble beasts. I will find my way there in due time.*

The dragons seemed to accept this instruction and winged off ahead, cutting their own paths home to Coldforge through the waning sunlight. After a time, Kalvuth sidled up to the Dragonsmith and gently prodded him in the ribs.

"Come on, Ancestors-favored Dragonsmith. Tell us of some stories inscribed into your armor."

"Please, Ranger. I would rather not recount them. The memory of this armor haunts me greatly."

Kalvuth nodded slowly and patted whatever he could reach on the great man. When he next spoke, his voice was much more somber.

"Believe you me, Viktor. You are in the company of folk who know those feelings better than any. A secret for you if you are interested." Viktor, not one to ignore information, leaned down as best he could to the Ranger. When he was close enough, the Ranger spoke. "The things we Rangers see in our day-to-day lives. The things we do in defense of peace and protecting innocent lives. They haunt us to where we cannot sleep at all."

"No sleep? But then, how are you functioning? Pray tell you are not merely drinking stamina potions to survive. The Healers say-"

"Aye, I know what the Healers say. 'Too long without rest

will rot your brain', they say and they have cut open the heads of folk who have died from lack of sleep to prove it." That sent a shudder down Viktor's spine. *Healing the injured was one thing, but cutting open dead folk? What could call for such barbarity? Had they lost their humanity in the pursuit of knowledge?* He was about to voice his concern when Kalvuth continued. "The brain withers if you go too long without sleep, but we Rangers have found a way around that."

"Pardon, Kalvuth, but... Do the Healers really cut open the dead? Why on Seran would they do that? Are they mad?"

"Nay, Viktor. They do it in search of ways to better aid the living. You know this well, but I remind you, life is not as clean as it is in your forge. We must do dirty deeds in service of those we protect. For folk such as you and me, that involves felling those who would prey on others. For a healer, sometimes that involves cutting open the honored dead to learn of the ways of the body." Kalvuth shrugged casually and popped his back. It was rare he got to speak with the Dragonsmith, but it was pleasant enough to try. He took a breath and considered his next words as he tried to gauge the Dragonsmith. Too much pressing could make the half-giant coil into himself and make him reluctant to talk at all, but not enough pressure would not give the Ranger the information he wanted. He was banking on the half-giant, not knowing what he was trying to do, but it was irksome that he was having to go to these lengths. Normally, giants and their kin were far more interested in storytelling than this one seemed to be, but the Ranger accepted he had his own reasons.

"What do you remember of your father, Viktor?"

"My father, hmm," Viktor began, reaching up to adjust his helmet. He was not sure how to speak of his father. Most of his memories were older than this Ranger and it would take some time to bring them to the surface. "Father was... strange. Always tinkering with some strange metal that he had found, disassembling or reassembling things. It was rarely that he had time for me, or my sister."

"You have a sister, Viktor? You have nary spoke of her in the times we have talked."

"She chose a different path and I write to her often, but she never visits. I cannot say that I blame her, for we live in one of the most dangerous areas of Seran."

"What does your sister do?"

"She is a healer, believe it or not, working at Mount Wounds-End."

Kalvuth nodded slowly and adjusted the pack he habitually wore. As they moved along the path back towards Coldforge. It startled him when Viktor spoke next, not because he expected silence, but because of what Viktor said.

"My story is not as pleasant as one would believe. Growing up was pleasant, even if father was distant. It was not until mother died that things were difficult. Father stopped eating, which led him to forget to feed his children. He drowned himself in work, as if he blamed himself when it was no one's fault. She sickened from what the healers called pneumonia and by the time he had brought her to Mount Wounds-End, she was already far enough along that death was certain."

Sucking in a breath, Kalvuth shook his head slowly. Pneumonia was a terrible way to die and to lose a mother was doubly painful.

"How old were you when she passed onto the Path, Viktor?"

"I was but ten. For five long years, my father suffered, and we suffered by that cause. It was a mercy when he handed the forge over to me and passed away, as we knew he would suffer no longer."

That must have been painful, thought Kalvuth as he examined the Dragonsmith with fresh eyes.

"What then? Surely your journeying didn't end there."

"Nay, it did not. When I started into my second decade of life, I felt a burning urge to adventure. A call deep in my blood. So, I handed the forge off to my assistant, in whom I had placed the entirety of my trust, and made my name as an adventurer. I was the Mastersmith of Coldforge no longer. In his stead, I had become Viktor the Brutal, adventurer with Krygan-Shawv Adventuring. It was a good life, and I amassed quite a fortune. Enough, in fact, that I could investigate funding an expedition beneath Coldforge, which is when we found the Star-Steel."

"And what happened then?"

"Well, as I was coming back to Coldforge after a successful venture, I met Seldred." Viktor took a breath, fighting back the mistiness in his eyes as he remembered the meeting, continuing after a few moments. "When I met her, it was a beautiful day. The clouds had retreated for the first time in record and the sun. *Kjetta himself* blessed our meeting. Her hair, deep red, was braided in the manner of the gah'Drin clan she was born in and her eyes twinkled the purest silver I have ever seen. Her face and indeed the rest of her body were covered in constellations of freckles and she was the most beautiful thing I had ever beheld. Her face," he chuckled for a moment, reaching up to dab away the tears that had flowed from his eyes, "was gentle. Kind even, as if she had seen the evil of the world and forsook it. When she smiled, she outshone the stars themselves and she would often wrinkle her nose when she was truly, deeply happy."

Viktor stopped for a moment to dab away his tears and to avoid letting a stray sob interrupt his memories. When he continued, he tried to paint the best picture he could through the pain. "She brought out the best in me. Tenderness, kindness, all things I had learned about and people told me I was capable of. Suddenly Viktor the Brutal became someone you could have a drink with, or talk to freely, instead of someone to hide away from. Six years we courted, as she learned she loved the town life more than living in a wagon and she grew as dear to me as life itself. She was the air I breathed, the water I drank. But she did not approve of my adventuring. 'Tis too dangerous, she would always say, and she begged me to stop. But ah... I was in my Restless Years. I could not settle down. Out of love as much as a desire to keep me home, we were wed by the Ranger Reawin, back when they still lived here."

Reawin was a truly honored name among the Rangers and was often named as the best example of what a Ranger could be. They were kind and merciful, but could be as terrible as the raging ocean. Calm one moment and calculating the next, they never stopped working for the greater good of the people. Kalvuth remembered Reawin fondly, for they were his saal'kwen and he did his best to carry on their ways. It was only after six centuries of working with the Rangers that Reawin followed their wife into the Afterworld and took their place in the Freelands of Veljra. But there was no sadness among the Rangers at their passing, for to pass in such a way was a much wished-for death. Peaceful, chosen by yourself and after having given your all to the cause, they considered it an honor to pass by your own wishes.

"It was wonderful and over a few years, she grew to accept the idea of me being gone for great lengths of time, provided I came back with something so maddeningly simple that it burned into my memory forever."

"What did she wish for?"

"A flower. One for every Hold, city, or Kingdom I visited. And I never failed. I always brought back something that defined that city and as I taught her to smith, she taught me to create flower crowns for her and I."

"It was near the end of my Restless Years when she sickened. I had just left on a quest to Khataar. I cannot remember the bauble I was retrieving, but it was myself and three others. A Ranger was there out of pure boredom. A mage, barely out of the College and an archer with the keenest shortbow ever."

That is strange, thought Kalvuth. *I was told that giants and their kin have perfect memories and can recall the smallest detail. Perhaps... He chose to forget?*

Out of deference to his friend, the Ranger kept their curiosity silent.

"We were six days out from Westerspring when a hawk arrived from the Town Healer, who was... Ysarl Whitehand, if I remember. Wonderful man. The hawk had a letter stating that my wife had sickened, but not to fear, she was in good care." He paused for a moment, trying to collect himself. The next words, however, came out as ragged sobs. "I should have gone back. I should have immediately returned. But I soldiered on, by the cause of treasure. I would have had my pick of any metals we found along the way." His voice dropped to a whisper, and even Kalvuth had a hard time hearing what he said. What he made out was a simple, "Seldred... please... forgive me."

Reaching up, the Ranger patted his friend's back gently. He suddenly regretted making Viktor relive that time in his life and realized he may very well rue his curiosity about the matter. He knew no way to comfort the half-giant and reasoned that touch would be the least he could provide.

"By the time I had returned to Northrealm, she was dying, despite the best works of the Rangers and the Healer. By the time I had reached Coldforge, running as fast as my legs would carry me, she was dead for almost a day."

At that, Viktor completely broke down, sobbing into his hands. The hands that had protected Coldforge many times, that had forged the weapons used to defend the innocent. They had been powerless to even comfort his wife in her dying days and for that, the Dragonsmith would forever blame himself. Again, he whispered his apology to his beloved and through the tears that nearly blinded him, continued to trudge towards home.

"That broke me. For many a year, I could not hold myself together and I could not bear to leave Coldforge ever again. This adventure is the furthest I have gone in a century."

Taking a breath, Kalvuth tried to shake off the pity he felt for the great man.

"Sadness insults the dead. Better to praise that they had lived and touched our lives than to be angry at their being called back to the Ancestors. You will find her again, Viktor, son of Ulfric. So, it is written in the doorway to the Afterworld. All that love each other will forever find each other, no matter how many lifetimes it takes."

The words felt hollow as they left Kalvuth's mouth, but they were true. The Ancestors themselves had taught the Rangers how the Afterworld worked; that life was endless, beginning repeatedly. He felt in his heart that Viktor would find his beloved again, even if at first he did not recognize their face.

"I have heard that so many times, Ranger, but it never helps. But... I thank you for trying."

The mood was quite somber as the sun dropped below the eastern horizon and Viktor's sobs were just about the only sound that came from the group for some time.

Finally working up the courage to speak again, Kalvuth looked from his friend to the Rangers and cleared his throat.

"Viktor, what is your favorite song?"

Viktor eyed the Ranger wearily for a moment and it struck Kalvuth by how much older he suddenly looked. It was as if that last story had taken the wind from his sails and indeed cast him adrift on a sea of emotion. It was something to behold, but the Ranger felt guilty. Certainly, it was good to face those memories from a more mature perspective, but the way it had come about seemed painful.

"I have many, Ranger Kalvuth. I have many that I hold dear and some that hurt too much to sing. The Coldforge Ballad is one of my favorites, but I am biased, for it mentions my father. Not by name, of course, but by deed."

"Come then, Viktor. Let us find less painful memories of which to speak. Begin the Coldforge Ballad for us."

Viktor shook his head, smiling weakly. Evidently, his mood was too far gone.

"I would prefer to be silent, Kalvuth. My singing voice is not what it used to be. But I have ne'er heard you or your compatriots sing. So, come then, I will stand as an audience while you sing one of your favorite songs."

Chuckling, the colossal man slapped Kalvuth's shoulder softly. Though he was gentle in the strike, it still off balanced the Ranger, who stumbled for a moment before recovering gracefully.

"Very well then."

Clearing his voice, the Ranger sang in a clear tenor, his voice drifting through the trees. Soon, he was joined by the rest of his company and they sang the song at full power.

"Afar and wide I go,
Upon far roads I travel,
To tell the story of my kind
And let my own unravel."

Viktor smiled as the Rangers sang the Wandering Song, and in the back of his mind, he wondered just how often they sang the song to each other.

"Come far and away, the road to me is calling,
Calling me astray, even as my home's in sight.
Ere break of day, I know I must go wand'ring,
Until at last, I make my camp at night."

Kalvuth beat the song's rhythm on his canteen and the other Rangers came in to give the song the power of acapella singing. The beat was strong and the song merry enough to lift even Viktor's dire spirits. Soon enough, he joined in the tune and adjusted his armor to sit more comfortably.

It was near Fifth Watch when they approached the town, and the guard let out a shout.

"Who goes there? Advance and be recognized!"

Kalvuth went to move ahead but was beaten soundly by the greater stride length of Viktor, who crossed to the head of the formation and into the light.

"Viktor, Kalvuth and company, returning from a raid on a bandit clan too near for safety."

"Hail, Dragonsmith! Hail Rangers! Welcome back. I trust

your quest was successful?"

"Aye! Now turn your weapons away, Reawin. I direly need to remove my armor and I feel my companions could do with some relaxation at the Dragon's Drink."

"Aye, Dragonsmith. By your word!"

Immediately, the town's guard shifted their stances from defensive to a more relaxed pose, their weapons drooping down to the ground. They remained watchful though and allowed the party to pass through their barricades and posts into the town. Viktor bade the Rangers safe travels and pleasant trails before making his way back to the Forge. Reaching up to press open the doors, he paused as he heard the familiar sounds of work within. *Even at this hour? Helve must not have been able to sleep.*

Pushing his way through the doors, the sight of twin blasts of inferno greeted Viktor as the dragons heated metal. Though it was darker in the forge than he was used to, the light of the flames gave truth to his thoughts. It was Helve, working extremely late on something. Slipping into the forge proper, he called out to his friend.

"Helve, Ancestors above, it is Fifth Watch! Have you not slept?"

Quickly placing the metal she was working onto the anvil, Helve continued to shape it and work the steel. Even from the distance he was at, Viktor recognized it- she was working with Star-Steel and indeed on a blade that was nearly her height!

"Nay, Viktor. My apologies. I sifted through the notes you had left on the workbench and worked more on this Script-Blade that you had noted down. The design is simple enough, and I know the engraving style well- almost, I wager, as well as you."

As he approached, Viktor noted that the steel was the right color and had been heated appropriately. Helve's shaping of the steel was flawless. Different, perhaps, than his own techniques, but masterful, as should be expected. She didn't talk about herself much, instead choosing to focus on forge work, but what Viktor had plied from her, after generous amounts of ale, was that she was born to a smithing family and had struck out to make her own name. Instead of following through with the dream of opening her own forge, though, she made her way to Coldforge, as if by blood-calling.

"Helve, we do not speak often. This is something I wish to change. I trust you completely, but I know not why. You came into my forge as if out of nowhere, and I immediately felt I could trust you."

The woman did not glance up from her work as she slammed her enchanted hammer down onto the metal, shaping it and sending ripples of energy through it. Viktor leaned his bulk against the colossal form of Alvarath before reaching up to scratch at the dragon's chin.

"What do you mean, Viktor? You know I can work. What else is there?"

"What of your family? Do you ever send them hawks? Ravens? Do you even know if they are alive?"

"Of course, they are alive. They live in the gah'Drin clan Wyrygg, back in Dragonmoor. I send them a hawk every other week, thanks to the Hawkmaster here, Magus Scilt. He has been a good friend ever since I came here."

That gave Viktor pause as he considered her words. She was gah'Drin? Why did that affect him so? This was raising more and more questions.

"Just a friend? Have you no one to go home to?"

"What drives your curiosity, Viktor? Are you trying to find an in with me, or are you just making conversation?" *Why am I talking about such things? Surely it affects me not that she is gah'Drin?* He took a breath and attempted to clear his head. Something was not adding up and he was going to find out why his curiosity had peaked tonight, rather than at *any* other time.

"I am unsure."

"Unsure, Viktor? That is strange for you. You have a reason for every movement you take, so this is new. Come then, what has you in such a tizzy?"

"I will answer this, but only if you answer my question, Helve."

"Very well. No, I have no one to go home to. I have not felt strongly for anyone save for-" She stopped herself for a moment, wondering why she had said that.

"Save for who?"

"It is nothing. I answered your question, Forgemaster. Now answer mine."

"I have been thinking about the past recently. Unhealthy, I know, but it happens from time to time and my mind ever wanders back in time to my beloved Seldred. Surely I have-"

"Aye, you have, and one of your more common mentions is how much I look like her. But there is something deeper, Viktor. Oh! Stand back a moment, would you? Alvarath! Vu'Locav! If you would be dears?"

The dragons rumbled with amusement as Helve held up the sword, which was taking shape quickly. As it was raised to a proper height, they issued forth their inferno, was Viktor nimbly ducked back to protect himself from the intense heat.

Normally, he had enchantments on his apron and kilt, but he had still not changed out of his armor. Helve glanced from her work for a moment and clicked her tongue.

"Tch! Viktor! Armor!"

"What? Helve, it is not–"

"No! If you are going to be in the forge, you need proper garb. Your armor is not enchanted like your forge-garb! Now go change, we will talk afterwards. Or, if you like, you can buy me a meal at the Dragon's Drink."

Putting his hands up in a gesture of surrender, Viktor made his way to the living area that had been built onto the forge, almost as an afterthought. It was a comfortable enough home, more than large enough for a small family and built so that the towering members of the Bludstyn clan did not have to fear smashing their heads on the rafters.

Walking to the chest he kept his armor in, Viktor began pulling each piece off almost reverently. Part by part, they were removed and put back into the chest, though he would rather have the chest hidden away once more instead of having it in the middle of his living-room. But he could not avoid such things sometimes, and he decided he would just accept the change. When he finally removed his helmet, Viktor glanced up at a mirror that had been placed on the wall at some point. He could not remember if he'd done it, or if it was new, such was his weariness. Looking at the mirror, he marveled at how old he seemed to look, and it reflected in how he felt. *How many years do I have left? How many years have I seen?*

As he sat musing, his helmet in his hands, Viktor realized a pair of eyes on his back. Placing the helmet down and turning, he saw Helve standing at the door, leaned against the frame.

He turned to face her and only then realized that he'd never seen her with her hair down, or realized that her eyes shone with the same passion as Seldred's and were indeed even the same color, which had to be an incredible rarity. Her skin was fair, almost as white as the snows outside, save for the constellations of freckles that covered her arms, face and Viktor assumed her body. As he looked at her, he thought it the first time he had ever seen her in his life.

"Well, Dragonsmith? Are you going to offer me a meal, or make me stand here while you stare at me all night?"

Viktor flushed deep red and screwed his face up, embarrassed beyond words for a moment. Then, after regaining his composure, he waved to her and finished removing his armor. He stood before her in *normal* clothes, which was an oddity itself. A white tunic, green trousers, and tan boots.

"Very well Helve, let us make our way to the Dragon's Drink."

17: Westerspring

Sighing, Fae realized she should've brought her *big* adventuring pack. Not just her market pack. Shaking her head, the elf wondered exactly when she'd have the chance to make it to her home once more to fix that error, and part of her wondered not when, but *if*. Shouldering her market pack, which was becoming stuffed with her foraging finds, she moved on after Kiri, trying to keep up with the elder wild elf. *Blast, but she moves with haste,* Fae thought to herself. She could keep up with most people, stay fighting ready through the longest battles, but this? This cross-country stuff was beating her down.

Finally, they stopped in front of what looked like a sheer rock wall. Arching an eyebrow, Fae glanced up and down the wall, looking for runes or any hidden traps. *Nothing. Just a wall.* She thought, hardly seeing Kiri pull her Ranger Compass pendant off. When she finally did notice, Fae watched the Ranger touch the spearhead and press it into a slot on the rock wall. There was a *click* followed by a loud *crack!* And a seam appeared in the wall.

"Come along then, Fae!" Kiri called, getting the other elf's attention.

"Aye!" Fae replied, sauntering up to the wall, which had opened to reveal a gaping doorway. Blinking, the elf stepped through the portal, her eyes adjusting as she made her way into the cave. The torchlight was plenty and warm, so her eyes adjusted easily, and the ground underneath, though she could tell it was stone, seemed... more wholesome than expected. Rounding a bend, she spotted the inside of the *tengjäv* proper. A massive cavern with a hearth nearly dead-center inside of it, stoves, cauldrons, kettles, and tables all around. The floor, save for where the hearth and stoves were, was wood—*fine* wood at that, the likes one would normally only see in a noble hall. *Ancestors, there are even woven rugs and carpets!* She realized as she stepped past an altar. Glancing at the worshiping table, she guessed who it was for. *Veljra, I assume. Mistress of the Wilds, the Hunt, and the Rangers.* Blinking for a moment, she stopped long enough to pay her respects, dipping her fingers in the cider and splashing a bit onto the statuette, as one was supposed to. The candles burned a bit brighter afterwards, but she didn't notice.

Chuckling in awe, the adventurer waited for Kiri to catch up before voicing her question. "How is this possible, Kiri?" She asked.

"Have you never seen a *tengjäv* before, Fae cos'Criux? If not, welcome." The Ranger pulled her mask down, a broad, friendly smile on her face. Reaching out, she patted the adventurer on the back before looking around.

The fires were burning well, spare fuel stacked in the proper spot. A kettle of what smelled like apple and braceroot cider simmered on one stove, the aroma of apples and spice filling the cave. For some reason, some reason Fae couldn't put her finger on, this almost felt more like home than her own little shack in the forest. Off to one end of the spacious cavern was a pair of ovens, loaves baking and a sand-glass keeping time. *Is this a Ranger post, or a home?* Kiri didn't seem to notice Fae's distraction, even as the younger elf drifted away into the distance, wandering through the *tengjäv*.

She went through some tunnels, wandering past a small, cozy room with desks, bookcases, and comfortable-looking chairs around a fireplace. *Reading room?* She wondered. Stopping in for a few moments, she examined the bookcases, hardly noticing the old Moriani sitting in one of the bigger, more plush chairs. When she finally noticed them, Fae let out a soft yelp and jumped back.

"M-my a-a-apologies, Ranger! I did not see you there!" Even as she backed away, the Ranger gave a soft smile and shook their head. *They look male,* thought Fae, but she'd long since learned to avoid assumptions.

Reaching up, the Moriani began making hand-signs. It took Fae longer than she liked to remember the hand-signs, but once she did, she recognized what they were saying.

"You have done no harm, friend. I am Alador." The Ranger signed. Fae bowed slightly.

"Fae cos'Criux, at your service." She offered a kindly smile and extended a hand. Alador took it warmly, they shook hands, and just then, Kiri popped in.

"Oh? Found some- oh! Alador!" Kiri's smile broadened and she walked over to the Moriani Ranger and planted a kiss on their forehead. "What are you doing here, mate?"

The Moriani smiled gently and signed a few words that Fae couldn't catch. Kiri, however, picked them up with no trouble and nodded.

"Needed time away from home, that feeling I know." Both Rangers chuckled. "Now, Fae, this Ranger is... well, they make Karos look *run of the mill.* Ancestors, even Thorvan Koza is miniscule in their presence." The wild elf said, eyes a-twinkle. Alador winced and shook their head. "But of course, the Bane of the Dollmaker refuses what they are owed." Chuckling, Kiri patted the ancient Ranger on the shoulder and squeezed. Fae nodded absently.

"This... how do you say? *Tengjäv?* It is so wondrous. Massive, too." Fae finally said. Both Rangers chuckled, and Alador nodded slightly, settling a bit closer to the fire. Kiri took the hint and led Fae away, taking her on a tour of the rest of the caverns.

"This room may interest you most, Fae," Kiri finally said a moment later. Pointing through a hanging tapestry, Kiri waved at the younger elf to step through. Immediately after following that instruction, Fae gasped. *This is incredible!*

Before her was a beautiful bathing cave, with wardrobes full of white towels, linen bath robes, benches, and a *massive* rock pool that looked as if it were made of a smoothed-out amethyst geode. There were basins made of quartz, and as she inspected everything, found one of the comforts she missed from living in a city. *Running water.* Blinking, she turned on the sink and let the water run for a moment. Not horrifically cold, but neither was it warm. Turning the sink off, she strode over to the bathing pool and touched the water. The warmth thrilled through her from the first touch. And abruptly, Fae knew. *I need a bath.* Slipping out of her armor and placing it on a bench, the elf pulled off her clothing a moment later, standing nude before she noticed the mirrors. Another yelp before she realized it was just her reflection. Chuckling at her own reaction, the elf grabbed a pair of towels and a bathing robe, placed them on the bench nearest the pool, and slipped in, feet first.

The moment the water hit her skin, Fae was in bliss. The last time she'd had a bath, a *proper* bath, mind you, had been... *ages, it feels like.* Long before all this trouble began, and she wasn't even sure when that was. It was hard to get the temperature of a bath right with a fire under a tub of water. So this? This was *beyond* her expectations. In the past, she'd been told that Rangers lived a life of scarcity; a life without comforts. So to have this? This was far and away, beyond what she'd ever expected of the people. But even those thoughts washed away as she dunked her head, letting the luxuriously warm water carry away her cares as it soaked into her skin and hair. Feverishly working to unbraid her long, titian hair, Fae worked the tail out and unknit the braids until she had the entire mass floating around her like a cloud. Again and again, she dunked herself under the water, until she felt adequately soaked. Coming up for air, she glanced to the edge of the bath, hoping that the traditional place for soap wasn't- *Yes!* She rejoiced as she spotted the familiar-enough container, likely containing soapsand. While not as easy on the body as *actual* soap, for her, it was a gift from the Ancestors.

"Careful, my love. One might think that blasphemy!" Came a voice out of nowhere. Again, Fae yelped. This time, she was too far from her normal weapons to be able to defend herself properly. Touching her right arm just above the shoulder, she sent a pulse of energy down her arm, causing her pathway nerves to glow with the expectation of sending hate to whatever threatened her. Looking around frantically, she saw- well, her mind hadn't quite made itself up on *what* she saw at first. A woman? Perhaps? Sitting on the edge of the bathing pool, watching her. Not with the normal look of someone planning evils, evils she'd escaped all her years. But the look of someone watching a beloved child play.

"What did you say?" Fae finally asked, still touching her shoulder. Her pathway nerves still glowed, though weaker than before.

"Thinking anything a gift from us might turn the wrong heads, Fae." The woman said, smiling warmly. Shucking out of a bathrobe made of the finest green silk, the woman stepped into the water and gave an approving sigh. Fae blushed fiercely as she caught sight of the woman's proportions, and in the back of her head, jealousy grew. "No, *daerlain*," said the woman, "no jealousy. Your body has proven its worth to you, and will again in time. There is no need to envy mine."

Gobsmacked at the apparent ability of this woman to tell her thoughts, Fae winced at her gently reproving tone. Forcing a smile, the elf watched as the woman slipped closer through the water. Where she expected to feel vulnerable. Scared, perhaps, there was only comfort. Calm.

"Who are you?" She finally asked.

"Why, my dear Fae," she began, a radiant smile on her face and starlight twinkling in her ruby eyes, "I am *home. Family. Hearth and heart.* I am someone whose influence you have longed for, in the back of your mind for as long as you have been alive."

Answering exactly nothing, thought the wood elf wryly. But the woman didn't seem to notice. Or care. She wasn't sure which it was yet. *And what exactly does she mean by that? Family? That never worked out for me.* Shrugging slightly,

Fae did her best to relax into the water, barely remembering her plan to scrub herself. The woman chuckled gently and continued.

"Oh, it has not. At least, not yet. *But, daerlain*, is family not the people you choose? Dire Company is a sort of family, are they not?" She said sweetly.

"If by family, you mean a bunch of semi-malevolent, deranged eccentrics who willingly break open crypts for the chance of a few Aureim." Fae muttered impishly. *And who am I but the Captain of those eccentrics?* The smirk was unplanned, but it came to her face nonetheless. The mystery woman chuckled gently as well.

"Aye, that is a good point. But my word remains true. You have been seeking family, a place to belong, as long as you have lived." The woman dunked herself a few times, soaking her raven curls before coming back up. "And your heart is beginning to realize it." Smiling again, the woman settled herself next to the elf. Leaning close, she whispered in Fae's ear. *"And I am here to give a secret."*

"And what secret is that, mystery woman?" Fae said, somewhat defensively, pulling away as much as she dare without seeming rude.

"You know who it is. You are not ready to understand *why*, but you already know who it is. Look to your past, longer than you have been you." Once she'd said that, the woman slipped away to the deeper section of the pool. "And you have not told me who *I* am, either." She smirked gently.

Fae finally remembered her plan to utilize the soapsand and moved over to the container, opening it and gazing within. There indeed was the grainy, sweet-smelling substance. But for some reason, some purpose Fae couldn't fathom, it smelled different today. It was a pleasant smell, a smell of... *leather, sandalwood, and earthiness.* Two of those were her favorite smells. The other was *beyond* a favorite. It was the smell of *home.* Blinking, she looked at the soapsand once more before applying the coarse lather to her body and scrubbing vigorously. The smell remained, and for the life of her, she couldn't fathom why it felt so familiar.

Leather. Well, the first thing that popped into her head was her own armor, but this didn't smell like that. This smelled like a different sort of leather. Aged, incredibly so, and laden with the memories of more campfires than she'd had days of life. Spiced with sweat, but not unpleasantly. More... comfortingly, in her mind. As if from someone who'd be safe to be around, because they *knew* life.

Sandalwood. An odd one, for certain. Not a scent she was terribly familiar with, but fond of regardless. The floral notes, the rich balsamic tones, all of it. Somehow, it made her think of someone she knew. Well, perhaps knew was the wrong word. Someone she'd met, and never known before. It was a confusing mess in her head.

Earthiness. The scent of dirt after rain, specifically. Forests and grasslands, cleaned and refreshed by rain and storm. She could almost hear the crack of thunder, feel the rain pelting her skin. And it was beautiful. Wonderful. *Comforting. Home.* She was a wood elf, so this was beyond being a favorite scent. It was a scent that meant *her* above all else, and now someone else. *Who?* She wondered.

As she scrubbed at her skin, Fae pondered the last time she'd caught those scents. Pondered who they might be associated with. The leather seemed easy enough - the Rangers. Certainly, she wasn't a dokk, with their near-perfect sense of smell, but the leathery, earthy smell that followed the Rangers around wasn't unpleasant at all. If anything, it was comforting to her, especially since she knew they knew what life was like on the roads.

Sandalwood. That one eluded her for some time. It was almost a sharp smell, and yet, for reasons she couldn't fathom, also a *round* smell. Gentle, but not out of softness. Friendly, but lying in wait for something. Something that slept its way through life, waiting for the right moment to burst forth. Reaching up, she unconsciously scratched the back of her neck. She'd completely forgotten about the woman bathing with her when her voice piped up.

"Have you sussed it out yet?" The woman asked, her voice buttery and warm.

"Nowhere near, my mysterious friend." Fae replied, still pondering things and scrubbing herself. Hair, skin, feet, every inch of her was scoured with the sand until she felt clean. "I am half-tempted to ask one of the Rangers about these smells."

"Oh, but that would be cheating, Fae," said another voice. The adventurer's head spun until she spotted Kiri. "You do not want to spoil the surprise, and I am certain Al'Talwha," Kiri bowed to the clay-skinned woman, who smiled in return, "does not want us revealing it."

Al'Talwha. Fae blinked, finally realizing the identity of the mystery woman. *But who else could it be?* She reasoned. She'd worn the cloth of hearth and home. Of comfort and kindliness. *Who else could it be?* Chuckling, Fae rinsed herself a few times.

"Well, then, ladies. Keep your secrets if you must, but I will find out someday." Fae said as she made her way to the edge of the pool. "Now, I am going to find something to eat. Fair famished am I, after that march with Kiri and a laden pack." The Ranger shared a chuckle with Fae as she stepped out of the bath.

Suddenly self-conscious around the other two women, Fae grabbed a towel quickly, before realizing neither one was looking at her with *judgment*. They were looking at her the way friends do. The way people who are uninterested but curious look at each other. So, she relaxed a little, knowing she didn't have to be *totally* embarrassed. Glancing to where her gear was, she found nothing.

"Erm," she began, casting accusing eyes on Kiri, "Where have my things wandered off to, Ranger?"

"Oh!" Replied the wild elf. "I took them and washed them. You will need a robe for now, but trust me, your kit is in expert hands. They even instructed me to give you one of our packs for now, until you have a chance to retrieve your own!" Kiri finished, eyes twinkling.

Fae shrugged and dried herself off until her skin almost ached and her hair was a static cloud clinging to her and floating off elsewhere. She felt almost comical until Kiri handed her a robe. As soon as she was garbed and the robe tied off, the wild elf handed her something else. *A brush.* Nodding her thanks, she took it and began dragging it through her hair, listening to the crackling and feeling the shift as she tamed her titian locks. Then, with a smile, she dismissed herself to wander the *tengjäv* some more, reasoning that the Rangers wouldn't mind.

Fae's wandering took her through the sleeping cave, with the individual stalls and beds arranged for various folks. As she passed the reading room, Fae glanced in to see if Alador was still sitting there. She was curious about the Moriani, what they knew. But they were nowhere to be seen, evidently busying themself elsewhere. So she wandered back into the main hall to look around and spotted a tented piece of paper next to a fairly decent spread of food. Approaching curiously, she spotted her name on the paper and reached to grab it. No one stopped her, so she unfolded it and found– nothing. *Just an invitation for food?* She wondered, glancing at the spread. It was fairly standard tavern fare, with foods her kind would find the most comforting. A few slices of venison, root and forage vegetables, and an odd-looking bread that smelled interesting enough.

Shrugging, the wood elf sat herself down and started eating.

18: Northrealm

As they ate, Viktor and Helve had been making quite a conversation. The woman was growing quite interested in the half-giant's tale and was not afraid to show it, both on her face and in how she paid attention. The stories of Seldred, which he at first seemed reticent to share, especially interested her. It was as if she were hearing about her own past, and she felt like she was. When she finally interrupted him between bites of food and listening to him talk, it was to speak of herself, to not let her friend dominate the conversation.

"Of course, Viktor, you have told me much of your tale, but know little of mine. As you know, I was born to a gah'Drin clan, but I have not told you the truth of it. My mother abandoned me to the clan and fled. My father was nowhere to be found, and to hear the Clanspeaker talk, I never had one. For all I care, the bastard can rot."

The burly half-giant nodded and waved at her to continue. Truth be told, he was thankful for the distraction of her speaking and ate his meal silently. Raising his hand to bring

Martin back over, he pointed at his mug apologetically. It was refilled and his back was patted before his attention shifted fully back to Helve.

"I have no siblings that I know of, and only send a hawk to the clan leader. He is the only parent I have known for my entire life. When I was of age, I struck out on my own. For a short time, I joined an adventuring company that had assembled under the banner of Krygan-Shawv but found instead that I did not enjoy that life. So, after one adventure, I tried my hand at farming and hardly made one season. But in my bones, I felt the call of the steel. I was in my early forties, already established as a competent blacksmith under my teacher, Arroli the Adamant. Of course, I had started much the same way any smith does- nails, fittings, horseshoes. I found I had a particular love for lanterns and would oft work intricate designs into them."

Pausing long enough to take a bite of her meal and a drink of her ale, she continued after a moment. As she spoke, she watched his reaction, watched every subtle movement he made. In no way was she planning to tell him she had learned how to read people from a Ranger, but she knew it was a necessary skill, especially with someone like Viktor.

"I am now in my fifties, though you knew not. No, do not grow apologetic. I never told you about my day of birth. It was unknown to me until I was in my thirties, as well. I was born on the 27th of Firstgreen. Anyroad, it was about a decade ago that I first felt the stirring to come north. So, I packed my things, said goodbye to Arroli, and joined a caravan bound for Northrealm. From there, my memory grows faint of how I ended up in Coldforge, but... well, you know the rest. I established myself at your forge and quickly became your

Second."

Viktor nodded and smiled. *And you have been indispensable ever since.* He was not sure if he wanted to say those words out loud, but he was certain that she could infer it from the way he looked at her. For some strange reason, he felt a calling to her, as if she were his Seldred reborn in a new body. He looked at her hair for a moment, which earlier had been tied in a sensible bun. Since they had agreed to this date, however, it was falling in cascades around her shoulders. He took a breath and sighed.

"It is no secret that I find many similarities between you and Seldred. I do not mean this as an insult."

"Nor do I take it as such. It is only common to find common traits in folk you spend your time around. But what you have said gives me great thought."

Both nodded for a moment and ate the rest of their meals. Once they were done, Helve grabbed her coin purse and laid enough to cover the cost of their food, drink, and a generous tip. Then she spoke once more, her business demeanor once more shining through.

"I feel that if I do not get back to that Script Blade, I shall never finish it. We shall have to do this again, Viktor. By the by, who is that blade meant for? I wager only one your size could wield it effectively."

"It is meant for Kingmage Harthos, and we are on a deadline. Rather than take the caravan, as is my normal way, once we are done, I will fly by dragon to deliver it and the spear to Harthos and his sister Hillevi."

As she absorbed the information, Helve made a mental note to do work beyond her best to ensure that the blade would be up to the Kingmage's exacting standards. She would have to be extremely precise, but luckily, the blade was already formed. Bidding farewell to the Forgemaster, she made her way back, her steps steady despite the two pints of ale in her body.

When Viktor returned to the forge, she was deep in her work, carefully grinding the blade to shape and preparing the wax to protect where she did not want the blade etched. Once she felt the blade held a keen edge, she coated it liberally in the wax and began scratching the designs. Unlike Viktor, however, she did not need to trace the designs in pencil- she was more than capable of free-handing the entire design.

"Helve, for Mydborh's sake, we have enough time that you can sleep. I can keep eyes on the blade while it etches, but you- you need rest. I have not seen you sleep in days."

"Then again, you have been gone for one. Who is to say that you merely missed it?"

"The darkness under your eyes."

Damn him, the woman thought for a moment, before shaking her head and grinning. His words made sense, though, and once she finished scratching into the wax in a careful hand, she placed it in a specially made acid bath to etch. Only then did she nod at the half-giant and agree to go to her rest.

"Very well, but I am sleeping on your couch."

"So be it. Grab a blanket from the chest in the living room."

As the woman made her way into the living area to rest, Viktor began looking over the designs she had drawn for the blade and sucked in a breath. Clearly, she knew this blade's purpose. While it was meant to cleave through flesh and even steel, it was just as much meant to channel vast amounts of energy through the etchings, which ran the entire length of the blade. It was a weapon meant for a Kingmage, simple as that. Her work was flawless- in fact, he could not hope to have done a better job.

She knows her work as well as you, Viktor. Vu'Locav sounded rather amused, and Viktor glanced around to see the glowing eyes in the dim forge. *I asked if she wished for light, but she declined.* Giving the draconic equivalent of a shrug, the magnificent beast laid his head back down to rest some more. *I will bear you to Starwatch-In-Karnost when the time is right. Alvarath will bring her.* Viktor was confused for a moment, wondering why Helve would want to accompany him on such a journey.

A few hours passed, and Viktor checked the etching to find that it was at the right depth. Removing the sword from the acid bath, he realized Helve was one step ahead once more- she had already drawn a matching design in the wax on the other side of the blade. Given that to go on, Viktor followed her practiced hand and scraped the wax away to reveal the star-steel blade beneath. Then, he repeated her actions and placed that side in the acid bath, resigning himself to wait until the task was done.

Once the acid had etched to the correct depth, according to Viktor's eye, he removed the sword from the basin and began melting the wax away with a torch. Then, he beheld the fruit of their labors. A great blade, spanning nearly five feet, covered with Sk'av'A runes and Indekari script, and humming with the combined energies of a frost dragon and a red dragon. It was a blade that could level nearly any foe. Holding it, Viktor felt a thrill run through his body, and he had to remind himself that the handle still needed pinning.

Nodding, he went to the handle and crossguard, which had

already been forged, shaped, and polished. He had wrapped the leather tight, and he found that even his large hands could sit comfortably atop one another on the handle. Quickly, he slotted the tang of the blade into the handle and found the pommel that had been crafted. It was in the shape of an eagle's head, which he found oddly appropriate for the great Nolvern man, and held a gem in each eye. Working quickly and precisely, he fitted the pommel and pinned it into place before smoothing out the work and examining it once more. Then he nodded, looking to the scabbard that one of his other forge-hands had made. They made it well, to his standards even, and it fit the blade perfectly. As he sheathed and drew the sword a few times to test the fit, he found that even the requested drystones had been integrated into the sheathe, to allow it to constantly have a razor's edge. *Perfection.*

With a cry, he roused the dragons and wrapped the Script Blade and Moon Spear into great hides to keep them safe. Helve stumbled out of the living area, still somewhat bleary. Both were unsure if they should dress in their court garb for this occasion, and finally Viktor gave voice to his thoughts.

"Helve, would you think it appropriate to be seen before the Kingmage in our forge-garb? I am unsure if I even have cloth appropriate for the court."

Helve shrugged and wiped the sleep from her eyes. Glancing at her own clothes, she quirked an eyebrow. *Is it appropriate?* She wondered to herself. *Certainly it is not unheard of,* she reasoned, *for a forgemaster to appear in forging garb before a king. But the Kingmage?* That brought a load of new questions. Quickly, she searched through Viktor's house, without so much as asking permission, to find him something at least *slightly* more appropriate than his oil-stained tunic, black trousers, and leather apron. Opening a chest and looking inside, the woman stopped short. *Why in the stars?*

Inside the chest was a *dress*, and definitely not one sized for the half-giant. *No, he is not haghta. This is far too small for his frame.* Puzzling over the dress for a moment, she hardly noticed the growling coming from the next chest. Glancing at it, Helve smiled gently and reached out, petting the growling chest. *How like him to have a mimic, but why protecting... this?* Again, her attention turned to the dress as the mimic next to her calmed down, seemingly recognizing some permission that no one had given. Pulling the dress from the chest, Helve looked it over. It was of fine make- the finest she'd seen in Coldforge, honestly. A neat, cream chemise, which felt as if it were made of silk, or perhaps fine linen. And the kirtle was the richest green she'd ever beheld, to the point Helve was wondering *how* it had been made. She wasn't knowledgeable about textile arts, but certainly *that* deep a green was not possible. Or so she reasoned.

Beneath the dress was a pair of neat buckled shoes, obviously of fine make and yet... simple enough to be attractive to her. Above those was a belt of green and blue interwoven stripes, along with a few pouches. Finally, sitting beneath everything else, she found a belt favor. *Odd*, she thought, *I thought Viktor had no heraldry.* Quirking an eyebrow, she moved the things off the favor and went to touch it.

The moment her hand hit the belt favor, everything seemed to go black around Helve. Suddenly, she was falling. Falling so far, so fast, she couldn't even tell time or place. The blackness rushed past her, inscrutable, and yet... her vision pierced it at every point, and she could see a thousand images, or perhaps a million. Her mind reeled with the sudden onslaught.

She saw *so many* moments of Viktor's life. Of her own. And then, out of the mists of the strange blackness, she saw *her.* Seldred, she assumed, judging the woman's form from what Viktor had told her. She was beyond breathtaking, even to the gah'Drin woman. But, at the same time, Helve didn't feel in competition with her at all. *Competition?* She thought for a moment, wondering where that thought had even sprung from. *What competition is there?* Certainly she *felt* close to Viktor, but close enough for there to be *competition* with a dead woman? *But am I competing?* She thought suddenly. Viktor had mentioned several things as points of similarity between her and Seldred. Things that both had been recognizable for, one and the same. Her head swam with the visions, more and more encircling her, drowning her.

Then it hit her. She wasn't seeing *Seldred's* life, because Seldred wasn't a different woman. She was seeing *her own past life.* Abruptly, it all made sense. The calling to Northrealm. The call of the steel. Coldforge's mysterious pull to her very soul. Viktor. It all made sense. The timing, even. She wagered that she'd been born on the very day Seldred died, just the same soul in a new body, taught something the Ancestors knew she would need to know. *Is this that knowledge?* She wondered, head still swimming.

Then everything went black again for what felt like an age of the world. When her vision returned, Helve was still kneeling in front of the chest, hand dumbly resting on a belt favor that wasn't Viktor's. It was and wasn't hers. *How will I ever explain this to Viktor? Will he even believe me?* She pondered for a moment before hastily, but neatly, packing everything back into the chest. *Perhaps forge garb will be just fine to be in the company of the Kingmage, seeing as how craftmasters we both be.*

She closed the chest and tried to forget what she'd seen.

Shaking her head, Helve backed away from the chest and its companion mimic, trying to push the questions that'd cropped up from her mind. Blinking, she turned and half-expected to see Viktor standing there, probably angry at her intrusion. He was nowhere to be seen, but the sounds coming from the forge told her what she needed to know; he was finishing up some detail or another, evidently clueless as to her investigations. Taking a breath, the short gah'Drin woman busied herself around the apartment portion of the Dragonsmithy, still curious whether Viktor even *owned* nice clothes. *Well,* she smirked, *nicer than what we have seen.* Chuckling gently, she rifled through his wardrobe, searching for anything that might be more fitting for an audience with the Kingmage. She'd heard about him, of course, and his sister. Both were imposing, but between them, she'd always heard that Hillevi, the little sister by mere *minutes,* was the more dangerous of the two. *So why is she not the Kingmage?* The moment that thought popped up, she knew the answer. *Because there are far too many old men who would rather burn the Empire down than see a woman at its head.* She shook her head, frustrated at the lack of foresight those men had. Then she continued snooping through Viktor's clothing, wondering if she was even looking for anything at this point, or had just grown curious what the man actually wore on the *day* he usually spent outside the forge.

"Ah-ha!" Helve cried out as she found a red wool tunic with gold embroidery around the neck and the half-length sleeves, both marked with a gold anvil, marking it as belonging to a master of the craft. Quirking an eyebrow, she inspected the garment. It was *massive*, at least, compared to her, so she assumed it was the right size for Viktor. Setting it aside on the couch in the half-giant's living room, she delved back into his wardrobe for a decently presentable pair of trousers. *That much is going to be near impossible*, she reasoned, expecting that every pair of trousers the half-giant owned would already be covered in oil, washed by acid, or otherwise damaged. But one pair stopped her short as she sifted through the clothing, which was a far larger collection than she'd expected from someone of such normally simplistic tastes.

After what seemed like hours sifting through the various pieces of clothing, Helve finally found a pair of trousers she thought appropriate for the occasion they were going to. Deep blue with gold stripes down the outside of the legs. Nodding, she tossed the trousers onto the tunic and selected the cleanest boots she could find. Not that the task was difficult, Viktor only owned three pairs, and the cleanest were the ones that looked the most appropriate. Then his belt, which she knew was part of his adventuring gear, and the normal few pouches. A coin purse, a drawstring pouch, a map pouch, and something to hold snacks in, in case the task was so important that they couldn't land anywhere.

Once she'd assembled the outfit, Helve looked at her own garb. She was in her forge garb again, and scoffed. *All this time spent picking out that oaf's clothing, and I have not given thought to mine.* Tutting at her lack of oversight, Helve stood up and called out to Viktor, who was still working on something.

"Viktor! I set you out some clothes for this, and I expect you to wear them. I am going to find myself something more appropriate as well!" Without even waiting for what she knew would be a confused response at her intrusion, Helve ducked out the door and made her way to her small cottage, one street over from the forge itself. Pushing the door open, she opened a basket full of magelight blooms, causing the strange plants to emit their brilliant glow. Going immediately to her own wardrobe, the woman began searching for a set of clothes for herself. Hemming and hawing, she looked over the offerings. She didn't want to be *too* formal, after all, but likewise, she didn't want to show up in oil-stained and singed garb and a leather apron.

Unlike Viktor, however, she knew her own wardrobe and what she had. Furthermore, the stout, short woman had already planned for the potential of going to see the Kingmage and his sister. *Which one is the true power?* She wondered for a moment. Hillevi, from what she knew, was an incredibly dangerous mage in her own right. Harthos was skilled *enough*, but she'd heard the rumors. He was physically imposing, standing almost a spearlength tall, and both could bring down incredible amounts of power. But Hillevi, she knew, was the more powerful of the two.

But, why does she sit in the shadows of the throne? She pondered further, knowing that she could easily fill the shoes of the Kingmage if she wanted. *But does she wish to?* Pausing long enough to scratch her chin, the woman blinked at that thought. Then it turned inward. If Viktor had to leave on some adventure, she *could* run the forge. It might be a bit of a nuisance without the dragons, but she could do it. *But do I want to?* She wondered. Certainly, there was a role to fill, and she knew she was capable. But the urge, the desire, that's what she was having trouble seeing. Shrugging, the woman went back to her clothing. Selecting a crimson wool tunic with blue knotwork neck and cuffs, likewise marked with the symbol of her trade, she looked over the tunic for a moment. Nodding, she placed it on her couch before finding her favorite *fancy* trousers. Not the most flashy, but then again, she never liked *being* flashy. Subdued blue, red knotwork down the sides. Over the top of all of it, of course, went her favorite greatcoat, her red leather belt and its pouches, and in the ways of the Nolvern and the gah'Drin, she made sure to wear a weapon, since she wasn't as physically imposing as Viktor. Looping on an axe frog, she dropped her favorite bearded axe through the metal ring to hang by its head. Just right for her size, she could use it one- or two-handed as needed. When she needed it in the shop, she could grip just beneath the head and use it for planing wood, which was the use she preferred for it. Smiling gently as the metal rang when the axe fell into place, Helve stepped back into her boots, buckled them tight, and stood for a moment, considering everything. Then she snagged her pack and headed out the door once again, making sure it latched behind her.

By the time Helve made the forge again, Viktor was dressed decently. *Almost looks like a professional,* she remarked to herself with a chuckle. He'd already packed the weapons into specially made cases to be presented to the Kingmage and his sister, and had slung both across his back, belting them in place for the ride ahead. Looking at Helve as she approached, the half-giant sucked in a breath.

Why, she looks incredible! Thought the man affectionately as he regarded his forge-second. There were times the woman stirred old pains in his heart, and times she made him wonder if he could love again. This was both at the same time, and it confused him for a few moments. Shaking his head, he took a breath and waved her over. The half-giant stood and called to

Vu'Locav and Alvarath before moving to retrieve the saddles they both used when riding the dragons. As soon as they were secured, Helve nodded to Viktor and threw the forge's doors open wide, allowing the beasts to exit and prepare for flight.

Vu'Locav stretched languidly as he plodded out of the Forge and into the gray light of the Eversnow Forest. Rumbling gently, the dragon looked around the area, watching as a few children came to see what was going on. Chuckling gently behind him, Alvarath stepped up beside his work-brother and leaned close enough to share a private joke between the two dragons. Both rumbled with amusement and looked at their respective riders. Vu'Locav, being the bigger by far, would bear Viktor. Alvarath, the white, would bear Helve, who was less of a burden than the Forgemaster.

Once both Viktor and Helve were seated and secured in their saddles, they gave a cry to the dragons, who propelled themselves into the sky, one after the other. Even at their best speed, it would be a seven-day journey, and Viktor knew they would arrive with plenty of time to spare. The ground beneath receded as the great dragons took to the sky, their massive wings sending powdered snow up in miniature blizzards. Both Helve and Viktor felt the unmistakable rush that always came with ascent on the great dragons, their hearts leaping into their throats. At first, they circled higher and higher, cresting the endless green, brown, and white of the forest and nearing the bottom of the perpetual cloudbanks that shrouded the Eversnow. Then they broke through the misty, shapeless mass into brilliant sapphire sunlight, completed their ascent, and began winging south and west.

Helve let out an elated whoop and threw her arms up, basking in the sunlight and the breeze blowing past her. Feeling the dragon's power beneath her legs was almost intoxicating, and this time was no different. Every movement of the powerful white dragon's muscles sent thrills through the short woman, and she almost felt giddy from the excitement of it all. *I finally get to meet the Kingmage and his sister!* She realized before letting out another whoop.

Viktor chuckled at his Second's enthusiasm. This was his... *third* time visiting the Kingmage? *Fourth?* Grinning, he slapped Vu'Locav's neck affectionately. The dragon let out an amused rumble. Certainly, for *him*, flying was as natural as breathing. *But for some of us,* remarked Viktor through their telepathic link, *it is not an everyday thing, old friend.* Again, the dragon rumbled as the ground flew beneath them. The crystalline sky was an incredible sight, no matter how often one saw it, and seeing far-off mountains from above was always wonderful.

Eight hours of flying later, Viktor's stomach began rumbling. Taking a quick glance, he tried to figure out where they were, and if there was a safe place to land nearby. Blinking, he pulled a map scroll from his belt; a prize gift, given by a Ranger. Unrolling it against the buffeting winds, he focused on the map. On where he was. Soon, the ink began to run, rearranging itself on the map until Viktor had a clear view of where they currently were. *About twenty leagues into Westerspring. Safe enough, I wager.* Signaling to Helve and Alvarath, he called out to Vu'Locav in turn. Soon, the dragons began descending, once more making lazy circles down toward the ground. The giddy feeling hit both riders once more, their stomachs in their throats, but it didn't last. Soon enough, the dragons struck ground with their massive feet once more, toes splayed out for stability.

As soon as their feet touched the ground, both dragons bent forward, giving their riders a safe descent to the dirt. Moments later, both took off again, shy Helve and Viktor, and went to hunt. *You are not the only hungry ones,* remarked Alvarath as they began to climb once more into the sky, *and you both need rest from the saddle.* Giving out a low rumble, the dragons began flying around the area, searching for prey to sate their hunger. Soon, both were out of sight.

Viktor glanced to Helve as she unbuttoned her greatcoat's collar, which she'd used to protect her features from the worst of the flight-wind. At an unspoken thought from him, she shucked her pack, setting it on the ground gently, and rummaged through it to find the rations she'd packed away. He was already echoing the action, pulling out what would be a feast for anyone of normal stature. *Good thing his pack is sized for him. A normal adventurer's pack would not hold half of a day's rations for the man,* thought Helve with a cheeky grin. Crossing her legs beneath her and setting her rump on the ground, the woman unfolded the ration pack she'd pulled from her ruck, and laid it out in front of her. A moment later, Viktor laid his out.

Looking over her ration pack, Helve made a mental tally of what was in there. She'd prepared each one herself, so she knew, and had packed for at least eight days. *I will need to pilfer from the Kingmage's larder... if that is an option.* Smirking, she looked down at the meal in front of her, sitting on a waxed cloth. A decent-sized bun she'd cooked a day ago, a wedge of hard cheddar, a large handful of dried apples, cranberries, highberries, and walnuts, and finally, several oatcrumble bars she'd made herself. Nodding, she began tucking into the food. It wasn't a large meal, by any stretch, but for her, it was perfect for now.

The half-giant watched his companion for a moment as she considered her food. Chuckling gently, he looked at his own fare as he unwrapped his rations. His differed greatly from hers, as he was likewise different from her. On his own waxed cloth sat a slab of kivlyha, dried and salted Nolvern reindeer meat. It wasn't the most flavorful of meals he'd had in his days, but between it and the other types of lyha he'd packed, it was... *acceptable, to say the least.* Apart from the meat, which was plentiful, he also had some squares of Nolvern kalkukka, a type of bread made with pieces of fish and pork, meant for traveling, as well as a small pot of butter. Finally, there was a generous wedge of gouda, which he loved not only for the taste, texture, and the hardiness, but also how well it sated even his massive form. Slicing a piece of cheese and placing it and some butter on a square of raksa, he began eating.

The kukka was dense, but pleasant, the butter wonderfully creamy, and the only thing Viktor found regretful was the lack of ale. *Oh, woe is me,* he thought sadly, lamenting his lack of alcohol. It must've showed on his face, because a moment later, and between mouthfuls of food, Helve spoke up.

"Something amiss, Viktor?"

Something in her voice. In the melodious mezzo-soprano voice stopped Viktor short, nearly causing him to choke on his lyha. Blinking at the woman a few times and coughing to clear his throat, he managed to stammer out a few words.

"What... did you say?"

Helve quirked an eyebrow as her silver eyes regarded her traveling partner, her forgemaster and friend. *That was... odd,* she thought for a moment before collecting herself and speaking again.

"I said, is something amiss, Viktor? I know you heard me, your ears are far better than that."

It was another moment before he answered, shaking his head gently.

"Something... oh, it is nothing. Just lamenting our lack of ale."

Smirking, Helve pulled one of her wineskins from her pack, offering it to him. Uncorking it, he took a sniff, then an experimental taste. It wasn't his *favorite*, as it was wine, a white wine at that. *Fine taste*, he thought to himself as he poured a cup and passed the skin back to Helve. Taking a sip, he let the wine linger in his mouth for a bit. It tasted lightly of fruit, reminding the half-giant of his last visit to Dragonmoor, and of course it had the warm nip of alcohol. He took another long draw and enjoyed the heating glow flowing into his body and the amazing aftertaste of the delicate white. Though he enjoyed ale most of all, Viktor knew the grapes needed to make a wine of this quality were rare and likely from Dragonmoor. Looking at Helve, he raised an eyebrow. She was already half a cup deep in the fermented juice.

"Where is this from?"

She chuckled gently and wiped her lips before answering.

"Do you mean, where did I get it, or do you mean, where was it made?"

"Both, I suppose."

Searching her memory for a moment, the woman pondered where she'd gotten in. *Was it... a decade? Two?* Scratching her chin, she took another sip of the wine before answering with a bit more confidence.

"I bought three bottles of it from a trader who came to Coldforge, say... Thirty-Five Forty? It is a Moriani White, and if I remember right, it is a Nilaetha Cellars... Thirty-Third Empire Four-Hundred-Thirty. As you can imagine, it cost me... about ten Sereim."

Viktor let out a whistle at the price of the three bottles. *That must have... well, that would have been at least five years' wages!* At first, he was in shock at the thought. *She must be far more skilled with her coin than I give her credit for.* While a miser may think of that as a reason to pay their people *less*, Viktor, on the other hand, began to wonder if Helve may be worth more, and as more than just a Forge-Second. *Maybe she should run the damn forge.* Moments later, he remembered; as Forge-Second, she *did*. In his stead. But the fact that she was willing to, and *so freely*, share nearly two years of her life, left him in awe.

"Helve..." He began, trying to find the words to give her his appreciation for her astounding kindness. She put a hand up, rolling her eyes at the very thought.

"Viktor, no. Let us not start that. You can thank me and become all sugary later. For now, let us finish our meal and stretch before flying on."

Chuckling, Viktor took another sip of his wine, though this time he savored it quite a bit more. Soon enough, though, the glass was gone. At first, he considered asking for another cup but chastised himself for the very thought. Going back to his food, the Dragonsmith ate a bit slower, but soon enough, cleared the wax cloth. Shaking off the crumbs and packing it neatly away, Viktor glanced around. It was midday, and though the shadowy clouds of the Eversnow still loomed near, the sky was clear in the near area.

The dragons were nowhere to be seen for another few hours, having ranged far to hunt to their satiety. When they came back into view, Viktor spotted them first as black dots on the sky, moving against the clouds. As they approached, the half-giant waved to signal to them. Slowly, the dots became shapes, and the shapes became dragons, which began circling down toward the two on the ground. Vu'Locav landed first, touching down rather delicately and walking out of the way of where Alvarath was planning to land. As the white dragon joined everyone on the ground, Vu'Locav quickly found a pleasant spot and promptly curled on the ground. Alvarath followed suit.

Both humanoids chuckled gently, and Viktor shook his head at the antics of the dragons. Shrugging a moment later, he plodded over to the red dragon and sat down against him, laced his hands behind his head, and dozed off. Helve stood watchful for a while, at least until Alvarath convinced her he would watch over everyone. *It is a decent time for a nap, Helve. I will protect us all, and remember, both Vu'Locav and I can wake far quicker than you two. So rest, my friend. We will continue a few hours from now.* Chuckling gently, the woman waved dismissively at the white dragon and found herself a comfortable spot against the white dragon's side. Within a few minutes, she too was asleep, snoring gently with her head pillowed against the dragon's scales.

Pronunciation Of Names

Njall – Nee-Awl

Sigmunt - Sig-muhnt

Heli - Heh-lee

Veljra - Vel-ee-rah

Kiri - Kee-ree

Karos - Kah-Rowss

Sardra - Sar-drah

Wastan -Wah-Stan

Ybril - Ee-Bril

Sahyrn - Say-heern

Koz'Ta'Riin - Kohz-tah-reen

Tas'Sa'Raath -Tahs-Sah-Rawth

Elz'Kal'Raan -Ellzuh-Kawl-Rawn

Cael - Kale

Möratuk: More-Ah-Took

Celedorn - Keh-Leh-Doorn

Kuzi -Koo-Zee

Kozlo - Cause-Low

Otho - Oh-Though

ces'Dalri - kes-dahl-ree

Narjas - Nahr-yass

Carwaan - Cahr-Wawn

Harthos - Hahr-Thoss

Cúledan - Koo-Leh-Dahn

Mykil -My-Kill

Pjotr - Pi-oh-truh

Alaya - Ah-Lay-Ah

Kizarian - Kih-zahr-ee-ahn

Poloa - Poe-Low-Ah

Mirenel - Mee-Reh-Nehl

Ashvathi - Ash-Vah-Thee

Joram - Yo-Rum

Hjalgroþ - Hee-awl-grott

Thäoldr - Thay-old-er

Vloran - V-Lor-An

Kitorath - Kih-tore-ath

Elsaia - El-Sigh-Uh

Tel'varael - Tehl-vah-rail

Thorvan - Thor-van

Koza - Koh-Zah

Veldan - Vell-Dahn

Nelya - Knell-Yah

Ardivari - Are-Dih-Var-Ee

Fae - Fay

Box - Bocks

cos'Criux - kos'Cree-ewx

Lyvan - Lih-Vahn

Myran - My-Rahn

Eldira - Eld-ee-ruh

Ulfric - Uhlf-Rick

Bludstyn - Blood-stin

Kavabalt - Kah-Vah-Ball-t

Calem - Kay-Lehm

Idorick - Ih-Door-Ick

Kar'Maerae - Kar-May-Ray

Ayara - Ay-Ahr-Uh

Las'Sa'Reeth - Lahs-Sah-Reeth

Parali - Pah-Rah-Lee

Ebert - Eh-Bert

Rollo - Row-Low

Samned - Sahm-Ned

Batam - Bah-Tahm

Vu'Locav - Voo-Low-Calve

Alvarath - Awl-Vah-Wrath

Viktor - Vick-Tore

Helve - Hell-veh

Arri - Ah-Ree

Skuld -Sh-kuld

Nils - Nihlsuh

Einar - Eye-Narr

Ralian - Rah-Lee-Ahn

Elruviel - Ehl-Roo-Vee-Ehl

Caladon - Kah-Lah-Dohn

Olin - Aw-lynn

Sunji - Soon-Gee

Skalla - Skah-Lah

Da'Shanaer - Dah-Shah-Nayr

Wythe - Why-the (as in, why the f-)

Varyna - Vah-Ree-Nuh

Razh - Rah-zhuh

Skel'Za - Skehl-Za

Adric - Ahh-Drick

Cos'Erick - kos-err-ick

Ynrasil - Een-Rah-Seel

Elyrea - Eh-Lee-Ree-Uh

Ulfgar - Oolf-Gahr

Frostnuin - Frost-New-Een

Berol - Bear-Ohl

Hyrwn - Heer-wun

Korzi - Core-zhi

Tezh - Teh-zhuh

Sungetiigd - Soon-Geh-Tiig-duh

Tomas - Tow-Mass

Kordanai - Core-Dah-Naye

Suteri - Soo-Teh-Ree

Hanmaer - Hahn-Mayer

Lognuk - Lowg-nook

ugh'Darsk - Uff-Dar-skuh

Tyrell - Tie-Rell

Caljen - Kahl-Yen

Ormere - Or-Mere

Taog - Tow-guh

Arthan - Arr-tan

Krygan-Shawv - Krih-Gan-Show-Vuh

Kalan - Kah-Lahn

Namryll - Nam-rill

Khula - Koo-Lah

Tallam - Tah-Lamb

Ellyn – Ehl-Lynn

Kigdan – Kigg-Dawn

Tyern – Tie-Urn

Ortan – Orr-Tan

Klimir – Klee-meer

Cala – Kah-Lah

tal-Edröhel – tawl-ehd-roe-hehl

Kinym – Kin-Yim

Siddi – Sih-Dii

Kamat – Kah-Maht

Ysarl – Ee-sarluh

Rijna – Ree-Nuh

Knal – Nawl

Var – Vahr

Tagik – Taj-eek

Klun – Clue-nuh

Ful'sa'Taan – Fool-Sah-Tawn

Ugtah – Ugg-Taw

Salrin – Sahl-Reen

Ug'Tahash – Ugg-Tah-Hash

Mulrah – Mool-Rah

Vaelyn – Vie-Lynn

Talakath – Tah-Lah-Kahth

Trensa – Tren-Sah

Kalvuth – Kahl-Vooth

Mydborh – Midd-bore

Jorun – Joh-Roon

Kivrasa – Keev-Rah-Sah

Aryil – Arr-yeel

Runvakt – Roon-vak-tuh

Aldin – Awl-Din

Turgon – Tuhr-Gone

Jorlin - Yore-Lynn

Sayra - Say-Rah

Sahralos - Sah-Rah-Lowss

Trässa - Tr-ess-ah

Iftra - Eef-Trah

Gelvrentael - Gelv-Rehn-Tale

Elliana - Ell-Ee-Ahh-Nuh

cos'Halara - Kos-Hah-Lah-Ruh

Vadayen - Vah-Dah-Yen

Isilda - Ih-Seel-Duh

Piyra - Peery-uh

Etric - Eh-Trick

Vansala - Van-Sah-Lah

Magus - May-Gus

Kefarion - Kehff-ree-on

Scilt - Skill-tuh

Taranith - Tah-Rah-Neeth

Dalan - Dah-Laan

Kurost - Koo-Rohst

Cathani - Cah-THan-Ee

Et'Ka'Saan - Et-Kah-Sawn

Aliyria - Alee-Ree-Uh

cos'Tunarik - Kos-Too-Nar-eek

Kessir - Kess-eer

Ethryll - Ehth-real

Elarac - Eh-Lah-Rack

Kathryll - Kahth-Real

Porrik - Poh-Rick

Tyfa - Tie-Fuh

Tygan - Tie-gan

Urvan - Uhr-van

Werrick - Wear-Rick

Kyon - Kie-on

Iridian - Eer-ee-dee-an

Korgrim - Kore-Grihm

Reawin - Ray-Wihn

Seldred - Sehld-Rehd

Alador - Ahl-Ah-Door

Al'Talwha - Awl-Tawl-Whuh

Nevian - Nee-Vee-Un

Pronunciation and Meaning of Terms

1. Ka teljt- kah tehl-yet (My Friend)
2. Sk'av'A- Sk-ahv-ah (Lifesong, the First Language)
3. Moot- Moo-t (Meeting)
4. dal'Korin- dahl-Kore-in (Lizard people indigenous to the province of Nevian)
5. Scala'dun- Scahlah-doon (The ruling body of the dal'Korin)
6. Valtagt- Vahl-Tag-tuh (See Tenderfoot)
7. ljas'atuk- Lee-ow-ss-ah-took (Ground-Fighting, Ranger hand-to-hand combat style)
8. Tenderfoot/Tenderfeet- (Ranger-in-Training)
9. wol'jalar- Wohl-ya-lahr (Fate-Water. Seer)
10. Kalatozi jevka wotik- Kah-lah-to-zhee yev-kah woah-teek (Until our paths cross again)
11. Tengarii - tehn-gah-ree (Ranger)
12. litik'ki - Lee-teek-kee (Honored)
13. kala'taj- kah-lah-tay (Brother)
14. Zenaz sul ta, ia ca'e kiji- Zeh-nazh sool-tah, ee-ah ca-ye kee-yee (Distance ahead, and the hunt)
15. kardo - kahr-doh (Old/Elder)
16. kijini ska- kee-yee-nee skah (Hunting-Wing)
17. Niruuz- Nee-rooz (Rune representing N)
18. Lufnat- Loof-Naht (Rune representing L)

19. Paili- Pay-lee (Rune representing P)
20. Po'ul'lar- Poh-ooh-lahr (Lover, Romantic sense)
21. Wulza- Wool-zah (Rune representing W and V)
22. rak'an'oþa'kaval- rahk-ahn-oathuh-kah-vawl (Family of Sworn Blood, Chosen family)
23. Skala'zan- Skah-lah-zahn (Formal greeting)
24. kaval'dagaan- kah-vahl-dah-gaan (Blood-spill family. Those who become family after sparring or fighting)
25. Jarl- Earl (Rank below King)
26. Se'he Tsalaemanka- See-hee Ts-ahl-aye-mahn-kuh (One of the Great Seas, Literally the Sea of Tsalaeman)
27. Veldan's Wounds (An interjection or swear referencing the battle-scars of the Chieftain of the High Ancestors, Veldan the Wisdom-Kindler)
28. Highberry (Nutritious, sweet berry that restores stamina and energy as well as feeding someone)
29. Twylan (Tree-person. Usually really tall)
30. Undaraar- Oohn-dah-rawr (Wanderer)
31. Anca'e - ahn-ca-ye (Of The)
32. Drolsenya - Drohl-sehn-yah (Woodlands)
33. Pul'gra'an - Pull-grah-ahn (Meat snack made of dried meat, berries, and rendered fat. Basically Pemmican)
34. Kiri'taj - Kee-ree-tay (Sister)
35. Longfather (Grandfather and further back)
36. Chattel (Property/cattle/slaves)
37. Vez - Vezh (Free)
38. Kurt - Kuhrt (Them)
39. Al'da - Owl-Dah (From)
40. Kadiyik - Kah-dee-yeek (Cage)
41. Ia Ee-yah (And)
42. Ekejta - Eh-kayt-ah (Remove)

43. Kurt'ak - Kuhrt-ack (Their)
44. Kenning (A word using figurative language in place of a definite noun)
45. Dú'wol - Dooh-wall (Shackles. It's actually a kenning meaning 'false-fate')
46. Urok'ni - Ooh-Rock-Nee (Orc, specifically 'thinking' Orc, as opposed to Tei'Urok, which are basically insane)
47. Kuz'no'litik - Kooz-noh-lee-teek (Most Honored)
48. Þrúnsaal - Throon-sawl (Mental Illness. It's actually a kenning meaning 'foe-mind')
49. Abryx - eye-brish (It is a crystal, quite similar to opal in looks, that seems to glow and warm up when it's worn around people who are meant to be in the wearer's life. The stronger the glow, the more important. The warmer, the more long-term)
50. gah'Drin - gah-dreen - Nomadic wagon-life people. Amazing storytellers and musicians.
51. Tejg Sungetiigd - Tayg Sun-Get-eeg-duh (Mount Wounds-End)
52. Av qis dran sa elyrök. Av qis dran sa tylca. Av qis dran sa tylbalt. Hyld Yrbos skjk kazin oksii pe sa.
    Ave kees drawn sah ellie-ruck. Ave kees drawn sah teal-kuh. Ave kees drawn sa teel-balt. Heeld Eerbos skyek cousin ox-ee peh sah.
    (I wish for you Mercy's Kiss. I wish for you strength. I wish for you steadfastness (stone-strength). My Yrbos close his eyes to you.)
    It is a prayer to give strength for those who are wounded.
53. Kajaat ne elvyklar - kah-yaat neh elvee-klahr (Interfere no longer!) (Used to demand something or someone get out of your way)

54. Carva'skav - Car-vah-skow - Raven Song (The name of a bow)

55. Skala'zaan - skah-lah zawn - Well Met!

56. Ka'kozaro - kah-koh-zah-row - My thanks!

57. Valk lor sak rakjivkii sa lirk - W/Valk lore sock rock-yeev-kee sah leerk - (May with your ancestors you wake.) (A blessing for the dead or dying)

58. Saal'kwen (proper; saal'qen) - sawl-kwehn - (mind-sculptor (teacher))

59. Lovik kejg - lo (w/v) eek kay-guh - (Aid us!) (Plea for aid)

60. Tengjäv - ten-gyehva - (Ranger Cave) (A Ranger hideout/house-cave)

61. Tyl Syrinta - teal see-reen-tah - (Strong Health!) (A blessing)

62. Ikii ia rakyivk - ee-kee ee-ah rock-yeev-kuh (Gods and Ancestors!) (The start to a prayer)

63. Nel ca'e armä - nehl caye arr-meh - (By the Steel!) (An interjection, mainly used by blacksmiths)

64. Kejg ekvi pe tajfa - kay-guh ekk-vee peh tie-fuh (We ask to commune) The opening to a prayer)

65. Aze - aw-zeh - (Oh!) (Interjection)

66. Skúlt - shkool-tuh - (Good)

About the Author

You can connect with me on:
- https://linktr.ee/cpuckettseran
- https://www.facebook.com/CPuckettSeran

Also by Cianan Puckett